UNLIT

A KINGDOMS OF EARTH & AIR NOVEL

KERI ARTHUR

KA PUBLISHING PTY LTD

With thanks to:

The Lulus
Indigo Chick Designs
Hot Tree Editing
Robyn E.
The lovely ladies from Central Vic Writers
Damonza for the amazing cover.

In the still crispness of a dawn not yet risen, evil stirred. It was a whisper, a promise that rode the breeze like an Irkallan ghost, insubstantial and yet threatening.

I leaned over the parapet, one gloved hand gripping the glass-smooth edge of the nearest merlon to ensure I didn't fall. Watchtower eight was situated at the very end of Winterborne's massive metal curtain wall. To my left lay nothing but a two-hundred-foot drop to the dark waters of Hook's Bay, an area that had once supported a vast fishing fleet, but was now as barren and as empty as the lands beyond this wall. Tenterra, like the bay itself, had been drained of life five hundred years ago when Winterborne's witches had joined forces and—in a last, desperate effort to save the gateway city and stop the Irkallan from entering Gallion—had drawn every ounce of energy from earth and air and cast it against it our foe. The ploy had certainly worked, but the price we'd paid for salvation was high. The once fertile farmlands of Tenterra were now little more than a two-hundred-and-fifty-mile-wide bowl of dust and broken riverbeds, and the skies above us had become volatile and unpredictable. Much of Winterborne itself had fallen into the seas; the sections that had survived were perched on a mountainous strip of land barely two miles wide and ten miles long.

The breeze strengthened as I leaned farther away from the wall, her chill fingers rifling through my short hair and chilling my scalp. I should have been wearing my helmet, but the close fit of the damn thing always felt suffocating. Besides, it wouldn't exactly save my life if I fell. Not from this height.

I couldn't see anything out there in the darkness. There was no sign of movement, nor should there have been given dawn's first fanfare was still a good twenty minutes away.

My gaze rose to the distant, craggy line that rather resembled a drakkon arching its back. It was the Blacksaw Mountains, and the home of the Irkallan. But if they were finally stirring from hibernation, we surely would have gotten word from one of the outposts that guarded both the Adlin and Irkallan borders.

No, whatever this evil was, it was closer than those mountains.

I flared my nostrils and drew in a deeper breath. The wind might share some of her many secrets with me, but it seemed she wasn't willing to reveal the source of that evil. Maybe she didn't know. Or maybe she merely teased. I shouldn't, after all, have even been able to understand her, let alone have any ability—however slight—to summon her.

Not that the wind or the earth *actually* whispered; it was instead the souls of all those who'd once controlled those elements. It's said that on death, earth and air witches were not reincarnated but rather joined the collective consciousness of their element, offering their wisdom, their opinions, and sometimes even their remonstrations to the next generation of those born with the ability to hear and control.

Which should *not* have been me. I was one of the unlit, a child born *without* magic in a world that revered it. The only thing that had saved me from a life of serfdom was the fact that I came from a Sifft bloodline—an ancient human race that could take on wildcat form at will. Thanks to centuries of DNA dilution, it was very rare these days to find anyone who could actually shift, but many of us did at least get some, if not all, of their other capabilities—greater strength, the ability to heal at a very fast rate, extraordinary night vision, and some degree of telepathy, though few could read minds without some form of enhancement device. I might have been raised in government care like every other child deemed to be unlit, but I'd also been trained from a very young age in weapon use and survival fighting, simply because of that Sifft heritage. When I'd come of age and the strength of my night vision had been confirmed, I'd been transferred over to the Nightwatch for more intensive training. I'd become a fully-fledged member at eighteen, and had been stationed on this tower for almost half that time again; this place—this area—was as familiar to me as the staining on my body.

Whatever I was sensing, it wasn't originating from anywhere around here.

I activated the earwig, a long-range communications device that used a mix of magic and technology to allow mind-to-mind communication and drew on body heat as an energy source. They hooked around the ear and had a pliable tail that slipped into the auditory canal. With it, we could converse with other Nightwatch officers and the communicators—true telepaths who monitored both short- and long-distance comms via a multi-enhancement chip inserted into their skulls, one that had the unfortunate side effect of slowly frying their brains. But communicators, like everyone else who was deemed unlit, had very little choice when it came to their career path.

"Ava," I said, "have you spotted any sort of movement at your end?"

"That," came the low and sultry reply, "would depend on which end you're talking about. It's been a long night, after all, and bathroom facilities are decidedly scarce on these towers."

I smiled. Ava and I had been born in the same month, and therefore not only shared a surname, but had been raised together, trained together, and had even explored the boundaries of our sexuality together. She was my cot sister, my friend, and the one person in this world I would do anything for—the one person in this world who would, without doubt, do anything for me.

"I definitely *wasn't* referring to your bowel problems."

"Huh." She paused. "There's nothing moving in either the gateway area or the vicinity immediately beyond it. Why?"

"Not sure."

While Ava was well aware of my ability to sometimes hear the wind's chatter, this line wasn't secure and I had no wish for anyone else to learn about it. I liked being a part of the Nightwatch and the last thing I wanted was to be shunted into a position designed specifically for those with minor magic talents. From what I'd seen, such a life wasn't all that great. Indeed, given the desire to produce magic-capable children, those who held minor magic were treated little better than bovines, kept confined and pregnant year in and year out, with no say in who they were bred to.

At least as a soldier I had more status and certainly more freedom—although none of the unlit could roam the entire city at will. The Upper and Lower Reaches—where those belonging to the ruling houses of earth and air lived, as well as those capable of personal magic, and the serfs and freemen who looked after them all—were out-of-bounds to the rest of us.

"That's not exactly helpful," Ava commented.

"I know." I pulled back from the edge, but as I did, a white light flashed in the distance—a small star-like speck that swiftly disappeared. It had that part of me that could hear the wind stirring excitedly. "Did you see that?"

"Clarify 'that.'"

"There was a flash of light to the northwest." The light sparked again. "Surely you saw it that time?"

"I did." She paused. "If I had to guess what it was, I'd say a beacon of some sort. Cap, you picking anything up?"

"There's no beacon out that way, and no incoming due from either the Blacklake or West Range encampments."

The captain's voice was little more than a harsh whisper. He'd lost an arm and almost his life when a sleuth of Adlin—who were eight-foot-tall hairy humanoid creatures with razor-sharp teeth and claws to match—had attacked the train he and six other Nightwatch officers were escorting to Winterborne from the Eastridge outpost. He now had a mechanical arm, but neither the surgeons nor the healers who'd saved his life had been able to do much for the vocal chords that had all but been destroyed when his throat had been ripped open. How any of them had survived let alone made it back to Winterborne was already the stuff of legends.

"Could it be an Adlin beacon?" They were certainly capable of rudimentary assault weapons and, in the last few months, we'd seen some evidence they were using glimmer stones—a black rock that drew in light and shone like a star at night—as a basic signaling device.

"None of the beacons we've found to date have had the capacity to be seen from such a distance," the captain replied. "Whatever it is, I doubt it's Adlin."

5

"Well, there's definitely something out there, Cap, whether it's Adlin or not," I said as the light flashed again. "It's too regular to be a random."

"Anyone else spotting it?" he asked.

Affirmatives ran down the line. There were ten watch-towers in all—eight along the curtain wall's curvaceous length and an additional two guarding the front of the gate-house. All of them were occupied by Nightwatch officers who were as close to full Sifft as anyone got these days.

Not that any of us really knew our true heritage. All who were declared unlit were taken away within hours of being born. We were told nothing of our lineage, and given no idea whether we were commonly born or from one of the witch houses. Our birth month always became our surname, but our first names were selected by whoever accepted us into government care. As names went, Neve March wasn't bad; some of my fellow Nightwatch officers had not been so lucky. Poor April had certainly been the butt of many a good-natured joke, not only because April was also his birth month, but because it was a name more suited to a female.

"There's nothing reading on the radar," someone else said. It was obviously one of the newer recruits, because I didn't recognize the voice.

The captain grunted. "Neve, looks like this is your baby. Requisition a scooter and go check it out."

I groaned. "Come on, Cap, I clock off in twenty minutes."

"You know the drill," he growled back. "You spot it, you deal with it."

"Can I least have some support?"

"No. The Adlin haven't been active in Tenterra for over a month, so there shouldn't be a problem." He hesitated. "I'll approve use of a rifle, however. Report to armory three."

Relief stirred. The blaster strapped to my right leg might be capable of bringing down the average person, but the

Adlin were as far from average as you could get. But access to more powerful weapons had been restricted of late, and generally reserved for escort details rather than mere scouting missions. According to rumors, metal supply from the smiths of Salysis had been severely curtailed thanks to a recent collapse in one of their major mines. "Appreciate it, Cap."

He grunted again. "I'll send Lort over to finish your shift. Get your ass into gear."

"On my way."

"Keep vigilant out there, Neve," Ava said. "Don't get dead."

"I suspect dead is not a look that would suit me."

"I suspect you could be right."

Grinning, I pulled off my right glove and pressed my hand against the reader. Once my fingertips were scanned, the light above the blast door flicked from red to green and the door slid open. I grabbed my helmet then clattered down the metal stairs, my footsteps echoing forlornly across the night. Some of the guards hated the solitude that came with being one of the Nightwatch, but I loved it—especially after twenty-eight years of being forced to share space in every other aspect of my life. There was no such thing as privacy for the unlit—not since half the city had fallen into the sea, anyway. Space was at such a premium here in what was known as the outer bailey—although Winterborne itself was a major city rather than any sort of castle—that there were now six of us sharing one tiny bunkhouse room and a bathroom. The only reason no one had come to blows was thanks to the fact Ava not only looked like a goddess, she had the persuasion powers of one, too.

Armory three was situated midway between my tower and the secondary wall, and was tucked underneath a huge claw of black rock that protected it from any possibility of attack from the sea. Jon May, the grizzled veteran who'd been in charge of this armory for as long as I could remember, pushed up from his seat and hobbled over to the scanner as I approached.

"Everett told me you were coming," he said. "I'm to supply you with a nitrate rifle and a couple of gut busters."

A gut buster was the nickname for a very serious handgun that fired multiple metal pellets in one round, and could literally tear anyone or anything *other* than an Adlin warrior apart. Which was where the rifle came in—silver nitrate bullets were basically the only things capable of stopping them in their tracks. And if the captain had ordered me supplied with both, then he obviously hadn't been entirely honest about the lack of recent attacks.

"Here's hoping I don't actually need any of them."

Jon's smile flashed, revealing stained teeth. "Amen to that, sister."

I followed him into the armory's shadowed confines. While most of the larger weapons such as the canons were stored deep underground, and were accessible only by special lifts that hoisted them into position whenever needed, there were three other armories like this strategically placed around the Lower Reaches, and four more behind the secondary wall—a wall that still bore the wounds of a war long gone.

This armory was the only one left that predated that war, however, and it was something of a museum when it came to weaponry. There were even swords hanging in the deeper recesses, though why anyone would resort to such a weapon in the face a foe like the Adlin or the Irkallan, I had no idea. Our ancestors were either a whole lot braver than we were, or decidedly more foolish.

An odd glimmer caught my attention and, as Jon stopped in front of the locker holding the nitrate rifles, I walked across to investigate.

The glimmer was coming from a knife—one that had an intricately carved handle and a short but decidedly danger-ous-looking blue-white glass blade. It looked ceremonial but the dark flecks along its edge suggested use.

"Jon, where did this blade come from?"

He glanced over his shoulder and grunted. "Don't know, love, but it's been here longer than I have."

"Any problem with me picking it up?"

"None at all." He pulled free a rifle, then unlocked the next unit and gathered ammunition.

I plucked the knife from its bed of dust. It felt light and well-balanced in my hand—a knife designed for throwing as much as close-quarter combat.

"Why would anyone use glass for a knife blade?" I care-fully ran a finger down its edge, and it sliced through the top layer of my glove easily. Still razor-sharp, even after decades of disuse.

"It's some form of specially hardened glass," he replied. "I've got a couple of swords in the back made of the same stuff. Tougher than steel, they are, and all but indestructible. Legend has it that they're called ghost blades, and were forged in the blood of the Irkallan."

"Huh." I shifted the blade from my right hand to my left and slashed it back and forth. It felt oddly right, almost as if it had been designed specifically for someone my size. "If the material is so damn good, how come we're not using it today?"

He shrugged. "Lost the method of creating it, most likely."

I glanced at the shelf again and spotted a leather strap sitting at the very back. I rose on tiptoes and grabbed it. It turned out to be a knife sheath made from an unusual laven-der-gray leather and, like the knife itself, was intricately carved, the swirling patterns almost resembling drakkon scales. Weirdly, despite the fact it must have been in this room for as long as the blade, the leather was still soft, still supple.

"What are the chances of me requisitioning it?" I slipped the knife into its sheath then strapped it to my left leg. I couldn't even feel its weight.

Jon glanced at me, surprise evident. "A knife isn't going to be of much use in an Adlin attack. If you're close enough to use that thing, you're dead."

"I know, but other critters do roam Tenterra." Or, at least, roamed her borders.

"And that's what you have blasters for."

I grinned. "Yes, but sometimes ammo does run out."

His expression suggested I was crazy, but all he said was "It's been delisted as an active weapon, so as long as you sign for it, it's yours. Come along."

I followed him over to the small office area, signed out the weapons and the ammo, then thanked him and headed across to the motor pool to grab a scooter.

Ten minutes later, I was speeding out of Winterborne and into the Tenterra dustbowl. The scooters were lightly armored vehicles shaped like rather fat tadpoles and, at a push, could fit two people in them. They were designed for scouting missions such as this and used a form of electro-magnetic repulsion technology that drew on the earth's energy lines to move. Those same crisscrossing energy lines also provided coordinates for the navigation systems. The scooters—unlike most military vehicles—were not only fast but also raised little in the way of dust, a major bonus given the numbers of Adlin that now roamed Tenterra.

Winterborne's gleaming metal wall soon became little more than a speck in the scooter's rear-vision screen. Dawn had begun to smother the stars and it lent the barren land-scape a moment of beauty. But that star-like flash that had drawn me out here had disappeared.

"Base, can anyone one still see that beacon?"

"Negative," came the reply. "But Ava worked out some rough coordinates before she signed off. Sending them through now."

"Ta."

Numbers flashed up on the scooter's control screen. I punched them through to navigation and released manual control. The scooter surged forward, the whine of her engines audible even through the helmet. It was a somewhat comforting sound, if only because it meant everything was working as it should.

The skies brightened as the sun began to rise over Drakkon's Head, the massive peak that was reportedly the main entrance to the Irkallan colony that ran deep under the Blacksaw Mountains. I sometimes wondered why the earth and air witches had never taken the war directly to the Irkallan—why they hadn't destroyed their land rather than ours. Nothing in the history books ever mentioned such an attempt, and if there *was* a sound reason for not doing so, it had never been recorded.

Of course, it could also be that we unlit had no need to know, so it simply wasn't a part of our education.

I was just over an hour out of Winterborne when I reached the coordinate location and the scooter began to slow. I couldn't see anything in the immediate vicinity and the sensors—which had a range of about a mile, depending on the terrain—weren't picking up anything. I switched the scooter to manual and began a long circular sweep of the area. About three-quarters of the way around the sensors began to beep—the directional lights indicated it was to the northeast, and the slow nature of the auditory signal suggested it was at least half a mile away.

It turned out to be a woman.

I stopped the scooter but didn't immediately get out,

instead giving the sensors time to do another sweep of the area. The Adlin had been known to use the bodies of their victims to lure soldiers to their deaths, and while this woman looked whole, I wasn't about to step beyond the punitive safety of the scooter until I knew for sure there was nothing and no one else out there.

When the sensors gave no further indication of movement or life in the area, I hit auto hover to keep them operational, took off my helmet and tossed it into the back of the scooter, then opened the door and climbed out. The wind stirred around me, whispering of the heat that was to come later that day. If there was anything more dangerous in this part of the world, she certainly wasn't inclined to tell me. I grabbed the medikit then slung the rifle over my shoulder and walked across to the woman.

The first thing I noticed was the fact that there was absolutely no indication of how she'd gotten here. There were no footprints or vehicle tracks, and the wind certainly wasn't strong enough to have already erased them. Aside from the thick silver bracelets on her wrists, she was naked, but her pale skin showed no sign of sunburn, which suggested she'd walked through the night rather than the day. But from where?

The second thing I noticed once I was much closer was the rough-cut, circular black stone lying near her left hand.

It was an Adlin beacon.

My pulse rate jumped several notches. I stopped beside her and scanned the area again. The brown landscape stretched on endlessly until it met the blue of the sky. If anything moved, it would be visible long before the sensors spotted it. But there was nothing near—nothing heavy enough to stir up the dust, anyway.

And yet I couldn't escape the notion that something *was* out there, watching us.

If it was the Adlin, we were in deep trouble.

I bent to press two fingers against the woman's neck. Her pulse was slow and strong, and her breathing regular. It was almost as if she was asleep rather than unconscious. There was no evidence of wounds or bruising on her back, rump, or legs. The soles of her feet were cracked and hard, suggesting she spent most of her time without shoes. But there was little dirt caked between her toes or covering her ankles—what did linger was black rather than the red-brown of the Tenterra desert—and no sign of the redness that came from walking through the night on soil heated by long days of hot sunlight.

I grabbed the mediscanner out of the kit and ran it over her. Other than noting she was dehydrated and carrying a very low body weight for her height, it backed up what was already evident by sight—although she was, apparently, eleven weeks pregnant.

I moved the glimmer stone and then carefully rolled her over. Despite her paler skin, she had what was considered to be typical Sifft features—an oval-shaped face, an aquiline nose, and well-defined cheekbones. Her hair was as black as mine, but also had thick streaks of silver—and silver so pure, be it in the hair or the eyes, was usually one of the signs of air witch.

I pressed the earwig and said, "Base? I've found my target. It's a woman, unescorted, with no apparent means of transportation."

"Is she alive?" The voice belonged to Jeni, one of the night shift communicators and my assigned comms point. She'd obviously been held over because I was out.

"Yes. Unconscious but unburned and unhurt." I hesitated. "There's an Adlin beacon with her."

"But no other sign of a trap?" Her tone was detached—without life or emotion. Another side effect of the

13

enhancement chips. "No indication she's been tampered with?"

I pursed my lips and quickly switched scanner mode. Thankfully, the screen remained green. "There's no indication of internal alterations or weaponry insertions."

"The captain said to bring her back but leave the beacon. Be wary, though—sensors are picking up activity about fifty miles southeast of you."

Which put it between Winterborne and us. I swung around. The horizon remained clear, but maybe the teasing wind was erasing any sign of movement. "Keep me updated, Base. Out."

I flicked off the earwig and returned my gaze to the woman, only to discover she was awake and watching me. But there wasn't a whole lot of awareness in her eyes—eyes that were a silvery-white rather than the gold of a Sifft.

"I'm Nightwatch eight-three from Winterborne." I kept my tone soft so as not to spook her. If the activity Base mentioned *was* the Adlin, then the last thing I needed was this woman screaming. I had no idea if they'd be able to hear her from such a distance, and no desire to find out. "Have you any memory as to how you got out here?"

She stared at me for a moment and then blinked. Awareness seeped into her eyes, but it was quickly overwhelmed by fear. She sucked in a deep breath, but I clapped a hand over her mouth before she could unleash the scream.

"Don't," I said, perhaps a little more sharply than was wise. "You'll draw the Adlin to us."

Her gaze darted left and right, her expression wild, confused. Fearful.

"It's okay," I added swiftly. "We're okay. We just can't do anything that'll attract attention. Okay?"

Her gaze returned to mine, and after a moment she

nodded. I hesitated, and then pulled my hand away. "How did you get here? Can you remember?"

She shook her head and opened her mouth to reply. No sound came out. Confusion and panic rolled across her features again.

I touched her arm, halting further attempts to speak. "Wait. I'll go get some water."

I rose and walked back to the scooter. The sensors were quiet and the horizon remained dust free, but the uneasy feeling we were not alone out here was growing.

The earwig buzzed. When I pressed it, Jeni said, "Eight-three, we're now picking up movement twenty miles out from you."

Which meant it remained beyond the range of my scanners. I glanced over my shoulder but still couldn't see anything. Maybe it wasn't the Adlin but rather one of the wildebeests that somehow eked out a living from this barren place. "Any idea what it is?"

"No, but it's not large enough to be a full sleuth."

"That's not exactly comforting." Adlin hunting parties were quite often only a half dozen or so in size rather than the full twenty-five. But half a dozen Adlin could easily take out a full escort detail. I certainly *didn't* want to be confronting one of the bastards right now, let alone six or more of them. "Are they moving toward us?"

"Yes, and rather rapidly. You'd better get moving, eight-three."

I flicked off the earwig again then grabbed the water bottle and walked back. After undoing the lid, I held it up and let the water trickle into the woman's mouth. She grabbed it, trying to drag it closer, to drink more, but I held it firm. "Just sip it," I said. "It can be dangerous to drink too much when you're dehydrated."

Something flashed in her eyes, something that spoke of

storms and thunder. The wind stirred around me, sharp and filled with ice, but, after a moment, she relaxed and obeyed. The wind, however, remained hostile, whispering promises of retribution. For what, I wasn't entirely sure.

After another second or so, I pulled the water away and repeated my question.

"I was dumped here." Her voice was little more than a scratch of sound, but held within it the force of an oncoming storm. Despite her hair not being a pure color, she was definitely an air witch of some power. "I'm not sure why."

I frowned. "Who dumped you?"

She shrugged. Frustration swirled through me, but it wasn't really my job to find out the whys and wherefores of her being here. My mission was to get us both back to safety.

As dust finally appeared on the horizon, I slung the water bottle over my shoulder, then grabbed the medikit and rose. "Do you think you'll be able to walk across to the scooter?"

Her gaze slid past me and she frowned. "Are we both going to fit in that thing?"

"It'll be tight, but yes." I held out a hand. "We need to move."

She half raised a hand then stopped, panic flaring across her features again. "You have to get them off me."

I frowned. "What?"

"The bracelets." Her voice was rising, as was the wind. It tore at my hair, my clothes, as if trying to strip me bare. "You have to get them off me. *Now.*"

"I will, but we haven't the time—"

She grabbed my hand and pulled me so close her nose was inches from mine. "Do it *now*. I can't be wearing these things. It's the surest way for the queen to find me, and I can't be found. Not again."

Queen? Both Gallion and Salysis had long ago freed themselves from the yoke of a ruling monarch. While

Versona—the lands that lay on the other side of the Blacksaw Mountains—had kept what we'd discarded, we'd lost contact with them not long after the war that had decimated Tenterra.

Did that mean this woman was some kind of refugee from those lands? She surely couldn't be an emissary, not given her words.

"Get them off me. You *have* to get them off me." Her words held an uneasy mix of desperation and fury that had ice running across the back of my neck. And I wasn't entirely sure its cause was the wind.

"Okay, but be warned, it's going to make things tight."

"Whatever comes cannot be worse than being found by the queen."

I glanced at the horizon; the dust cloud was thicker, and far closer than before. We really couldn't afford this delay, but it wasn't like I had any choice. Not with the wind continuing to tear at me.

I swore under my breath, but shifted my grip and studied the bracelet. The workmanship was absolutely beautiful, the silver pure and bright, and the decorations carved into its surface intricate and unusual. I couldn't immediately see any sort of catch, but a closer inspection revealed a hairline break on the reverse side of the bracelet.

"Hurry," the woman growled. "They're coming."

"Which is why we should be in the scooter rather than wasting precious time trying to get these things off."

"If they're not removed," she bit back, "running will be of no use."

"Why?" I slid the glass knife out of its sheath and wedged the delicate tip into that crack. I hated the thought of breaking the blade but short of blasting the bracelet—and half her arm—away, I had little other choice.

"They are a beacon, of sorts," the woman said, "and are

powered by my life force. When no longer attached, they will not hold any ability to summon."

"That dust"—I pointed with my chin as I shoved the tip of the knife deeper. The hairline crack widened fractionally —"is being raised by Adlin. Are you saying these bracelets are somehow connected to them?"

She twisted around and studied the dust cloud. The wind grew stronger, but its whispering was faint and incomprehensible, at least to me. After a moment, she said, "No, they're not. They're connected to something far worse."

"I'm not entirely sure there *is* anything worse than an Adlin hunting party." I twisted the knife and, with a metallic click, the bracelet opened. Dust bloomed as it hit the ground.

"Then you would be wrong. Look, I can't explain what I can't remember. You just have to trust me."

Even though the wind was now begging me to do just that, instinct was screaming the very opposite. I had no idea why. Maybe it was just a natural distrust of the odd, almost otherworldly fury I kept seeing in her eyes—though, for all I knew, those brief flashes were entirely natural for an air witch. Aside from the occasional escort placement, I'd never had that much to do with witches of either kind.

The second bracelet came off easier than the first. I shoved the knife home then hauled the woman upright. She gasped and bent over, her body shaking and seeming to struggle for breath.

I hadn't been that rough—had I? "Are you okay?"

"Yes." Her voice was tight. "It's just been so long since I've moved with any sort of speed that I was surprised."

A curious statement given her position here in the middle of nowhere, but my gaze drifted back to that dust cloud and fear stirred. If that dust *did* signal an approaching party of Adlin warriors, then they were already far too close for my liking.

I shifted my grip and wrapped my arm around her body in an effort to support her. "Let's go."

She balked. "I need the bracelets."

"Didn't I just remove them because they were damn dangerous?"

"Yes, but they're pure silver and very valuable. I'll not leave them here in the desert."

I swore under my breath, then scooped up the two bracelets and clipped them to my utility belt. "Can we go now?"

"Yes."

She began to walk toward the scooter, but her pace was frustratingly slow. It was almost as if she was trying to remember *how* to walk. Instinct itched, but I swiped it away. Right now, I needed to concentrate on getting us out of here rather than the puzzle this woman presented.

I boosted her into the rear of the scooter and quickly strapped her in. The sloping roof meant she had to bow her head, a position that would soon get rather uncomfortable—but better that than dead.

I jumped in front of her, slid the door closed, and then switched off the auto hover. The engine kicked in, the noise almost deafening after the silence of the Tenterra wasteland.

"Base, we're on the move."

Even as I said the words, I hit the accelerator. The scooter jerked forward; there was a responding crash and woman behind me swore. "Be careful."

"You be careful. I'm trying not to get dead."

I punched in the coordinates for Winterborne, but the direct path put us on a collision course with the Adlin. I ordered a more circular route then hit the autopilot. The scooter began a sweeping curve as it accelerated to top speed. I unclipped my blaster so that it was easier to grab, then loaded both the gut busters and the rifle. There was nothing else I could do. Nothing except hope the Adlin decided we were too much trouble to pursue.

"Have you got a name?" the woman said.

Her voice was barely audible over the screaming engines. They weren't exactly designed to run at top speed for very long; I hoped they held up.

"Neve. You?"

She hesitated and, after a long moment, said, "Saska."

The earwig buzzed. "The Adlin are echoing your movements," Jeni said. "They're now two miles away and closing fast."

"Thanks, Base." I picked up the rifle and placed it across my lap. "How did you get to be out in the middle of nowhere, Saska?"

"I told you, I don't know."

The wind rose at her reply, buffeting the scooter and sending it drifting sideways. "Getting pissed off at my questions doesn't do either of us any good. Why don't you put all that hostility to better use, and direct it at the Adlin instead?"

"I'm not sure what you—"

"I mean that." I waved a hand at the window and the dust being torn up by the battering wind. "It's hindering our speed and making us easier to spot. Direct your power at the Adlin instead—draw up a cloud so thick and a wind so strong they can't move with any speed against it."

"That's not me." But her voice was confused. Uncertain.

"Then who's drawing the wind to us? Because it's sure as hell not me." I might be able to call on the wind, but I'd never been to raise this much force.

Not that I'd ever really had a reason to try.

She didn't say anything. I wished I had the skill to touch her skin and read the secrets I suspected she was keeping, but that was a task for the readers. Besides, I had more important problems right now—like the scooter's sensors finally kicking in, signifying the Adlin were now within a mile of us. We weren't going to make it to Winterborne. Not without help.

I touched the earwig. "Base, this is Nightwatch eight-three. We're going to need assistance."

"The captain said we've no units close enough to render any. Alter course and head for the Blacklake encampment. He'll order them to fall out." Jeni paused. "Be aware that we're picking up secondary movement at twenty-two miles out from your position. They appear to be shadowing you."

"How big a sleuth?"

"We're not entirely sure it's Adlin. The readings aren't quite right."

"How can the readings not be right? It's either Adlin or wildebeest. Nothing else lives in this godforsaken place."

"We're getting tech to check out whether it's a fault or not. But it's not them you have to worry about right now."

Something I didn't need reminding of. "Tell Blacklake if they don't hurry, we're going to be Adlin meat."

"ETA estimates are twenty minutes."

Which meant they were going to be about ten minutes too late to prevent a running battle happening between the Adlin and us. Fear rose, swift and sharp, twisting my gut and momentarily snatching my breath. But that was okay; fear could be controlled and channeled. It could make you sharper, more alert, more dangerous. Every single Night or Daywatch officer was taught that, and every single one of us had learned the truth of it.

But it was a truth I wasn't looking forward to once again confirming. Not when I was about to go into battle alone.

"Tell them to get here faster. Oh, and Base? I have the woman's name for you—Saska."

"No surname?"

"No, but I think she's an air witch."

"We'll check if any have been reported missing."

"Thanks. Eight-three out."

I punched in the Blacklake coordinates, turned off the sensor's audible warning, and then reached for both gut busters. The scooter did a sharp right turn and began speeding away from the Adlin. I knew it really wouldn't make all that much difference. I could see—and hear—them now.

At least the wind was no longer battering the scooter but had instead shifted behind us, seeming to urge us on to greater speeds. But we were already at full tilt.

It definitely wasn't going to be enough.

If the scent of fear coming from behind me was anything to go by, Saska was also aware of it. But that fear apparently wasn't strong enough to unleash her abilities, to reach out for the air and the storms and fling them at the Adlin. I wondered what had happened to her to cause such a cataclysmic breach between mind and abilities, but it was a thought that swiftly died as a long, drawn-out roar reached above the noise of the screaming engines.

"Can't this metal bucket go any faster?" Saska said, voice tight.

"Yeah, but only if I throw your ass out of it."

"You won't... will you?"

"As tempting as it might become, no, I won't."

The Adlin were almost upon us. Tension crawled up my spine and sweat broke out across my brow. I didn't wipe it away, didn't move. I just waited.

The noise behind us died.

Here they come....

The scooter lurched to the right as one of them cannoned into it, then bounced, briefly hitting the soil as another jumped on top. Claws raked roof, tearing into but not breaking through the metal skin. Saska screamed, the sound deafening in the small cabin.

"That's *not* helping," I said, voice harsh. "So for freedom's sake, shut up and get as low down as you can."

I raised a gut buster as she obeyed, but didn't immediately fire. I wouldn't—not until those claws broke through. As long as the scooter remained intact, we had a chance. A slim one, but I'd take that any day over none.

Another hit sent the scooter sliding sideways. I glanced to the left and saw four Adlin, teeth bared and eyes bloody with rage and hunger, running beside us. Three more appeared to our right. Eight all told.

May the gods of earth and air help us....

Another thump on the roof. The scooter dipped under the weight, and the engine's screams became high-pitched as it struggled to maintain speed and height under the additional weight.

A third thump, one that made the metal echo. Not another Adlin this time, but rather a blow. The roof dented, then several claws pierced the metal and began peeling it back. I fired both gut busters. The boom was deafening in the confines of the cabin, but the metal pellets did their job, tearing through the roof and into the Adlin above us. They screamed but weren't dislodged. Their claws bit deeper into the shredded metal; I fired again. One of them fell and the scooter surged forward.

It still wasn't enough.

A thick, hairy arm slashed down through the gap in the roof. Claws wrapped around the gun in my left hand, tearing into my skin in the process. Pain reverberated through me as blood flowed down my arm and fingers. I fired the other gun. There was a roar in response and fluid dripped into the cabin—fluid that was black and rancid-smelling. But despite its injuries, the Adlin wasn't letting me go. Instead, it began tugging me upward, trying to pull me free from the craft. All that held me in position was the belt around my waist.

I swore, reached across my body for the knife, and then slashed at the Adlin's arm. The glass blade bit deep, severing skin, muscle, and bone with ease, and suddenly I was free. As the Adlin's arm dropped to the scooter's floor and black blood began to pulse all over me, I grabbed the rifle and fired upwards. The Adlin's entire head exploded and his body tipped sideways.

The minute his weight slid from the roof, the scooter surged forward. Hope rippled through me, but a quick look either side soon killed it. The Adlin were still running beside us, although I could only see four of them now. Even as I wondered what the others were up to, the scooter jerked and the craft's fat nose began to rise. The missing Adlin had obviously jumped onto the scooter's tail and were pressing it downward. Dirt filled the air, a choking cloud that quickly cut visibility.

I swore, straightened my arm over Saska's trembling body, and fired the rifle again. Twin holes appeared in the scooter's sloping tail, and the head of the nearest Adlin disintegrated. The other one roared in fury and two more hairy figures appeared to take the place of the one I'd shot. The tail dug deeper into the soil and the whole craft began to shudder. It would tear itself apart if I couldn't make the Adlin release it. I reloaded and fired, then reloaded and fired again. Hair and muscle and body parts went flying, but the ones I killed were being held in place by the ones who lived, and the scooter was coming to a slow but inevitable halt.

The front of the vehicle jerked upward. I twisted around, had a brief glimpse of two Adlin as they slipped under the craft's nose. Something hit us hard; the whole vehicle twisted, the metal groaning as the nose rose again and became almost vertical. It threw me back into the seat but I somehow kept a grip on the rifle and once again fired, blasting a hole through the foot well but catching no Adlin.

Again, the craft shuddered. But before I could reload, before I could do anything, the tail was torn away from the passenger pod and we were sent tumbling, end over end, across the barren Tenterra soil.

2

W e came to halt upside down but relatively intact. The air was thick with dust and the windows were caked with the stuff, meaning I had no clue where we'd landed or where the Adlin were. The sensors were ominously quiet. Something must have broken when we'd been sent flying. The engines, however, were still at full bore, and the acrid smell of smoke teased the dusty air. I hastily shut everything down and an odd, creak-filled hush fell over the pod.

Nothing moved except the wind, and she was urging us to get out, to flee before the Adlin fell upon us again.

But if we'd *did* flee, we'd die. The Adlin had kept up with the scooter's top speed—what hope would we have on foot?

I reached up with a bloody hand and gripped the ragged edges of the hole I'd blasted into the foot well, and then unlatched the seat belt with the other. Once back on my feet, I twisted around and glanced at Saska. She was hanging upside down, her eyes closed and her expression slack. It was hard to tell whether she was conscious or not.

"Saska, you okay?"

She jumped at the question, but didn't open her eyes. "Yes."

The whisperings of the wind got stronger, and brought with it an ominous howling. The Adlin were coming at us yet again.

I gathered my weapons, then pressed the earwig. "Base, this is eight-three. The scooter is down. I repeat, the scooter is down."

Static was my only reply. I cursed softly but resisted the urge to rip the thing out of my ear. While I might not be getting a response, there was always a chance that Winter-borne could hear me. And, if not, they should at least be able to track my position through it—but only as long as the tail remained inserted in my ear canal.

"Well," I said as I began reloading all the weapons, "unless Blacklake can break the land-speed record, it looks like it's just the two of us."

"Yes." Again her reply was remote.

I glanced at her sharply. Air spun tightly around her, air that was as sharp and electric as a storm on a summer night. On a surface level, she might have appeared uncertain about her air witch abilities, but her subconscious self certainly had no such doubts.

The bite in the air got stronger, louder, and the pod began to shudder and shake. But rather than lifting it up, as I half expected, the wind began to tear at the broken metal, ripping it further apart, creating a hole big enough to fit a person through.

There was a soft click and Saska fell free of her restraints, grunting as she landed partially on her head and partially on her back. The wind began to wrap around her and I suddenly realized what was about to happen.

"You are *not* going to leave me here alone, witch."

I slung the rifle across my shoulder, clipped the gut

busters to my utilities belt, and then lunged forward and wrapped both arms around her waist. And none too soon. The wind had barely finished demolishing the rest of the pod's wall when it pulled her free, taking me with it in the process. It swept us upward, into the blue of the sky, and then hesitated. Fingers of wind began to tear at my grip on Saska. I closed my eyes and for the first time ever, attempted to meld with the air, reaching as deep into its heart as I could. Pleading my case, asking it to save me too.

The fingers stopped pulling at my hands and, after a moment, the wind wrapped around us both and held us steady. A cocoon of cloudy, gossamer air that was as soft as spun cotton and yet as cold as ice then formed to conceal us. When that was done, we were ripped up and sideways at speed.

I had no idea where we were going. The wind might have listened to my plea but she wasn't talking to me right now. Nor was Saska. All I could do was hope we weren't being taken toward even bigger trouble.

Only a few minutes seemed to have passed when our speed diminished and the cocoon began to unravel. Below us, brown soil stretched on forever, empty and without life. I could see neither the Adlin nor the Blacklake rescue party, and there was nothing even remotely familiar.

The wind delivered us onto the ground then gently eased away. I loosened my grip on Saska and rolled away from her, staring up at the blue sky while I sucked in air and thanked whatever gods might be listening for our freedom.

I guessed it now was up to me to ensure we remained that way.

I sat up. While I still had all my weapons, none of them would protect us for very long if the Adlin found us. As for injuries... I finally allowed myself to look at my left hand. The black graphene-and-Kevlar-layered leather glove had undoubtedly saved me from losing it, but neither had gone undamaged. While I could still move three of my fingers, my pinky felt dead and lifeless. There was also a great gash that stretched from my knuckles to my elbow, and it was from this that most of the blood was coming. Weirdly, it wasn't hurting. Maybe I was still in shock. Or maybe the desperate knowledge of what our fate might yet be if we didn't find some sort of sanctuary in this barren, blighted place was simply smothering it.

If I wanted *any* chance of survival, the first thing I'd better do was stop the blood loss. I stripped off my jacket, and then grabbed the knife and cut the sleeves into strips. I didn't bother taking off my glove—it was probably helping to keep the wound together—and simply wound the strips of material as tightly as I could over my hand and forearm. It would make grabbing and firing weapons harder, but realistically, a lack of movement in one hand wasn't going to make a great deal of difference if we were caught.

I shoved my jacket back on then pushed upright. There was nothing on the horizon, no sign of dust, and absolutely no indication of where we were. I unclipped the small compass from my belt and held it away from my body. The needle swung about for a second or two, then settled on north. Winterborne lay to the south, Blacklake to the west. All of which wasn't much help when I had no idea where we'd actually landed and therefore how far we were from either of them. I bent and roughly shook Saska. "Wake up."

"Can't," she mumbled. "Everything hurts."

I'd heard that sometimes when a witch used too much of their strength to summon and control wind and weather, their body could be thrown into such a state of shock that could take hours—if not days—for them to recover, but I wouldn't have thought *that* would have applied here.

But then, what would I know? I wasn't witch trained and

had never asked the wind to do much more than throw up the occasional dust devil.

"Where did you ask the wind to take us?" I said. "Where did it leave us?"

"Home," she said. "I told it to go home."

"And is your home Winterborne?"

"No. Yes." The wind stirred, briefly teasing her hair, and then she waved a hand. "West. We went west."

Meaning we were probably closer to Blacklake than Winterborne. Which was handy, given the garrison had emptied out to rescue us, but only if they weren't headed in the opposite direction to where we now were.

"We need to start walking."

"I can't."

"You must." I reached down, grabbed her hand with my one good one, then planted my feet and hauled her upright. She cursed me, her language colorful and inventive. *No gently raised witch, this one*, I thought with a grin.

"Lean on me." I gripped her waist with my bad hand—as much as I was able to anyway—to steady her.

She flung an arm around my shoulders and, after a stumble or two, we began walking in a westerly direction. Although our pace wasn't great, it was at least momentum.

Time ticked by. The sun got higher, and no matter how hard I scanned the horizon, there was no sign that anyone or anything was coming to rescue us. But there was also no sign of the Adlin, so I guess that evened things out.

We continued walking. The barrenness of this place seemed to stretch on, with no relief in sight. Wherever the hell the wind had blown us, it obviously wasn't anywhere near the Blacklake encampment. While I hadn't actually been there, I'd done escort duty to Farsprings, and that place was a veritable garden, thanks to its closeness to the river and the attention the two witches who did duty there gave to the soil immediately around the encampment. I could see no reason why Blacklake, with the river running across its western flank, would be any different.

As the day grew hotter and the air shimmered, walking became more and more difficult. My arm burned, the pain a pulse that was as rapid as my heartbeat, and an odd light-headedness was beginning to take hold.

That's when I saw it.

The dust.

Relief stirred and I staggered to a stop. The approaching cloud was thick and heavy, and spoke of numbers.

"I think the cavalry just found us, Saska."

"No."

The reply was so softly spoken I wouldn't have heard it if not for the wind snatching it up toward me. That same wind spoke of the dust and the things that came.

It wasn't the Blacklake soldiers. It was the Adlin.

They'd found us.

Somehow, the bastards had found us.

I couldn't run. Nor could I call the wind—not to lift us up and whisk us away. I didn't have the strength to maintain such an order, even if the wind would obey a call like that from me. Maybe Saska could... but even as that thought crossed my mind, her knees buckled and she became a dead-weight that almost dragged me down with her.

I let her go, took a deep breath, and tried to think. To plan. After a moment, I pressed the earwig and said, "This is Nightwatch eight-three, sending out a code red call. We are on foot and in trouble. The earwig is malfunctioning and the scooter is destroyed. Adlin have our scent. We have, perhaps, ten minutes. If you're out there, if you're listening, come save our asses. And if you can't do that, come get our bodies."

Or whatever was left of them after the Adlin had finished with us.

I glanced around again, looking for someplace to make a stand, to give us hope, but there was absolutely nothing but flat, hard earth….

Maybe *that* was our salvation.

I gathered the wind to my hand, directed it at the soil, and asked it to dig. Maybe she sensed my desperation and need, because she gathered speed and strength as she clawed at the soil. Dust flew all around us, a choking cloud that would flag our presence to anyone who was out there. It didn't matter, because the only things that were out there were the Adlin, and they were already well aware of us.

A short trench that was three feet wide and almost double that in depth was soon created. I directed the wind sideways to create a cave, then jumped into the trench and dragged Saska in after me. There was very little room to maneuver but that was the whole point.

The fierce, trumpeting war cry of the Adlin bit across the howling of the wind. I closed my eyes and urged the air to hurry. She picked up strength, tearing at my hair and clothes, threatening to suck us into the vortex that was hammering through the rocklike soil. Chunks of earth began to explode all around us. I shifted to protect Saska's naked body, but it was mostly the smaller pieces that hit us. The larger chunks were flung upwards and shot sideways. Maybe the wind was doing her bit to help us.

When a deep enough cave had been created in the soil, I asked the wind to ease, then shifted my grip on Saska and dragged her to the very back of the earth shelter. It was about twelve feet in length and three wide, and a little too grave-like, when I thought about. But at least the Adlin, with their big bodies and wide shoulders, would have trouble getting down here en masse.

Their roaring cut out again. I grabbed the gut busters, double-checked they were fully loaded and undamaged, and then returned to the cave's opening. For a minute, everything was silent. Nothing moved other than the floating dust.

Then a big, hairy body appeared high in the air before thumping feet first into the trench. He wedged tight at hip level and began to pound and tear at the soil. I dropped the guns, grabbed the knife, and slashed at his legs, severing tendons and biting deep into bone. He roared and twisted, the earth shuddering under the force of his blows. Dust and stone rained around me, but I continued to saw at his legs, until one was amputated and the other hanging by threads. Blood poured from the remains of his limbs, a black river that spoke of death. This time, it was *his* rather than mine. But the trembling earth told me there were at least five others up there, if not more.

The movements of the Adlin stuck in the cave's entrance got weaker, his strength seeming to drain as swiftly as his blood. His body jerked, shifting upward several inches, before he was torn from the entrance and a fierce, battle-scarred leathery face appeared. I jumped back, grabbed a gut buster, and fired. The pellets tore into the Adlin's face, shredding his nose, cheeks, and mouth, and taking out one eye. But he didn't move. He simply opened his broken, bloody mouth and screamed at me. His breath smelled like death. I aimed slightly higher and fired again. This time, the pellets took off the top of his head and much of his brain.

As his body fell toward me and half covered the entrance, claws slashed down from the left. I threw myself backward, but one claw snagged my boot and dug down into flesh. I swore and fired the gut buster; hair and skin flew, and bone was revealed, but again the Adlin didn't seem to care. He simply dragged me forward and up. I swore, grabbed my knife with my left hand, and slashed awkwardly at the claws drawing me toward death. The glass blade was diamond bright in the shadows of our earth hollow, and it cut across

the Adlin's knuckles as swiftly and as easily as paper, separating its flesh and releasing me from its grip. The creature
screamed and slashed with the remains of his hand, trying to
hook me again. I scrambled backward, out of his reach and
out of immediate sight.

The severed claw was still stuck in my leg, and though it
hurt something fierce, I didn't pull it out. I had no idea what
damage it had done, but blood was filling my boot and I
suspected it might get worse if I removed the claw. I tugged
off my jacket, cut some more strips of material from it, and
hastily wrapped my calf to immobilize the claw and stop it
from causing further damage. The Adlin were now tearing at
the tunnel opening, desperately trying to widen it. I reached
across for my weapons and waited. I didn't have the energy
to do anything else.

Dust once again filled the air, and heavy chunks of earth
littered the cave entrance. Maybe they were trying to bury us
rather than eat us…. The thought died as another Adlin
jumped into the hole. I raised the rifle and fired. The nitrate
bullets killed him in an instant and his body filled the
entrance, momentarily stopping the others. But it left me
with only the knife, the gut busters, and my blaster. The
latter was useless against the Adlin, but that's not what I'd be
using it for anyway.

There was no way I'd let either of us be taken alive by
those things.

I briefly closed my eyes and tried to quell the fear—and
the anger—that rose. Every Nightwatch member knew death
was a possibility. I just hadn't thought mine would find me
facing the enemy alone out in the middle of the Tenterra
wasteland.

The Adlin's body was soon hauled from the widened
entrance but another didn't immediately fill its place. Maybe
they'd finally learned what fate would befall them if they did.

While they didn't appear to have human intelligence, the Adlin certainly weren't stupid. They were more than capable of creating primitive weapons, so they were certainly able to grasp the consequences of their actions—at least when the hunting rage wasn't on them.

But that could be said about many a human, too.

A thumping sound began immediately above us, echoing lightly as dust floated down from the ceiling. As the thumping got louder—harder—I realized they were trying to bring the roof down. The heavy blanket of dust now swirling through the cave caught in my throat, making me cough. I hurriedly tore several strips off the bottom of my shirt to use as a filter then edged forward, wondering if it was possible to shoot any of them. The minute I moved, an arm swooped down through the trench and tried to grab me.

I resisted the impulse to fire at the questing claws and simply kept out of their reach. I had maybe a dozen rounds left in each of the gut busters; I couldn't afford to waste them. Not if it was going to take at least two rounds to take out one of them.

The jumping continued and cracks appeared in the roof. I swore and reached for the wind. She stirred lightly around me then ran away, and for a minute, I thought I heard someone swearing. Which was stupid, because the wind, as much as she sometimes appeared to be playing games with me, wasn't capable of any sort of emotion.

The cave's roof cracked. As I looked up, a huge chunk of stone and soil came tumbling down. I leaned sideways to avoid it then pressed the earwig in frustration. "For freedom's sake, is anyone out there? This is Nightwatch eight-three, about to become Adlin lunch if someone doesn't get to us within the next couple of minutes."

Unsurprisingly, static was my only reply. I cursed it and fate and anyone else who might be listening, then slid on my backside to the rear of our disintegrating shelter. I unlatched the blaster, counted the bullets in the chamber to ensure I kept two for Saska and myself, then gripped the gut busters and waited.

More and more chunks of soil came down, until a crack of blue sky was visible. Another thump, and then feet appeared. I unleashed the gut busters and just kept firing. There was little point in conserving bullets now.

Blood and bone and freedom only knew what else began to rain through the widening cracks above us. The Adlin didn't seem to care about the damage I was inflicting on them; they just kept on jumping. The low-ammo light began to blink—a slow flashing that was little more than a countdown to our death.

The booming retort of the weapons echoed all around us, sounding like a dozen rather than merely two. One of the gut busters fell silent, but that odd echoing continued.

Imagination? Wishful thinking?

I cocked my head and listened. It was neither. There *were* other weapons being fired out there.

Hope surged but I clamped down on it, hard. Until every Adlin warrior was dead and I saw the evidence of salvation with my own eyes, I couldn't allow myself to hope.

The heavy machine-gun fire continued for another few minutes, then silence fell. I waited. A few more minutes passed, then dust stirred, a heavy cloud that drifted into our broken shelter, making any sort of vision next to impossible.

"Nightwatch eight-three?" a deep voice said. "This is Blacklake Prime. How are you both faring down there?"

Blacklake Prime. Winterborne hadn't just called out the regular troops; they'd sent the commander of the whole outpost. It made me wonder who the woman I'd rescued was, because they certainly wouldn't have done it for me.

"I'm injured, and our witch is unconscious."

"Is she hurt?"

"No."

"Good. I'm sending a healer down. Don't shoot him."

A smile touched my lips. "I don't know what you've heard about the Nightwatch, but we're not inclined to shoot our rescuers."

"I thought it best to mention, given the way you were spraying bullets around." Amusement ran through the rich tone of his voice. "If I didn't know any better, I'd think you had an armory down there."

"No armory. I just decided it was better to go out in a blaze of glory."

Feet appeared at the main entrance to our cave, then a brown-clad man dropped into the trench, his fingers briefly brushing the ground before he rose again. He was carrying a medikit and looked a whole lot younger than me, although that could merely be the impression given by his rather wild-looking red hair.

"I'm Mace Dien, chief healer at Blacklake."

So, once again, not just any old healer, but the man in charge. Saska *had* to be someone of importance—maybe even someone from one of the ruling houses.

"Neve March." I held out my good hand and, after a moment, he shook it. "Saska is unconscious, but I think it's due more to overusing her abilities. I did run a scanner over her when I found her, and it came back negative for injuries."

His gaze briefly scanned her then came back to me. "She's not the one needing attention right now."

I smile tugged my lips. "Perhaps, but she's the reason you're all here, is she not?"

He didn't bother denying it, just moved inside our shelter and crouched down beside me. "Tell me if this hurts," he said, and lightly placed a hand on my injured leg.

It felt like I was being touched by a hot iron, and it set off a wave of heat and pain so fierce it had a hiss escaping and sweat popping out across my brow.

"I'll take that as a yes." His gaze shifted to my left arm, and he made a "show me" motion with a couple of fingers.

I raised it as ordered but it was a far harder task than it should have been. Obviously now that adrenaline was no longer coursing through my body, reaction was setting in.

Again, he touched me, and again it felt like fire. He screwed his nose up and met my gaze. "They both need immediate attention, but I can't do anything in this pit. If I give you a painkiller, do you think you can stand being hauled out?"

"Yes." No matter how much pain it caused, it would never be as bad as what the Adlin would have put us through had they caught us alive.

"Good."

He opened the medikit, which turned out to be extremely basic, containing little more than vials of painkillers and a couple of needle-free injectors. But then, he was a healer, and they tended to work alongside regular medicine and doctors, using a mix of psychic power and magic to heal wounds. They also tended to spend a lot of their time on the battlefield, patching up bodies to ensure survival until proper medical attention could be given.

He injected both my arm and my leg, then closed the kit back up and rose. "Okay," he said, offering me his hand. "Take it easy getting up. You've lost a lot of blood and could be very lightheaded."

There was no "could be" about it. I gripped his hand, took a deep, steadying breath, then nodded. He carefully pulled me upright, but it didn't really matter. My head still spun, my knees buckled, and my stomach rose rather alarmingly. He gripped my elbow to steady me, and then shifted his grip to my waist, holding me upright in much the same manner as I'd held Saska up earlier.

"One coming up," he said as we shuffled forward.

It was an effort that had sweat running down my spine and forehead. Damn, I felt weak.

Once we'd made it into the open air, hands reached down and hauled me up. The fierceness of the sunshine had my eyes watering but it didn't stop me from seeing the mutilated remains of the Adlin. There weren't just five or six bodies scattered about, but over a dozen of them. It was a far greater number than what had initially attacked us and it made me wonder why. Adlin might be fierce hunters, but it was unusual for a hunting pack to allow others in on the action once the chase had begun.

The two men who'd hauled me upright shifted their grip and then carried me across to one of three heavily armored, tanklike troop movers. These things weren't designed for comfort, and were cramped and basic inside. This one had two medibeds situated at the rear of the vehicle. The soldiers carefully placed me the bottom bunk then gave me a nod and retreated. I closed my eyes and tried to ignore not only the sick weakness washing through my limbs but the impulse to punch the air in victory and shout obscenities at the ghosts of the Adlin who'd been slaughtered in this place. Both urges were undoubtedly a reaction to surviving the unsurvivable, but it wasn't like we were out of the woods yet. The Adlin had showed an amazing tenacity, and part of me couldn't help but think our problems weren't over yet.

Footsteps echoed as someone entered the mover, and I reluctantly opened my eyes. The man who had entered was tall, with the brown skin and hair that was commonly found amongst those who were earth witches, and eyes that were a startling green.

"Trey Stone, Blacklake Prime." He stopped near the bunk

and crossed his arms. "That's one hell of a chase you led the Adlin on, March."

"It was either run or die, and I really wasn't in the mood for the latter today."

"Obviously." His gaze scanned my face but showed little reaction to the very evident stain on my cheek. Which was odd, because it was the first thing most people commented on when they initially met me. "Was there any indication of how Saska Rossi came to be naked and unescorted in the middle of nowhere?"

"No indication at all, Commander."

But the fact that she was a Rossi really *did* explain why everyone had gone to such lengths to rescue us. The Rossis were a very powerful family of air witches, and one of the six ruling houses in Winterborne.

Stone was another.

And while it wasn't surprising to find an earth witch stationed at Blacklake—all outposts had both air and earth witches on their rosters—it was certainly unusual for the placement to go to someone from a ruling house. It was even rarer for that person to become prime.

"And how did you get to be here, so far away from your scooter?" he asked.

I gave him an edited version of events and he frowned. But before he could question me further, the two men who'd carried me reappeared with Saska. Stone stepped back to let them pass, then glanced at me again. "We're returning to Blacklake. I'll inform your captain we've found you alive and relatively intact."

"Thanks."

He headed out of the carrier, moving with a grace and lightness that was rare in those of earth. Or maybe it simply rare in those born into the lower houses, or in those who usually held duty at the five border encampments.

Mace climbed into the cabin, followed by half a dozen other men. He curtained off the rear of the carrier then strapped Saska in before repeating the process on me.

As the roar of the engine coming to life filled the air and the whole carrier began to rattle, he said, "I'm afraid your wounds aren't going to wait until we get back to Blacklake."

I shrugged. "That's okay. I have no problems with healers."

"Good to hear, although it wouldn't matter if you did, because I'm all you've got. And you won't be awake to protest, anyway."

"I'd rather not—"

"Every Nightwatch I've ever treated has said that." He placed a hand on my forehead. Heat leapt from his skin to mine, and an odd sort of peace began to descend. "The expectation of toughness must be off the scale amongst your lot."

"It's not." The words came out slightly slurred as the peacefulness began to extend across my body. "I just hate..."

...*being incapacitated when others are facing danger in my stead.* But the words never made it to my lips. The peacefulness claimed me and I knew no more.

It was the warm wash of water that woke me. For several seconds I didn't move; I simply enjoyed the sensation as I gathered my senses and tried to figure out where I was.

And that obviously wasn't in the troop carrier. This place was quiet and filled with the fresh scents of herbs and femininity rather than machine oil and men.

The gentle breeze that stirred past my skin spoke of night and stars, and told me nine hours had passed since our rescue. There was no pain emanating from either my arm or my leg, although a quick twitch of my left hand revealed a still unresponsive little finger. But that might have been because there was something tight wrapped around it.

I opened my eyes. A woman with gray hair and a lined face met my gaze and smiled. "You're not supposed to be awake yet."

"I do a lot of things I'm not supposed to do."

A quick look around revealed I was in a hospital ward. The whitewashed walls were made of stone and lined with small windows that probably wouldn't allow much daylight in, but also wouldn't let anyone climb in or out. While I was currently the only occupant, there were at least a dozen beds in the room, each one possessing a silent array of medical machines both over and beside it.

"So I hear." The woman dunked the cloth into a tub of water and continued to wash me down. It was, I thought with a slight frown, a rather pleasurable experience. Which was weird given the situation and the lack of attraction. "Like you and the witch surviving against impossible odds."

"*That* was good luck and her abilities more than anything I might have done." I raised my hand and saw that it was still in a partial splint. "What's happened to my finger?"

"It was smashed and severed. They've managed to reattach the flesh, but the bone was almost beyond repair. They've inserted metal knuckles and joints and are hoping the grafts will take."

The skin at the tip of my finger was pink, which at least indicated the blood vessels were working as they should.

"And Saska? Where's she?"

"In the state apartments. Can't have someone of her ilk staying with us commoners, now, can we?" It was said with a smile, and without rancor.

"We surely can't." I echoed her smile and held out my good hand. "I'm Neve."

She wiped a hand on her skirts then shook mine. "Treace. Chief nurse and all-round dogsbody in this place."

"How long am I likely to be held in this place, Treace?"

Her smile grew. "I was wondering when we'd get to *that* question. It's usually the first one I'm asked."

"And do you have an answer in this particular instance?"

"Not really. Not until Mace appears to examine your wounds, and he's currently up with the Rossi woman." She dumped the washcloth back into the water and grabbed a towel. "But your leg has healed rather nicely and I'm thinking it'll be sooner rather than later."

She began drying me off. It was a rough caress that had shivers of delight running through me. Which again was decidedly odd, because I wasn't normally *that* sensitive to touch, especially when it involved someone I wasn't physically attracted to. Maybe it was just a hangover from near death—a renewed appreciation of life and everything it involved.

There was a soft knock on the door at the far end of the room, then it opened slightly and another woman poked her head through the gap. "Lord Kiro wants to interview our Nightwatch officer, if she's feeling up to it."

Treace glanced at me. "Are you?"

"That depends on who Lord Kiro is."

Her smile remained in place, but her eyes told a different story. Lord Kiro was someone she was uncertain—maybe even afraid—of. "The Rossi clan sent him here to confirm Saska's identity. Apparently she's been missing for nigh on twelve years now."

Meaning *he* was from the Rossi clan? "Why does he want to talk to me? I don't know her—I just rescued her."

Treace shrugged. "I'll send him away if you wish."

I hesitated and then shook my head. "It will only delay the

inevitable. But I'd like something to eat once he's gone, if that can be arranged."

"It surely can." She pulled the bedsheet back over my body, and then nodded an acceptance at the other woman before heading out the door to my right.

I pushed up into a sitting position and tugged the sheet up over my breasts. While nudity didn't faze me, I'd heard those of earth and air were a whole lot less comfortable in their skin than the Nightwatch tended to be. Of course, we lived in cramped quarters and shared bathing facilities, while those who lived in either the Upper or Lower Reaches not only had the benefit of their own huge dwellings, but also privacy and the ability to be alone when not on duty.

While I waited for Lord Kiro to appear, I glanced down at my left arm. It, like my left cheek, my right hip, leg, and the entirety of my foot, was stained, but the leathery skin looked lavender in the half-light of the hospital. It was an unwanted legacy of the past and the war, when the Irkallan had not only overrun all the villages and farms that had once dotted Tenterra, but had also raped those who'd survived the slaughter, be they men, women, or children. Those of us who carried this unwanted reminder of that time were no longer outcast or looked upon with revulsion—for the most part— but because we were also rarely gifted with any ability in magic, few considered us to be ideal partners. Even those who were totally ungifted—the blacksmiths, bakers, builders, even the Nightwatch with whom I lived—would not consider undertaking the committal ceremony with someone such as me. It was a fact I'd long ago accepted, even if in the deeper recesses of night and dreams I sometimes ached for more.

The stain actually looked quite pretty in this light, but it was somewhat spoiled by the scar that now ran from my knuckles to my elbow. Although it would fade with time, it was currently an ugly, ragged pink line that spoke of death's closeness. But I guessed I was lucky that two scars and a reconstructed digit was *all* I'd come away with. It could have been a whole lot worse.

The door down the far end of the room opened and a tall, silver-haired gentleman stepped through. Despite the fact he looked to be well past his fifties—maybe even his sixties—his power rode before him like a wave and sent electricity racing across my skin, making it jump and itch. But it wasn't the power of the air and the storms; it wasn't even the power of the earth. It was deeper—and more personal—than that.

I resisted the urge to scratch and watched him warily. He was dressed in black from head to toe, and it was a color that suited him, for it emphasized both the strength of his body and the fierceness of his power—a power that both appealed and repelled, all at the same time.

"Neve March, we owe you a great debt." He snagged a chair, dragged it up to my bed, and sat down.

I resisted the ridiculous urge to edge away from him and forced a smile. "I was only doing my job."

"I don't think there are many who would act as you did." He paused, his gaze sweeping me, lingering briefly on the stains that were on show. "I don't think there are many who could."

I frowned at the odd emphasis he placed on "could." "All Nightwatch are trained the same. I did nothing more than what was expected of me."

"Perhaps." He leaned back in his chair and crossed his arms. I had a vague feeling he was somehow here to judge me, but why that would be the case I had no idea.

"Tell me about finding Saska and how the two of you managed to survive the Adlin."

My frown deepened. "Surely she's already done that?"

"Her version is decidedly sketchy on details."

"She was semi-unconscious for much of it," I replied. "But it thankfully didn't stop her from raising the wind. We'd be dead if not for that."

"Indeed."

While there was nothing in his tone or his expression that suggested disbelief, it nevertheless wrapped around me like a glove—a glove that felt like silk and steel combined, and one that had goose bumps skittering across my skin. It wasn't all fear—far from it. But I didn't dare acknowledge what the rest of it was, because to do so would give it power. And it was a power, the wind whispered, he would not hesitate to use.

"Please," he continued, "I'd really like to hear your version of events."

I studied him for a second, a deep sense of unease growing. Something was going on, something I didn't understand and couldn't immediately fight. But I obeyed, only omitting my part in the wind's actions.

By the time I'd finished, he was leaning forward, his arms resting on the edge of the bed close to my hip, as if drawn there by anticipation of the story's end. Yet I was no storyteller and he already knew how this particular tale ended.

"That is all quite extraordinary," he said. "Saska's powers have certainly grown in the twelve years of her absence."

His tone suggested that should not have been the case. "Has she remembered where she's been in that time?"

A glimmer of amusement appeared in his pale eyes; he knew a redirect when he heard one. "No. Nor can she remember who the father of her child might be or how she came to be in possession of an Adlin beacon. It's a puzzle, and one her husband will undoubtedly desire an answer to."

If Saska was committed, then she must have gone through the ceremony as soon as she'd come of age, as she appeared to be no older than me.

"I gather a full scan has been run on her?"

He smiled, knowing full well what I was *actually* asking. "Of course."

His tone suggested it was the first thing they'd done, and surely meant the babe *wasn't* Adlin.

"Who fathered her son is of no real consequence, of course," he continued. "Not if he is born into magic."

Because, in the end, the capacity for magic—be it earth, air, or personal—mattered more than bloodlines or relationships. It was the reason why so many of the children born into ruling families had Sifft blood but possessed no magic. In the past, they'd erroneously believed that shifting was a form of magic, when it was nothing more than complex DNA coding.

"Is her husband coming here to escort her back to Winterborne?"

"That task has been conferred to me." He shifted back in the chair, but one hand brushed my hip as he did so. Despite the sheet that lay between my skin and his, awareness surged and pleasure rushed through me again.

Why on earth was I in such a hyper state? Why was this weird, unwanted rush of desire even happening, first with the older woman and now with this man—a man who was obviously here for reasons other than what he'd stated?

He was still watching me far too closely and I had a vague feeling he was very aware of my sensitive state. Which, erect nipples aside, should not have been the case. He wasn't Sifft, and shouldn't have been able to scent desire.

"Whose idea was it to dig an earth shelter?" he asked, after a moment.

"Mine." I paused, feeling rather like a wildebeest caught in a powerful spotlight, knowing trouble was coming but unable to see or move past the glare of the lights. "Why?"

"Because while air witches can control wind and weather

for as long as their strength holds out, the earth is not theirs to command."

I frowned. "But she didn't command the earth. She merely asked the wind to cut into it."

"Even that should not have been possible. Earth and air are two completely different elements and a witch who controls one cannot impact the other."

I shrugged, trying to ignore the confusion within as much as the questions that rose at his statement. "Maybe the wind sensed her desperation."

"Maybe." He studied me for a moment then pushed to his feet and held out a hand. "I would like to officially thank you on behalf of the Rossi clan."

I hesitated, not wanting to touch him but knowing he'd consider it offensive if I didn't. But the minute my fingers were encased in his, energy surged, a wave of heat that prickled across my skin like desire and yet had a far darker purpose. Lord Kiro might possess a very powerful and seductive type of personal magic, but he was also a reader—someone who had the ability to touch the flesh of another and draw out his or her innermost secrets.

I had no secrets—nothing other than a tiny fraction of magical ability I wasn't supposed to possess. And as far as I knew, readers weren't capable of uncovering such information—that was the job of auditors.

"Believe me," I said, keeping my voice even. "No thanks are required."

"Many would disagree." He frowned down at our hands, as if confused, then said, "Saska would like to see you when you feel up to it. Tonight, if possible, but certainly before we leave tomorrow."

Because of course a common Nightwatch officer would not be transported in the same vehicle as those from a ruling house—even if said Nightwatch officer had saved one of their asses. I pulled my hand from his and said, "Sure. I'm just waiting on dinner now, but maybe afterward?"

"I'll let her know." He gave me a half bow, then turned and strode from the room.

But the tension that rode me didn't leave, even after he'd well and truly departed. Something was happening, something over which I had no control and no understanding. Something that involved that man, Saska, and perhaps even the ability I wasn't supposed to have.

Restless and uneasy, I flicked off the sheet and swung my feet off the bed. The scar on my leg was as puckered and ugly as the one on my arm, though at least it was no larger than a babe's fist. I eased down onto my left leg then carefully switched my weight to my right. A niggle of pain ran across my nerve endings, but the leg seemed to hold up. I took a step, then when nothing happened, walked over to the window and looked out.

Just in time to see a huge ball of flame arc over Blacklake's curtain wall and smash down into the courtyard.

3

Almost immediately a high-pitched wail cut through the silence and made the hair on my arms stand on end.

It was the attack alarm.

I spun and ran back to the locker at the base of my bed. Saska's bracelets and all my weapons were inside, but my clothes weren't; instead, there was the brown uniform of a Blacklake officer. I guessed mine had been too damaged to repair. I hastily dressed, then clipped on my utilities belt, weapons, and knife.

"Whoa there, young lady," Treace said as she stepped back into the room. "Where do you think you're going?"

"We're under attack—"

"Yes, and our people can handle it. You can come with me to the raid shelter—"

"Sorry, but I can't." I grabbed one of the meat patties from the tray she was carrying. "I'll eat the rest of that later."

I raised the patty in salute then ran out into the hallway, eating it as I paused to get my bearings. I had no idea how this place was laid out, but to find the curtain wall all I had to do was listen for the sound of fighting—and *that* was coming from the right.

I spun and ran down the hall, weaving my way through the men, women, and children going in the opposite direction. The doors opened as I approached and I paused again, my gaze sweeping the courtyard ahead. The hospital appeared to be situated against the inner bailey wall, and just in front of a massive but empty moat. Between it and the main curtain wall lay the outer yard, much of which was currently on fire. To my left, there were steps leading up to the barracks, under which lay machinery sheds. To the right, what looked like workhouses, kitchens, and a mess hall. Directly in front of me was the great tower, a massive metal construction that was undoubtedly the command center. If I wanted to join the fight, I'd better head there and ask for a station. To do anything else was not only disrespectful to the Blacklake battalion, but also dangerous.

I spun left and ran for the drawbridge. There were several men stationed near it, ready to draw it up should the outer wall be breached—but it wouldn't be, surely. While an Adlin's claws might be able to pierce stone as easily as flesh, the metal used on these walls—like the metal used at Winterborne—was slick and thick, and impervious to anything the Adlin or even the Irkallan might throw at it.

A soft whistling had me looking up. A ball of fire the size of a head was coming straight at me. I threw up my hand, as if to ward off the heat of it, and called on the wind to divert it. She answered surprisingly fast, gusting briefly but fiercely, changing the course of the flaming ball just enough to smash it into the ground several feet away. Fire chased my heels as I raced across the yard and then into the great tower. Surprisingly, there were no guards there. I gripped the metal railing and began to climb, my footsteps echoing in the vast, shadowed space.

From up above, a voice said, "Who goes there?"

"Neve March, Nightwatch officer, seeking permission to join the fight."

There was a pause, then, "Permission granted to come up."

Which was not permission to join the fight, but better than being sent packing to the raid shelter. I raced up the remaining two flights and came to a large landing area. Several heavily armed men were on watch here; only one of them acknowledged me.

"This way."

He pressed his hand against a nearby print reader and the heavily armored door to his right slid open. I stepped through and paused. The room was a long oblong shape that had two levels and contained not only a full complement of communicators, but computers, scanners—which were full screens rather than the basic light units used in sprinters and haulers—as well as other military personnel doing who knows what.

My gaze was immediately drawn to the grated windows that ran the length of the room. Beyond the curtain wall below us, spotlighted not only by the powerful search beams that dotted the wall but also the bonfires they were using to ignite their projectiles, were the Adlin. There were at least five sleuths out there, and that was very unusual. Winterborne certainly hadn't seen those sorts of numbers for years.

I tore my gaze away and looked around until I spotted Blacklake's prime. He was standing behind a series of scanners on the top level and talking into an earwig. I walked over and waited.

He glanced at me, held up a finger, and continued issuing orders. I watched what was going on in the room, fascinated. It was a rare glimpse into the other side of a battle.

After several minutes, he hit the earwig to end communications then looked at me. "What the hell are you doing here, March?"

"I'm trained to fight, Commander. Put me to use."

"We have this under control." His gaze swept me briefly. "And Mace would have my nuts if I let you out on the wall without his clearance."

I raised an eyebrow. "How do you know I haven't got it?"

A smile tugged one corner of his lips but before he could reply, a communicator stationed at a bank of computers— which detailed the position of the six soldiers in her contact group—the next level down said, "Just got the go from station one, Commander."

"Is two ready?"

Another communicator said, "Yes."

"On my mark, then." He paused and studied the row of sensor screens in front of him. Each one not only repre- sented a different section of Blacklake, but also an over- laying chart of the earth's crisscrossing energy lines. The Adlin were green blobs that moved from one intersection point to another, their numbers indicated by the size of those blobs. The commander waited until all the green blobs had drawn close to the wall and then said, "One and two, go."

The order was swiftly repeated, and silence fell. The commander leaned forward, his expression intent as he stared out the windows. I stepped closer, wondering what was about to happen.

Most of the Adlin were clustered inside the dry moat bed that ringed the curtain wall; some of them flung crude projectiles at the walls to protect those who hauled long siege ladders into place. The Blacklake soldiers fired at those nearing the top of the ladders, but not, I thought with a frown, with any great zeal.

A soft rumbling invaded the silence and the heavy stones

under my feet started to vibrate. The force of it sang through me, and though its voice was muted, I knew what it meant.

The earth had just been called into the fight.

The rumbling grew louder, stronger, and, out in the night, beyond the empty moat, the earth began to twist and shake and split. Fire spilled from its pits, only to be swallowed whole. The rudimentary trebuchets soon met the same fate.

The Adlin roared and threw themselves at the walls with greater intensity. The earth's writhing eased, but a different kind of rumbling began to grow. In the stark brightness of the spotlight stationed on the far right edge of the curtain wall, I spotted a foaming, glittering rush of water that was at least two-meters high. The Adlin saw it at the same time and began to run, but the water was far faster. It hit them, swallowed them, and swept them away to freedom only knew where.

A fierce cheer went up from those stationed on the wall and inside the command center, and everyone began to talk and relax.

"That," I said to the man standing beside me, "was a rather awesome display of power."

He pushed away from the sensor screens and glanced at me, one eyebrow raised. "You've surely seen the earth respond in such a manner at Winterborne."

"Yes, but not water." I paused, glancing at the window again. The tide had once again become a trickle, but the few Adlin who were not caught by the first rush were on the run. "You have the Black River dammed?"

"It runs across our western flank, so it is easy enough to do. Ruma, you want to take over operations? Contact me if there're any problems."

A strong-looking black woman glanced up and said, "Will do, Commander."

His gaze came back to mine and, in a clipped voice, he said, "Follow me."

He brushed past me, and that troublesome, achy awareness stirred again. I frowned as I followed him down the metal stairs, our footsteps echoing in time through the shadows. I wished there was someone I could talk to, someone who might know what was going on, but I dared not ask. Dared not reveal the secret I'd been carrying since I'd come of age. To do that would be the end of my life as a Nightwatch officer—the end of everything I knew, and everything I held dear. If my ability to talk to the wind—however minor —was revealed, they'd either place me into one of the ruling houses, where I would serve as a "battery" to those of greater power, or I'd be taken as a mistress by one of the men in the hope that I would bear a child of greater ability. For someone stained as badly as me, there was little other option. Not unless I wanted to run and live life somewhere beyond the reach of the ruling Forum. And there weren't many such places in Gallion or even Salysis these days.

The commander strode across the outer courtyard, briefly acknowledging those who were containing the fires still burning across the stones. The guards at the inner drawbridge nodded as he passed but there was no saluting or formal snap to attention. Unlike the primes at some of the other outposts, Trey Stone didn't appear to stand on ceremony.

As we passed through the heavily fortified inner gatehouse, the raid alarm sounded again, this time in three short, sharp bursts.

"That's the all clear," the commander said over his shoulder. "It tells those in the shelters it's safe to emerge."

I caught up to him. "Do all the outposts have such shelters?"

"All those who have a civilian population, yes." He glanced

at me, one eyebrow raised. "Why the surprise? You have them in the outer bailey at Winterborne, do you not?"

"Yes, but as far as I'm aware, we haven't needed to use them since the war." I paused, briefly taking in the surrounding buildings and wondering where we were headed. "Was tonight's attack usual for this area?"

"No, it was not."

There was something in his voice that had my gaze snapping back to him. "In what way was it different?"

"They've never attacked in such numbers before, nor have they ever used assault weapons, however rudimentary they might have been." He paused and nodded at the soldier who opened the door to a long, three-story stone and metal-clad building. "They were after something. Or someone."

"Saska." I blew out a breath. "But why?"

"I have no idea."

The room we entered was a vast space filled with tables, chairs, and cushioned areas for lounging. Bright tapestries lined the walls and a huge fire dominated the far end of the long room. It seemed nothing more than an old-fashioned great hall built along the lines of castles of old, but a closer look revealed the presence of light switches and power connections. It might have been an outpost, but those living and working here were not expected to go without their creature comforts.

We didn't stop in the hall, however, but continued past the great fire to a staircase all but hidden behind it. Two flights up we reached the antechamber for what I presumed was his private suite. And the fact we'd come here sent all sorts of alarms through me—but not because I thought he intended, in any way, to make a sexual overture.

Two comfortable-looking chairs sat in front of a smaller, but no less warm, open fire. He sat down and motioned me toward the other.

I hesitated. "I'd rather stand, Commander."

"Yes, I know you would, but this is an informal chat rather than a formal one. So sit."

As I reluctantly did so, he pressed a button on the table next to his chair. A few seconds later, a woman appeared. She was comely and young, with blonde hair and blue eyes—and wanted to be far more than just a handmaiden if the look she gave the commander was anything to go by.

"Mari, two glasses of red, please."

She curtseyed and disappeared before I could protest. "What is going on, Commander? What do you want of me?"

"What do I want?" He pressed his fingers together and considered me. "The truth would be a good start."

"The truth of what?"

"Of what really happened out there."

I frowned. "I told the truth in the troop carrier. I'm not sure what else you want."

"I want to know why those Adlin were so bloody determined to capture one or both of you."

I half smiled. "I bear the scars of their determination to kill, Commander. It's certainly not me they're after."

"Perhaps."

It was the second time a man of power had said that, and it sat as uneasily with me this time as it had the first. I leaned forward and splayed my fingers wide to capture the fire's heat, although I was far from cold. That heat came not just from the discomfort of questions I could not—dare not—answer, but from a fierce, raw wash of energy emanating from the man sitting entirely too close. It was both earthy and sexual, and it ensnared my senses and made them hunger.

I made a vague attempt to shake such thoughts and desires from my mind and said, "The questions that should be asked here is, how did a woman who has been missing for

twelve years come to be alone and lost in the Tenterra wasteland? And why was she in possession of an Adlin beacon?"

"Oh, they're questions that will undoubtedly be asked,
and by more than me and you." He crossed his legs, the
movement casual and elegant. "But I very much suspect that
there are other questions only you can answer."

"Such as?"

Mari returned with two glasses and a bottle of wine. She
poured us both a drink then said, "Is there anything else,
my lord?"

"Not tonight, Mari. Thank you."

She bowed and disappeared, but not before I'd caught the
brief flash of annoyance she cast my way. My guess about her
desires had been right.

I swirled the red around in the glass. It was rich in color
and full in body, and teased my nostrils with the smell of
blueberries and violets. But it could not overpower the raw
scent of masculinity coming from the man in the other chair.

Whatever this awareness was, I wanted it gone. Quickly.

He was watching me, I knew, but not really in the way of
a man who was attracted to a woman. It was more like
hunter and prey. He wanted something from me, but that
something wasn't sex. I took a sip of wine and tried to ignore
both my hyper-awareness of him *and* the growing uneasiness. The silence ran on. And on.

Whatever his reasons for me being here, he wasn't in a
hurry to reveal them.

"This wine," I said eventually, "is far better than anything
they serve at the base canteen."

He snorted. "It should be, given the price the merchants
charge for the stuff. Tell me about that earth shelter, March."

"Neve," I said automatically, and then cursed inwardly. I
didn't need to be on intimate terms with this man, not even

when it came to something as simple as being on a first-name basis. "And there's really nothing much to tell."

"Lady Saska is a woman of some power, but even the most powerful air witch alive has no authority over the earth. The wind couldn't have dug that trench and cave for her."

My gaze met his. "So Lord Kiro said. That does not alter the fact of what happened."

"Lord Kiro happens to believe you are not telling the truth."

And he would be right. I raised an eyebrow and hoped the inner agitation didn't show. "And what lies does he think I'm telling?"

"He, like me, believes that it was you who dug the trench."

I raised the wine to my lips and somehow resisted the urge to gulp it down and ask for more. I sipped it, licked the sweetness from my lips, and then said, "So he thinks I somehow snatched the ability to control the earth from some hereto unseen and unknown place that harbors such magic, and used it to save us?"

Amusement touched his expression, and it softened his aristocratic features. While he couldn't be classified as captivatingly handsome—as so many of those in the ruling houses were—there was still something about this man's features that drew the eye.

"There are no places of wild magic left in this misbegotten land," he said. "So no, he does not think that."

"He's foolish to think anything else," I replied bluntly. "I'm unlit, Commander, and that can never change."

He drank some wine, the green of his gaze filled with shadows and questions. "The auditors have been known to get it wrong."

My smile held little in the way of amusement. "But I'm

also stained. Have you ever known—ever heard—of one such as I possessing such power?"

His gaze drifted to the stain on my cheek. I half expected a slither of distaste to appear, but again, he surprised me.

"No. Not the ability to command interaction between earth and air, at any rate."

"Then I don't know what else to say, Commander. I can only repeat the truth of what happened, and if that is not believed then—" I stopped and shrugged.

"Lord Kiro is arranging for Lady Saska to be re-audited once she's back at Winterborne and recovered. I expect we'll have our answers then."

Those answers, I knew, would only lead to more questions—questions that would involve my part in doing the impossible. But even if the auditors were assigned to me and did detect the sliver of magic I now possessed, it wouldn't provide them with answers. Although I had to wonder, if an air witch had no power or control over the earth itself, why had I been able to do just that? It was certainly the air I'd called for help, not the earth.

"I hope so, Commander." I drained the rest of the wine, placed the glass on the small table between our chairs, and then rose. "If that's all, I should return to the hospital ward."

"Yes, I think perhaps you should." He pressed a second button and then stood.

Though there was still a good five feet between us, something flared. Something that was once again earthy and base, sexual and yet not. It echoed not only through me, but the rough stone under my feet. It was unlike anything I'd ever felt before, and it left me both breathless and frightened. Because whatever it was, it was not only powerful but also very *dangerous*.

And he felt it, even if it was only evident by the slight narrowing of his eyes.

I took a step back but the movement didn't shatter the power of whatever that surge was.

"Rogers?" he said, his gaze not wavering from mine. "Can you escort March back to the hospital, please?"

"That's not necessary—"

"I disagree." His voice was mild even if his gaze was still too watchful, too wary. "And a guard will be placed on your door should you decide to go wandering again without clearance."

"I'm not dangerous—"

"Oh, I think you are, Neve March." The small smile that briefly tugged his lips did little to ease the darkness in his eyes. "Few others could do what you have done. Few others could even survive it."

He wasn't, I suspected, talking so much about our escape from the Adlin, but the means by which we'd done it. Trouble had indeed stepped into my path the minute I'd decided to meld with the wind, and it obviously wasn't stepping away. "Then you misjudge the training and skill of the Nightwatch, Commander."

"Perhaps."

As footsteps warned of the approaching guard, I spun on my heel and walked across to the stairs. A brown-clad figure appeared down the bottom. I motioned him to stop, then glanced back at Stone.

"I hope you get your answers, Commander."

"I intend to. Good night, March."

I wasn't sure whether his comment was a promise or a threat, and was just as unsure about the response it evoked within me. I nodded in reply and clattered down the stairs.

But I had a vague feeling I had not seen the last of Black-lake's prime.

Treace clucked over me like a mother hen as I stripped off and climbed back into bed. She swung the nearby machine over me to check that I'd done no damage to either my hand or my leg, then reheated my meal and made I sure I ate it.

"You need to build your strength, young lady, not be wasting it willy-nilly," she said at one point.

I smiled. "I'm fine—"

"Yes, I'm sure you are," she said, with a roll of her eyes. "Nevertheless, you *will* stay in this bed until Mace gets here, won't you? Because I will tie you down if I have to."

I grinned. "And how many of your patients have said 'yes please' after such a threat."

She laughed. "Far too many, I tell you. Sleep tight, lass. We're just outside if you need anything."

And so were the guards—one on each door, in fact. Trey Stone was certainly determined that I would remain exactly where I was supposed to. As the lights dimmed in the room, I shuffled down into the bed and dragged the sheet over my shoulders. The strange awareness had finally begun to fade, even if my body still hummed like a fiddle too tightly strung. I closed my eyes, drew in the silence and peace of this place, and slept.

And if I dreamed of green eyes and earth, I had no clear memory of it.

Mace visited me the following morning. After checking my wounds, he muttered something about wishing he could harness the healing skills of the Sifft for the greater good of all, and ordered me to keep the brace on my finger for one more day. Treace then brought a hearty mid-morning meal, the news that I was cleared to leave Winterborne, and a demand from Saska that I come and see her immediately.

I showered and dressed, then clipped the bracelets onto my utilities belt and strapped on the blaster and gut busters. The rifle I slung over my shoulder. I wasn't about to leave anything here—not when doing so would involve all manner of paperwork and deputations when I got home.

Last night's guard had been replaced by a slender, dark-haired woman. She gave me a friendly enough nod, but didn't say anything as she led me into the inner bailey and across to a long, sturdy-looking building I presumed were the State Apartments. It was interesting that the commander had his quarters over the great hall rather than here. Maybe he simply preferred to keep the apartments for visiting guests—Blacklake might be an outpost, but he was still a member of a ruling family and a male at that. I doubted he'd be left out of family events or decisions.

Saska's quarters were on the second floor and were a vast, comfortable space that not only possessed a four-poster bed, but also several couches, a private eating area, and an open fire. There were no tapestries on the whitewashed walls here, but rather paintings depicting landscapes and farm build-ings. I wondered if they were meant to represent Tenterra as it had once been.

Saska sat near the fire, but turned as I entered. The look she gave me was remote and regal. The woman who'd sworn at me like a soldier had obviously been well and truly leashed.

"Neve," she said, voice cool. "I'm glad you could make it before we were shipped out."

It wasn't like I really had an option but I merely stopped and did the required half bow. "I'm glad to see you appear to have recovered from your ordeal, Lady Saska."

"Indeed." She raised one eyebrow. I wasn't entirely sure if it was in amusement or disdain. "Aside from the troublesome lack of memory of how I managed to get there, I'm surpris-ingly well."

"Good." I unclipped the bracelets and held them out to her. "These are yours."

She didn't take them. In fact, something close to fear or revulsion rolled across her face before she got her expression back under control.

"They were never mine. The first time I saw them was out in that desert."

I frowned. "I thought you said the queen gifted—"

"I said *no* such thing." Her cool tone hinted at anger. "And I will *not* have you spreading such lies, do you hear me?"

The wind that stirred around me contained a similar frosty bite, but also a warning for me to hold my tongue—that it wasn't worth antagonizing her just yet. The wind rather unusually seemed to be on my side rather than hers right now.

"I hear." Whether I obeyed was another matter entirely. Although, who would I tell? It wasn't as if anyone would take my word over hers.

"Good." She waved a hand dismissively. "You may do with them what you wish."

"But—" I hesitated, my gaze falling to them. They were heavy in my hands and obviously pure silver. Selling them would go a long way to ensuring I had a good sum of money behind me come retirement—if I made retirement, that was. That wasn't always a certainty in either the Night or Daywatch. But I couldn't in good conscience accept them so readily. It wasn't right—not when they might be some kind of family heirloom. Their design was certainly old enough. "You asked me to save them because of their value. This is far too much of a reward when I was only doing my job."

"Then give one to Stone. I care not."

She picked up a nearby mug and took a drink. I couldn't help but notice her hand was trembling. There was definitely something about these bracelets she wasn't passing on.

"So be it." I clipped them back onto my utility belt. "Is there anything I can do for you before we leave?"

"No. I merely wished to express my thanks for your actions yesterday. I'm told I'd be dead were it not for you."

I smiled. "That's not entirely true. Both you and the wind contributed to our survival."

"Indeed." She paused, her gaze returning to mine. "My husband intends to give a masque to celebrate both the rising of Pomona and my return. I wish you to be present."

Pomona was a festival dedicated to the goddess of the same name, and was both a celebration of the end of summer and an entreaty for a successful harvest. While Tenterra might have been made a wasteland after the war, the Gallion farmlands—which lay just behind Winterborne —hadn't been as fully drained, and had quickly become plentiful again. The Pomona Masque was a big celebration, even in the outer bailey. Guard duty was restricted to a bare minimum, drink flowed, and the coupling rooms were never empty. I really didn't want to waste such a celebration feeling awkward and out of place in some highborn's house.

"I appreciate the honor, Lady Saska, but—"

She raised a hand, halting me. "You *will* come. It is only fitting that my saviors are appropriately presented to those who gave up hope."

I wondered if one of those people was her husband. Wondered what he really thought about his long-lost wife being found. I guessed I was about to find out.

I bowed in acquiescence. "As you wish."

"Good. I will arrange the appropriate invitation once I return home."

"Thank you." I hesitated. "Will there be anything else?"

"No." She turned to the fire, dismissing me physically if not verbally. I retreated from the room. The dark-haired guard waited for me in the main corridor, and escorted me to the outer bailey, where two troop carriers waited.

Blacklake's commander stood in front of the first one. My escort led me to him then, with a nod from Stone, retreated.

His gaze skimmed my length before returning to my face. "How are you feeling today, March?"

"Better, thank you, sir." I unclipped one of the bracelets and held it out to him. "The lady Saska asked me to give this to you, as a token of her appreciation."

He took the bracelet and studied it. "This isn't the work of the smiths of Salysis."

"I thought it might be some sort of heirloom."

"If it were an heirloom, she wouldn't be giving it away." He rolled the bracelet around, a frown gathering. "I've never seen workmanship like this before. It's almost Versonian in style, but couldn't have come from that place."

Because their lands had been sundered from ours by the Irkallan and a vast landslip, and all communications with them had long been lost.

"It *is* old," I said. "So it's possible it came from a time before the war."

"Maybe." He slipped the bracelet onto his belt. "Either way, I know someone who would appreciate such a trinket."

My thoughts instantly went to the young, blonde-haired woman who tended his chambers. He was obviously a generous man if he gifted his serfs with such things.

"I also want to thank you for your timely intervention yesterday, Commander. If you'd been delayed but a few minutes longer—"

"I would probably have found more Adlin carcasses."

I half smiled. "Unlikely, given I was almost out of ammunition."

"Not when you had an air witch—and possibly more—at your command." His gaze went past me as someone approached from behind. The speculation I'd briefly glimpsed fell once again, replaced by the cool efficiency of a man in charge. "You're in the lead carrier, March, and part of the protection detail for Lady Saska."

A soldier stopped beside me and offered me a bandoleer for the rifle and several clips for the gut busters.

I slung the former over my shoulder and attached the latter to my utility belt. "Thank you, Commander."

He nodded and stepped back. "Assume your position, March."

I nodded, formally saluted him, then spun and headed into the first carrier. Once Lady Saska and Lord Kiro were secured in the second vehicle, the engines were booted and the big machines rumbled forward.

It was a long and uneventful journey home. As Winterborne's massive curtain wall began to dominate the evening horizon, I couldn't help but wonder if Saska was as grateful to see it as I was, or whether her feelings ran to wariness or even fear. After such a long absence, she had to be uncertain of her position within her own family as well as in her husband's bed. Although, given her countenance this morning, I suspected whatever emotions she might be feeling would be hidden under a mask of dismissive coldness.

The carriers swept through the gatehouse and came to a halt in the inner bailey. Mak November—the day shift captain and a man I'd once been involved with—was waiting, along with a full escort of guards in the heavy blue-and-gold uniforms of the Rossi family. Beside them, hovering just a foot or so off the stone, was a heavily curtained, sun-powered, short-range carriage.

Saska and Lord Kiro were greeted by the captain, then quickly ushered into the carriage and swept away. Only then were we allowed out.

"Check those weapons back in, then make your report, March," Mak said, voice brusque. No surprise there given how badly our relationship had ended. "Captain July wishes you back on the line this evening."

If I were the betting type, I'd say it was Mak behind the order more than July. I might have been the model of soldierly decorum since our breakup—mostly, anyway—but Mak had never really forgiven me expressing my *exact* opinion of him in the bitter moments after he'd told me he was marrying someone who was "nice and unstained."

I saluted and then headed across the yard to armory three. Several day duty guards greeted me, but it was more a perfunctory, almost absent gesture than one containing any real warmth. The Nightwatch and the day guards rarely mingled, except on the odd celebratory event such as the upcoming masque.

Though there was still an hour before his shift should have started, Jon had already claimed his usual seat.

"Where's Henry?" While I was surprised to see Jon, in truth, I'd much rather deal with him than his counterpart. Henry was several years older, and a whole lot crankier.

"He's had to go to the infirmary—some sort of stomach bug. The cap asked if I'd step in for the last couple of hours." His smiled flashed. "Good to see you back in one piece, lass."

"It was a rather close run thing, let me tell you." I slipped off the bandoleer and rifle, and followed him across to the armory's door. "And I will have you know that the knife proved to be very handy."

"Ha!" He hobbled around to his desk and opened the records folder on the desktop. "I'm guessing that means you should keep it."

My gaze jumped to his. "But it's noted in the inventory— won't that get you into trouble?"

He waved his free hand as he began scanning in my weapons. "As I said, it's been delisted. It's yours if you want it."

"I do. I owe my life to this thing."

"I'm thinking the busters and the rifle might be due a word of thanks, too." Amusement crinkled the deep lines in his face.

I grinned. "Maybe just a little bit."

He handed me the stylus. I signed the weapons back in then gave him a sketchy salute and headed out. The bunkhouses lay at the western edge of the main wall, where the vast White Cliffs fell three hundred and fifty feet down to the Sea of Giants—so called, I was told, because of the white limestone stacks that still dotted the bay. There were no walls between the bunkhouses and those cliffs—there was no need for them, as both the Irkallan and the Adlin had a morbid fear of water. Even spring water caused them pause if it was deep or wide enough.

The room I shared with Ava and four others lay at the top of the five levels, and backed up against the old wall. It was a good position, because we had no one above us and neighbors only on one side rather than two. The price we paid for this was six in a room but none of us was willing to swap this relatively quiet position for a little more space.

I'd barely stepped through the door when Ava all but threw herself at me. She was slightly taller than me, with a lithe, softly rounded body that belied the steel of her core. She had the dark hair and lightly tanned skin of the Sifft, but features that echoed the rare beauty of those from Uraysia— a wider, more exotic-looking facial structure, a mouth that was made for kissing, and eyes that were as black and as heavenly as a starless sky, with the epicanthic fold enhancing rather than detracting from their beauty. Her body, pressed so firmly against mine, was trembling, her nipples erect and hard. Awareness stirred, and though it held none of the power of what had beset me both in the hospital and in Stone's chamber, it was at least welcome this time. I wrapped my arms around her waist and held her lightly, filled with relief that I was still able to do so.

"You didn't get dead." Her breath warmed the base of my neck. "I'd feared the worst when I found out what happened."

I frowned. "Didn't the captain pass on the news of my survival?"

She snorted and drew back, but kept her arms wrapped loosely around my neck. "Numbnuts was on. Such a nicety wouldn't even enter his brain space."

I chuckled softly. Ava had never forgiven Mak for his treatment of me, or the manner in which he'd acted since our breakup.

Mind you, nor had I. I was just a bit more circumspect about it after Captain July had chastised me for publicly running Mak down one drunken day.

"Hey," a deeper voice said. "I thought we had a rule— there's to be no canoodling between two of us without approval from the missing third?"

Ava's snort was louder this time. She loosened her grip on me and turned around. "Well, if you want to sleep the whole damn day away, dearest April, who am I to judge?"

"You can sound so damn condescending at times, woman." He tossed off the blankets and jumped down from the top bunk. He was a big man with blond hair, blue eyes, and a smattering of golden hair that ran across his chest and down his washboard abs. It was a trail I'd followed many a time with touch and tongue. "It's a wonder any of us can tolerate you."

"You do so because of the aforementioned sex. The others do so because the cook is sweet on me and it gets us extra rations."

April laughed. "That is also very true."

He flung an arm around each of us, then tugged me closer

and kissed me soundly. "Shall we go find an empty coupling room to celebrate?"

Ava punched him lightly. "Is sex really all you can think about at a moment like this?"

He considered the question for a second, and then said, "Yes, I believe it is."

I laughed and nudged him. "In this particular case, it's the anticipation of such that has gotten me through the long drive back from Blacklake."

"See? It's not just me." He gave Ava a told-you-so look then caught both our hands and led us out the door. "Let's go find that coupling room."

We did. And the sex that followed was a damn good validation of both friendship and life.

And yet that niggling sense that something was wrong, that my life and my world were about to change in ways I couldn't begin to understand, wouldn't go away. The wind whispered softly through my dreams, but her voice was unclear and muddy. I had no idea if she was trying to warn me of what might be coming, or merely playing games yet again.

In the nights that followed, the niggling fears did not become reality. Life went on as it normally did, and I heard no word from Saska, Lord Kiro, or even Commander Stone. While it should have eased my mind, the opposite seemed to be happening.

It was on the fifth night after my return that the Adlin were first spotted.

"All towers report," came the captain's gruff order. "We have sleuth movement a mile out. Anyone sight anything?"

I leaned out as negatives ran down the line. A sliver moon held court in the sky tonight and it cast little in the way of light. But if the Adlin were only a mile out, we should have been able to spot them—Sifft night sight was almost as good as any mechanical aid currently in use.

"No sign of movement here," I said, when my turn came.

"Keep sharp, everyone, because they're out there."

Not only out there, but howling.

But no attack came. Not then, and not for the long, uneasy nights that followed.

I had a weird feeling they were waiting for something.

Or for *someone*.

The wind had its own theory about what was going on and who might be involved, and part of me couldn't help but wonder if the wind was right.

Because the name it kept whispering was none other than Saska Rossi.

4

———

Which, in reality, was ridiculous. Saska might have had an Adlin beacon with her, but the Adlin *didn't* take prisoners. Not live ones, anyway. Even Ava dismissed the idea as absurd when I mentioned it to her. And it wasn't as if I could confide in anyone else—not without outing my meager abilities.

The Adlin continued to howl night and day, and though both the Night and Daywatch made several strikes at them, little changed. The Adlin simply disappeared before our attack force could get too far beyond the gates. It left us with nothing more to do than wait and watch. Anything else would simply be a waste of armaments. But their actions went against everything we'd ever learned about them, and unease spread across the ranks.

Six days after their first appearance, just as I'd finished my shift and was walking back to the bunkhouse, a young lad dressed in the blue and silver of the Rossi household stopped in front of me, forcing me to a halt.

"Neve March?" he said. "I have a message for you."

He held out an old-fashioned, folded piece of parchment

and my stomach sank. I'd hoped Saska had forgotten her request for my presence at the masque but it seemed I was out of luck.

I reluctantly accepted the parchment and carefully unfolded it. It said, in quite ornate handwriting, *Lord Rossi and his recently returned beloved require the presence of Neve March this coming Monday for the Masque of Pomona and the ongoing harvest celebration. A leave of absence has already been sourced from Captain July.*

A leave of absence? That rather ominously sounded like I was required for more than one evening. And while I'd heard many tales of hedonistic festivities that ran over days rather than the one night those of us in the outer bailey were given, I hadn't actually expected my presence to be required for the entire event.

It made me wonder just why they wanted me there—and whether Lord Kiro, with his sharp eyes and restless suspicions, was the main force behind this invitation.

I swallowed the bitter uneasiness that rose up my throat and forced a smile. "You may tell your lord and lady I accept with pleasure."

"Thank you." He spun and raced away.

Both Ava and April were waiting for me inside our bunkroom, as it was something of a ritual between us to relieve the tension and stress of the night with some mattress time. They were the only ones currently here, as Moss and Chet preferred to drink away their tensions before sleeping, and Pen had a lover who wasn't from the watch, meaning she was undoubtedly making full use of his more private dwellings rather than the coupling rooms.

"Talk about a perfect piece of timing," Ava said as she and April strolled naked and wet from the washroom. Desire, thick and luscious, teased the air, but it was unaccompanied by the scent of sex. Coupling in a bunkhouse was a brig-worthy offense—apparently the powers that be believed the rule cut down on friction and other petty nonsense. "I was just about—"

She stopped abruptly, her gaze scanning my face. "What's wrong?"

"This."

I handed her the invitation. April leaned over her shoulder and read its contents as well.

"Oh my," Ava said. "This is certainly something."

"But not," April said, "deserving of such a woebegone expression."

My gaze rose to his. "You don't understand—"

"No, I'm thinking *you* don't understand." He plucked the invitation from Ava and lightly waved it in front of my face. "This is a five-day break from duty, and one that comes with unending feasting and debauchery. Why is *that* suddenly a problem?"

In any other circumstances, it wouldn't be. I was more than willing to celebrate the upcoming harvest with as much fervent wantonness as the goddess might require—but that *wasn't* what this was about. I was sure of it.

"But it's tomorrow night," I said. "And I have nothing suitable to wear and no chance—"

April's loud snort cut off the rest of my sentence. "Clothes are *not* a requirement at masques, dear Neve. Not for long, anyway."

I hesitated, and glanced at Ava. She knew I distrusted all things Rossi right now, but even she didn't appear to see a problem.

"Look," she said, placing a hand on my arm. "The masque is attended by both the six ruling houses and the six non-ruling. It's not like you will have to spend every single hour with the Rossi. I doubt they'll do much more than an official thank-you, and then you'll be free to enjoy yourself. As for clothes, you can borrow my silver sheath dress. It's classy enough for even the Upper Reaches."

"It's probably just the uneasiness of the whole Adlin situation that's the issue," April added. "But what you need to be thinking is that you're there representing the Nightwatch, and you need to show those people we unlit are more than able to keep up with their nonsense."

I snorted softly and rose up on my toes to drop a kiss on his cheek. "You're right. This is a once in a lifetime opportunity, and I really need to make the most of it."

"Right," April said. "Now that's settled, let's go have sex."

I rolled my eyes and met Ava's amused gaze. "You two go. I need a shower and some alone time."

She squeezed my arm in understanding, then pushed April toward the door. "You heard her, out."

"Bossy as well as condescending," he murmured. "Just as well I love your body."

She snorted and lightly smacked the back of his head. As their footsteps disappeared down the walkway, I stripped off, stowed my blaster and knife in my locker, and then headed into the bathroom. But a long, hot shower did nothing to shake the certainty that something beyond my comprehension was happening. I felt like a pawn in a game of chess, one where the players were hidden and I had no idea who were the white pieces and who were black.

Sleep was slow in coming, and once again haunted by the wind, although if she trying to warn me about something, it remained unclear.

The following morning another courier intercepted my path back to the bunkhouse, although this time he was clad in dark green that was shot with gold. Not the Rossi but still a ruling house, I suspected.

"Neve March," he said, with a slight bow. "I have a parcel for you."

Said parcel was gorgeously wrapped in pale gold silk. I touched it, briefly and in awe, and then jerked my hand away lest the rough skin on my fingertips catch the material. "Are you sure it's for me?"

"Yes."

"But who would be sending me such a thing? What house wears these colors?"

"There's a letter inside, Miss March. That's all I am allowed to say."

It was a statement that raised a whole lot more questions but I reluctantly accepted the parcel. The courier bowed again and walked off.

"For freedom's sake, what is it this time?" April said, as I walked into our room.

"A present of some kind." I stopped at my bunk and sat down.

Ava perched beside me and ran her fingers carefully across the top of it. "The material is as fine as I've ever seen. Who sent it? The Rossis?"

I shook my head. "It's not their colors."

"Then whose?"

"I don't know."

"And won't until you open the thing," April said, ever practical.

I hesitated, then flipped the parcel over and carefully undid the ties holding it together. The golden material fell away to reveal a dress—a dress that was pale lavender gray, the same color as my stains and had obviously been designed to blend with them. Underneath it was a mask in the same color but intricately patterned with a deep gold, and a silk belt that had the same colors, but ended in a knot of deep green. The same color, I thought, that the courier had worn.

"Oh my," Ava whispered. "That's *beautiful*."

Yes, it was, and even as I placed the dress carefully to one side and picked up the note underneath the mask, I suspected who'd sent it.

From one reluctant participant to another, the note said. *Your carriage will be waiting at seven tonight.*

Ava frowned at the note. "That's rather cryptic, isn't it?"

"Not to the man who sent it."

"Does that man have a name?" April asked. "Or are we expected to beg for such morsels?"

I screwed up the note and tossed it at him. "Idiot."

"*That* is no answer but a fact," Ava commented. "Give, sister."

I drew in a deep breath and released it slowly. "I believe the dress comes from Trey Stone."

"My, my, you are walking in exalted circles these days, aren't you?" April said. "Care to direct a little highfaluting tail my way sometime?"

"It's not as if I've gotten any such tail, so it's unlikely I'll be able to cast any your way."

"So, if you're not getting any, why would the firstborn son of a ruling house be sending you a dress?"

Trey was the firstborn? Then why on earth was he at Blacklake, let alone its commander? "Because he's the prime at Blacklake, and was involved in Saska's recovery. If this note is to be believed, he's been ordered to this shindig and is just as reluctant as me."

"I can't believe that," April said. "Although it *is* rather odd for a firstborn son to be sent to an outpost in *any* capacity. Those in the upper class usually avoid real work like the plague."

I placed the mask on the bed then rose and gingerly draped the dress against my body. It was an off-the-shoulder design, with a full sleeve to cover my stained and scarred left arm while leaving my right arm and shoulder exposed. The swooping material barely covered my breasts, and the left side of the long skirt was slit to my hip. Every move I made would reveal plenty of unstained leg while hiding the other. The silky soft, translucent material would skim my body beautifully, emphasizing my curves while—via discreetly placed panels—leaving me some modesty.

"They'll think they're in a presence of a goddess," Ava murmured, eyes shining with appreciation.

"Only if you're there with me."

She snorted. "If you don't come away with a generous patron after this, I'll eat my helmet."

"I don't want a patron, in *any* capacity."

She smacked my leg. "Don't be an idiot. You can't be a Nightwatch forever. What are you going to do when retirement beckons?"

I thought of the bracelet in my locker and smiled. "Buy myself a small allotment far away from Winterborne. I might even invite you two along, if you promise to behave."

"I'll certainly visit if you do achieve such an aim," Ava said, "but I, for one, intend to end my days living a higher lifestyle."

"Which is why you're currently fooling around with a cook on your days off," April commented. "That makes perfectly good sense."

Ava shot him a look that would have put a lesser man well and truly in his place. April merely grinned.

"That cook is about to take up a position in the Fisk house as junior pâtissier," she said with a sweetness that belied the ice in her eyes. "As his current bedmate, I will be given visiting access into the Lower Reaches and therefore be in full view of the non-ruling houses who inhabit that place. How hard do you think it'll be to attract their attention once I set my mind to it?"

"You, my dear, are a schemer," April said. "It makes me so proud."

She snorted. "Yes, because you have such a long history of successful schemes behind you."

"You cannot win if you do not first lose, my sweet."

Ava blinked. "That sounded almost… philosophical."

He grinned. "I know. Amazing, right?"

She shook her head and then returned her gaze to me—or rather, to my hair. "What are you going to do with this?" She brushed her fingers through the short, wavy strands, her expression thoughtful.

I shrugged. "There's nothing that can be done with it."

"You could get some of those color fudges the unlit teenagers in state care have been using of late," April said. "A streak or two of gold would look quite pretty."

"*That*," Ava said, glancing at him incredulously, "is a damn good idea. Off you go."

"What about sleep? And sex?"

"The former can happen after we've got the supplies to gussy up our girl for tonight," she said. "As for the latter, I'll book a double period for the coupling room for us tomorrow morning."

"Ha! Done deal." He departed, whistling cheerfully.

"Whoever that man eventually falls for is going to be one lucky person," Ava murmured. Her gaze returned to mine, and the amusement in her dark eyes faded. "Are you okay?"

I took a deep breath and released it slowly. "I'm scared out of my tiny little mind—not so much by the thought that I'll be treated as some sort of novelty or freak, but by whatever is coming."

She wrapped her arms around my shoulders and hugged me gently. "It is not as if the wind has often spoken truly to you," she said. "It is more than likely she merely teases now."

"I know." Just as I knew she *wasn't* teasing, and that her fears were as real as mine.

"Then stop with this nonsense, ignore the wind, and try

to get some sleep today." She pulled back and brushed some stray strands of hair from my eyes. "You can't be having shadows under your eyes at such a fancy shindig."

A smile teased my lips. "It doesn't matter if I do, because they won't see them thanks to the mask."

"That," she replied sternly, "is *not* the point. Now get your ass into that shower then climb into bed. I'll ensure no one disturbs you."

I did as ordered. And for the first time in days, the wind didn't enter my dreams. Maybe she'd heard the unspoken threat in Ava's voice.

I was alone when seven o'clock ticked around. The Nightwatch drew duty from six to six, and I couldn't help but wish I was with them rather than heading off to some grand house for a celebration I had no desire to attend. I wasn't one of them and, once the mask came off—as it inevitably would—I'd be viewed as nothing more than a curiosity. And, despite my words to Ava, I had absolutely no desire to be courted or bedded because I was different—been there, done that with Mak.

Perhaps I could sneak out after the official introductions and thank-yous were done. Celebrations here in the outer bailey wouldn't kick off until the autumn equinox, which this year fell on Thursday—three days away. Surely *that* was enough time to satisfy the Rossis' sense of appreciation?

I took a deep breath then pushed away from my bunk. If I delayed much longer, someone would be sent to fetch me. It would be better to appear a willing participant; anything else would just get the gossips going—and there was enough of that already. I gathered the bag containing enough clothes and toiletries to get me through the upcoming days, and then slipped my feet into my flats. Although shoes were frowned upon at any harvest festival, I wasn't about to stride across the grime of both the stairs and the bailey barefoot. I doubted there'd be a footbath in the carriage.

With the mask dangling from one hand, I headed out. The wind stirred around me, as cold and uneasy as I felt. But she wasn't talking to me, wasn't telling me what she feared. Maybe she didn't know. Or maybe she was merely amplifying the doubts and fears that were already mine.

Those doubts and fears increased greatly when I discovered it wasn't only the carriage waiting for me, but Trey Stone himself.

I stopped abruptly. "Why are you here, Commander?"

He was wearing a loose, dark green shirt that was as sheer as my dress and allowed teasing glimpses of the lean but muscular body underneath. His trousers were the same color but made of a thicker material that hugged his legs from thighs to knees before falling loosely to his bare brown feet. There was a green silk belt around his waist, but it ended in a knot of lavender the same color as my dress.

"I told you I'd be here at seven." His gaze skimmed me, and appreciation stirred through his eyes. "That dress is rather becoming on you, March."

"You said the *carriage* would be here. There was no mention that you'd be with it." I hesitated, knowing I sounded rather ungrateful. "But thank you for the gift, although you shouldn't have done it. It has set too many tongues a-wagging."

"Good, because that was part of the intent." He held out one hand. "Come along, I won't bite."

I forced my feet down the rest of the stairs and somewhat reluctantly accepted his help into the carriage. His skin, like mine, was slightly rough, and yet it in no way felt unpleasant.

There was great strength in those hands, just as, I suspected, there was great strength in the man.

The carriage was specifically designed for two people, with one seat on each side of it. I took the one facing the driver so that I might see the grand houses as they approached, then kicked off my shoes and tucked them into my bag. The commander climbed into the other seat, then reached back and knocked on the carriage wall separating us from the driver.

"We're good, thanks, Bernie."

The carriage moved forward smoothly, her engines emitting little more than a soft purr. I resisted the urge to cross my arms and tried to relax into the seat. But it was a hard thing to achieve when that nebulous, earthy energy was stirring between us once again.

"Why are you here, Commander? What game are you playing?"

His smile teased the corners of his bright eyes. They looked almost emerald in this light—rich, warm, and friendly. But there was also a tension in him, one that spoke of a warrior ready for battle. Not against me, although I rather suspected I would play some part in it.

"Oh, there are plenty of games afoot, but I'm certainly *not* involved in them thus far." He pressed a button to his left and a door slid aside, revealing an ornate green flask and several glasses. "Drink?"

I shook my head. The way my stomach was currently churning, I'd probably bring it right back up.

"I gather you now have every intention of getting involved."

"Yes." He poured himself a drink then contemplated me over the top of the glass. "And I want you to help me."

"Commander, I'm unlit and out of place amongst your kind. I could never—"

"Could never what? Have fun? Enjoy yourself?"

I smiled wryly. "I'm thinking that's *not* the sort of help you're wanting."

"In part, it is." He stretched out his legs and crossed his ankles. "As an unlit, you have no allegiances, no enemies, and no stake in whatever is happening. You'll see things I never will, by virtue of the fact that you're untainted and untouched by everything that is the twelve houses. I need that if we are to stop whatever is coming."

The wind stirred past me, telling me to listen, to help. I frowned. "What do you think might be coming?"

"War. But not, perhaps, the type we have been expecting for nigh on five hundred years." A hint of anger crept into his voice. "Those Adlin did *not* learn to make the beacons or trebuchets by themselves."

I sucked in a breath. "Surely you don't think someone from the twelve houses is working with them?"

"Right now, I'm unsure what to think. But something is going on; there've been too many troubling incidents of late. Someone needs to investigate whether they stem merely from courtly machinations, or something far more dangerous."

"Why has the job fallen to you? Is it because of your position at Blacklake?"

Another smile teased his lips, but one that held a bitter edge. "For the most part, yes. But I'm not here in any official capacity. I haven't spoken to anyone at the Forum, and only my father knows the true depth of my fears."

"And what does he think?"

Something close to pain stirred through his expression. "He thinks me a fool. But then, *that* is an opinion he's long held."

While it was not unusual for a son to fall out with his

father, it appeared there was something deeper than a mere difference of opinion behind this particular event.

I glanced outside for a moment, noting we'd already moved through the inner gatehouse and were slowly making our way up the wide but twisting road that led up to the plateau of the ruling houses. The accommodation in this lowest section was mainly multilevel terraced housing, and was little bigger than the bunkhouse I lived in. For the most part, it contained those freemen who served but weren't bound to any of the ruling houses—blacksmiths, weavers and millinery folk, carpenters, even ladies and men of ease. Interspersed with these houses were the workplaces for the various crafts. As we moved farther up the hill, we'd come to the homes of those with personal magic—the healers, illusionists, the bards, and the danseuse. Only once we'd gone through a secondary gate that was more decorative than defensive would we reach the estates of the lower ruling houses and the plateau.

I reluctantly returned my gaze to his. "Is that why the firstborn son of a ruling house has accepted a position at an outpost rather than taking his rightful position at the Forum?"

A smile ghosted his lips. "You've been checking up on me."

"The minute this dress arrived. But it's not like anyone within the Nightwatch was able to tell me much."

"Quite rightly, I would think."

"And in that statement lies the arrogance of a ruling house."

His smile grew. "And *that* propensity to not hold back is the very reason I wish your help."

"It's a propensity that has gotten me into trouble more often than not. And you didn't answer my question, Commander."

"No." Though his expression gave little away, there was an odd mix of sadness and anger emanating from him. "I ceded my position as my father's second in the Forum to my younger brother Karl. It is he who now carries the weight of family expectations."

"Then why haven't you confided your suspicions to him?"

"Because it makes little sense to burden him further until I have proof. I hope to either gather that confirmation within the next five days, or be able to acknowledge it for the stupidity my father thinks it is."

The wind didn't think it was stupidity. I rather suspected the earth didn't, either. Why else would he be here? He might be stationed a long way from Winterborne, but the earth was an unbroken connection that ran between the two. If he was a powerful enough earth witch—and I very much suspected he was—then he would hear the tales of this place not only through the connection of the stone, earth, and metal elements that made up so much of the buildings within Winterborne, but also through movement of people across the land itself.

"So what is it, exactly, that you wish me to do?"

"Tonight is the unofficial portion of the masque. It is a night for introductions and seductions, a night where nothing more than a good time should be had."

"If I'm to bed anyone, Commander, it'll be because I desire it, not because you wish me to."

"And that is as it should be." He paused. "However, either of us bedding anyone willy-nilly would not only muddy our purpose here, but would also be unseemly."

Trepidation stirred through me, and it wasn't helped any by the sudden glint of amusement in his eyes. "And why is that?"

"Because you and I are an informal item."

"Meaning we have sex on an irregular basis?"

This time, he laughed. It was a warm, rich sound that sent delight skittering across my skin. "Not exactly. It means we are sexually together, but have made no promises nor undertaken the committal ceremony. It means that if others wish to lie with one of us, permission must be sought from both parties. It is a means of protection for us both."

I raised an eyebrow. "And why would you need protection, Commander?"

"Please, you need to call me Trey for this charade to have any chance." His amusement faded, only to be replaced by something much darker—something that spoke of old ghosts. "I may be the black sheep of the family, but I am nevertheless a firstborn son of a powerful ruling house. It's not an understatement to say there will be those present tonight who'd think such a liaison would be worthwhile, for both their own status and that of their family."

"No one would ever think that about *me*, though."

"Perhaps not, but I think you'll gather much attention and more than a few propositions before this night is over. And I believe such interest will only increase once your mask comes off." Something of a wry smile touched his lips. "If there's one truth about the twelve ruling houses, it's the fact that none can resist chasing the unattainable and the different, especially when it comes so exquisitely packaged."

This time, the wry smile was mine. "I'm well aware that my stain will draw attention, Commander—"

"Trey," he cut in.

"—but I don't think it'll be considered such a prize once I'm introduced as Nightwatch and therefore unlit."

"Oh, I think you underestimate the allure of the unknown. Besides, you won't be announced as Nightwatch. Kiro agrees it would not be beneficial."

"You won't confide in your own family, yet you confide in

him?" I couldn't help the edge in my voice, or the distaste that lingered on the word him.

Trey's eyebrow rose. "And why would you have formed such an opinion of the man in the brief time he was with you?"

I hesitated then mentally shrugged. He'd brought me here to be honest, so honesty was exactly what he'd get. "There's a darkness to his energy that I don't like."

"Perhaps what you sense was nothing more than his suspicions about *your* dishonesty."

I was shaking my head even before he was finished. "It was more than that. More than just his ability to read people, too."

"Interesting that you caught *that* when so few are even aware he's a reader—and it totally verifies my belief that your help will be invaluable."

Perhaps. I hesitated. "Who is Lord Kiro, exactly? He doesn't wear the color of any house, and yet he bears the moniker of Lord."

"He was born Kiro Vaun, and is the second son of a healer of some repute. The Forum tithed him both the title and a house at the entrance of the plateau for services rendered to the ruling houses over the last thirty-five years."

"So he'd be what? Sixty? Seventy?"

A smile touched his lips. "You'd think so, wouldn't you? But he is, in fact, much younger—fifty-one."

I blinked. "He's been in the service of the Forum and the ruling houses since he was *sixteen*?"

"Yes. He is both a forecaster and reader of incredible strength, but all magic, even personal, has its costs. His ages him."

I remembered the dark restlessness of his energy and a shiver ran through me. "I rather suspect those are not his only gifts."

"No. But many readers are also sexually alluring. It is often the best way to ferret out secrets."

"So does he seduce *only* with his words and energy?"

Trey raised an eyebrow, his expression one of amusement. "What do you think?"

"I think it is a combination of words, aura, and physicality. But why would the lords of this place turn a blind eye to the bedding of their own women?"

"It's not just women, and it would depend on the circumstance and information required. There are certainly a few who are *extremely* unhappy about Kiro's methods." He glanced at the window and abruptly sat forward. "We near the secondary gate, and there are a few formalities you need to know."

"Only a few?" My voice was dry. "I would think *that* is something of an understatement."

He acknowledged the statement with a twist of his full lips. "First and foremost, you curtsey to everyone you are officially introduced to, be they upper or lower house. No lady ever serves herself from the outside tables—she either accepts such things from the trays serfs carry around the room, or requests such from one of the men who are in attendance of her."

"Which will only be you, so be prepared for a lot of walking back and forth."

That eyebrow winged upward again. It was truly amazing how much one could discern from such a movement—like the odd mix of amusement and irritation currently evident— even if little otherwise showed on his expression. "Perhaps we should have a small wager on who is right on that account?"

No, we should not. But I nevertheless found myself saying, "That would depend on the stakes."

He hesitated, his gaze challenging as it pinned mine. "If I

win, you tell me the truth of what happened out there in the Tenterra desert."

Such a bet would be nothing short of foolish, and yet I could almost hear Ava in my head, egging me on, telling me this was a golden opportunity that shouldn't be missed. But I couldn't in all conscience ask for anything that might further my placement in the watch or even secure something for my retirement fund. Not when all he wanted was the truth.

But the refusal of the bet would all but confirm that something had gone on. That I was lying.

And he was aware of the position he'd just placed me in, damn him.

"If I win," I said slowly, "I want the truth about the break with your family and why a first son would cede his rights to a younger brother and take a position at Blacklake."

He didn't react for a moment, then a slow smile spread over his face. "I am so glad, Neve March, that it was you who was sent to rescue Lady Rossi that day."

A statement I had no idea how to respond to. He stuck out his hand. "Agreed."

I hesitated, then gripped his fingers. And wasn't surprised that the indefinable *something* surged between us again. His eyes darkened fractionally, and I had to wonder if what he was feeling was even more sexual in nature than the mix I was receiving.

"Agreed," I said softly, and then pulled my hand from his. "Is there anything else I should be aware of?"

"While the Rossi house is hosting this year's Harvest Masque, all six upper ruling houses provide accommodation for the lower ruling houses and their entourage. Because I was a late and unexpected inclusion in this year's festival, we are being hosted at Rossi, as my suites had already been allotted."

"We?"

Again that smile ghosted his lips. "As my informal lover, it would be considered a breach of etiquette to house us separately."

"Except that Lady Saska knows the truth of our relationship."

"Actually, she doesn't."

I studied him for a minute, listening to the wind, hearing her tales of the machinations that had begun from almost the minute he'd saved us. "*That's* why you took me back to your suites for an informal chat."

"Yes. The wind was watching us that night."

"What the wind witnessed wouldn't exactly have led Saska to believe we were in a relationship."

"Except for the fact I dismissed my maidservant and we spent much time in companionable silence. *That* is the province of old lovers, not new."

I wondered what he would have done had it been any other Nightwatch officer who'd been sent after Saska. But maybe it wouldn't have mattered, given all he really wanted was a fresh pair of eyes to view those from the twelve houses?

"The masque itself lasts for two and a half nights," he continued, "and it is in this time most of the political and committal alliances are made."

"Why just then? Why not over the whole five days?"

"Because just as the equinox signals the end of summer days and the slip toward winter, it also brings to an end any formal entreaty and marriage negotiations between the houses for another year."

"So the other two and a half nights are just a party?"

"Yes. We will keep to our rooms during the day. The official revelation of identity comes at midnight on the night of the equinox, which is when we will officially be introduced and thanks given."

I frowned. "So how are we introduced before that?"

"Merely as Lord T and Lady N."

"Which, combined with the colors you're wearing, will tell everyone exactly who you are, mask or no mask."

"Yes, but it will heighten the intrigue of who my consort might be, because your colors offer no allegiance other than the green that denotes our liaison."

Which explained why he was wearing the knot of lavender gray at the end of his belt. "That intrigue will only last as long as the official introductions."

"I think not." He glanced out the window as the carriage began to slow. "Our bags will be taken directly to our quarters. Don your mask, Lady Neve, for the game begins."

The carriage came to a halt. I looked out the window as we waited for the door to be opened, butterflies gathering in my stomach. What little I could see of Rossi House was a vast white stone and silver structure that was both imposing and beautiful. It was a house designed with impossible angles and sweeping curves, and one that would fall in an instant if our enemies ever got this far.

But if they ever did, the ruling houses wouldn't be here to see it. They would have already retreated, leaving Winterborne a deserted wasteland in much the same manner as they had Tenterra, to start anew somewhere else. Such an eventuality had even been factored into the building of this place, with the creation of a sea canal that divided Winterborne from the rest of Gallion. Vast earth and stone bridges might now connect us, allowing easy movement between the two, but none would be hard to destroy. Not for a combined attack from the ruling houses that were responsible for their existence in the first place.

The door was opened and Trey, his mask in place and revealing little more than the glitter of his eyes and the fullness of his mouth, stepped out. He immediately turned and held out his hand. "My lady?"

A smile twisted my lips, one that seemed to be echoed in his eyes, but I nevertheless place my fingers in his and stepped carefully from the carriage. He released me but remained close, and as a young page bowed and asked us to follow him, pressed his hand lightly against my spine to guide me. My attention, whether I wished it or not, was both on him and the impact his touch was having on my body rather than all the wonders that had been built onto this plateau.

"Rossi House," Trey murmured, as we climbed the long, sweeping stone staircase, "like all other ruling houses, cedes the entire top floor of their home to entertainment. Guest suites and private wings are on the second, while the ground floor consists of kitchens, washrooms, and serf accommodation."

"It would be nice to have the leisure of such space."

"Do not judge by surface appearances," he said. "It can often be deceiving."

"I somehow think your upbringing contained a whole lot more freedom and choice than mine ever did."

"Perhaps," he said, his tone heavy. "And perhaps not."

A liveried footman met us at the heavily ornate double-width silver doors atop of the stairs and led us through a vast open space of glittering white-stone walls and high-vaulted ceilings. The colors of all twelve houses adorned the left side of the long room, and a multitude of tables filled with food and wine lined the right. We moved past two large parlors that were fitted for comfort and ease taking, before finally stopping on a landing that looked out over a ballroom that was even bigger and grander than the hall. There were no flags or adornments on these walls; there was no need for them when the guests themselves provided a rainbow.

The footman stopped, and then said in a loud voice, "The lord T and the lady N."

Just for an instant, conversation ceased and the weight of all their stares hit. I trembled under the force of it, my skin cold and stomach churning. I didn't smile. I didn't react in any way; unattainable was the word Trey had used, and that impression was what these people were going to get. It was, I suspected, the only way I was going to get through the evening.

After an altogether too long a pause at the top of the steps, Trey lightly pressed me forward. I was glad of his steadying touch as I concentrated on moving gracefully and *not* falling. The murmur of conversation started up again, and some faces turned away from us. Most did not.

The next five hours became an almost dizzying array of introductions and small conversations. He didn't leave my side in that time, giving me the chance to fall into my role. And while it didn't become any easier as the hours passed, I did at least feel better once my nerves were under control. But I certainly wouldn't go as far as saying I was enjoying myself. Not when I kept waiting for the moment someone would denounce me as the fraud I was.

Trey captured two glasses from a nearby drink boy, and handed me one with a smile. We were standing in one of the quieter corners of the room, a shadowed and half-hidden nook.

"How do you feel about circulating by yourself for a little while?"

"Terrified." I took a sip of the dark wine. It tasted of blackberries and plums, and though it was slightly more acidic than the one Trey had served, it nevertheless tasted damn fine to my palate. "But I'm not here for my looks."

He gave me a quizzical look. Or, at least, that's what it

appeared to be given the constraints of the mask. "Why are you so harsh on yourself when it comes to appearance?"

"Because when it comes to appearance, it's all I've ever been judged on." My gaze met his, and I could feel the old anger stirring. "Have you any idea what it feels like to know, from a very young age, that while you might be considered beddable, no one will ever commit to you?"

"No, but—"

He paused, and part me wanted to retort, *but what? That it is the reality of my life and position, and I should just accept it?*

But there were footsteps approaching, a heavy sound that spoke of a man rather than a woman, and it snatched away the moment. Such bitterness shouldn't be aired at a celebration or place like this, anyway. So, as ever, I tried to pretend there was nothing wrong, that it wasn't there deep inside, eating away at me like a canker.

Trey smiled and leaned forward, lightly brushing his lips across my bare cheek. Surprise rippled through me, but before I could react in any way, he whispered, "And so it begins."

Someone cleared his voice behind us. Trey turned and studied the rotund figure in the sand-colored robes for a few seconds before saying, in a rather dismissive tone, "Lord V, how may I help you?"

I frowned, running rapidly through all the colors of the houses, and the names of everyone I'd been introduced to. Trey had filled me in on their backgrounds after each introduction and this man had certainly been one of them—I remembered his rather odd mask, which was more an ornate helmet with eye shields. After a moment, I placed him—Lord Vaseye, from the non-ruling earth house Myrl.

Vaseye cleared his throat again, looking very ill at ease with Trey's coolness. "I wonder if I might speak to you privately for a minute or two?"

"Is it of great importance?" Trey asked. "Because I'm rather delightfully occupied right now."

Vaseye's gaze flicked to me—or rather, to the breast the dropped shoulder of my dress was barely covering—and his cheeks grew even redder. I hadn't thought that possible.

"I believe it to be so, yes."

"Then I will come. Sorry, my sweet." Trey turned back to me and leaned in, as if to kiss. And indeed, his warm lips did brush my cheek, but only because he murmured, "Meet back here at three. We can retire and compare notes."

"Don't be one second late," I murmured in return. "Or the knife that sleeps in my bag might just find a home in your heart."

He laughed, a rich sound that drew more than a little attention. "Warning heeded."

He stepped back, gave me a bow, and then walked away with Vaseye. I resisted the urge to gulp down the rest of my wine and wandered out of our nook, ignoring those in my immediate vicinity who sought to catch my eye as I walked around the edge of the vast room and studied the crowd.

This masque was not, in any way, what I had expected. Yes, there was some flirting, some caressing, even the odd stolen kiss or two, but it was not the alcohol- and sex-fueled indulgence that most of us in the outer bailey had believed it to be. Maybe that would come *after* the equinox, when all the maneuvering and alliances had finished for another year, but right now, it was positively restrained. Hell, the watch parties would shock more than a few highbrow sensibilities if Vaseye's reaction to a barely covered nipple were anything to go by.

There were plenty of shadowed nooks inset into the white walls around this vast room, as well as more brightly lit seating areas. Most of the former were surprisingly unoc-cupied—although given the restraint in the room, maybe that wasn't such a surprise. The latter were filled with serious-faced men or older women whose bodies were adorned with all manner of bright jewels, chains, and bracelets, and who chatted animatedly as they cooled themselves with ornate fans.

The bright silver bracelets two of those women wore looked from a distance to be very similar to Saska's, but there was something about the countenance of the older woman that made me wary about approaching her.

Music started up from somewhere ahead. It was a lovely, sprightly tune, one I recognized and had often danced to. As I moved toward the sound, a blue-clad figure stepped firmly into my path and forced me to stop.

He bowed with something of a flourish, his gaze sweeping my length before it rose to linger a little longer than was polite on my breasts. I gently cleared my throat and his gaze jumped to my face, a slight tinge of pink touching his cheeks.

"Lady N," he said, "may I have the honor of this dance?"

I hesitated, studying him over my now empty wineglass, desperately trying to remember his name. He was wearing blue, so that meant Rossi allegiance. After another moment, it came to me—Tavish. He just happened to be the youngest brother of Saska's husband, Marcus, and could be an excellent source of information.

Tease, the wind said. *Leave him with heated dreams and desires so that he might be more pliable on the morrow.*

The wind, it seemed, was feeling rather wicked this night. And she was also speaking to me far more clearly than she ever had before. In fact, her whisperings were so clear she could have almost been another woman standing beside me. Was it this place? We were in the Rossi stronghold, after all, so her strength and power would likely be infused into the very walls.

"Alas, Lord T, I have promised my first dance of the night to *my* Lord T. And he, rather annoyingly, has currently disappeared." As his face fell, I stepped closer and brushed the rim of my glass across his chest. "I would, however, be very appreciative of another glass of that delightful red."

He bowed, took my glass, and hurried off. I couldn't help but wonder how old he was—for a surety, he was not only a lot younger than me, but also a whole lot more innocent. He came back within minutes and handed me a full glass of wine with another flourish. I smiled and raised my glass to him. "Good deeds never go unnoted. Perhaps we can talk more on the matter tomorrow night?"

"That," he said, with a gleam of anticipation in his eyes, "would be *most* welcome."

"A date then." I clicked my glass against his. "Tell me, how goes the lady S? Has she recovered from her trials in the desert?"

He hesitated. "I don't know, as she keeps mostly to her suite."

"But I'd expect her lord was glad to see her returned?"

"One would expect that, yes." He glanced past me, and his face went pale. He bowed. "I mustn't delay you any longer, Lady N. Until tomorrow night, then."

He spun and hurried off. Someone had obviously scared him off, but who?

I turned, and the reason for Tavish's sudden departure became crystal clear. I certainly would have done the same, had our positions been reversed.

Because the man who strolled toward me with dark nonchalance was none other than Lord Kiro himself.

5

He was, once again, dressed from head to toe in black, a color that suited the dark caress of his energy. His silvery hair and eyes glimmered like ice in the brightness of the room, and his mouth—oddly lush and eternally kissable —was painted black to match his rather devilish mask.

I blinked at the direction of those thoughts, and thrust them firmly from my mind. Part of this man's personal magic was that of enticement and seduction, and knowing that placed the power of it in my hands more than his.

So I held my ground and took a sip of the wine, watching him approach with what I hoped was an expression of disinterest.

He stopped and bowed politely. His energy was a darkly seductive wave that had pinpricks of heat skittering across my skin. While I couldn't control the reactions of my body, I gave it little heed, and simply did the required curtsey.

"Lord K, what a pleasure to see you again."

"Indeed, Lady N. You are looking much more—" He paused, his gaze scanning me, a leisurely caress that felt so real it stirred desire and made me ache. When his eyes finally returned to mine, they burned with heat. But whether that was real, or merely part of his power and whatever he was trying to pull from me, I couldn't say. He smiled. "— delectable in that outfit."

"My Lord T has very good taste in dresses, it seems."

"Indeed." He swirled the wine in his glass, the movement languid—a sensation that seemed to echo through me. "I have to admit, I was rather surprised to learn you were an item."

There was something in his voice that made me think it was said more for those who might be listening than me. I raised my glass, took another drink, and then licked the remaining droplets from my lips. I might not have his power of seduction, but I could certainly play his games. His gaze followed the movement and something flared within his eyes. Something that *wasn't* desire, but rather an acknowledgment of my resistance and a spark of even greater determination.

"Why?" I murmured. "You should be well aware that restraint isn't practiced where I come from."

"Indeed. But Lord T is not known for his hedonistic tendencies."

"Then perhaps you don't know as much about him as you thought."

"Perhaps." He stepped into my personal space, an impolite act that would set tongues wagging. But that's exactly what Trey wanted—and something I could certainly twist to my advantage.

Or so the wind assured me.

I raised my free hand and placed my palm against his chest. His skin, even through the black silk, was unusually warm under my fingertips, the muscles taut. From a distance it would look like an act of desire; only Kiro knew it wasn't.

"How does the lady S recover from her trials in Tenterra?"

"Is that what you were asking young T about?"

I raised an eyebrow. "Of course. What else would I be seeking?"

"I fear I don't know."

He placed an odd emphasis on the word "fear." I was under no illusion that he in any way feared me, but he certainly didn't trust me. And while I might be holding a secret, he seemed to think it was bigger—and far more dangerous—than it actually was. It was time I called him out on it.

"And I fear I do not understand your suspicions of me." I cocked my head to one side and studied him for several seconds. "Perhaps you have walked too long in this world, and see secrets and dishonesty where there are none."

He laughed, a warm and surprisingly real sound that caused heads to turn. And, no doubt, set tongues wagging even harder. "Perhaps you are right."

His tone suggested otherwise. I gave him a cool smile and murmured, "Whatever you think of me, Lord K, believe one thing—I would give my life for the protection of Winterborne. How many in this room do you think would do the same? Would you?"

"I have given over my entire life to that very practice."

Which didn't answer the initial part of my question, but I let it slide. "Then perhaps you've been jaded by a lifetime of such service, and see wrongs where none exist."

"Lady N, you are an intriguing woman." He paused, and added with an edge that spoke of suspicion, "I can see why Lord T is enamored with you."

"Perhaps he merely sees what is there, and what is *not*."

It was a response that addressed what he *hadn't* said, and his gaze narrowed. I smiled, stepped back, and said in a slightly louder tone, "It has been a delight talking to you, Lord K, but I'm afraid I must move on."

With a perfunctory bow, I turned and did just that. His heated gaze burned into my back even as whispers and surprise followed me. I ignored them and continued to the area that held the musicians and bards. I passed the remaining hours there, talking to many but promising little. It wasn't just men who approached but also women, young and old. Many of these were openly inviting of a sexual liaison, and it took me by surprise. Fluid sexuality was common among those of us who were deemed unlit or who held no magic, but I'd honestly expected it would be more frowned upon here amongst those who held power or who lived in the shadows of it, especially given the relentless pursuit for children born of magic. Although perhaps—if what Trey had said was true and Lord Kiro *did* apply his dark energy to both men and women—it was not so much frowned upon, as given official blessing only at such events and celebrations as this masque and the summer solstice.

If that were the case, then, for the first time in my life, I felt sorry for them.

When the hour of three finally approached, I unhurriedly made my way back to the nook. But before I could reach it, fingers caught my arm and pulled me to a gentle stop. I turned, one eyebrow raised in query, and discovered it was a woman rather than a man. Her dress was the rich gold of the Hawthorne line and it hugged her curves delightfully, while the mask did little to hide the perfection of her face. But it wasn't just her beauty that had my heart pounding, but also the two very familiar silver bracelets that decorated her wrists. This was none other than the younger of the two women I'd noticed talking earlier.

I bowed my head and murmured, "I'm sorry, my lady, but I don't believe we have been introduced."

"I'm Lady P, and I was most desirous to talk to the woman who has intrigued half the masque this night."

She was tall and lithe in build, with pert breasts, silvery hair, and ice-colored eyes. What I could see of her face was both intriguing and captivating.

She held out her right hand, as if in invitation. I hesitated, unsure what was expected of such an offering. A kiss, most likely, but there was a stubbornness within me that refused to abide by such haughty expectations.

Something flared in her eyes; determination most certainly, but something else also. Something that was deep, dark, and foreign.

"It's a pleasure to meet you, Lady P." I gave her another formal half nod. "What can do for you?"

"I was wondering if, perhaps, you would be available for a discussion of a more personal nature?"

She dropped her hand, letting it skim down my waist and exposed left hip in a flirtatious manner. Her touch was light, her fingers warm, and the desire that stirred within me was strengthened by not only her closeness but also the richness of her scent—a heady mix of wildflowers and lust. Lady P was definitely out to seduce. And while the strength of my reaction would normally have made me a more than willing partner, suspicion nevertheless stirred. Because despite the desire, there was a coldly determined light in her eyes, one that suggested she wasn't here of her own volition.

It was a suspicion the wind agreed with.

"Alas," I said softly, "I'm now late for such a meeting with my lord."

"Then perhaps," she murmured, her hand slipping to my rump as she closed the space between us. Her breasts pressed against mine, allowing me to feel the racing of her heart. There was no doubt she wanted me, even if the suspicion there was more than lust at play here lingered. "We should make it tomorrow night, at a time when your lord is well occupied with others."

Suggesting she didn't only want our liaison to be unofficial, but also that she was aware enough of Trey's movements to be certain he wasn't going to be around the following night. And all of *that* just deepened the suspicions.

I hesitated and then shrugged one shoulder, as if it was of no importance to me.

"Perhaps I shall agree to such a meeting out on the balcony at midnight, and perhaps I will not." I let a seductive smile tease my lips. "Shall we see what the night brings, Lady P?"

"We shall." Her lips brushed my cheek, leaving my skin tingling as she stepped back and bowed lightly. "I wait in anticipation, Lady N."

So, she'd certainly been asking after me, given I'd never mentioned my name.

"Indeed you will," I murmured, then bowed and continued my journey. And once again was aware of a heated gaze watching my departure.

I was somewhat relieved to find Trey already at the nook, waiting for me.

"Lady N," he said, offering me another glass of red, "I'm delighted you managed to find your way back to my side."

Amusement touched my lips. "Did you doubt it would be otherwise?"

"Oh, yes." He pressed a hand to my spine once again, and guided me toward the internal balcony and the staircase down to the guest accommodation area. "It seemed your attention was in much demand. Just as it would seem I've won our wager."

"I wouldn't be so confident about that—not until *after* the equinox unveiling."

"Oh, I have every confidence an unveiling will only increase the intrigue."

I didn't bother replying. Only time would tell which of us was right. A footman met us at the bottom of the stairs and proceeded to guide us through the myriad of lushly decorated halls until we came to an elegant silver and glass door situated toward the rear of the building.

"We've taken the liberty of supplying you with a range of food and drink. If you desire anything else, please ring the bell, my lord." The footman opened the door and then stepped aside to allow us entry.

"Thank you," Trey said. "But I think we shall be all right for the rest of the evening."

"As you wish, my lord." The footman bowed and retreated.

I walked inside. The suite was of a simple design, consisting of a large lounging area, a plush bathing area that could be curtained off or not, and the offset and partially walled bedding area. There were also several large glass doors that led onto a balcony. Beyond that lay the sea. I could hear her call through the whisper of the wind. The only other door in the area, aside from the entrance, was into what I presumed was the privy. There were a number of paintings and tapestries on the walls depicting scenery, and a multitude of colorful rugs on the stone floor.

That floor was warm against the soles of my feet, and contained an odd sense of power.

I frowned and walked across to the long, kneeling-height table that sat in the middle of the main room. It held trays of sweetmeats, breads, and cheeses, and there was also a decanter of wine and an ornate silver coffeepot set atop a heating pad.

Trey stripped off his belt and mask, tossing both onto one

of the well-padded blue-velvet chairs as he headed for the coffeepot. "Drink?"

"Please."

I took off my mask and stretched out on one of the fur-covered cloudsaks, crossing my legs at my ankles. It was a position that revealed the long length of my unstained leg and a good portion of my right buttock. Trey handed me a coffee then sat down on one of the hassocks to my left—an optimal position to view what was on show. If he noticed, there was no immediate evidence of it.

"So, what did the night and this celebration reveal to you?"

I took a drink, winced at the bitter taste, and then quickly updated him. "I guess the most intriguing is the fact that although Lord Marcus is hosting this event to celebrate the return of his lady, neither of them appeared."

"A curious anomaly many commented on. Any theories?"

"No, but I did talk to Tavish briefly. Saska apparently keeps to her rooms and sees no one. I got the distinct impression Marcus isn't pleased about her return."

"Which is far more information than I managed," he said. "Although I *did* learn Marcus has a hetaera who has given him three sons, one of them born long before he and Saska were committed."

A hetaera was one step up from a mistress. It basically meant she was treated as the lady of the house by everyone within it, but wasn't formally acknowledged as such. Saska's return would have been a great blow to her hopes and her standing in this place. "Was she there tonight?"

"No, but she'll apparently be in attendance tomorrow night." He smiled. "Which is rather fitting, given it is the night of knives."

"Really? Why?"

"It's a symbolistic representation of the cutting of old ties and the forging of new. That knife you threatened to plunge into my heart will be a most appropriate adornment."

"And an appropriate response if Lord Kiro decides to test the boundaries of my patience."

His smile grew. "Did you glean anything else from young Tavish?"

"No, but only because Kiro intervened."

He raised his eyebrows. "Did he indeed?"

"He seemed rather determined I should not flirt with that young man."

"Perhaps that's because he has designs on him."

"No. There was nothing sexual in his interference." I hesitated. "He *did* try to seduce me, however, even though he does not trust me."

"Neither is surprising. He knows you keep secrets."

"Everyone keeps secrets. Most are not worth worrying about." I shrugged. "Besides, I'm not one of those women whose lips are loosened after a tumble, however exceptional it may be."

"I'm guessing, then, you have not been bedded by a man such as Kiro?"

"No, and I have no desire to be, either. No matter how much his personal magic might push such onto me."

Something glittered in his eyes, something that almost suggested satisfaction. But all he said was "Anything else?"

I hesitated. "I saw two women wearing bracelets similar to the ones Saska gifted to us."

An eyebrow rose. "And this caught your attention because?"

I took another sip of coffee but it was far too strong for my palate. I wrinkled my nose and placed the cup back onto the table. "Because you said you'd not seen their like before."

"That's hardly surprising given I've been absent in any real capacity for just over seventeen years."

"Seventeen?" I blinked. "How young were you when you went to Blacklake? You can't possibly be more than a few years older than me."

"I would wager I'm at least five years older," he said. "As for the reasons—isn't that part of our wager?"

"It is indeed." Five years would make him thirty-three and that was a very young age to become commander. Given the respect he generated from his people, it wasn't a position he'd been handed, either, but rather one earned.

He stretched his long legs out until his toes touched my lower thigh. It was little more than a light press of skin against skin, and yet it caused a reaction more intense than anything Lord Kiro, with all his sexual prowess and magic, could ever hope to achieve.

If Trey felt a similar reaction, he was doing a damn good job of concealing it.

"That's not the only reason the bracelets caught my interest," I said, in a vague attempt to concentrate on the reason I was here. "Out in the desert, when Saska asked me to remove them, she said they were a gift from the queen, and that she could be tracked through them."

He leaned forward at that. "There haven't been royals in Gallion for eons."

"Precisely."

"I suppose she might have been delusional. It's possible she was out in the Tenterra sun for too long."

"You saw her skin, Commander. Did it look like she'd been out in the sun to you?"

"No." A smile briefly ghosted his lips. "Describe these women to me."

I did so, and he frowned. "The older woman sounds like Lady Hedra Harken—"

"Who is?" I cut in.

"Saska's mother."

"Meaning it's even odder Saska went on to deny seeing the bracelets before she woke in the desert when they're identical to the ones her own mother wears."

"Yes." He rubbed his chin, expression thoughtful. "The other lady would probably be Pyra. I haven't had much to do with her but I believe her to be the youngest of Brent's five daughters."

"She made some effort to seduce me."

"Did she now?" Speculation lit his eyes. "And why is that, do you think? Because your tone makes it obvious you don't believe it's simple attraction."

I smiled. "Oh, she *was* attracted. But her overtures were a little too deliberate, and I don't believe she was there of her own volition." I hesitated. "Is possible that Lord Kiro set her onto me?"

He laughed. "No. Kiro sees your resistance to his wiles as a challenge. He wouldn't send others to do what he can't."

"Meaning you didn't tell him to back off?"

"No."

"Why not?" I picked up the waist belt and waved the green end of it lightly. "Is that not the purpose of this thing? You know Kiro is an unwanted suitor."

"Yes, but that doesn't apply in this case. Kiro believes someone *within* Winterborne's ranks is responsible for both Saska's disappearance and her mysterious reappearance. He has full approval from the Forum to do whatever might be necessary to uncover who that person—or *persons* —might be."

"I'm not that person, Commander."

"He's well aware of that, but you nevertheless keep secrets, and until he uncovers them, he'll keep up the pursuit."

"Even though he knows I'm here to assist you?"

"Yes."

I grunted unhappily. Putting up with Kiro's heated overtures on top of everything else was not what I wanted—or needed—right now. "What should we do about Lady Pyra?"

"I shall discreetly inquire about her." He hesitated. "Although the best means of finding information would be from the source itself. If you could lure her away with the promise to spend time—"

"'Spend time' being a polite plateau term for have sex?"

"Yes." His smile flashed again. "We'll provide you with a quick-acting draught that'll make her talk and then sleep. She'll wake with no memory of what went on."

I raised an eyebrow. "And what if I actually want to have sex with her?"

"Then we'll provide a slower-working draught." He studied me for a moment. "Which would you prefer?"

"The latter." Not only because I *did* desire her, but because it'd be safer. She might not remember being questioned but the lack of satiation might well raise suspicions.

"Ah, good." He paused and took a long drink. "I'll give my blessing to such an interlude when she seeks it."

"Oh, she has no intention of seeking permission."

"Indeed? Intriguing."

"Yes." I paused. "Should I be expecting to approve a liaison for you?"

"I haven't agreed to such as yet."

Meaning he'd certainly been approached. I couldn't help but wonder who he was waiting for.

He took another drink, and then said, "It would seem our targets tomorrow night—aside from Pyra and our so far absent hosts—need to be Lady Hedra and Marcus's mysterious hetaera, whoever she may be. Whatever is going on, its epicenter revolves around this house. I can feel it in the stone of this place."

The only thing I was feeling right now was the unacknowledged thrum of desire that seemed to burn between us.

"And what of Lord Kiro?"

"He'd provide no future problem if you'd tell him what you conceal." There was the faintest hint of reproach and annoyance in his voice.

"Kiro may be investigating whatever dark deeds are being played out in this place, but I don't trust him."

"Kiro is many things, but he'd never betray either the Forum or Winterborne."

"Are you sure of that?"

"As sure as I've ever been about anything."

Which only made me wonder all the more about the relationship between the two men. I doubted it was in any way sexual, but there was certainly something that bound them.

I pushed to my feet. He made no move to follow. "If the game proceeds tomorrow night, I'd best be fresh for it." I hesitated, and raised an eyebrow. "Are you coming to bed, Commander?"

It was both an invitation and a dare, and I wasn't entirely surprised when he merely shook his head.

"For intrigue's sake, it's better if I don't."

Because, I knew, many of those in the ruling house had as much Sifft blood in their veins as magic, and would therefore note the unfulfilled desire that rode me. It would increase the questions surrounding us, given we were an acknowledged pairing, however informal, and perhaps make the hunters within the ruling ranks even more determined to ensnare.

And though I understood all this, I couldn't help asking, "For intrigue's sake, or is it more an aversion to my stain?"

He didn't immediately react. He simply studied my face in such a way that heat began to infuse my cheeks.

"Your face," he said eventually, his voice soft. "Is exquisite, staining or no. Whoever has made you believe otherwise is a fool."

The words made me smile, even though I'd heard their echo before. I'd believed it back then and it had led to heartache. It wouldn't be in any way smart to believe them again, no matter how genuine they sounded.

No matter how much a part of me wanted to believe.

"Any intrigue I might hold will be of no matter once I meet with Pyra. The race to see who will be the first to taste my so-called delicacies will have been won."

"On the contrary," he murmured, "the mere fact you've chosen Hawthorne's youngest daughter to bestow your first favor on will only enflame determination."

"And so, the wheels of deviousness continue to turn." I shook my head. "I hope you don't regret your decision in the long hours of sleep to come."

"Trust me, I'm not made of stone, Neve, even if I bear it for a name."

"*That* is yet to be seen." I kept my tone light. "I hope you realize I have *no* intention of making your vow of celibacy easy."

"And another challenge is presented," he said. "It'll be interesting to see who wins this particular battle."

"It will, won't it?"

With a nod good night, I stepped around the large cloudsak and headed for our bedchamber. When I was halfway there, I caught the end of the dress, tugged it over my shoulders, and then tossed it lightly to one side. A soft groan followed me as I disappeared behind the half wall.

But he didn't follow me in. Not then, and not in the restless, hungry hours that followed.

Lord Marcus appeared at the masque early the following evening, but Saska was again noticeably absent. He was a tall, much older man than I'd been expecting, possessing a receding hairline and silvery eyes. He wore a long loose tunic in the rich hue of his house, and an ornate longsword strapped to his waist. I couldn't help but wonder if the length of that sword was any indication of a determination to cut ties with his newly returned beloved. His expression—or what was evident of it through the mask—certainly spoke of discontent and anger combined.

"Our host does not look happy," I murmured.

We stood near the far edge of the dance floor, watching the occupants move to a slow and sensual melody. It wasn't a dance I knew, so I was glad when Trey made no fuss about my refusal to take part. I had no desire to reveal the awkward truth about my education—or lack thereof—when it came to things such as formal dances and manners, which were undoubtedly taught here from a very young age.

I sipped some wine and ran a hand down the silk of my dress to hold it in place against the teasing wind. Trey had rather generously ordered me an entire wardrobe. The evening outfits were all in the same pale lavender, but the daytime items were a softer, grayer tone. The dress I wore tonight had two full sleeves that ended with gloves, and a high neck that acted as a collar. The lavender material skimmed my waist then fell from my hips in a series of sheer loose panels that provided teasing glimpses of calf, thigh, and rump with every movement. It had also been designed with no back—the material at the front simply wrapped around my hips and skimmed across the top of my tailbone. Trey had one hand wrapped rather possessively around my waist, and it was causing all sorts of internal havoc. Which, I knew, was precisely his intent. The man was evil. And, despite his protestations, he really *was* made of the material whose name he bore. Certainly none of my overtures this afternoon—be they naked or not—had borne any fruit.

"We should go introduce ourselves," he murmured. "It would be impolite otherwise."

"I imagine it would."

He guided me through the crowd toward Marcus, whose gaze skimmed past us and then abruptly returned. Recognition stirred in his eyes—he was well aware of who we were, masked or not. And if the glower he all but threw my way was anything to go by, he was certainly unimpressed with my presence in his house.

So why would he go to the trouble of inviting me?

"Lord M," Trey said smoothly as he bowed. "May I present to you—"

"I know who she is," he snapped, and then seemed to remember where he was. He drew in a breath and offered the required formalities. "Lady N, welcome to my house. I hope the goddess gifts you with a bountiful harvest for this coming year."

I curtseyed. "And you, my lord."

"Is your lady not present, my lord?" Trey asked.

"No." There was much fury in that single word. Again, he struggled to compose himself. "She has taken ill since her return. Mayhaps the babe troubles her."

And maybe, the wind whispered, *it is something else.*

"Do you think she might see me?" I asked. "It's unseemly she spends such a time of celebration by herself."

Marcus studied me for a moment, and then nodded abruptly. "It is worth a try, I suppose. If you can convince her to come out of hiding, even if only for an hour or so, I would be appreciative."

He snapped his fingers, and a blue-clad pageboy instantly appeared. "Escort the lady N to my lady's rooms."

Trey released me. I bowed to Marcus, and then followed

the page out of the ballroom. In the colder silence of the halls, the wind's chatter seemed to increase, whispering of dark secrets and even darker actions in play. Details, however, remained scant.

The Rossi family's private accommodation consisted of one entire side of the V-shaped house, and its halls were even more ornate than the guest and entertainment spaces. It was a place of gold and silver, with rich hues on the walls and the floors in the form of tapestries and carpets. Lady Saska's apartments lay at the rear of the building, in what would be a wide, blunt end of the V-structure.

The page stopped at the ornate silver-and-blue door and pressed a buzzer. After several seconds, footsteps approached.

"Yes?" The woman who opened the door was middle-aged and friendly looking.

"The lady N is here to see Lady S."

Obviously, even though we were now beyond the boundaries of the masque, initials still had to be used in public.

The maidservant hesitated. "One moment, and I shall ask m'lady if she wishes to be disturbed."

The door closed again. The page shuffled his feet from side to side, looking rather impatient—at least until he caught my amusement and remembered his manners. I felt like telling him not to bother, but refrained. In this place, my attitude had to appear no different to any of the others here.

The footsteps approached again. Although I'd half expected to be turned away, the maidservant rather surprisingly opened the door wider and bid me to enter. "Please, Lady N, come in."

I thanked the page then entered. Saska's rooms were—unsurprisingly—far grander than the one I shared with Trey. The lounging room was vast, and filled with enough cloud-saks, hassocks, and divans to seat several households. To my right, there were three doors—the sleeping quarters, bathroom, and separate privy, from what I could see of the rooms beyond—but to my left, there was an entire wall of sliding glass partitions, several of which were open. The wind whistled in, filling the room with the salt of the sea and a feeling of anger. Whatever was going on in this place, she did not like it.

The maidservant led me out onto the balcony. The wind was even fiercer out here, her touch cold and almost violent, tearing at my dress and mask as if she meant to strip me bare. I hastily slipped off the mask and handed it to the maidservant, who, after announcing me, curtseyed and rather sensibly went back inside.

Saska leaned against the stone cap railing, her silver-touched black hair streaming out behind her like a wind-torn thundercloud.

For a minute I wasn't even sure she was aware of my presence, but then, in a voice that was little more than a whisper, she said, "The wind admonishes me."

I stopped beside her and leaned my forearms against the rail. The stone was as cold as the wind, and just as furious. This close to Saska, I could see the paleness of her lips and the shivers that assailed her.

"And why would the wind do that, Lady Saska?"

"I do not know."

The wind battered her, forcing her to grip the railing tightly to prevent being flung backward.

After a moment, she whispered, "She's angry with me."

Obviously. The question was, why?

"You're her voice in this world," I said carefully. "What is it that you're not saying for her?"

Saska's gaze came to mine. Her silver eyes were remote—distant—and I had a vague feeling it wasn't me she was seeing or hearing. There were others—others who might or might not be real—who had her attention right now.

She stared at me for so long I didn't think she intended to answer, and then she swallowed heavily. "I can hear them, you know."

I frowned. "The whispers of the wind?"

She waved a hand almost impatiently. "No, the *other* voices. The ones that belong to *her*."

"Her?" I hesitated, gathering skirts that threatened to end up around my ears. The wind spun around me, her voice filled with amusement. She might be angry with Saska, but it seemed she was feeling very flirtatious with me. "Do you mean one of the women at the masque?"

"I'd thought that by taking them off," she continued, as if I hadn't spoken, "it would break our connection. But I was wrong. And *she* is very angry."

So she wasn't talking about the wind as much as that other, nebulous she—the person who'd given her those bracelets. The woman she had designated "queen."

"Why would the queen be angry with you, Saska?"

"Because I ran. Because it makes communications difficult." She shivered again and rubbed her arms. "I cannot do what she asks. I simply cannot."

A sliver of alarm ran through me. Was Lord Kiro right—was the epicenter of whatever was happening to be found right here in this house? With Lady Saska herself? "And what does she want, Saska?"

She blinked, and that odd remoteness disappeared. Whatever had momentarily possessed her had fled.

"Neve," she said. "What a surprise."

I curtseyed lightly. "I came to see if you're okay, Lady Saska. You are missed at the masque."

She snorted. "Certainly not by my whore of a husband.

He has his hetaera to accompany him in my place, after all. Did you know the bitch has borne him three sons?"

"So I heard." I touched her arm lightly. "I'm sorry for the position you've been placed in, Lady Saska, but it's not unexpected given your length of time away."

She glared down at my hand for a moment, but she didn't shake me loose and something within her oddly seemed to relax. "I guess. But it rankles nevertheless."

"Then why hide in your suite? Why not go out there, into that masque, and show everyone who is the true mistress of this house?"

She stared at me for another lengthy amount of time. The wind continued to stir around us, but its force was gentler against me than her. And for once, I could hear what it said to her; it wanted her to do as I suggested. That the whispers would be lessened if she were not alone.

The wind knew what afflicted her. It just wasn't ready to tell me. Which was frustrating but not unexpected. She was beholden to Saska, not me.

"You don't stand on ceremony around me, do you?" she said eventually. "You give your thoughts and opinions honestly, and that is rather rare around here. The wind says I should trust you."

I half smiled. "The wind is wise. And I didn't save your ass in Tenterra, Lady Saska, to threaten it in any way now."

"Indeed." A small but nevertheless real smile touched her lips. I had a vague feeling that didn't happen all too often. "Then let us get out of the chill of this wind, and go create some havoc at the masque."

I smiled and turned to walk alongside her. Once inside, her maidservant hastily smoothed her hair and dress, and then placed the mask upon her. Once I'd donned mine, a pageboy was summoned and we were escorted back to the ballroom, where she was grandly announced.

The hush that fell upon the room was deep and rife with speculation. It ran across the silence like electricity, and oddly seemed to take in me as much Saska. But that was no surprise given I was by her side, acting as escort.

It was a position she entrenched by holding out her hand for me to take. I did so, and we walked down the stairs at a slow and regal pace. If Saska sensed the tense anticipation in the room, she didn't show it. Indeed, what little could be seen of her expression through the mask was serene and remote.

Marcus approached us as we reached the bottom of the stairs. He bowed slightly, and then said, "Lady S, I am so glad you've decided to join us."

"Are you indeed?" Saska murmured. "Here I was thinking you'd rather be rutting with the cow who coveted my place."

It seemed I wasn't the only one who wasn't afraid to speak their mind.

"There has never been anyone else in my heart, m'lady," he returned, just as softly. The fury and distaste I could see in his eyes did not spill over into his expression or his words. "But no man would or could have remained celibate for such a length of time. Nor, indeed, any woman."

It was a none-too-subtle reminder that she was pregnant with another man's child. It didn't infuriate her, as I'd half expected. It did the opposite. Waves of horror seemed to flow from her and, just for an instant, I thought she was going to turn and run.

Then she glanced at someone over his shoulder and abruptly straightened her shoulders. "Just so, my lord. Perhaps if you'd be so good as to reintroduce me to everyone?" She slipped her hand from mine, but not before she'd squeezed my fingers lightly and whispered, "Thank you."

As the two of them walked away, I found my gaze searching the nearby crowd, wondering who Saska had glanced at. There were no familiar figures and no one that stirred unease, either in me or in the wind.

I frowned and went in search of Trey, but once again found myself being stopped by the young Lord Tavish. "Lady N," he said, with a grand flourish. "It is the following night, and I am eager to resume our conversation."

He was, I couldn't help but note, rather intoxicated. He'd obviously been gathering courage in the richness of wine, and it made me rather suspect he had not indulged in the type of conversation he was hoping to get from me. Perhaps virginity was more highly prized here in the Reaches than it was in the outer bailey.

I tucked my arm through his and lightly guided him forward. His body was trembling at the light contact and I couldn't help but wish Ava were with me. She would have relished teaching Tavish the fine art of seduction.

"I am afraid, my dear Lord T, that I am not the woman you should be seeking for the type of conversation you desire."

I said it as gently as I could, but nevertheless felt the surge of frustration and annoyance in him.

"But you *must*, because if you do not, my father—" He clammed up suddenly, and heat touched his cheeks.

"Your father will what?" I prompted.

He took a deep breath and blew it out softly. "My father sees the benefits of having Lord Kiro in his debt."

"But why—?" I stopped abruptly. Trey had mentioned rather casually that Kiro might fancy Tavish for himself. He obviously knew far more than he was admitting. "Your father surely wouldn't agree to such a liaison if you yourself are not amendable."

"You don't know my father," he said, rather gloomily.

"Then get yourself to both a lady *and* lord of ease who have studied the finer arts of Astar or the god Drago; lose that which your father plans to barter and enjoy yourself in the process."

Astar was the goddess of female sexuality and empowerment. Her followers believed a woman should fully explore the pleasures of both her own body and those of her sisters before ever indulging in those of the opposite sex. Such intimate knowledge empowered us in the presence of a man, and made us more able to guide him toward greater pleasure for us both. Her counterpart was the god Drago, whose followers not only believed that a man must spread his seed as far as possible, but that pleasure could and should be taken in what*ever* form it presented, be it man or woman.

I'd undertaken Astar's initiation rites as soon as I'd come into puberty, and while I was no priestess, neither I—nor indeed, anyone else in the Nightwatch—could ever be accused of not following the teachings of either god as fully as we were able.

"Laying with a lady would not temper Lord Kiro's desire."

"Perhaps not, but there are plenty of gentlemen within that quarter who would offer a similar service."

He frowned. "I know, but I dare not—"

"Then choose someone within this room *other* than me. I'm sure there are plenty here, of both sexes, who'd be willing to spend time with a Rossi lord." I paused, and then added softly, "And after all, does your brother not have a hetaera?"

"Lida?" He snorted. "Even *I* know that woman is nothing but a schemer. Marcus had best watch his back, because she's not one who'll take being scorned lightly."

That raised my eyebrows. "He no longer lies with her?"

"Not since his lady's return."

"He must love Saska greatly."

Another snort greeted that statement. "He does nothing of the sort, but there are formalities that must be observed, and my brother has always fallen on the side of doing what appears to be right."

"Have you managed to talk to her yet?"

"No. But she's come back mad if the whispers of the serfs are anything to go by." The drink, it seemed, had loosened his tongue greatly.

"What do they whisper?"

"That she hears nonexistent voices, and goes on and on that she can't do what they ask." He shook his head. "It was bound to happen, of course, given she was lost for so long."

"She can't have been too lost if she carries the child of another."

"That's true." He considered this for a moment, and then said, "Do you think, perhaps, she was not lost but rather sent to a sanitarium?"

Given Kiro was suspicious of her sudden reappearance, I very much doubted it.

Someone cleared their throat behind us. I looked over my shoulder, and was somewhat unsurprised to see Kiro himself. Tavish went red, bowed to us both, and yet again retreated.

I raised an eyebrow as I turned to fully face Kiro. "You seem to have an unusual effect on the young Lord T. It's almost as if he doesn't wish to be in your presence in any way, shape, or form."

"That's certainly not my wish nor my desire."

"And yet it's your desire that scares him."

His gaze narrowed. "The young Lord T has obviously been very loose of lips this evening."

"Drinking too much fine wine will do that." I tilted my head and studied him. "Tell me, Lord K, what does it take to loosen your lips?"

"More than you have, my lady."

"And yet, here you are, dogging my steps because of some

ill-defined secret you think I keep. A lesser woman might perhaps believe that you merely use it as an excuse."

The smile that teased his lips hinted at amusement, but it failed to touch the darkness in his eyes. "Your Lord T is right —you are an unusual woman. I look forward to further ripostes." He retrieved a small vial of reddish liquid from his pocket and offered it to me. "Place this in Pyra's wine. It will release any disinclination to answer questions, but will take an hour to make her pliable for questions."

Once I'd plucked it from his hand, he bowed lightly and disappeared. I caught a fresh drink from a passing tray waiter, downed it quickly, and then claimed another. It made my head buzz a little too much, but at least it went some ways to drowning the knowledge that Trey had been discussing the possibility of my seducing Pyra with Kiro.

I scanned the crowd, looking for Trey, but the room was too big and had far too many shadowed corners. The wind stirred around me, whispering it was time to seek the lady P. I took a deep breath and released it slowly, but it didn't really ease the sudden uncertainty about the path I'd chosen. My attraction to Pyra was real enough, but this place—these people—were leagues above me, and I suspected the games they played might be too.

If I seduced Pyra, I'd be in great danger, of that, I had no doubt.

And yet, the danger to Winterborne was even greater. I was a Nightwatch soldier, trained from a very young age to do whatever it took—to step willingly into death's path if necessary—to protect this place. And if bedding Pyra to uncover her secrets gave this city a chance to survive the darkness hinted on the wind's whisperings, then there really wasn't a choice.

I downed my drink, gathered two more, placed Kiro's drug in one of them, and then went in search of her.

She was waiting in the far shadows to the left of the doors, her back resting against the railing and her mask dangling idly from one hand.

"Lady N," she said, her voice warm, "I was beginning to suspect you'd decided against our liaison."

"I have to admit, it is only the intrigue of what you might wish to discuss with me that has brought me here."

She laughed softly and accepted the glass of wine from me. "I think we both know talking is not what I desire."

The wind stirred around me, whispering the need for innocence. "Indeed, we do not."

She studied me, her gaze suddenly speculative. "Tell me, lady N, are you acquainted with the teachings of the goddess Astar?"

More than just acquainted, I wanted to say, but once again the wind urged against it. "I'm afraid not."

"Ah, then you are in for such a revelation." She paused, her anticipation sweet on the air. "Perhaps we should retire to your suites so that I might enlighten you?"

"Lord T might well interrupt—"

"Your Lord T is well and truly occupied. I've made sure of that." She drained her glass, then stepped forward and linked her arm through mine. "Shall we go?"

I hesitated, and then nodded. She guided me down the stairs and—obviously well acquainted with the layout of this place—waved away the pageboys who would have guided us to the suite I shared with Trey. Once we were inside and the door locked, she poured us both another drink then handed it to me gravely. "To the revelations and pleasures of the flesh."

I echoed her words and silently hoped the truth serum wouldn't take any longer than an hour to work. While I had no doubt I'd enjoy my time with her, the vague sense of uneasiness I'd felt earlier had returned twofold. What I learned here tonight might well be a key to solving the mystery of what was going on, but it was also about to place me in great danger.

If the wind agreed, she wasn't saying.

Pyra smiled. "Are you ready, Lady N?"

"I think so."

"Good."

She stepped forward and kissed me. It was a gentle thing, little more than a promise of the heat to come. Then, with a prayer to the goddess, she stepped back and began to undress.

Initiation was never hurried. It was an unveiling, a blooming of both the senses and sensuality, one designed to heighten the experience and the pleasure for a first-time initiate. Which I wasn't, of course, but it was nevertheless beautiful to watch her slow dance to nakedness.

Then it was my turn. I echoed her movements, my body tingling with expectation and the knowledge of what was to come. She gasped when my stains were revealed, but it was a soft sound of surprise and perhaps even passion rather than horror.

She stepped closer and our dance continued, filled with reverent touches that became ever more intimate, until it was no longer just hands, but also tongue. And so it continued until sweat sheened our bodies and desire was so sweet and heavy on the air it was almost liquid. Only then did the goddess allow completion, and while it might not have been what the deeper recesses of my body truly desired, it was nevertheless a more fulfilling initiation than what I'd experienced the first time.

We retired to the bed and continued to worship the goddess for nigh on an hour, after which Pyra murmured a prayer of thankfulness and closed her eyes, a smile teasing her well-kissed lips. I fought the tiredness pounding through my body, fought the need to drift into sleep right alongside her, and said softly, "What secrets do you keep, Pyra? What is your involvement with Lady Saska?"

"She's my sister."

I yawned hugely, and then said, "Sister of blood, or sister of the flesh?"

"Neither. She is my apiary sister."

I knew an apiary was a hive, but had no idea what she meant in this situation. For all I knew, it might have been some sort of secret sisterhood here in the Upper Reaches. "And who else is a member of this apiary?"

She mumbled something I couldn't quite catch, and then added, "But there's no one else currently in Winterborne."

Meaning there were others elsewhere? "What of Lady Hedra? She wears the same bracelets are you."

Again, I didn't catch her reply. I leaned closer and said, "Repeat that."

She did, but even softer. The drug seemed to be working faster than Kiro had implied. And I had to wonder if perhaps I'd accidentally ingested some of it via her lips, because the need for sleep was pounding through my body.

Instead of trying to clarify Hedra's position in whatever was happening, I asked, "And what is the aim of this apiary?"

"To obey."

My eyes closed. I forced them open again. "Who is it that you have to obey?"

"The queen."

So this queen, whoever she was, wasn't a figment of Saska's imagination. "And where can we find this queen?"

"Everywhere and nowhere. She's in our minds and under our very feet."

Meaning we were dealing with a witch capable of using both air *and* earth magic? Hadn't both Kiro and Trey claimed that was impossible?

I yawned hugely; it was becoming a struggle to remain awake, to think. "And does she use the bracelets to communicate with you?"

"Yes."

I closed my eyes for longer this time, and tried to think of another question. But my brain was fuzzy and unfocused. Alarm ran through me, but it was a distant thing and couldn't reach past the fog that was encasing my mind. Whatever question I might have asked died unspoken as sleep finally claimed me.

It was the wind who woke me. She reached through the fog with little courtesy or gentleness, her whisperings harsh and cold in my brain. I stirred, swearing at her, only to become aware of the slight dip in the bed; someone had either climbed in or out of it. I reached out sleepily and realized Pyra was no longer tangled in the sheets with me.

Move, move, move, the wind whispered urgently, tugging at my hair, my arms, and my legs. I rolled over compliantly and forced my eyes open.

To see a flash of silvery white as a knife plunged toward my heart.

6

It might have been the wind that woke me, but it was training that saved me. Even though sleep still rested far too heavily on my limbs, I jackknifed sideways and lashed out with a bare heel. There was a grunt as I connected with flesh and the knife that would have plunged into my chest buried hilt-deep into the bed instead.

The wind hit me like a punch, knocking the air from my lungs and flinging me backward onto the floor. The same air that had hit me now screamed in warning. I rolled sideways and somehow staggered upright, only to be knocked down again as something smashed into my face, cutting my skin and leaving me bleeding and dizzy.

I shook my head, trying to rid myself of the lingering sleepiness and saw, out of the corner of my right eye, another flash of movement. I rolled under the vase aimed at my head then surged upward, flinging myself at the woman causing the mayhem. A squeak of surprise left her lips as she jumped off the bed onto the floor. But before I could follow her or pin her, the wind hit me, forcing me backward. I swore, and she spun around me, apologetic even as she kept pushing me, until my back was pressed against the far wall and the force of her was so great I could barely even draw breath.

"I'm sorry it has come to an end such as this." Pyra climbed to her feet. "I would have liked to have dallied with you a little more."

"You don't have to obey the voices," I said, even as I admonished the wind for doing this to me.

Reach, she advised. *You have the power.*

If that were true, I wouldn't currently be pinned to the wall. But I did as she bid and reached into the maelstrom, trying to get past it, trying to gain control, to get some help. The air quivered and twisted and fought, and the power of her confusion seemed to echo through the stone beneath my bare feet.

"Don't do this, Pyra," I said, desperate to buy time. Time for the wind to break her control, time for me to get free so that I could fight. Or even time for someone to hear all the noise and come to my aid. Because surely in a place such as this, someone *had* to be near.

Pyra smiled and reached for the knife—my knife, I noted somewhat ironically. "That's not possible."

"And yet Saska fights them."

Something flickered in her eyes; something that was bitter, and not wholly human. "Saska will be brought to heel once you're out of the way."

"I have nothing to do with her resistance."

The vibrations running under my feet were now so strong that the stone floor was beginning to heave and writhe. *Quake.* And yet how was that even possible? The only other time we'd experienced such an event was during the bitter final moments of the war, after the earth witches had drawn so much power from the surrounding land that it caused massive landslips on either side of Winterborne and plunged thousands to their deaths.

"You have everything to do with it." Pyra's voice was flat. "It was no coincidence you found her. She called you. She still calls you. You're her strength and her touchstone."

And *she* was mad. There was no other explanation for thoughts like that.

She walked toward me, her fingers white with the fierceness of her grip on my knife. But the air pinning me in place was also hampering her movements; it wasn't stopping her, but it was at least slowing her, making her fight for every inch she gained.

When she realized this, she raised the knife and flung it. It flew straight, unhindered by the turbulent air, but she was no knife master and her aim was far from true. It hit the wall, drawing sparks from the stone as it dropped to the ground. It came to rest with its hilt across my right foot; almost immediately—and rather weirdly—the blade began to glow with a rich blue fire.

Pyra screeched and rushed at me. But the floor was now heaving with ever-increasing ferocity, and massive cracks appeared across the stones that lay between us, forcing her to slow. Yet for all that the air screamed, for all the noise the earth was now making, no help had arrived. There was no one to stop her, no one except the wind, and she could only help me so far against an air witch as strong as Pyra. My one chance was the earth—if it would only rise up and trap her....

The thought had barely crossed my mind when the huge slabs of rock punched up through the floor, one after the other, until Pyra was completely encased in a prison of stone.

The air pinning me suddenly swung around, attacking the stones in a useless attempt to draw Pyra from her prison. She screeched again, and the air became violent, flinging the furniture around the room, until it became a dangerous maelstrom of razor-sharp edges that could skewer flesh as easily as a knife.

None of it touched me. The wind, although she couldn't entirely deny Pyra's commands, was providing me with a small cocoon of safety.

I dropped to my knees, my head swimming and my whole body shuddering with the effort of simply breathing. For several minutes, I didn't move; indeed, couldn't have moved, even if my life had depended on it.

But help was coming. I could feel it in the tremor of the stone under my legs.

"Mother of mercy, what on *earth* is going on here?"

It was Trey, arriving to help, even if it was a little too late.

"Neve," another said sharply, "control the wind."

And of *course* he'd brought Kiro. *Damn him.* But the words didn't leave my lips, because even though I hated the thought of him seeing me like this, I also understood Trey's reason for bringing him here. There were dark deeds afoot in this place, and that was far more important than the fate of an unlit soldier who could hear the wind.

But I couldn't obey his command. This wind wasn't mine.

I hugged my body against the pain running through me, and fought the urge to weep. Tears wouldn't help, but I had no idea what actually would. The sensitivity was back again, fiercer and sharper than before. Not only could I feel the presence of the two men in the thrum of their energy beating through the stone under my legs, but also Pyra's fury, the cry of the wind, the demands of a voice that was both one and many, all of them foreign in tone....

I blinked. The voices that both Saska and Pyra had spoken about were *real.*

But why could I suddenly hear them?

"Neve," Trey said, voice sharper, "control the wind."

"Not," I somehow ground out, "me."

"Some of it is," Kiro snapped, "otherwise you'd be dead."

"No," I denied, even though the truth was evident in the small bubble of air that protected me.

The stone began to rumble again. I forced my eyes open and saw that the prison containing Pyra was retreating back into the earth, revealing the fact she was pinned by two boots of stone.

"Release the air, Pyra." Trey's voice was flat but hinted at the fury I could feel via the stones. "Or those cuffs encasing your feet will spread to your entire body, and you'll become little more than a pretty ornament in this place."

"You wouldn't *dare*." Her fists were clenched, her eyes wild, and her voice clear despite the roar of the wind. If she felt any trace of fear, it wasn't evident. "It'd be considered an act of treason under the laws of this place."

"Not if he has my blessing," Kiro replied equably. "The Forum has given me full freedom to use whatever means necessary to uncover what's going on, and you, my dear, are part of whatever it is."

"And what of her?" Pyra flung an arm out, pointing at me. "She's caused this mess. She tried to kill me; I was only defending myself."

I licked my lips and somehow said, "He's a reader, Pyra. He'll uncover the truth of it soon enough."

The violence within the alien whispering got sharper. Pyra shook her head, as if denying what they were saying. Fear flashed across her countenance, but it was more fear of those whispers than what Kiro might reveal.

"I am indeed a reader," he said, "and it would be far easier on you if you willingly revealed whatever information you hold."

I shifted slightly, trying to ease the ache in my leg. Something cold pressed harder against my shin. The knife... and as even as that realization went through me, the voices sharpened and became clear.

But they were only saying one word that was repeated over and over—*kill, kill, kill.*

"Pyra, no!" I screamed, even as I reached for the wind and tried to stop her. Pain unlike anything I'd ever felt before hit me, and the plea shriveled on my lips.

Leaving me to do nothing but watch as the wind swung around and all the deadly missiles that had been rotating within the room were suddenly aimed at the woman still pinned by the stone cuffs.

They shredded her. She didn't even scream. She didn't have the time. The wind died with her, and what missiles remained clattered heavily to the floor.

I closed my eyes and sent a silent prayer of thanks to the forces of earth and air. If they hadn't, for whatever reason, helped me, the bloody mess of body parts staining the white floor would have been mine.

"That," Kiro said eventually, his voice soft, "was not what I'd been expecting."

"No."

Soft footsteps approached. Trey, not Kiro, the stone told me. He knelt in front of me, his gaze a heated caress that skimmed me. Even though he made no immediate move to touch me, I couldn't help whispering, "Don't."

"No," he repeated. I had a vague thought he knew precisely what was happening to me. "Lord Kiro, it would be best if you go back to the masque and reassure everyone that nothing of consequence has happened. Some would have heard the anger in the wind, and many would have felt the tremor. I've asked the earth to whisper reassurances that the tremor they felt was a minor event caused by an untrained child, but still—"

"I will," Kiro said. "But what of Lady Pyra? We need to know what went on in this room, and what part Neve has played."

"Yes, but she's in no state to deal with questions right now." His gaze still hadn't left me, and my body shook under the force of it. But the strange awareness was growing stronger—deeper—because the wash of his breath, soft and distant, felt as fierce against my skin as any summer storm. "As for Pyra—the earth will take care of her."

"They all know she left with Neve and will suspect wrongdoing."

"Which may yet play into our hands."

Kiro's gaze joined Trey's and I felt like weeping under the double pressure. For freedom's sake, what was happening to me? If the wind knew, she gave no answers, and the earth had never deigned to even help me until today.

"There are questions that desperately need—"

"Yes, but she undoubtedly has *just* as many. Pyra tried to kill her, Kiro, and the quake was the result of protecting herself. This has to be dealt with *now*, and then we need to bring her fully into our confidence."

There was a long silence then, "You will perform the ceremony?"

"Yes. We have no option right now."

"And yet the ceremony is not without its dangers. We can call in a priest—"

"There isn't enough time. Look at her, Kiro. The power all but consumes her."

Consumes me? My whole body might be on fire, and every breath—every quiver of movement might feel like a blow—but I wouldn't have said the sensations were so intense that I'd fall under the pressure of them.

Kiro hesitated, then said, "Be careful, Trey. We'll continue this on the morrow."

"Come back at three. Not before. And tell the maidservants to keep well away until then."

"As you wish."

The stone trembled under the weight of Kiro's steps as he walked away. As the suite door closed and the sound echoed around the broken room, I forced my eyes open and looked into Trey's. There was sympathy there, as well as understanding.

And desire so fierce perspiration began to dot my skin.

I swallowed heavily and said, "What is the deal between you and Kiro?"

A smile tugged his lips. "Of all the questions I expected you to ask, *that* was not one of them."

"You know what's happening to me, don't you?"

"Yes, and I'm afraid the cure will make things a whole lot worse before they can get better."

"I don't think that's possible."

"Then you'd be wrong. As to what's happening—" He took a deep breath and released it slowly. "What you're experiencing is the end result of raising magic you neither understand nor fully control."

I frowned at him. "But I didn't—"

"You *did*. Who else was here to raise the earth? It certainly didn't answer Pyra's call."

"But how is that even possible? I'm *unlit*—"

"The hows and whys aren't important right now. We need to perform the ceremony of Gaia immediately. It will bind you to the energy of the earth and stop these uncontrolled events. You'll still need training, of course, but it will ease the risk to both you and everything around you." He hesitated, and the wash of his desire increased, making me tremble under its force. "But I have to warn you—the ceremony is sexual in nature. Given we have no time to call for a priest, I'll have to take his place as the earth's representative."

While I was all for having sex with Trey, *any* sort of touch in this hypersensitive state would be nigh on unbearable. "What happens if I *don't* do the ceremony?"

"You'll be torn apart by the forces you cannot yet control." His voice was grim. "And you might just take a good portion of Winterborne with you."

"Then there is no choice."

"No. Can you walk?"

I snorted—a soft sound that somehow hurt. "You already know the answer to that."

"Given your propensity to keep doing things you shouldn't, I had to ask." He paused again, and the amusement that had briefly flirted with his lips fell away. He reached to the side, picked up a smooth piece of what looked to be the remains of a chair's leg, and said, "Place this in your mouth and bite down into it."

Fear stirred through me. "Why? What do you intend to do?"

"Pick you up."

He placed the wood against my lips. In my current state of being, I could taste the varnish on its surface, feel the eons of life from the tree it had once been. Could smell the minute droplets of blood that had been sprayed across one edge.

"Trust me," Trey said softly, "you'll want this."

After a moment, I opened my mouth and accepted the gag. He shifted to my right side, the movement washing waves of air across my skin and sending another shudder through me.

"Ready?" he asked.

No, I wanted to say, even as I nodded.

He hesitated, then slipped his hands under my knees and behind my back and, in one smooth movement, lifted me. It felt like every nerve ending in my body was being ripped apart. The pain I'd felt before was bad, but this—this was a tsunami. I bit down on the chair leg so hard my teeth cracked its surface, but it didn't stop the scream that ripped from my throat. Nothing could.

And though he held me so very gently against his body as he carried me from the bedroom, the rub of his silk shirt against my flesh felt like sandpaper tearing away layers of flesh.

We moved outside, onto the patio. The icy air stung my skin, drying the blood on my face but providing no release from the heat and the pain. I could feel through the night's vibrations that the party still went on above us, could hear the music and the violence of the sea far below us, but none of it came close to the overwhelming sense of power and desire coming from the man holding me so close.

He didn't stop at the railing. He simply climbed over the capstone and stepped out onto the ten or so feet of dangerous wilderness that now separated us from the long drop to the sea.

"Are you intending to throw me over that cliff?"

It came out more than a little garbled, given the chair leg, but he obviously understood, because he laughed. It was a soft sound that caused both pleasure and pain. "No, I most certainly am not."

Good. But this time, I didn't say it. Couldn't.

"When I set you down, Neve, I need you to kneel and hold out your hands, palm up. Can you do that?"

I nodded. He stopped, carefully placed me on the ground, and then pulled away. The pebbles and twigs that littered the ground felt like knives digging into my skin, and the wild grasses became lashes of leather. I bit deeper into the chair leg, fighting the bile that rose up my throat and the blackness beginning to affect my vision, and slowly, carefully, assumed a kneeling position.

Knees touched mine. The contact was skin on skin and electric. My heart began to beat a whole lot faster. I forced my eyes open and discovered he was as naked as I. And lord, was he beautiful; his brown skin gleamed like warmed chocolate under the moon's cold light, his arms and his chest were well muscled, his abs well-defined, and his erection thick and fierce.

Whatever doubts I might have had about his desire for me were in that moment irrevocably shattered.

He carefully removed the chair leg from my mouth, and then placed his hands on top of mine. Though his touch was light, it burned through my nerve endings and sent a shudder through my entire body. Despite that, energy stirred between us, energy that was sexual and yet not, and came not just from him, but from the very ground underneath us.

Ground that was heated and beginning to heave anew.

I carefully licked parched lips and somehow said, "What does this ceremony involve aside from sex?"

"We have to raise the power of the earth and immerse ourselves completely in her." He paused. "You have to trust me, Neve. What follows will first undo you and then heal you. But you won't be alone. I'll be your anchor, both physically *and* metaphysically."

"*That* doesn't explain anything."

"No. But we're out of time." He slid his hands up to my wrists and held them tight. It felt like I was being branded.

I swallowed heavily, and then nodded. I had no true understanding of what was going on or what might happen in the next few minutes, but I trusted him.

He took a deep breath and released it slowly. His body was trembling with expectation and there was a fierce light in his eyes, one that spoke of desire and something more. Something that was as deep, as powerful, and as old as the earth itself.

"I will tell you what to say," he said softly. "Do not worry about the forces that rise. I'll not let you get lost in them."

I nodded. And so it began.

What he said, I repeated, and with every sentence, the

earth grew warmer, the night became sharper, and that intangible, heady rawness that had been surging between us grew ever stronger, ever deeper, until contact was not just hands and knees and the sheer force of the energy we were creating threatened to tear the world apart.

And then it *did* tear apart—the earth rose, wrapped warm earthen fingers around us, and drew us deep into the heat of her ample bosom. The sky and the stars disappeared and there was nothing but the heartbeat of the earth around us. It was a force that swept through every particle that made up the entirety of my being, inspecting, judging, and testing. The strands of my DNA were stretched beyond the possibility of breath and life, and all that the earth mother was, and all that I could be, became one and the same. And oh, it felt so beautiful, so enriching, to be a part of such power, that I didn't want to let it go. Even as the earth began to reassemble my being, I fought to remain, to languish in the heat and the wisdom of all those who'd come before me, and whose spirits now resided alongside mine. But there was iron at my waist and thick heat in my body and the urgency of such could not be ignored. As the earth opened her fingers and gently deposited us back into the world, the power of our joining reached a crescendo more powerful than anything I'd ever felt before—one that tore a scream of pleasure from my throat even as it left me weak with satiety.

Awareness returned slowly, and with it the true realization of what had just happened. I was sitting on Trey's knees, my arms wrapped around his neck and my chest pressed hard against his. His shaft was becoming flaccid within me and his hands were pressed firmly against my buttocks to hold me in place.

"You really *didn't* have to go to such lengths to seduce me," I murmured, not wanting to move. It felt warm and safe in his arms, and the pain and heightened sensitivity seemed to have fled, leaving my body tired but at peace. "I would have said yes had you but asked."

He laughed softly, a sound that rumbled rather delightfully through my breasts. "I'm afraid Mother Earth demands more than just an oath. She demands complete immersion of body, soul, *and* passion before she accepts an initiate into her being."

I frowned and pushed away from him. "What?"

He brushed the sweaty strands of hair away from my eyes, his touch gentle. "She has accepted you as one of us."

I stared at him for a long, rather stunned, silence. "But I've never heard the whispers of the earth, only the wind—"

I stopped abruptly, but far too late.

"And so the secret we've long suspected is finally revealed." Amusement touched his voice, but there was concern in his expression, and it sent a shiver of trepidation through me. "It *was* you who directed the wind to cut that trench into the ground."

"Yes, but you said that was impossible—"

"Impossible for an air witch," he cut in. "But not for a witch who can hear the whispers of both."

"But I'm *unlit!*" It was all but torn from me. I didn't want to be a witch. Didn't want to be forced from the Nightwatch and all that I knew and loved. "Besides, I didn't think it was possible for a witch to hold more than one power."

"Generally, it's not. Witches are born into one of three categories—earth, air, or personal. It's been so since time began, and it's only in the last few hundred years that we've seen the beginning of a change."

I frowned. "Since the war, you mean?"

He nodded, and then slapped my rump lightly. "Shall we continue this discussion in warmer surrounds? The air is getting cold."

The air stirred around me in irritation, and a smile

touched my lips. "The air thinks you've grown soft within the warm walls of your outpost."

He laughed again and pushed me upright. Once he'd also stood, he twined his fingers in mine and led me inside. My gaze went to the utter destruction of the bedchamber and came to rest rather unerringly on the remnants of flesh and the slowly drying stain that was all that remained of Pyra.

Why had she been directed to kill herself? What did the queen fear she might reveal?

"Don't feel sorry for her," Trey said, his voice holding a cold edge. "Because she certainly would *not* have felt anything resembling compassion or sorrow for you."

I glanced at him. "I thought you didn't know her?"

"I've discreetly asked around about her. She wasn't well-liked in this place." He hesitated. "Why don't you go shower while I take care of the mess?"

"But—"

He pulled his hand free and lightly pushed me forward. "Go. Blood stains your face, and I cannot tend to your wounds until they are washed."

Frustration born of the need for answers stirred through me, but I nodded and headed for the curtained-off bathing area. The earth rumbled and rolled as I showered, but it was nowhere near as violent or as noisy as the quake I'd called into being. Which was no surprise given Trey was behind whatever the earth was currently endeavoring.

The wound on my face turned out to be long but not deep; it skimmed the edge of my left eye and the stain on my cheek before disappearing just under my ear. There were a few bruises and a couple of minor scratches over the rest of my body, but all in all, I'd been rather lucky. It could have been a whole lot worse if the wind had not fought Pyra's commands.

By the time I'd finished, Trey was just coming out of the

bedchamber. All the broken furniture, torn wall hangings, and twisted bedding remained scattered everywhere, but there was no evidence the floor had ever buckled and moved, and absolutely no sign that someone had committed suicide within the room.

"What happened to Pyra's remains?"

His smile held little in the way of warmth or amusement. "I shoved her deep within the earth. She deserves neither an official burial nor a marker, not when she was involved in a betrayal of Winterborne."

"You can't be sure whatever she's involved in is as deep as that." I paused. "Does such a burial mean her spirit won't rise to join the greater consciousness?"

"It does indeed."

"A harsh fate if her scheming *isn't* part of a plot to bring down Winterborne."

"If I turn out to be wrong, then I'll exhume her remains and pass them on so that she can be buried in a fitting manner. But I'm not."

Part of me still hoped he was, but only because I didn't want to think anyone would want to bring Winterborne down. "And her bracelets?"

"They're safely hidden within the walls. I'll retrieve them if and when we need them." His gaze scanned me critically—a look that spoke more of a commander checking one of his people than anything more intimate. "Would you like a healing cream for that wound on your face?"

I shook my head. "I'm Sifft. It'll be healed by tomorrow."

"Good, because the official welcome and de-masking is tomorrow night." He motioned to the nearest double cloud-sak. "Have a seat. I'll grab us both a drink so we can continue the conversation."

I sat down on the cloudsak and crossed my legs. Not a very ladylike position given I was naked, but then I was a soldier, not a lady. "Why are you so sure a plot to bring down Winterborne even exists?"

"Because there's been some unusual vibrations happening under the earth for many years now, and while the earth cannot—or, more worryingly, will not—tell me its source, it seems to be aimed at Winterborne."

"So its source is coming from here somewhere?"

He began gathering a tray of sweetmeats, cheeses, and breads. "*That* is unclear."

"Then how did you get involved in this search? Black-lake's a very long way from Winterborne."

"Which is precisely why Kiro asked for my assistance." He placed the platter on the floor near my feet, and then poured two glasses of rich red wine. He handed one to me then sat down beside me, his body warm against mine. "But he also asked because I owe him."

I raised my eyebrows. "Why?"

He hesitated. Just for an instant, an odd sort of defensiveness flashed across his face. I touched his arm lightly. "You don't have to tell me, Commander."

"Trey, please, at least in this place. And I should, because it goes to the heart of why I know so much about your situation." He paused. "You once asked how I ended up at Blacklake."

I reached forward and made a sandwich of thick cheese and bread. "And you said you'd only tell me if I won the bet."

"I think we've gone past such games at this point."

"I'm glad."

"So am I. Although restraint remains the best option—at least until tomorrow night's unmasking."

"A statement that *doesn't* preclude the possibility of inter-course," I noted, amused.

He smiled. "No matter what you think, I'm *not* made of

stone. But what I'm about to tell you mustn't be repeated anywhere else in this place; this you must swear."

"You have my word on that, Commander."

"*Trey.*" He hesitated. "The first part, everyone knows. Eighteen years ago I had a liaison with Jaci Fisk, as she was known back then. Said liaison produced a child."

I just about choked on my sandwich. "You what? How old were you?"

"I was six months away from my sixteenth birthday."

Which was technically underage by the Forum's rule, and a punishable offense. "What happened?"

"While it was a mutually agreed act, she admitted to deliberately getting pregnant in the hope I'd commit to her when I came of age. Such a joining would have raised both her status *and* that of her house."

"The Fisk house being Lower Reaches?"

"Yes—and not known for producing anything more than mediocre witches." He paused. "Anyway, because I was underage at the time of the child's conception, my father had the right of refusal over any possible agreement. He forbade it, stating if there *was* to be a committal, it would come *after* the babe was born."

"When the auditors revealed what the child was?" Or, more precisely, wasn't?

He nodded, and his expression began to glow with something close to rapture and utter, utter love. It was so powerful, so strong and beautiful, that tears prickled my eyes. Oh, to be the recipient of such depth of emotion... a dream, I knew, but nevertheless a pleasant one.

"And she was perfect in every single way imaginable," he murmured, obviously no longer really seeing me, "but she was stained, and also unlit. My father, as you can imagine, did not react well."

"So there was no committal?"

He laughed, the sound bitter. "No. Not *just* because of the babe, but because the admittance of such conniving killed any feelings I might have had for her."

"And the child went into state care?"

"They practically ripped her out of my arms to do so. I had such a row with my father that night—it's the reason why we speak little even now." He paused, the joy I'd briefly seen falling to moments of old pain, anger, and hurt. "Two days later, I was accepted for the position of earth witch at Blacklake. Five days later, Kiro helped me smuggle my daughter away from state care and out of Winterborne."

That he—someone who'd been raised in the luxurious rule of this place—would even consider such a thing, let alone go through with it, not only left me speechless, but fighting the tears that were stinging my eyes. To give up everything he'd known for the sake of his child—a child he'd held for no more than a few minutes—was a phenomenal thing to do. Especially given he was barely sixteen at the time.

I blinked rapidly and managed to ask, in a somewhat normal voice, "Why would Kiro help you, when for all intents and purposes he was going against Forum rules?"

"Because years ago, when he was little older than I was when my daughter was born, he fell in love with my mother, but the union was considered unacceptable by her father. Kiro didn't hold the power that he does now." He half shrugged. "What he did for me, he did out of the love he still holds for her. She asked him to help me."

"So you owing him a huge favor is the reason you're here rather than at Blacklake?"

"I owe him more than one favor, but yes."

"And your daughter? She lives with you still, at Blacklake?"

"Oh yeah." His expression was both proud and little

rueful. "I may be the commander, but *she* runs Blacklake. They've spoiled her rotten since we arrived, and she's not beyond making full use of it if she so desires." He paused, his smile and eyes saying all that needed to be said about the depth of his love for her. "Which, to her credit, she mostly doesn't."

I hesitated, but couldn't help asking, "Has she siblings?"

He blinked, and his gaze came fully back to the present. "I would have called another earth witch to undergo the ceremony of Gaia if I was committed, Neve."

The smile that twisted my lips held a bitter edge. "There are many, both here in the Reaches and in the outer bailey, who do not hold the sanctity of a commitment so highly."

"And was it such a person who gave you this appalling low opinion of your own attributes?"

There was a flick of anger in his voice and it made me smile. "Perhaps."

"Give me his name and I shall knock some sense into him." He paused, and frowned. "Recant that. I'd rather you spend time with me than chase a past lover."

I laughed softly. "And here I was thinking you were determined to remain celibate until *after* the unmasking."

"That would be more ideal, yes, but there *are* two and a half days of debauchery to follow that, remember."

"To which I'm most certainly looking forward." I tried to swallow my yawn, but didn't quite succeed. "Sorry, it's not the company."

"No, it's an aftereffect of the ceremony. Most initiates barely make it through half a plate of food before they succumb to sleep."

"There is too much I need to know to allow that."

"Much of which can be said tomorrow, when Kiro comes back. For now, I'll continue with Eluria's story, as he already knows the details."

Eluria, I knew, meant precious flower. It made me like him even more.

"Long before she reached maturity, it was very obvious she could hear the earth. I began teaching her control almost as soon as she could walk and talk."

"So from the very beginning you knew I was lying."

He nodded. "When she reached maturity and came into her full potential, it was evident she was a powerful earth witch. I consulted Kiro, who told me that, although rare, it was certainly not an unknown situation. But it was happening *only* to those unlit whose skin holds major staining."

"That still doesn't explain why we're classified as unlit. We're very obviously not."

"It's the theory of those few who have studied the phenomenon that the Irkallan blood not only breaks down the barrier to magic, but also provides some sort of immunity to it."

I raised an eyebrow. "How can you use magic and yet be immune to it?"

"I don't know the ins and outs of it," he said. "I simply know its truth."

I finished my sandwich then picked up one of the sticky sweetmeats. "What happened to the unlit unfortunate enough to be uncovered as witches?"

The smile that twisted his lips held little in the way of humor. "You already know the answer to that. It's the reason I keep Eluria well away from Winterborne and beyond the sight of any witch."

"You have witches at Blacklake."

"Who have been there for decades. They wouldn't betray us."

"So why the subterfuge when I was there?"

"Just because I believe no-one there would betray either

me or my daughter doesn't mean they *wouldn't* pass on information if they suspected you were a witch-capable unlit. The subterfuge was meant to protect you—and it was Kiro who suggested it."

"And why would he do that? I'm nothing to him."

"No. But you *are* both a soldier and a Sifft, one who has had little to do with either the Reaches or us witches. We needed an outsider, one we could trust, and who would see what we couldn't."

"But what happens afterward? When the puzzle is solved and we're all returned to our normal lives? Will I find myself facing the fate you seek to keep your daughter from?"

"Whatever you think of Kiro, he's a fair man."

"Which is no answer."

"No." As I yawned again, he added, "You need to sleep. We can continue this tomorrow."

"I'm not going anywhere—not before you fully explain why it was so necessary to perform the ceremony of Gaia. You surely couldn't have been serious when you said I might have destroyed half of Winterborne—"

"Oh, but I was. A witch who has *not* performed the committal ceremony has little control over the elements that flow through them. Not only do they risk tearing themselves apart with the power they evoke, but also everything and everyone around them. Tonight, with you, it was only the floor of the bedchamber. The next time it might be the curtain wall or something even more catastrophic."

It was a sobering thought. "Does that mean I have to undergo a similar induction for the air magic?"

"It would be best, although you seem to have far greater control over that element."

"But won't that jeopardize the reason I'm here if what I am becomes common knowledge?"

"It won't. Kiro will ensure the priestess who draws you through the ceremony is of a discreet nature."

"So the earth and the air have different demands sexually when it comes to the ceremony?"

He smiled. "The air is temperamental and changeable, so she's naturally considered the more feminine power. The earth is stronger but slower to change, and therefore considered male."

"And yet she's called the earth mother, *not* earth father."

He laughed. "That's also true. Perhaps it's more a case of the earth mother having basic needs, and therefore it's priests rather than priestesses who are called upon." He pushed out of the cloudsak with far more grace than I seemed capable of. "You should stretch out and sleep."

"What are you going to do?"

"Go make sure the maidservant is paid for her silence, and get her to discreetly organize another bed. I'm *not* sleeping for more than a day in one of those things."

"Soft, just like the wind said."

He snorted, but his gaze skimmed me and the smell of desire began to taint the air. He scrubbed a hand across his chin, the sound like sandpaper in the brief silence, then gave me a sharp nod and departed. I smiled, reached for the nearest fur, and then made myself comfortable on the cloudsak.

And, rather unsurprisingly, slept.

Kiro reappeared on the dot of three. I was at least awake by then, but the lethargy I wouldn't admit to after the ceremony last night hung on my body like a weight, and it was something of a struggle to even think.

The maidservant let him in. Trey appeared a heartbeat

later, one towel wrapped around his waist while he dried his short hair with another.

"Kiro," he said, dropping down onto the nearby hassock. "What news leaves the lips of gossips this day?"

Kiro sat in the chair opposite us both, his gaze sweeping me in a critical manner. "They're all abuzz with the news of a liaison between the mysterious Lady N and Lady P, especially given neither appeared back at the masque."

"Will there be any problems?" Trey asked.

"No. There are several servants in her household who'll swear she arrived back at her own suites little more than an hour after leaving the masque. What happened *after* that will, of course, will be the target of much conjecture once it is discovered she's missing."

"And her husband? Will he cause a problem?"

"Hard to say given he hasn't spoken to me since I did a full reading on his lady when she first reappeared a year ago."

"Wait—what?" I glanced from Kiro to Trey and back again. "Did Pyra disappear like Saska?"

"Not just like her," Kiro said, voice grim. "But *with* her. They were part of a train coming back from the West Range outpost that was attacked by the Adlin."

The West Range lay at the end of the Blacksaw Mountains, very close to the sea. A lack of major attacks from the Adlin for over half a millennium had led to the outpost becoming something of a holiday resort. Even April, Ava, and I had gone there, though I personally wasn't all that keen on the place—mainly because the sand had a nasty habit of getting in all the wrong places.

"But surely it was well guarded if it contained witches from Upper Reaches?" I said. "And in any event, wouldn't the witches be more than capable of protecting themselves?"

"Apparently not, because the train was totally decimated. But the bodies of the five women—all of them powerful witches—were not recovered. They were presumed taken by the Adlin to be consumed at a later date."

"And here I was thinking Adlin had an 'eat until engorged and hunt again later' approach to their food." And maybe being immediately eaten *wasn't* the worst that could have happened to Saska and me.

"Generally, they do."

The edge in his tone had my eyebrow rising in query. "So this has happened before?"

"Once, some thirty years ago, from what I've discovered so far. It was an event that involved the lady Hedra Harken—"

"Surprise, surprise," I muttered.

His lips twisted in acknowledgment. "And the ladies Maya Myrl and Kora Sanna. The latter two were never seen again."

"When and where was Hedra found?"

"Two years later, out in the middle of the Tenterra desert." He paused. "She was pregnant. Saska is the product of her captors, whoever they might be."

Just as Saska's child would be. Was it a coincidence that both mother and daughter had suffered an almost identical fate? I suspected not—and the wind agreed with me.

"It obviously wasn't the Adlin, then." Not given Saska showed no sign of that heritage. "I'm gathering you've done a full reading on them all?"

The dark energy that was his magic stirred, reminding me of a viper rattling in frustration or anger. Interestingly, though its power caressed my skin, it didn't hold anywhere near the pull that it had on other occasions.

"Yes. There's no awareness of what happened to them in the time they were missing, or who their captives were." He paused. "To be honest, the totality of the memory loss makes me suspect it was deliberately done."

"So why do you think the Adlin were so furiously determined to recapture Saska? That's *not* normal behavior for them, I can guarantee you that." I gathered the fur around my chest then knelt up to pour three mugs of coffee. I handed one to each of the men then gripped mine and sat back down.

"I don't know." Kiro took a sip of his coffee, and then gave me a nod of thanks. "But the possibility of an Adlin alliance with enemies unknown is something that scares me greatly."

And if *he* was scared, then the rest of us should be damn well terrified. "The Adlin might now be capable of rudimentary weapons, but they certainly haven't the knowledge to produce silverwork as fine as the bracelets Hedra, Saska, and Pyra wear. Whatever is happening, those bracelets are a part of it."

Kiro's gaze narrowed. "Why would you say that? What happened here between you and Pyra?" At my amused look, he rather dryly added, "*After* the seduction, that is."

I gave them a detailed rundown on everything Pyra had said, then added, "Those voices are real, by the way. I heard them."

"How?" Trey's voice was flat and perhaps a little fearful—no surprise given he had an unlit daughter to worry about.

"It was just before she turned the wind on herself. I shifted to ease the ache in my legs, and my knife pressed into my right leg."

"Your stained leg?" Kiro asked.

I nodded. "It was then I heard them—they were chanting, *kill, kill, kill.* I'd thought they meant you two, but I was, of course, mistaken."

"Let me look at this knife," Kiro said, voice sharp.

Trey motioned me to stay and got up instead. Two minutes later he was back with both my knife and Pyra's bracelets. Kiro accepted the knife and rolled it over in his hands several times. "I have never seen its like before. Where did you get it?"

"From armory three. According to Jon, they're called ghost blades, and were supposedly forged in the blood of the Irkallan. He doesn't know where they came from, but there's apparently swords and more kept in the older recesses of the armory."

"Interesting." He offered me the knife, hilt first. "Can you hear the whispers now?"

I put my coffee down then gripped the knife with my right hand. The glass was cool and oddly inert against my skin. "No."

"Touch the blade to the bracelets."

I did. "Still nothing."

"Now shift the blade to your stained hand."

I did so, and almost instantly the whispers started. This time they were chanting, *retrieve, retrieve, retrieve.*

"You can hear them, can't you?" Kiro said.

I grabbed my coffee and took a sip, but it didn't ease the sudden dryness in my throat. "But why?"

"At a guess, the knife is some sort of conductor, but one that taps into communication lines rather than being a recipient of them."

"Which doesn't explain why it only happens with it comes in contact with my stained hand."

"No, but your staining is the reason your magic has gone unnoticed. Perhaps it also allows you to tap into other magic, but only if you carry the right implement."

"That's a whole lot of perhaps."

"It's all we have at the moment, I'm afraid." Kiro paused. "What about the bracelets?"

I reluctantly reached for one; it was nothing but cold metal in my stained hand. "Saska told me that the queen would find her if she wore them, so maybe they're more a tracking device than a means of communication. She said she still hears the voices even though she no longer wears them."

Trey held out a hand. I tossed him the bracelet and then said, "The more important question would seem to be, what do those voices want the women to retrieve?"

"Hedra and Saska would be our logical targets to uncover that particular secret," Kiro said. "But it might also be worth trying to get into Pyra's suite and seeing if any information can be found there."

"Her family is being housed in the Harkin house," Trey said. "Which makes it difficult for either of us to get in there, given you're not welcome and I have no reason to be there."

"What, there's no ladies of seducible age in that entire house?" I queried, amused.

Trey half smiled. "Pyra was Brent's youngest and the others are all committed."

And he would obviously never consider breaching such a bond—even at a festival like this, when the ties that bound were released for five nights, and the freedom to be with whom you wish, however you might wish, had the goddess's blessing. "What about the Harken line? No uncommitted there?"

"Yes, but males, one and all."

"And you are not partial to any of them?"

"Nor males in general, I'm afraid." His gaze met mine and something warm ran through me. "I do have full appreciation of Astar's many teachings, however."

"Indeed, Commander? Perhaps that is something we might explore—"

Kiro cleared his throat. "Concentrate on the matter at hand, please."

I laughed softly and glanced back at him. "But we are—or

are you not planning to ask me to lure Pyra's husband away from the ball?"

"Lure yes, anything else no. All we need is for you to ensure he takes you back to his suite. Once there, you can drug him, and be free to search both Pyra's and Hedra's suites."

It mightn't be as easy as that, and we both knew it. "And his name?"

"Ewan."

I cast back through all the men I'd met over the last few days, and then said, "Is he a whip-lean, rather aristocratic-looking man with dark gray hair and pale blue eyes? I think he was wearing a horned mask of some kind."

"Yes," Trey said. "Why?"

"Because he just happens to be one of the many men who approached me on the first night." He was also one of the ones for whom a gentle no had not been enough.

"Good. He's taken a succession of masked ladies back to his suite over the last few days, so no one will raise an eyebrow at your presence there." Kiro glanced at Trey. "I think our task tonight should be shadowing Hedra and Saska."

"*If* the latter comes out of her suite."

"Oh, she will." Kiro's smile held an edge of satisfaction. "It's the night of the unmasking, and she'll want to reclaim to her place by Marcus's side rather than ceding it to his hetaera."

"I wonder who whispered that possibility in her ear," Trey said, clearly amused.

"Rumors do have a tendency to get around at events like this." There was a gleam in Kiro's eyes as he pushed upright. "I'll see you both in a couple of hours."

"You need to answer one more question, Lord Kiro."

He stopped and glanced down at me, one dark eyebrow raised in question.

"What happens when all this is over? Will you, or will you not, report the change in my status?"

"I see no reason to do such a thing if you pose no threat to Winterborne. *That* is my priority, and has been ever since—" His mouth twisted and he glanced at Trey briefly. "Unless and until Winterborne's safety relies on the revelation of such secrets, they will be taken to my grave."

Relief stirred through me. He gave me a sharp nod and departed. Trey's gaze swung back to mine; once again it was critical and decidedly nonsexual. Even the raw energy that surged between us seemed to be testing me, judging me. The earth mother was as concerned about the state of my health as Trey, it seemed.

"How are you feeling?"

"Weaker than a newborn, but otherwise healthy."

He nodded. "You need to eat. Lots. Initiation tends to sap your strength for days, but we, unfortunately, haven't got that sort of time."

"Why are you both so certain there's a time limit to whatever it is that is happening?"

He hesitated and then shrugged. "In my case, it's nothing more than intuition. That, and the uneasiness in the earth."

"So why isn't she telling you what is going on?"

"I'm not sure, but I suspect there's one or more powerful earth witches behind it. There could be no other reason for her reticence."

"But Hedra, Saska, and Pyra are all air witches."

"I know. But the other women who went missing held earth power, even if they were from a minor house. If Saska and Pyra survived being snatched, it's possible they did too."

"Then where the hell are they?"

"If we knew the answer to *that*, this mystery might well be solved." He hesitated. "There's one other thing Kiro didn't mention—Hedra, Pyra, and Saska all bore children in the time they were missing. The latter two have had at least eight each, if not more, if the healers are to be believed."

"But Saska was only missing for twelve years!"

"Indeed." His voice was grim. "It would seem that whoever held them treated them as little more than incubators."

But for what darker purpose? And where were those poor children now? What was being done to them? I scrubbed a hand across my face. "This situation just seems to be getting darker and darker."

"Yes."

I cursed under my breath and studied the bracelet on the table for a minute. "And what about those things?"

He glanced at the one he was holding. "What about them?"

"They need to be kept somewhere safe. It's possible they're what the voices are looking for."

He rose and picked up the second one from the table. "Then perhaps you need to take them to Saska before the masque, and ask her about them."

I frowned. "Pyra very nearly succeeded in killing me. Saska is a far stronger air witch."

"And yet, Pyra said you're the reason for Saska's resistance, that you're somehow a touchstone for her." He frowned. "Why do you think that is?"

"I honestly don't know."

"Perhaps that's another question you should ask." He put both the bracelets down on the table. "I'll organize something to eat. You'd best be getting ready."

I nodded, flicked off the fur, and rose. His gaze skimmed me again. "Celibacy," he muttered, "has never been so hard."

"Celibacy," I replied, amused, "is rather overrated."

"At this point, I'm tending to agree." He held up a hand as I stepped toward him. "The mission comes first, whatever the cost."

"That cost," I said, my amusement growing as my gaze skimmed down to what his towel *wasn't* hiding, "is, as you said, probably going to be very hard to bear."

"Don't I know it." He waved me past. "Go get dressed. I'll arrange everything else."

I deliberately walked close enough that my arm brushed his. He groaned softly, but made no move to touch me, to stop me. The damn man might not be made of stone, but there was certainly a whole lot of steel in his makeup.

Saska's maidservant once again led me toward the outside balcony. The wind was bitter, and the rain fell in thick sheets that would drown me the minute I stepped out. I hesitated, eyeing the wild night warily. The wind whipped around me, chilling my bare stomach and tugging at the scarf-like layers of my skirt. I felt no threat in her touch, but I wasn't hearing her voice, either.

"I have a coat, if you wish it, Lady N," the maidservant said.

"Thanks, that would be great."

As the maidservant hurried off, I brushed my fingers against the knife strapped to my left thigh, feeling safer for its presence as I studied the shadows. Saska was once again standing in the far corner of the balcony. Her dark blue dress was plastered to her body, and she looked decidedly frailer than she had out in the desert. The weight loss made the small bulge of her belly look huge by comparison to the rest of her, even though the scanner had said she was little more than eleven weeks pregnant a week ago.

The maid came back with a long, fur-lined coat. I gave her my mask and the bracelets to hold while I donned it. Once I'd zipped it up and securely tied on the hood, I reclaimed the bracelets and stepped out into the storm. The rain hit me hard, instantly freezing my unprotected face and feet. The wind was a little more reticent in its attack, preferring to scoot around me rather than forcing me to battle against it.

I walked across to Saska and once again leaned on the capstone beside her. Far below, the sea crashed against the ragged cliffs, its force such that I could feel the shudder through the stones under my toes. Thunder rumbled overhead, an ominous warning that worse was to come. A heartbeat later, lightning streaked across the sky, a display of power that was at once beautiful and threatening.

"Nights like this are inspiring, are they not?" she said eventually.

"Yes, they are."

She raised her face to the sky. Silvery droplets clung to her lashes and water sluiced down her cheeks, but she didn't seem to care. "My mother used to tell me the firestorm that followed thunder was nothing more than the gods disagreeing, and that there was little to fear in such fierceness."

"So what do you think the gods might be arguing about tonight?"

She smiled, but it was a hollow thing. "Perhaps that is a question you should ask my mother. She's the one communing with them, not I."

"Is it the gods she talks to, or merely a queen?" I asked softly.

"They are one and the same."

"And where does this queen reside, Saska?"

She shrugged. "She is everywhere and nowhere. In our thoughts, and in the ground; she sees all, she hears all."

"But is she flesh and blood?"

"Yes." Her gaze came to mine, haunted and desperate. "But her desire for revenge has all but consumed her."

"What does she want to avenge?"

"Death."

I frowned. "Whose death?"

"Everyone's."

Which made no sense. I placed the bracelets between us. "What can you tell me about these?"

She didn't even glance down at them. "They were Pyra's."

"Do you know what happened to her?"

"No. Nor do I want to. I fear her fate is what awaits me if I do not obey their wishes."

"If their wishes are to retrieve the bracelets, then you have them right here beside you."

"*That* is not what they command of me, but rather my mother." Her gaze came to me briefly, her silvery-white eyes distant and stormy. "Your presence mutes their voices and gives me strength."

So in that, Pyra was right. "Why do you think that is?"

She shrugged. "Perhaps it's nothing more than a kinship born of air. You can hear her, I know."

"But not control," I said, as alarm surged. The last thing I need was someone like Hedra—who appeared to be the main force behind whatever was happening here in Winterborne —spreading rumors in the wrong ears.

"She likes you."

"Who?"

"The wind. That's why she saved you, and why she whispers not in the ears of the others."

I briefly closed my eyes and thanked the wind and the collective consciousness of all those who resided within her. "So what are the whisperers asking of you that they are not asking your mother?"

"Something far darker." She paused and picked up one of the bracelets. "But they are very desperate to get these back."

"Why? What is so special about them?"

She twirled one around her fingers. Its silver surface reflected the power and the beauty of the storm around us, seeming to glow with a white-blue fire that oddly reminded me of the glow the knife sometimes had.

"They are limited in supply, and not made by the queen's people but rather those of Versona."

Communications between Versona and Winterborne had been irrevocably shattered after the war, though why that should remain the case in this day and age, with all the technology we now had, I couldn't say. All I knew was what the history books said—that their efforts to protect their lands had, like ours, seriously disrupted the weather patterns close to their shores. To this day, our ships couldn't find a way through the constant storms and waterspouts that battered the seas between us. Even the few ships that *did* make it through the first barrier then had to battle the fierce wind that drove them onto the jagged rocks that had risen like a wall after the Versona earth witches had severed the connection between our lands and theirs to stop the Irkallan. To my knowledge, no shipmaster bothered with the Versona trade route these days. Not when easier trading was to be found in Elprin and Cannamore.

"Are you saying the queen has somehow found a way to do what the rest of Winterborne can't?"

"No. Indeed, any communication remains impossible given the wide trench that divides and the shadows that conceal."

"Then where did the bracelets come from?"

"They were found in ruins of Catlyn, in a store deep underground. There are only twenty-nine in existence, so every one of them is precious."

Catlyn wasn't a place I'd ever heard mentioned before. Certainly it had never featured in the little history we'd been taught about Versona. "And they're a communications device?"

"Yes." Her smile twisted. "And no."

She drew back her arm and pitched the bracelet out into the air. The wind caught it, toyed with it, and then swept it beyond sight. She picked up the second, but didn't immediately toss it into the hands of the darkness and the wind.

"At least by ridding the world of these two," she said. "It gives them two less options for controlling either us or our children."

The wind stirred, begging me to be gentle, to not go there. But I had to, if only for the sake of those children. How could we help them if we didn't know anything about their plight? "So your children wear these things?"

Her gaze came to mine. Once again it was haunted, anguished. "They take them, you know. Take those who are gifted and kill those who are not."

Kill? Dear god, who *were* these people? At least here in Winterborne, those of us who were unlit were given a chance at life, even if it wasn't always under the best circumstances.

"How many of your children have met this fate?" I asked gently.

"Three." A tear slowly tracked down her cheek. "Three perfect little girls, who were not even stained."

I touched her arm lightly, though in truth I wanted to grab her, hold her, to try and protect her against such memories. Maybe in the face of such evil, it would be too little, too late, but I had a feeling Saska was in sore need of it. And yet the wind whispered she would not—could not—appreciate such comfort. Not when she felt so undeserving of it.

"You cannot allow history to repeat itself, Saska. You have to keep strong for the child you now carry."

"I know," she whispered. "But it is hard. So *very* hard."

"Resistance is never an easy path to take against evil, especially when your strength is at such a low level. You need to eat—not just for the health of your child, but also in defiance of the voices."

Her gaze came to mine, but again, she didn't appear to be really seeing me. "It's for the sake of my child that I should step over this barrier and throw myself to the rocks beneath this cliff. It's a far better fate than what awaits under the queen's rule."

I wrapped my fingers around her arm. "You cannot do that—"

"You *don't* understand. You can *never* understand."

She placed her fingers over mine and, just for a moment, a connection formed. A connection that was air, mind, and something deeper, something that went to the very heart of our DNA. In it, I saw earth, darkness, and pain. The air was putrid, thick with despair and the screaming of babies. Light flashed; its source wasn't the sun but rather the gleam of a rudimentary flare off a silver blade. I saw the hand that gripped that knife, and it was the color of my staining, but the fingers were thinner and longer than mine, with razor-sharp nails a good inch long.

I'd seen hands like that before, but only in pictures. They were the hands of an Irkallan. And yet those creatures *couldn't* be at the heart of all this. They'd been in hibernation for centuries and there'd been no indication at *all* that they'd come out of it.

No, there had to be some other reason. *Had* to be.

"They want you dead, you know," she continued.

Her words shattered the fragile connection, leaving me shaking and more afraid than I'd ever been in my life. I licked my lips and said, "Who? The queen?"

"Yes. She fears the strength I draw from you, sister."

"I rather think it's your strength she fears, not mine."

"I have no strength." Her gaze drifted back to the storm and the cliff's edge. "That has been proven to me time and time again."

In that darkness filled with despair, I knew. "You say that, and yet escaped them."

"I didn't escape. Not really."

The words were almost inaudible, and yet they might have been shouted, so sharp did they seem on the wind. Never before had five words so filled me with fear. While I genuinely believed she was desperate to escape the grip of the queen, I couldn't ignore the possibility that her presence out in the desert had been nothing more than a deliberate ploy to further infiltrate Winterborne.

I gently placed my hands either side of her cheeks and made her look at me. Her skin was like ice under my fingertips, and she was trembling, though I wasn't entirely sure whether from the cold or fear of what might yet be coming.

"Did you, or did you not, escape them?"

"I did. And she was furious. But now, she uses me, and it makes me wonder if that was her plan all along."

"Doubt makes the voices stronger," I said. "Do not give them that edge."

"You do not understand their persistence. You do not understand their power."

No, I didn't. But I didn't have to understand to sympathize, didn't have to understand to see what the relentless stream of noise was doing to her mind. A mind that seemed to be unraveling even as I watched.

But if that happened, if she lost this battle, we were all in trouble. Both intuition and the wind were telling me that.

"Saska, you can do this. You are stronger than you know —your presence here is evidence enough of that." I paused. Pressing her for information was probably the worst thing I could do, but we had to know what was going on—especially if Trey's intuition was right and events would come to a head in the next couple of days. "What can you tell me about the queen's plans? What does she want of you?"

She gently pulled free from my grip, her mouth twisting. "She tells me nothing. She only gives me orders."

"What is she ordering you to do, Saska?"

Moisture tracked down her cheeks, and I wasn't sure if it was rain or tears. She didn't answer. She simply stared out over the storm-held darkness. I let my fingers rest on the hilt of the knife. The voices jumped into focus, and they were fierce and angry. But all they were chanting was, *do it, do it, do it.*

"Saska, please—"

She opened her mouth, as if to reply. The voices sharpened, lengthened, becoming a long, high-pitched squeal that stabbed through my brain like a fiery lance. I jerked my fingers away from the knife hilt and the sound disintegrated. But its echo remained, beating through my head like a drum.

Saska's body was still shuddering, shaking, under the force of the mental assault. The wind stirred around me, and my gaze jerked down to Saska's hands. She was still gripping the remaining bracelet, and it was glowing with a fire as fierce and as cold as a blue moon. I wrenched it from her grip and tossed it into the air. The wind caught it and carried it far, far out into the ocean.

Saska practically collapsed, her breath little more than thick wheezing that shook her entire body. "I cannot stand this. I will not."

I hesitated and then said, "Perhaps the healers can give you a potion that will ease the turmoil and take you into a deep sleep. The voices cannot force you to do something if you're in a chemically induced slumber."

She lifted her head and stared at me for so long uneasiness stirred. "You're right. Abee?"

The maid came hurrying out; she was soaked in an instant. "Yes, ma'am?"

"Ask a healer to come here immediately."

The maid curtseyed and disappeared again. Saska's gaze came to mine. "Be wary of the Adlin. They will attack."

"What?" I said, alarmed. "When?"

"Soon." She hesitated, her mouth twisting in bitterness. "I would tell you more if I could, but I know it not. They erase; they are always erasing."

Was *that* what the sharp lance was? The queen—and whoever else it might be behind the voices and the bracelets —erasing what they didn't want shared? Just because I'd heard it as little more than a squeal of sound didn't mean Saska had.

It also explained the weird gaps in her memories, and Kiro's inability to uncover any information from the three women—no matter how strong his powers, or how deeply intimate the reading, he couldn't uncover what was not there to find.

"So this queen—she's Adlin?" It was a logical conclusion given it was the Adlin who had originally snatched them, even if the hand I'd glimpsed in her memories was Irkallan.

"No. She merely uses them as she uses us."

"Meaning they've enslaved them and are using them as incubators?"

A smile touched her lips, and it held the first hint of warmth I'd seen for a while. "She doesn't need to enslave them—not when she controls the one who now leads them."

The entire Adlin population under the total control of another race? It was a prospect I found rather hard to accept. And yet their actions in Tenterra when I'd rescued Saska had certainly been beyond their norm.

She wrapped her arms around her thin body. "The wind

166

bites at me. I think she wishes me ill."

"Nonsense. You're just projecting your own fears onto her." I tried to inject as much positivity as I could into my tone, because in truth, there *was* bitterness in the wind's whispers. I touched Saska's arm lightly; I might as well have been touching ice. "You need to come inside. Catching a chill will do neither you nor your child any good."

"No."

I thought for a moment it was a refusal, but she allowed herself to be gently guided into the warmth of her suite. The maidservant came rushing into the room, and she was carrying several blankets. I helped Saska strip, eased the blanket around her trembling body, then glanced at Abee and said, "Is the healer on the way?"

"Yes, ma'am. And I've taken the liberty of ordering some hot soup and bread for you both."

"I have to go back to the masque, but thank you." I guided Saska to the nearest cloudsak then squatted beside her. "Shall I wait with you for the healer?"

"The longer you remain in my presence, the more determined they are to get rid of you." She hesitated, then added softly, "Watch your back, sister, because they are fiercely angry with you at this moment."

"I fear them not." I squeezed her arm then released her. "If you need anything—no matter what it might be—have me paged."

She smiled, but her gaze wouldn't meet mine. "I will. Go. I'll sleep the sleep of the dead, and enjoy the peace of it."

I studied her. She was exuding an odd sense of calm now and *that* stirred uneasiness within me. "Are you sure?"

"Yes. Sleep is all I need. A long, uninterrupted sleep." Her gaze finally came to mine; the clouds I saw there did little to dispel the unease. "Thank you. You saved me out in Tenterra. You save me still."

"Saska—"

She touched a cool finger to my lips. "Enough. You should go enjoy yourself while you can. And if you remain determined to seek answers, then perhaps you should go back into Tenterra, to the place where you found me. Everything you need to know can be found there if you look to the ground and what lies beneath it. Now go."

Her gaze and her touch left me. She drew the blanket up closer to her chin and closed her eyes. She wasn't sleeping; it was a dismissal. The questions that remained—and there were more of them than ever after that final statement— would not be answered tonight. I reined back my frustration and rose. "Night, Saska."

She didn't reply. I took off the coat, handed it to Abee, then put my mask on and left.

Once again, Trey was impossible to find but Lord Kiro made his way to my side almost as soon as I walked into the ballroom. "Lady N," he said, smoothly ensnaring my elbow and guiding me toward the edge of the vast room, "walk with me."

The desire to say no twitched my lips, and he obviously sensed it, because he dryly added, "Please."

I took a glass of dark red wine from the tray of a passing drink boy and sipped it as Kiro led me toward one of the nooks.

"What can I do you for, Lord K?" I said, once we were both seated.

He crossed his legs, his foot lightly brushing mine. A ruse for those who might be watching more than an attempt to seduce—there was no heat in that brief touch, no underlying sense of power. "There's a feel in this room I don't like. I came to warn you to be wary, both with Ewan and when you're circulating."

"Do you think he's the source of whatever it is you're sensing?"

"Perhaps. Certainly there's some anger directed his way." His mouth twisted, though it was hard to classify the result as a smile. "Lord E, apparently, likes his sex a little rougher than some of his more genteel conquests would prefer."

I snorted. "Surely his reputation for rough play has preceded him, given a masque is held every year."

"Oh, I'm sure it has, just as I'm sure it's disbelief and curiosity that has led many ladies to his bed."

"The ladies of the Reaches," I noted, "need to be a little more outspoken about what they do—and do *not*—want in bed."

"Ah, but that might well cost them and their family a lucrative commitment."

"And that's all that matters here? What about love? Besides, Ewan's already committed, so a relationship with him isn't likely to go anywhere vital."

"Unless of course, a child born with magic comes out of the liaison." Kiro raised an eyebrow, but there was darkness and old pain in the deeper reaches of his eyes. "But I won't have you thinking it's all business here in the Upper Reaches. There are as many liaisons that happen for love as happen for advantage."

I guessed if there was one good thing about being stained *and* classified as unlit, it was the fact that I knew, from the very start of any relationship, that even if love did strike, it was unlikely to end in anything lasting.

I took a drink and then said, "Saska confirmed the voices wanted me dead. Perhaps what you're sensing here is the beginnings of another attempt."

"This doesn't feel specifically aimed at you. What else did she tell you?"

Instead of immediately filling him in, I said, "Do you know of a place called Catlyn?"

He frowned. "I believe there was a Catlyn temple on the far side of the Blacksaw Mountains near the Songbird River. But when Versona's earth witches severed the ties between our lands and theirs, it would have been destroyed."

"Well, not all of it was, because that's where the bracelets came from. From what I've witnessed, and from what Saska has said, they not only enable sharper telepathic communication, but are also a means of implementing punishment and memory erasure."

"And everyone who is a part of this scheme was given them?"

"It would appear so." I hesitated. "Tell me, has there been any indication that the Irkallan are active?"

His gaze sharpened. "No—why?"

"I caught an image in her mind, and it looked an awful lot like drawings I've seen of Irkallan limbs."

"If those creatures were out of hibernation, we'd surely know. They're warriors first and foremost, and would not hesitate to attack the forces that now sit on their borders." He paused, his gaze narrowing in thought. "I will, however, ask for scouts to be sent into the Blacksaw Mountains, just in case."

Relief stirred. We'd know soon enough whether the image I'd seen was merely the madness of a disintegrating mind. "What about Heska?"

"Given she's the only other woman in this place possessing the bracelets, we'll need to round her up as a matter of urgency and make her talk."

I nodded. "There is another possible problem."

He raised an eyebrow. "That being?"

I told him everything Saska had said, from it being only the stained children who were kept to the possibility that Saska might have been allowed to escape. But it was the imminent threat of an Adlin attack that naturally caught his attention.

"I'll contact your captain immediately and warn him." He thrust up then paused, dug into his pocket, and handed me a small vial of clear liquid and a carefully folded piece of paper. "This potion is fast-acting, so do not linger here once you have administered it."

With that, he nodded and strode away. I put my glass down and unfolded the small piece of paper. It turned out to be a hand-drawn floor plan of the Harken residence, including X's to mark where the guards were located and where Ewan's suite was in relation to Pyra's, Hedra's, and even Lord Marcus's. I slipped both it and the drug into the skirt's hidden pocket, and then began the search for Ewan. I saw Trey first—he was in standing in one of the shadowed recesses not far from Hedra, a drink in his hand and something close to distaste in his expression. It cleared the moment he saw me. He blew me a kiss for those who were watching, then raised his glass, as if in toast. But one finger was pointing in the direction of the long outside balcony. It seemed I was about to have another round with the wild weather.

I downed my drink, whisked another from a passing waiter, and then headed for the balcony.

The rain and the wind were even fiercer here than they had been around Saska's side of the building. I paused on the threshold, my gaze searching the drowning shadows. Surely even the most ardent Romeo would reconsider seduction in such atrocious conditions?

A blue-clad footman stopped beside me and bowed lightly. "Can I help you, m'lady?"

I hesitated. "I was actually looking for a Lord E. I was told he was out on the balcony."

"Would Lord E be from the Chetwind house?"

"He would indeed."

"Then he has taken refuge in the ramada. If you take the door to your far right, the covered pergola will take you there."

"Thanks."

He nodded and slipped away. I finished my second glass of wine, claimed two more, and headed for the door. To say the wind was bracing was an understatement. She whipped around me in utter glee, tossing the scarf layers of my skirt around and pulling at what little material there was in the cropped top. Ewan was going to get an eyeful without the benefit of undressing me at this rate. The wind laughed, but her teasing lessened. I headed down the long, flower-draped pergola. Goose bumps fled across my skin but the stone was at least warm under my feet. Whether the stone was actually heated, or it was simply Mother Earth taking pity on me, I couldn't say.

At the far end, within the darkness of the ramada, a light flickered. In its pale glow, I could see the elongated outline of a man. It didn't take him too long to see me.

"Lady N," he said, as he stepped fully into the light. His gaze skimmed me and came up hungry. "You're not who I was expecting, but you're surely a sight for sore eyes."

"You took the words right out of my mouth." I slowed my pace, as much an effort to delay the inevitable as heighten his expectation.

"Am I to take it that you, too, have been stood up?"

"Perhaps." I handed him the glass. I hadn't yet placed the potion in it, simply because I no idea if Ewan actually drank wine. He certainly hadn't been carrying a glass when he'd pursued me the first night. "And perhaps not. A woman doesn't want to appear too eager to a possible suitor, after all."

"Indeed." He placed the wine on the nearby table and stepped closer. "And what must one do to turn the possible into a definite?"

"I don't know." I allowed my gaze to drop, skimming his body in much the same manner as he had mine. "It would depend, of course, on the offer."

"And what should the offer entail for it to be successful?" He placed his hands either side of my hips, drew me close, and then leaned in for a kiss. I shifted slightly, allowing it to brush my mask rather than my lips.

"Someplace warmer would be a good start."

"I'm sure we could create enough heat here to warm us both if we but tried." His hands skimmed up my waist then under my crop top, and, after a moment, he brushed his thumbs across my nipples. They peaked, but it was an automatic response rather than one born of any real sense of desire.

"And I'm sure I'd be far more comfortable in warm surroundings." I stepped back, away from his touch. "If that's *not* an option—"

He laughed softly. "Of course it is. I was only teasing." He swung to the side and offered me his arm. "Our carriage awaits."

He escorted me back down the pergola and around the covered outside of the building. His carriage—a small brown vehicle not dissimilar to the one Trey had used—was indeed waiting. A soggy-looking man in silver stood by the open door, a sturdy umbrella held at the ready.

We quickly climbed in. As before, I took one side, Ewan the other, but the inside space was smaller, the benches harder and more upright. The footman slammed the door shut and, in very little time, we were underway.

"And where do we go, Lord E?"

"To my suite at the Harken residence. And please, call me Ewan." He leaned forward and caught my hands—one of them gloved, the other not. "There's been many a whisper about you. I have to admit, I am desirous to see what might lie under the pretty wrapping."

"And what if it is something you don't like, my lord Ewan?"

"Like what?" He slid his hand up my left leg, the material of my dress parting before his touch like a silken sea. "It's not like you're stained, my lady."

My smile held a bitter edge, but he didn't notice. "You have something against the stained?"

"No, but they're hardly worth the waste of time or seed, are they now?"

"I think you do them a grave injustice."

"Perhaps." His touch paused when his fingers hit the knife scabbard, but it was anticipation rather than fear that began to ride the air. "The lady bares a stinger."

"The lady also knows how to use it."

The warning seemed to inflame his passion rather than thwart it. He chuckled softly, then leaned forward and tried to kiss me. Again I offered him only my mask-covered cheek.

"I think you play with me, lady." His touch slid to the inside of my thigh. "Perhaps I should play with you."

"Perhaps it's more that I prefer to anticipate an event rather than simply dive in." I paused, and took a drink of wine. "And perhaps it's the fact that I prefer the taste of alcohol on a man's lips."

"Ah." He pulled his hand away. "I'm a mead man myself. It's rough and rustic, but it suits my palate."

"Rough and rustic is more than suitable for this sort of occasion."

The scent of desire became sharper. He knocked on the

wall between the carriage and the driver and said, "Hurry it along, man!"

The vehicle slid forward fast but smoothly. Ewan didn't say anything; he just watched me, his gaze hungry. I returned the look evenly and sipped my wine.

Within minutes we were pulling up to another grand house. The storm tore at the carriage as it stopped and the wind howled in fury. Not at me, not at what I was doing, but at something that was happening within the building. Curiosity stirred, but I couldn't risk speaking to the wind or even investigating what was going on until Ewan was sleeping.

If he thought there was anything out of place or unusual about the sudden ferocity of the storm, he didn't mention it. Maybe he was simply too enflamed by possibilities to hear her. The carriage door opened, revealing a long, metallic tunnel being pushed out toward us. Once it was strapped to the carriage, Ewan stepped out, then offered me his hand. I gave him my glass and then said, "Please, lead the way."

He laughed again but spun and strode through the rattling and somewhat insecure tunnel until we reached the main building. There he handed my glass to a waiting manservant and ordered another red and a tankard of mead for himself.

The inside of the Harken household was every bit as ornate and as colorful as that of the Rossi. The only difference I could see was the color of the stone—it was slate gray rather than silver, and shot with veins of dark blue.

Ewan's suite was, according to Kiro's map, on the second floor right wing of the structure. Pyra's room adjoined his, but there was no door connecting the two. Lord and Lady Harken lived in a similar situation within the other wing of the building.

Our drinks were already waiting on the low table when

we arrived. The suite was smaller than the one I shared with Trey and there were no dividing walls or curtains separating the sleeping chamber and bathroom from the main room. The only room that had its own space appeared to be the privy. Thick curtains covered the row of windows to our right.

As Ewan strode toward the table, I found the light switch and plunged the room into utter darkness. He spun around immediately. "What on earth—"

"Were we not talking about anticipation before, my lord?" I walked toward him, my steps light and sure.

"But I can hardly see you!"

Hardly was good. Hardly meant he possessed no Sifft blood and therefore wouldn't see my stains and raise a ruckus. "Sometimes it's what you feel rather than what you can see that brings the sweeter victory." I reached into my pocket and pushed the potion's stopper free, then pressed my free hand against his chest and lightly guided him backward. He all but fell into the cloudsak. "I believe that we should proceed my way first, and then perhaps try yours? Would that be agreeable to you, my lord?"

"I believe it would." Hunger stretched his lips. "I am in your hands, dear mystery lady."

"As indeed you could be very soon, if you play your cards right." I knelt at the table, my back to him, and poured first the mead and then the potion. After swirling it around, I lightly raised it to my lips, pretending to drink it even though the liquid didn't touch them, and then said, "A rough and ready brew indeed."

I turned and handed it to him. He took one long drink then placed it to one side. I pointedly cleared my throat and, with a grin, he finished the mead. How long, I wondered, would the drug take to work? Kiro's definition of fast might be very different to mine.

I pushed to my feet, then took off my mask and tossed it to the nearby hassock. His eyes should have had time to adjust to the darkness by now, but he didn't react in any way to the stain on my cheek; his night sight really *wasn't* good. I pushed aside my skirt, undid the knife sheath, and tossed that beside the mask. The crop top and my skirt slowly followed.

The breath that escaped his lips spoke of desire.

"Stand, my lord."

He did so, rapidly, and reached for me. I lightly slapped his hands away. "Anticipation, remember?"

He laughed again and obediently stood still. I slowly stripped him, then, when he was naked, stepped forward, pressed my body lightly against his, and whispered in his ear, "Now for the fun part."

He didn't move. He just waited. I let my fingers roam across his face, neck, and shoulders, making my way slowly downward. His breath hitched when I brushed his shaft, though I didn't linger there, but simply continued downward. He was shaking by the time I'd finished, his desire so fierce that I was almost drowning in the scent of it.

But he was swaying now, and it was very evident he was fighting to keep his eyes open. I lightly pushed him back into the cloudsak, then picked the tankard, filled it with mead, and offered it to his lips. His eyes closed, snapped open, and then closed again. I ran my hands lightly up his legs and brushed my fingers against his ball sac to test his awareness. He didn't react. He was asleep.

Relief slithered through me. I strapped on my knife then hastily dressed. The air stirred around me, filled with whispers of wickedness. Something had definitely happened in this place, even if she wasn't exactly telling me what.

I padded to the door and carefully looked out. According

to Kiro's map, there were guards at either end of this corridor, but neither were currently visible.

I slipped out of Ewan's room and padded down to Pyra's. It was unlocked, so I quickly went inside and closed the door behind me. Whatever the wind had seen, it hadn't happened in this room. Indeed, the place was so immaculate it was hard to believe Pyra had spent much time here.

She didn't, the wind said. *She and Hedra were kept together.*

Kept?

The air stirred, but she provided no answer. Maybe she figured I'd find out soon enough.

I walked on, my feet making little sound on the warm stone under my feet as I approached the sleeping area. There wasn't much in the way of possessions to be found, nor was there any evidence of wrongdoing. I frowned and went over to the bathing area. Again, there was very little here, and what there was—shampoo, washcloths, and soap—hadn't been used.

I pulled out Kiro's floor plan and studied it. Six sets of guards stood between my next target and me. But those guards weren't expecting any sort of intrusion—not on a night like this, when the wish of the goddess was one of merriment and celebration rather than intrigue and danger.

So rather than trying to slip past them, why not do so openly? Or, better yet, get *them* to escort me there? The voices already wanted me dead, so what did I really have to lose? The worst that could happen would be for the guards to refuse—and truly, how likely were they to do so when the request came from someone who at least *some* of them had seen walking in here with a guest of the house?

I tucked the plan back into my pocket, then pulled the mask back into place and strode out the door—which I slammed to ensure they heard me coming.

I'd barely gone three paces when a silver-coated footman

came running around the corner. He slowed when he spotted, me, tugging down his waistcoat and clearing his throat. "Can I help you, m'lady?"

"Your lady has summoned me to her quarters—and at quite an inconvenient time, I might add. Lord Ewan is most displeased." I paused and leaned forward, adding in a conspiratorial tone, "I wouldn't recommend anyone disturb him until I manage to return."

He nodded, but his expression was unhappy. "Lady Hedra relayed no such orders to me, m'lady, and that is most unusual—"

"Yes, yes, but your lady is not unknown for unusual behavior of late, is she?"

He had the good grace not to confirm that particular statement. Instead, he simply half bowed, and then said, "If you'd follow me, we can clear this up very easily."

"Thank you."

I gathered my skirts and followed him through the long, silent halls until we reached the section that belonged to the lord and lady of the house. He paused at the door and gently knocked. Unsurprisingly, there was no reply. He glanced at me. "She's not here, m'lady."

"Well, she can't be too far given she directed me to come around immediately. I'll wait for her inside."

"I don't think—" He paused at the sound of a long moan. I knew it was the wind, but it sounded very human. He frowned again, and knocked harder. "Lady Hedra, are you all right?"

Again, it was the wind that answered, but softer this time. He paused, glanced at me, and then opened the door.

Though I'd fully expected the room to be empty, it wasn't. But it was certainly empty of life.

Marcus Rossi lay sprawled in the middle of the room, a knife sticking out of his back.

7

The footman gasped and opened his mouth to call for help. I gripped his arm fiercely. "Think, man. The lord of a major house murdered in your mistress's bedroom? How do you think that will play out for the guards in this house?"

Not to mention any hope I had of understanding what had gone on here.

"This can*not* be covered up—"

"No, it shouldn't. But the appropriate people must first be advised. It's not for you nor I nor anyone else to disturb this room until then."

He studied me, his expression troubled. "What would you advise us to do, m'lady?"

"I think someone should be discreetly but immediately dispatched to fetch Lord Kiro." I hesitated. "Tell him that Lady Neve has discovered something he needs view immediately. He will know what to do."

"And you, m'lady? You cannot stay in this room of death? That would be—" He paused. "—unseemly."

I smiled at his concern and couldn't help but wonder if

the sensibilities of the Reaches ladies really were that delicate. "Someone has to ensure no one disturbs this room."

"There are other guards, m'lady—"

"Yes, but one of them might well have let the killer in." I motioned to the closed and curtained windows. "How else did he get into this room if not by the main door?"

He glanced at the curtains, his expression troubled. "I cannot in good conscience allow you to stay in here alone—"

"Fine," I said, a touch impatiently. "Ask a guard you trust beyond doubt to stay here with me."

He hesitated, and then nodded. In a very short amount of time, a guard slipped into the room, his face becoming ashen when he spotted Rossi's body. But he didn't say anything, simply stood at the door and watched me suspiciously—even though he was well aware I couldn't have done this deed. Not when he'd witnessed me coming in with Ewan only half an hour previously. Rossi had obviously been dead longer than that; the blood on the back of his tunic was already stiff and dry.

After what seemed an interminably long time, there was a soft knock at the door. "Who is it?" the guard asked, one hand on his gun.

"Lord Kiro. Open up."

The guard drew his gun, then cautiously did so. Kiro brushed him aside and stepped into the room. Behind him was Trey. Both men stopped when they saw Marcus.

"This isn't what I had been expecting." His gaze met mine. "You've searched the room?"

"No. We merely ensured the room remained untouched until you arrived."

He nodded and glanced at the guard. "Outside. Ensure no one else enters here, but speak no word of this to anyone else. Understood?"

The guard nodded and retreated. Once the door was

closed, Trey walked across and touched my arm lightly. "Are you okay?"

I smiled. "I'm no tender Reaches lady. I've seen more than my share of death, and most of it far more gruesome than this."

"I wasn't referring to this event, but rather the reason you came to be here."

My smile grew. "Ewan dreams of things he'll never get."

"Ah. Good." He returned his attention to the body. "Why on earth is Marcus here? In Hedra's room, of all places?"

"I don't know." Kiro walked across to the body and squatted beside him. "As far as I'm aware, he and Hedra could barely tolerate each other."

"Maybe his anger with Saska drove him here," I said. "Maybe he hoped Hedra could somehow reach her."

"You're the only one that can apparently reach her," Kiro said. "And that hasn't gone down well with Hedra, let me tell you."

"Hedra's in league with the voices, so that's no surprise." I walked across to the windows and pushed aside the curtains. The doors were definitely locked. "Is it possible someone's setting Hedra up?"

"It's possible, but a body is no easy thing to move over such a distance, and other witches would have at least sensed something odd was happening." Trey stopped on the other side of Marcus's body, his gaze sweeping him critically. "I saw no such awareness rippling through the masque."

"Then he was killed here?"

"Yes," Kiro said. "There's a good amount of blood on the floor underneath him."

"And the knife?"

"Is ceremonial, and one that bears the markings of the Harken house." Kiro pushed upright. "We'll need to arrest

Lady Hedra, but to do that, I must first discuss the matter with the Forum leaders."

Trey glanced at him. "You think she did this?"

"No." Kiro grimaced. "There is a taint of passion about this murder. Hedra has no such emotion left in her."

"If it's an act of passion, surely the most logical suspect should be his hetaera, Lida."

"She wouldn't have murdered Marcus. Her standing in the Rossi house depended on his survival and favor." He frowned. "Besides, she's not a strong enough witch to have gotten in here unseen."

"Unless she had help," Trey stated. "Lida's family lost a lot of face when Saska was welcomed back into the fold so readily by Marcus."

"And she has three sons, hasn't she?" I asked. "Could one or all of them be behind this act?"

"Possibly all." Kiro's expression was thoughtful. "But Jamson, as the eldest, has the most to gain by this death. Until Saska's child is born and proven to hold magic, he's the rightful heir, born of a hetaera or no. If Saska's son *is* born into magic, then Jamson will act as regent until Saska's child is of age."

"If Saska was barely sixteen when she disappeared, how can Jamson—" I stopped, remembering what Trey had said about Lida being Marcus's lover long before he committed to Saska.

"His marriage to Saska was political. Jamson was fifteen when the commitment ceremony happened." Kiro paused, and frowned. "I'd originally thought he and Lida were behind Saska's disappearance, but a reading of them both proved otherwise."

If Kiro had bedded Jamson at fifteen in order to do a full reading, his suspicion must have been backed by a fair amount of evidence, given it was illegal to couple with anyone that young. Unless, of course, it was given full Forum backing, and that *might* have been the case. Marcus's own brother had said he'd do whatever he thought proper to keep up appearances, so he might well have appealed to the Forum to allow a full interrogation of Jamson, if only to prove the innocence of his firstborn son.

It was also possible such an act might have been seen as a betrayal by Jamson, one that had possibly festered and grown in the years since.

"Just because they were innocent then doesn't mean they are so now," Trey commented.

"Indeed," Kiro said. "And *that* should probably be our first line of questioning. The lady Lida resides in her suites within the Rossi household. Perhaps it would be best if you bring her here."

"And Jamson?"

"Is at the masque." Kiro's gaze came to me, and a slight smile touched his lips. "Perhaps his retrieval should be left to our lady N."

I raised an eyebrow. "And why is that, my lord?"

"Because Jamson is heavily invested in following the preachings of the god Drago, and has been seeding as many Reaches females as he possibly can."

A statement that had me wondering if such licentious behavior was a result of being taken by Kiro at the tender age of fifteen. "I'm not the one who can gain the secrets of a man's soul by bedding him."

"You won't have to. Last time I saw Jamson, he was heavily intoxicated. I doubt it'd take much to get him blathering like an idiot."

I frowned, and waved a hand at Marcus's body. "If he was intoxicated, he's hardly likely to have been capable of doing this."

"Unless the intoxication was merely an act to ensure

there are plenty who can swear to his whereabouts at the time of Marcus's body being found."

I guess that was possible. "And what of Hedra?"

Kiro hesitated. "I have a man watching her. Once we've talked to Lida and Jamson, I'll deal with Hedra. Even if she's not responsible for this murder, she remains a threat."

I glanced at Trey. "You were shadowing her movements, weren't you?"

"Yes, but she never left the masque."

"Which means nothing, as it's more than possible this murder happened earlier than that," Kiro said. "We'll have to wait on the coroner's report."

"Why not request her incarceration now, just to be sure?" Trey said. "I'd sleep safer knowing she'd been neutralized."

"I cannot formally arrest her without privately advising the Forum first." Kiro's mouth twisted. "I might have been given full rein to explore what goes on, but there are still some protocols involved when it comes to the heads of the twelve houses and their ladies."

"Do you want me to bring Jamson back here?" I asked.

Kiro hesitated. "Only if you believe he's played some part in this murder. But be wary. Jamson has a rather nasty streak in him, and if he *is* drunk, he'll be all the more dangerous."

"I can handle myself."

"I know. But still, stay wary. And call in help if you need it." Kiro's gaze switched to Trey. "It would be best if Lida is brought here without gathering too much attention."

"Easier said than done, I suspect."

"You have my permission to tape her mouth and hands if required."

"And *that* won't garner any additional attention, will it now?" Trey said, then caught my hand and led the way out of the room.

"So what does Jamson actually look like?" Though our

footsteps made little noise on the warm stone flooring, the footman who'd initially escorted me to Hedra's room reappeared. With a slight bow, he asked us to follow him, but kept a discreet distance.

Trey hesitated. "I've only seen him from a distance, but he's tall and lean, with hair that is more dirty yellow than white."

"And he wears the color of the Rossi house?"

"Yes. His mask rather resembles a snarling dog."

I snorted. "Which is somewhat appropriate, if what Kiro said is true."

"It is."

Trey's carriage was waiting out the front, and the odd silver tunnel had been rolled out to protect us from the weather. Trey helped me up into his carriage, his fingers gripping mine perhaps a little longer than necessary.

In very little time, we were back at the Rossi household. Once we'd reentered the main hallway, he pulled me close and slipped one hand around my waist to my spine. A show for those who were watching, I knew, but not one I was about to object to.

"I know you're Nightwatch and more than capable of handling yourself," he said softly, "but Jamson runs with a pack and none of them are pleasant."

I frowned. "Then why is his presence abided?"

"Because he's the current heir of a major house." His expression was flat, but that edge of old pain and anger resurfaced. "As I have said, some of the ladies in this place will go to great lengths to capture such a man, no matter how heinous they might find him."

"It seems to me that there is a very dark heart to the glitter that is life here in the Reaches."

"I think you might be right." His mouth twisted, though it

held little in the way of humor. "Why do you think I remain at Blacklake? It's not just for the sake of Eluria."

"But the price of such freedom comes at a cost," I said. "Blacklake is not without its dangers."

"Yes. But she's become a strong, independent woman well able to protect herself." His smile grew, became filled with a warmth and humor that did strange things to my pulse rate. "In that, she very much reminds me of someone else."

"And just who might that be?" I asked, pressing a little closer.

His grip tightened briefly. "A witch named Saska, perhaps?"

I slapped his arm in indignation and he laughed softly. "Or not." He leaned forward and kissed me. It was little more than a brush of lips, but it held a heat, a promise, that had desire rising. "Unfortunately, we both have people to hunt down. This discussion can be continued later." He hesitated, and then added, "Please be careful."

"And you."

"I am not the one about to face a drunken pack on their home ground."

He stepped back and bowed before walking across to the stairs leading down to the next level. I adjusted my slightly skewed mask then moved into the ballroom, pausing at the top of the stairs as I searched the room for someone who fitted the description I'd been given. Once again, a blue-suited footman approached and bowed lightly. "Maybe I can be of assistance, m'lady?"

"I'm looking for Lord Jamson."

Distaste briefly flashed across the footman's face. "I believe he's with friends in the blue room."

"And where might that be?"

"If you follow this wall around to the right," he said, waving a hand at the wall behind us, "it is the last door before you come to the white terrace. Be careful, m'lady. He's in a mood."

"Then perhaps you should wander past that room at some point in the near future, in case help is needed." While I was more than able to protect myself, it was still four male witches against one woman armed with only a small knife and very unreliable powers.

"I'll do as you suggest." He bowed and left.

I followed the wall around. There seemed to be a lot more people in the room tonight, but I guessed that wasn't surprising when the equinox was only a few hours away now. The music was rambunctious and loud, and the dance floor so crowded there was barely room to move. Even so, I heard the half scream as I neared the blue room. It was a sound that abruptly cut off, but the hairs along the back of my neck nevertheless rose.

That sound had come from a woman's throat, not a man's.

I tried to open the door, but it was locked. I pressed closer, listening intently. There were at least three men inside; a couple of them were talking and laughing, the other making rather crude suggestions as to what should be done next.

Underneath all *that* was a whimper of distress.

It didn't take a genius to figure out what was happening. Anger surged through me and with it came the wind. She ran under the door and, a heartbeat later, had it unlatched. I quietly stepped inside. The four men didn't even notice. Three of them were too busy discussing the actions of the forth, who was plundering a woman strapped facedown against a table.

I took three quick steps, raised a fist, and swung it as hard as I could. As the blow hit the first man's chin and smashed him sideways, I spun and lashed out with a bare heel at the second. It hit him hard in the gut, forcing a grunt of pain as he staggered backward several feet. The third man spun around, his expression shocked even as he swung a clenched fist at my face. But the blow was wide and slow, and I had plenty of time to duck it. A quick, hard uppercut had him tumbling backward over a chair. He hit the ground awkwardly and didn't move.

The fourth man—a man with dirty yellow-blond hair—swore and swung around, his thick cock rampant and bloody as he grabbed the air and flung it at me. It threw me back several steps before I was able to brace myself against it. The man I'd hit in the gut grabbed my arm, but I twisted out of his grip and thrust him as hard as I could against the nearest wall. I didn't wait to see the result, but dove under another blow of air and grabbed Jamson by his ball sac.

"One move, be it from you or the air," I ground out, "and I shall rip these things free from your body and feed them to the Adlin."

He made an odd sound of distress and pain, and became a statue. I wasn't even sure he dared to breathe. I slid my knife free and pointed it at the man I'd thrown against the wall. His nose was broken and there was blood all over his face and mouth. I hoped like hell it was *very* painful. The air stirred again but held no immediate threat. Perhaps Jamson's friend was in too much pain to concentrate on any form of retribution.

"You got a name?" I growled.

He hesitated, and then spat. The bloody globule landed near my toes. "Franc."

"Untie the woman, Franc. *Now*," I added, when he hesitated and glanced at Jamson.

He shuffled forward and did so. The woman scrambled free of the table and hastily lowered her skirts. If her clothing was anything to go by, she was a chambermaid rather than one of the guests. She was also, I suspected, little older than sixteen or seventeen and, if the blood I'd seen was any indication, uninitiated in the ways of Astar. My hand tightened against Jamson's sac, and his knees buckled. He didn't fall, but only because I shoved him back against the table.

"Are you all right?" I asked softly.

She nodded, but wouldn't meet my gaze. Her cheeks were red, her eyes puffy with tears, and her mouth pinched.

"What's your name?"

She hesitated, and then said, "Kara."

"Kara, do you wish to press charges against these men?"

She rapidly shook her head. I wasn't surprised given her position here would probably be, at best, tenuous if she did, but it nevertheless angered me that these men would so easily get away with such a serious assault.

"I'll support you in any hearing if you wish to do so."

Again she shook her head. "I just—" She hesitated, and sniffed. "I just want to go. Please, can I go?"

"Of course you can. But if you need—" The words died on my lips. She was already out the door.

Franc once again spat out blood and then said, "You will pay for this—"

"Oh, I don't think so," I cut in. "And if you don't want your friend here to become a eunuch, I suggest you quit the threats and drag your companions around so I can keep an eye on the three of you."

I squeezed Jamson's ball sac as I said it, and he made another of those half-gurgled screams. His sweat and pain stung the air, but the smell did little to ease the anger within me. That anger very much wanted to not only rip his balls off but slice up his manhood to ensure he could never again violate anyone—innocent or not—in such a manner.

Franc reluctantly obeyed. Once he'd dragged the two unconscious men into my line of sight, he stopped beside them and crossed his arms. "This action will be the end of you," he said. "We will ensure—"

"Look, if we're going to throw threats about, let me give you one or two," I said. "First off, I'm here under the orders of Lord Kiro, who is currently investigating the murder—"

"Murder?" Franc said. "We haven't murdered anyone—"

"Not in this room, maybe, although who knows what might have happened if I hadn't walked in when I did."

"Oh for freedom's sake, it was only a damn maid—"

He didn't get any further, because my knife buried itself in his thigh. He screamed and went down, clutching his leg with both hands as blood began to pulse. I squeezed Jamson's balls harder then released him; he made an incoherent noise and dropped to his knees.

The door opened and the footman who'd given me directions entered. His gaze swept the room and, just for an instant, something close to delight crossed his expression before he got it under control.

"Is everything all right, m'lady?"

"Everything is perfectly fine, thank you." I tore a strip of fabric from my skirt then walked over to Franc, throwing the material at him before bending to retrieve my knife.

"No, it's not," Jamson wheezed. "Arrest this witch, she attacked us—"

"Four Upper Reaches lords brought down by one woman? Won't that be the talk of the masque," I said. "Are you sure you want to advertise that? Because I don't mind ensuring everyone knows the precise reason *why* I attacked the four of you."

Jamson glared at me. His friend didn't even do that much —he was too busy tying the material around his thigh in an effort to stem the bleeding. I returned my gaze to the footman. "Could you have a guard placed on the door? None of these men are to leave until Lord Kiro arrives to interrogate them."

Jamson snorted, though the sound came out weirdly given he was still battling to breathe and obviously remained in pain. "Taking advantage of a maid is hardly a crime worthy of Kiro's—"

I raised a hand in warning and he cut the rest of the comment off. The footman bowed. "I shall order it done, m'lady."

"For freedom's sake, why are you taking orders from her? She's a damn nobody!" Jamson said. "I'm the Rossi heir apparent and you're mine to command—"

"And Lord Kiro's orders," I cut in, "override everything else."

"You're *not* Lord Kiro—"

"No, but I *am* here on his orders—and that can be easily confirmed by simply requesting his presence here immediately."

"I think perhaps that would be for the best, m'lady." The footman hesitated. "And perhaps I should ask a healer to attend Lord Franc?"

"He doesn't deserve it, but I guess you'd better."

He ducked his head to hide his smile and retreated, closing the door behind him. I cleaned my knife on the coat of one of the unconscious men, and then said, "Right, tell me about Marcus Rossi."

Jamson drew in a deep, shuddery breath, and then said, "He's my father."

"And you wanted him dead."

He snorted. "So what? I'm not the only eldest son who wishes death on his parent."

"But I'm betting few of the others have actually followed through with the desire, as you have."

"What on earth are you blathering about, woman?"

The confusion on his face was very real. He might be a drunken abuser, but it very much looked like he wasn't guilty of patricide.

"I'm talking about your father, and the fact he was murdered this evening."

Jamson blinked. Surprise, horror, hope, and fear—the emotions tumbled across his face in quick succession. "Seriously?"

"Yes. And given you have the most to gain by his death—"

"If I was going to murder anyone," he retorted, "it'd be the bitch carrying the spawn of another. He or she is the real threat to my position, thanks to the fact it'll be born of his legal wife."

"So you're saying you didn't in fact murder your father? Or did you perhaps arrange for someone else to do it?"

"I didn't kill him and I didn't ask anyone else to do it, but I'm damn glad someone did."

That was, beyond any doubt, a truthful statement. His hatred of his father and his elation at his death were evident in his voice and in his eyes.

A knock at the door had me glancing around. "Enter."

The door opened and a gray-clad healer walked in. His gaze quickly scanned the room and a smile twitched his lips. Jamson and his friends really weren't liked up here in the Reaches, it seemed. "M'lady," he said, with a quick nod at me. "I've been told to advise you Lord Kiro is on his way. A guard has been placed at the door to ensure these four remain here."

"Excellent." I sheathed my knife. With Kiro on his way, there was little point of me remaining here. I had the answer I'd been sent here to find; it was up to Kiro to decide what to do with these men now. "When you finish with these four, could you check on a maidservant called Kara for me? She was the victim of an attack by these delightful souls."

"Indeed? I'll ensure Lord Kiro is also aware of that when he arrives." His gaze was cold with anger when it rose to mine, but it wasn't aimed at me. "And I'll certainly find Kara and ensure she's okay."

"Hey," Franc growled, "I didn't actually do anything—"

"No," I said. "You just stood back, offered suggestions, and cheered Jamson on. Which is just as bad in my books. You're damn lucky that knife was aimed at your thigh and not your rotten heart."

"Amen to *that*," the healer murmured.

Franc shot him a dark look, but wisely refrained from saying anything. Jamson was also quiet, but I could feel his gaze on my back, and it was as deadly as a knife—and that might just become a reality if I wasn't very careful. I had a feeling the Rossi heir did *not* appreciate being shown up in any way, shape, or form.

Of course, he had to find me first. It was doubtful that—even when my face was revealed at the equinox unmasking—he'd think to look in the Nightwatch for me. Aside from Saska and the now dead Marcus, Kiro and Trey were the only other ones who knew my background, and I doubted they'd reveal it, as it would void the very reason they were using me. No Reaches man or woman—no matter what the house—would reveal any information, let alone their most intimate secrets, to someone considered so far beneath them. They might find a stained witch intriguing, but once they discovered I was actually nothing more than a Nightwatch officer with a small amount of magic... well, I'd be seen as little higher than a serf—as someone they could use but certainly never trust.

I headed back out into the ballroom, then paused, not entirely sure what to do next. After scanning the crowd and seeing no one I knew, let alone anyone I wanted to talk to, I walked back to the foyer, vaguely hoping to catch Kiro on the way through. But there was no sign of him—if he was on his way here, as the healer said, then he wasn't coming via the main entrance. Which didn't really surprise me; Kiro, I suspected, had a long habit of doing the unexpected.

I walked across to the main doors and studied the long line of carriages outside. The one bearing Trey's colors wasn't present, so he was obviously back at the Harken house with the lady Lida. I contemplated joining him, but before I could move, the wind whispered around me, bringing with it a distant but familiar sound.

The Adlin were howling again, but it was stronger—angrier—than before. It was also a sound that spoke of an imminent attack.

The itch to run down to the gates, to take my place amongst my fellow Nightwatch, had me taking a step forward before I could stop it. The reality was, the Nightwatch and the walls were more than capable of taking care of the Adlin without my help. Even if the Adlin used trebuchets against us, as they had in Blacklake, it wouldn't help them breach the walls or the gates. They were too thick—too strong—to be brought down by fire, however fierce. And not even the heaviest rock the Adlin could cast against the walls would mar their mirror surface and give them climbing holds. Even if the fire did reach the outer bailey area, it was, for the most part, more stone and earth than wood, and wouldn't easily burn or smoke.

So why did the wind speak of trouble and treachery?

I frowned and stepped further into the night. The air was bitterly cold, and fat drops of rain fell from the edge of temporary canvas cover, chilling the back of my neck before running down my spine. Far below me, I could see the lights that lined the inner wall, and, beyond that still, the black ribbon that was the main outer wall. From a distance, everything seemed to be as it should. There were no alarms, and nothing to indicate an attack. And yet the wind continued to suggest all was not as it looked.

Damn it, why did she speak so clearly to me sometimes, and not at others? Was it simply because I hadn't gone through the initiation ceremony? Or was there something else going on? Certainly she'd been clearer within the walls of the Rossi household than anywhere else, but standing out here on the porch rather than inside shouldn't have made that much difference.

As I caught the ends of my skirt to stop it flying over my head, something weird happened. The wind dropped and everything went still; even the storm seemed momentarily hushed. Then, with a huge whoosh, the air rushed backward, as if drawn unwillingly down the hill. Even the breath from my lungs was snatched, and it left me momentarily dizzy. I threw a hand against the sidewall to keep upright, and felt the shudder go through the stone. But power wasn't being drawn from it—not in the same way that the air was being sucked down the hill. It was more a reaction to what was happening—it was as if the earth was issuing an odd kind of denial.

A heartbeat later, the attack alarm sounded.

Not up here in the Reaches, but down below, in the outer bailey. Lights flared along the inner wall, throwing the area immediately around it into brightness, and highlighting the scramble to get to the walls.

Because it was the night of the equinox, and there was only a skeleton crew manning them. If ever there was a perfect time for an attack, then this was it.

I clenched my fists against the increasingly urgent need to take my place amongst them, to fight beside the people I'd grown up with, the people I cared about. Ava and April would be down there somewhere, running to answer the call to arms. I should be with them, not up here playing games with people who'd never accept me.

Except it wasn't a game. Not when the very safety of Winterborne might well hinge on us uncovering the true depth of the plot Hedra, Saska, and the now dead Pyra were involved in.

Besides, even if more than half of its personnel were drunk, the Nightwatch could cope with an attack. The walls wouldn't be breached, not by anything the Adlin could throw at them.

It is not the Adlin you have to worry about, the wind whispered, in a voice that oddly sounded like Saska, *but rather treachery from within. The Adlin did not call the air.*

The image of Hedra, feet bare against rough, wet stones, her hair shining brightly against the rough blackness of the inner wall, flitted through my mind.

Hedra was supposed to be here, in the ballroom, her every movement being watched, so how could that image be fact?

Trust, the wind whispered.

But if Hedra is in Winterborne as a spy for whoever's behind this plot, why would they risk exposing her?

Because her position here has become tenuous. Because of you. Because of your actions. She will make her mischief and then she will run.

Not if I can help it. I ran into the storm and was soaked in an instant. I didn't care. The driver of the first carriage in the long line hastily jumped down from his covered seat as I approached, his face one of confusion and concern.

"M'lady, can I—"

"Find Lord Kiro immediately. Tell him Lady Hedra is in the outer bailey." I brushed past him and jumped into the cabin.

"M'lady wait!"

I didn't. I just hit the start button, grabbed the steering stick, and pressed the accelerator to the floor. The carriage lurched forward, rattling and shaking as it picked up speed. I zoomed through the gates and followed the wet roads down the hill, slipping and sliding around the various corners. More than once the carriage threatened to smash sideways up the wide pavements and into the ostentatious entrances of the many houses that lined the roadside, but each time I battled the steering stick and managed to keep disaster at bay.

The closer we got to the inner wall, the more strident the alarm became, and the more urgent the wind's whisperings. My breathing was little more than short, sharp gasps, but it wasn't fear. It wasn't even the exertion of battling with the carriage.

The air was simply becoming scarcer the closer I got to the outer bailey.

If a soldier couldn't breathe, they couldn't fight.

Was that Hedra's plan? To snatch the air from the lungs of everyone in the outer bailey, then simply walk down and open the gates to the Adlin?

What on earth would that gain her?

Even if she killed every last soldier in both the Night and Daywatch, both she and they would still had to contend with the military forces manning the secondary wall *and* the entire force of both air and earth witches in the. Upper Reaches. Hedra wasn't a strong enough witch to steal the breath from them all, of that I was sure. She'd die, the Adlin would die, and she would have outed herself as a traitor all for naught.

Or was the plan simply to let the Adlin cause their havoc while she ran back to her queen, as the wind had suggested?

I rounded the last corner and hit the long straight stretch of road that led down to the inner wall. There were guards lining the top of it now, and more struggling to climb the walls. All of them were armed. Normally, the reserve force would only be called out under the direst of circumstances, so what on earth was happening in the outer bailey?

Were Ava and April safe?

I took a deep breath that barely even tickled my throat let alone filled my lungs, and tried to remain calm. I had to concentrate on finding Hedra, on stopping her, if everyone both here and in the outer bailey were to have any chance of halting the larger threat of the Adlin.

I hit the brake as I neared the locked-down inner gates. The carriage slewed sideways for several feet before it came to a shuddering halt. I threw my mask on the seat and then climbed out. Two men and a woman were running toward me, all of them wearing breathing masks. I hoped like hell someone had thought to issue them in the outer bailey.

My own breathing remained short and sharp, but my lungs weren't burning. The wind stirred just enough air around me to keep me upright even if that fierce vacuum continued.

"Did the lady Hedra come down here sometime in the last half hour or so?" I had to shout to be heard above the noise of the sirens.

"Yes," the woman—a regular soldier rather than one of the reserves—said. "But she's caught in the outer bailey."

"What happens there?"

"We don't know," she said, and then motioned toward the Upper Reaches. "You should return to your house, m'lady. It's not safe here."

Meaning she hadn't seen my stain. "I need to get into the outer bailey—"

"There is no way inside," she said. "The doors are secured and cannot be opened until the all clear is given."

I swore softly. "Where's your captain?"

"Up on the wall, but—"

I didn't wait for the rest of her answer. I just headed for the nearest steps that climbed the steep wall, the wind at my back, feeding me air, telling me to hurry. If the soldiers chased me, I couldn't hear them.

My lungs were burning when I finally reached the walkway at the top of the inner wall. I ran to the parapet, one hand gripping the nearest merlon as I leaned out.

Below me was chaos. There were soldiers everywhere, but many of them were either on their knees gasping for breath, or unconscious. I couldn't see either Ava or April amongst those littering the ground, so maybe they'd made it to the wall. Not that it would make them that much safer— not against a wind that was sucking away the air. I scanned the rest of the area but couldn't see Hedra anywhere. Maybe she was standing in the shadows of *this* wall.

At least the gates were still closed... but for how much longer if this wind continued to batter them was a question I really didn't want an answer to.

The wind stirred again, bringing with it the sound of running steps. I glanced to my left and saw several armed soldiers coming toward me. While they'd probably release me the minute they confirmed my identity, every instinct said I couldn't afford any sort of delay. That if I wanted to stop Hedra and save my friends I had to get down there, into the outer bailey, as soon as I could.

Run, the wind whispered.

Run where? It wasn't like the wall provided any real choice, given it, like the outer bailey wall, ended with a sheer drop to the sea.

Trust, the wind whispered. *Run*

I did, even as I wondered at my sanity for doing so. The soldiers behind me shouted at my reaction, and I had no doubt orders were being issued along the line for soldiers to stop me at all costs—and no sooner had that thought crossed my mind when it started to happen. I swore and barreled through a couple of ill-prepared attempts but the farther I got along the line, the harder it became.

Jump, the wind said again.

I glanced over the parapet and the long drop down to the outer bailey. *Not on your life.*

Or my life, in this case.

Trust, the wind said. *No harm will come.*

I ducked under the blow of a soldier, and barely avoided the desperate attempts of two others. Rain-slicked skin helped, but for how much longer?

The wind didn't reply. Instead, she amplified a sound that chilled my heart—a male voice ordering weapons to be fired.

They'd kill me rather than let me get any farther along this wall.

It left me with little choice. I took two steps and leapt high over the parapet.

And hoped like hell the wind kept her promise.

8

E verything became a blur as I dropped down the sheer edge of the inner wall. Far below me lay the hard stone rooftops of the bunkhouses, but hitting them rather than the ground wouldn't make all that much difference. There was probably only a couple of hundred feet difference between the two and—from this height—the result would be the same: my flesh splattered ingloriously across the stone.

The wind didn't seem inclined to check or hinder the speed of my drop, and it made me wonder—far too late—if perhaps the voice I'd heard advising me to jump belonged to Hedra, using my trust of wind's voice against me.

But as I drew closer to the ground, the air surged, buffeting and bruising my body even as she gripped me. The speed of my fall began to ease, but the urgency I could hear within her was growing.

I hit the wet rooftop hard enough to send a shudder of pain through my entire body, and stumbled forward several feet as the wind abruptly released me, and I struggled to keep my balance.

A shout had me reaching for my knife and spinning

around. The air was so thin that even though I hadn't been here long, my lungs were beginning to burn and my head was pounding. There were unconscious soldiers everywhere on the ground below, their clothes and hair fluttering in the almost violent exodus of oxygen toward the gates. But some of the Nightwatch had managed to grab breathing apparatus, and many of them were now heading up the stairs to the walls. Walls that were shuddering under multiple impacts, something I could feel through the stones under my feet.

So where was Hedra?

There was no sign of her in the immediate area. I ran to the edge of the roof, leapt down to the walkway and pounded along, the sound of my steps lost in the cacophony of noise coming from both the sirens and the roar of the Adlin. On the second bunkhouse level, there were at least a dozen unconscious Daywatch soldiers lying across the walkway, and several had breathing masks they hadn't been able to strap on in time. I scooped up one, hurriedly tying on the small tank before pulling on the mask. It didn't immediately help either the burning in my lungs or the pounding in my head, but that was to be expected. I jumped over the railing and dropped down to the ground. No one paid me any attention—all those who remained awake and aware were focused on the wall and the Adlin, none of them realizing the real threat lay within the walls, not without.

I paused, and looked around. Logically, Hedra wouldn't be out in the open. She'd either be hidden in the deeper shadows, out of the immediate sight of any Nightwatch officer, or perhaps even in one of the two emergency shelters used to protect noncombatants caught within the outer bailey during an attack.

Former, the wind whispered. *Ahead.*

Ahead was *not* a useful instruction given the sheer size of the outer bailey. Nevertheless, I ran on, my grip fierce on the knife as my gaze constantly swept the shadows, looking for any hint, any sign, of life.

The pull on the air got stronger, seeming to crystalize in thought and determination. Urgency beat at my brain even as the wind tore around me, harrying my steps, pressuring me to greater speed. I all but flew across the wet stones, and still, there was no sign of her.

For freedom's sake, I need more help than this! If you wish to help me save Winterborne, then tell me where Hedra is!

For an instant, I thought the mental plea went unheard. Then the wind hit me, pushing me to the left. In the shadows near the box that normally held the guard who monitored day-to-day entry into the upper areas stood Hedra.

Unfortunately, the same wind that showed her to me also revealed my approach to her.

She clenched her fist, but instead of throwing me backward with a tumultuous blast of air, as I half expected, she ripped her hand back, as if the air was a rope attached to something very real and very solid.

I felt the shudder in the stone first, and then heard a strange, almost metallic groaning; immediately after this, metal began to pierce the air—metal that was thick and heavy and smelled of machinery oil.

And it was coming straight at me.

I cursed and hit the ground, my hands over my head in a rather useless act of protection. The wind shifted its force just enough for the deadly projectiles to smash into the inner wall above me rather than into my body, but I was nevertheless covered in a rain of metal, cogs, and freedom only knew what else. Pain shuddered through my body, but it was minor compared to the fear.

Because the metal projectiles were nothing other than the remains of the apparatus that operated the gates. Without it, there were only the two steel girders that were automatically dropped into place to provide additional support to the gates in the event of a mass attack.

But those girders were shuddering and shaking in position as the wind tore at them with increasing force.

Stop, I silently screamed at the air. *You have to stop it. You can't open the gates.*

Can't stop, the wind whispered. *It is not a matter of will, but rather control.*

And Hedra was the far stronger air witch here, even if she wasn't from one of the ruling houses.

I cursed and pushed upright. The wind swung around me, battering me, hindering me, but not, I knew, with the force Hedra wanted. Still, it was enough to snatch the mask from my face and rip the lines free from the small air cylinder. As it was sent tumbling, twisting up into the air and out of reach, Hedra screamed. Not in fear, but in fury. I could hear her now—she wanted the wind to grab my body as it had grabbed the mask, to send me flying, to smash me against the wall the machinery had hit.

Wanted it to rip *her* free of this place, to take her well beyond the walls and the Adlin where she would meet the Queen's forces and be safe.

The wind tore at me, sending sections of skirt flying but leaving me otherwise intact. And it left *her* on the ground.

I staggered forward, my knuckles white with the force of my grip on my knife. I had one chance—just one chance—to stop this madness. The temptation to throw my knife and end her life here and now was fierce, but the wind whispered against it. It was still bound to obey Hedra, if only partially, and would divert the blade if I did so.

If she saw me coming, she gave no sign of it. Her concentration now seemed to be solely on the gates. I didn't dare look at how close she was to succeeding in her aim of opening them; my goal was to stop her, and every inch of concentration and energy was now being poured into that.

Inch by inch, I drew closer. But every step felt like a goddamn mile; my lungs burned, and my heart pounded so rapidly I swore it was about to tear out of my chest.

Then the inevitable happened. The crossbeams were flung free of the latches holding them in place, and the two extremely heavy gates that protected Winterborne opened with a crash that reverberated through every inch of the outer bailey.

"No!" I screamed, and lunged at Hedra.

She saw me, but far too late. She raised a hand as if to batter me away physically as well as magically, but my knife punched through her chest and sliced into her heart. Her eyes went wide as the realization of death hit and the wind died. The silence that briefly followed was eerie. If the wind mourned her passing, then she did not speak of it.

As her body crumpled to the ground, I swung around, sucking the returning air into my burning lungs as I prayed that the Adlin hadn't noticed the gates were open.

It was a forlorn hope at best, and one that died very quickly.

A sea of thickset, hairy beings scrambled in through the opening. Nightwatch officers were pouring down from the walkways, and it was literally raining metal as they fired everything they had at the incoming Adlin. But there were far too many Adlin and far too few soldiers armed with nitrate rifles to do too much damage.

I bent and pressed my hand against the stone. *Bury her deep. Keep the bracelets safe and out of sight. Tell no one about her presence or where she lies.*

The earth didn't speak to me, but after a moment, a rumble ran through the ground, and the stone split asunder. Hedra's body dropped without ceremony into that gash. It swiftly closed again, leaving no trace of the woman who had betrayed us all.

But the stones under my feet continued to shake. Power surged through it, through me, a force that was both masculine and familiar. The rumbling increased as the ground began to heave and rise, becoming a wave of almost molten rock that raced toward the doorway, sweeping the Adlin before it, forcing them back. As this first wave pushed them beyond the gateway, a second wave began to form. At the same time, thick gray fingers of stone crept up the gatehouse walls and began pushing at the doors. They shifted, slowly at first, but with increasing speed. More Adlin appeared, scrambling over the still-moving wave of earth and then throwing themselves through the rapidly closing gap. Some didn't make it, becoming little more than a smear of blood and hair as the doors slammed shut. The second wave then crashed upon them, quickly forming a retaining wall and providing extra weight to hold the doors closed.

But there were at least two sleuths now locked within the outer bailey walls. And while some of them were attacking the defenseless men and women who lay on the ground, most were running to the right, to the stairs that led up to the bunkhouses.

Why? What on earth did they hope to achieve by fleeing there rather than attacking? They wouldn't find much in the way of protection, especially given the lack of maneuvering space on the narrow walkways and within the small rooms....

A throaty roar caught my attention. I glanced around sharply and saw an Adlin coming straight at me, his eyes filled with rage and his teeth bared and bloody. I swore, flung some air his way to slow his steps, then spun and ran. I wasn't about to face even *one* of those damn creatures armed with just a short-bladed knife.

But the creature was faster than I'd ever be, and was gaining on me far too rapidly. As the shuddering earth warned me of the creature's closeness, I scooped up a couple of blasters and then spun around, firing them nonstop even as I continued to run backward, my steps guided by the whispering of the wind. The Adlin's body shook and shuddered under the barrage of the blaster's bullets, but it wasn't stopped. Nothing except a nitrate rifle could do that, and there certainly weren't any of those lying about in the near vicinity.

"Duck!" a familiar voice screamed.

I did so without question and, a second later, the Adlin's head was blown apart. As his body lost momentum and fell to the ground near my feet, I twisted around. Ava strode toward me, a fierce grin on her face and a bloody wound stretching down her left arm from above her elbow to her knuckles.

"That," I said, accepting her help up, "was a very nice piece of timing."

She gave me a quick hug, and then shoved a rifle in my hands. "Let's go get the rest of these bastards."

"Where's April?" I said, as we strode forward.

"Don't know. His festival shift was from ten until two, and I didn't see him afterward."

"We need to find him." My gaze scanned the bunkrooms above us. The Adlin were still running through the second and third levels, but I couldn't see any sign of opposition. The soldiers I'd seen up there might have survived the air being sucked from their lungs, but it looked like they'd not survived the ravages of the Adlin.

I pushed away the possibility of death being April's fate and caught the ammo loop Ava threw me. We reached the base of the stairs and headed up.

After a quick sweep through the first level to ensure there were no Adlin lying in wait, we joined six others and made our way toward the second level. A pack of seven Adlin immediately came at us, their screams ripping across the air, hurting my ears. We fired as one, and the Adlin went down, their bodies torn apart by the spray of metal. We reloaded and checked each bunkhouse to ensure no creatures remained. All we found was bodies. The remnants of at least a dozen soldiers were scattered in either the rooms or on the walkways, but it was obvious none of them had been caught unawares. They'd either died when the air had been sucked from their lungs, or had gone down fighting the Adlin with whatever they could get their hands on. But wood and steel was of little use against the greater strength and reach of the creatures.

We cautiously moved up to the last level—our floor. My gut twisted as we neared the coupling room April, Ava, and I usually used, but it was empty of both life *and* death. Relief spun through me, but it was a tempered with the knowledge that while he wasn't here, he could still be dead.

We took out the remaining Adlin and then continued checking the rest of the rooms. They'd not only gotten as far as ours, but had also, in fact, torn it apart. Furniture had been broken, the bedding torn into pieces, and our personal lockers smashed beyond repair, their contents spilled all over the floor. Even the walls and the ceiling had not escaped the Adlin's attentions.

Ava stopped in the middle of all the mess and looked around with something close to bemusement. I walked past her, looking for my uniforms. I eventually found a shirt that was only missing one arm, a pair of pants that were whole aside from a slight rip along the seam near my thigh, and—most importantly of all—a pair of boots for my beaten-up feet. Once I'd stripped off what remained of my sodden skirt and top, I quickly dried myself on the remnants of a towel and then got dressed.

Outside, the siren finally stopped and with it went the sound of the Adlin's howls from beyond the walls. The silence was almost eerie. I sat on the edge of the bed and contemplated the mess, wondering again what they were doing here. The destruction in the other rooms had been nowhere near as bad as this.

"You know," Ava mused, "If I didn't know better, I'd say they were searching for something."

Suspicion of *what* that thing might be stirred and I stood abruptly. "Ava, can you see that bracelet I brought back from Blacklake anywhere?"

She shook her head. "Mind you, it's rather hard to spot *anything* in this."

"We need to find it."

"We need to find April," she said. "The bracelet and this mess can wait."

"No, it can't, trust me on that."

She frowned me, but nevertheless helped me search. We went through everything, searched everywhere; we found the gorgeous jewelry Ava had tucked away for a special event, and April's dagger made from an Adlin's claw, but the bracelet was conspicuously absent.

"It's gone," Ava said. "Though how that is possible I can't say. None of them escaped us."

Yes, the wind said. *They did. The roof.*

I turned and ran the door. Ava followed me out. I stopped at the railing but couldn't immediately see anything, so I climbed up, balancing preciously before leaping for the roof. I caught the edge and hauled myself up. Ava soon followed me.

What we discovered was more bodies—bodies that *hadn't*

been there when I'd jumped down from the inner wall. Bodies that were both Adlin *and* Nightwatch.

"Well, these buggers are well and truly dead." Ava lightly nudged an Adlin with her toe. "None of them appear to be carrying anything, though."

"No." I walked over to the edge of the building. Far below me, in the Bay of Giants, the ocean pounded against the white cliffs, a fierce and murderous force no human or Adlin could survive. Not that the Adlin would even consider jumping given their fear of water in general. So why did they come up here? They had to have known there was no escape. And as powerful as the Adlin were, there was no way even *they* could throw the bracelet across the distance that separated Winterborne from the white sand that lined the bay's gentler shoreline. And by the time they *had* come up here, Hedra was dead, so the wind couldn't have helped them. Unless, of course, there was another witch involved, one we didn't know about.

Hell, it might even be Saska, for all I knew.

No, the wind whispered. *The Adlin are accompanied by another witch. It is he who commanded the wind to snare the bracelet and bring it to them.*

I briefly closed my eyes. Yet another traitor... or was it perhaps one of the many children Saska and the other stolen witches had given birth to?

"Neve! You up here?"

It took me a moment to recognize the voice—Trey. "On the roof, Commander."

Ava walked over to the other edge and peered down. "So is this *the* commander? The one who sent you the dress and whisked you away to the Upper Reaches?"

"Yes."

"Huh." Ava paused. "I must say, he's rather nice-looking. Well caught, you."

"It's hardly likely to be anything more than a passing fancy," I said, my gaze on the distant shoreline. "I'm unlit, remember?"

"Unlit maybe, but not undesirable."

I smiled and didn't answer. Although the rain had eased, the sky remained thunderous, and there was little light glimmering on that distant shore. But it didn't matter, because I could feel movement, through the stones and the earth. There was at least one sleuth, if not more, running away from that shore.

Why would they risk so much for the return of one bracelet?

I blinked at the thought. There wasn't *just* one bracelet involved. There were two.

And if they'd gone to extremes here to retrieve it, what would they do at Blacklake?

I ran back to the other edge of the roof and jumped down, sprinting forward without really looking, and just about collided with Trey as he came up the walkway.

"Whoa," he said, catching me firmly. "What's the hurry?"

"The bracelet," I said. "They were after the *bracelet*."

Understanding flashed across his eyes. He didn't say anything; he just grabbed my hand and ran back down the bunkhouse levels. Captain July was walking across the courtyard toward the infirmary area, but stopped the minute he saw us.

"Commander Stone," he said. "I believe we have you to thank for the earthworks that saved Winterborne."

Which was why the energy had seemed familiar—it had been Trey who'd called the earth into action.

"Indeed, Captain." Trey came to a halt and released my hand. "And now I must ask a favor of you. We need to get to Blacklake immediately."

The captain frowned. "It's not safe, Commander. The Adlin still roam—"

"I know, and I don't care. I have reason to believe Black-lake will come under a similar attack, and I will *not* remain here while they fight for their lives."

The captain hesitated. "A speeder could be ready inside twenty minutes; the problem is the gates—"

"What I've done can be undone," Trey said. "If you can arrange the immediate preparation of a speeder and weaponry for myself and Neve, I'll make an urgent call up to Lord Kiro, requesting the presence of several earth witches. They can help you restore the gates into full working order."

He glanced at me. "Neve has been given a leave of absence. She's not even supposed to be here—"

"She's here under my orders, Captain; in fact, I will formally request her secondment to my division until the current situation is dealt with."

The captain's frown grew as he glanced at me. "Neve?"

"It's only temporary, Captain, and I'm more than happy to help the commander out."

"Then head over to three and see what weaponry they have left." He glanced back to Trey. "Contact Kiro, Commander, and I'll do my part."

"Meet back here," Trey said to me, and then left.

"Neve, what's going on?" Ava said, as she came up behind me.

I turned around. "I'm off to fight a second battle at Black-lake. Find April for me; I need to know he's okay."

"Why on earth do you have to go?"

"Because the commander wishes it." I hesitated, wondering how much I should tell her. "While the invitation to the masque was real enough, I'm not there to enjoy myself. I'm helping the commander ferret out a couple of spies—"

"Spies!"

"Quiet!" I looked around to ensure no one had overheard us. "This can't become common knowledge."

She gently cupped my face, her fingers cool against my skin. "It won't, you know that. But how deep does the deception go?"

"The woman behind this attack is—was—an air witch from a non-ruling house. But there are others involved, others who come from higher houses."

Ava swore. "I wondered how the bastards managed to blast the door open. The truth is, they didn't. They had help."

"Yes, although I can't tell you why they went to all that trouble to retrieve one bracelet. To me, the prize doesn't justify the cost, whatever the end design might be."

"Until you know the end design, you can't actually say that with any certainty," Ava said. "Why hasn't the commander gotten the carabinieri involved? Surely they should be the ones investigating this?"

"Lord Kiro is in charge of the investigation. I dare say he'll call in the cops once all the threads of the plot have been uncovered."

Ava nodded then leaned forward and dropped a kiss on my cheek. "Don't get dead on me, Neve."

I smiled. "Like most bad smells, I'm rather hard to get rid of."

She snorted and slapped my arm—and hard enough to sting. "Stop putting yourself down, woman, whether in jest or not."

"Yes, ma'am." My grin grew as I stepped back. "I'd better get going. Kiss April for me when you find him."

"I'll clip him over the damn ear for causing us both so much damn worry first," she said. Then, with a nod, she headed for the infirmary.

I spun and jogged across to armory three. Jon was looking a little worse for wear—there was a roughly patched but still bloody cut that stretched from his forehead down to his neck, and his bad leg had been splinted and was obviously in need of further attention, but his smile was wide and his eyes shone.

"The bastards thought I'd be easy meat," he said, as I slowed down. "They soon learned otherwise."

"Next time it might be best not to let them get so close before you take them down."

He laughed and slapped my arm. "You could be right there, lass. What do you need?"

"Weapons. The captain's given approval—"

"Aye, he's sent through a message, which is why the armory's open and waiting. Come along."

We once again headed inside. I waited while he hobbled across to the near-empty storage lockers, my gaze scanning the shadows. The nearby shelves and lockers had been emptied, but down the far end, I glimpsed the shapes and shadows of the ancient weapons. Curiosity stirred and I walked down. The farther I got, the darker it became. It seemed the powers that be weren't about to waste electricity where it wasn't needed.

The shelves of old guns and other odd bits of machinery soon gave way to the even older, medieval-style weapons Jon had mentioned a week ago. But it was the glass swords that drew me; having used the knife a number of times, I could certainly see the benefit of having a longer blade. I picked up a couple, testing their weight and feel, but most of them were too heavy or too long for someone my size. But on the shelf close to bottom I found one that was perfect. Once I'd also found its scabbard, I headed back.

"What have you got this time, lass?" Jon said.

I grinned and showed him the sword. "The knife has come in handy, so I figured something bigger might be doubly so."

He snorted and shook his head. "You're definitely certifiable. But it's yours if you want it."

"And I do."

I signed out the sword, the ammo, and the weapons, and then went over to requisitions to grab a new earwig—one that was multi-tuned, enabling communications between the various outposts and us when we were on escort duty. The speeder had been lifted up from the underground garage by then, and the heat from her engines rippled the air as she hovered in the middle of the courtyard. The speeders were triangular in shape and could carry up to four people across both land and sea faster than any other vehicle in the armory. But they were not without their problems, and were extremely fragile. Even rough weather could tear them apart.

Trey, Kiro, and two other men I didn't recognize came out of the inner gateway as I approached the vehicle. The captain appeared and handed Trey a ledger. Once the vehicle was signed over, Trey motioned me to get in. I did so, placing all the weapons and the ammo in the storage bins before climbing into the driver seat. Trey spoke to the captain and the other three men for several seconds and then climbed in behind me.

As I closed the main door, the two strangers approached the gatehouse and a heavy rumble began to fill the air. The retaining wall sitting against the back of the gate began to slide away, until a clear enough path appeared for the gates to be opened and the speeder to go through.

"Ready?" I asked, as I punched in the coordinates.

"Hit it," Trey said. "Push this damn thing as fast it can go."

Which was precisely what I did. The speeder shot out of Winterborne, gathering speed as it accelerated over the remnants of the first wave of dirt. Dust plumed behind us, a beacon that would call to any Adlin left out here. It didn't matter. They wouldn't catch us on foot and they didn't have the knowledge or the technology to do anything else. Trebuchets might have provided a problem had the Adlin been able to mount them onto a vehicle or at least fire them with some sort of accuracy, but they didn't.

We shot through the darkness, the whine of the engines filling the air. The tension in the man behind me grew with each mile that passed, until it felt like every breath was filled with it. I wanted to tell him that it would be all right, that his daughter would be all right, but after what had happened at Winterborne, I dared not. We had no idea just how far this treachery might reach. He might trust the witches stationed at Winterborne, but witches weren't the only ones who could destroy machinery and open gates. A single soldier armed with several well-placed bombs could achieve the very same thing. A week ago, I wouldn't have thought such a betrayal possible, but my perception had certainly changed.

We didn't see any Adlin and the sensors weren't picking up any evidence of movement. I had no doubt they were out there somewhere, just as I had no doubt they'd been sent to Blacklake solely to retrieve the other bracelet.

The Blacksaw Mountains soon loomed large in the front windscreen. Trey leaned over my shoulder and said, "Can you contact Blacklake from here?"

I glanced at him. "You can't?"

He half smiled, though it didn't lift the tension from around his eyes. "I took the earwig out when I left Blacklake. The Reaches gentry don't wear them, and I didn't want to stir too much curiosity."

"Good idea." I triple tapped the earwig to get the right communicator and then said, "Blacklake, this is Nightwatch eight-three inbound from Winterborne with Commander Stone. Are you hearing me?"

Static was my only reply. I frowned and tried again.

"Blacklake, this is Nightwatch eight-three, relaying a request for a status update from Commander Stone. Please reply."

More static.

Trey swore and scraped a hand across his chin. "Either communications are out or they're under attack and haven't the time to reply."

"I can't see any indications of an attack on the sensors, Commander," I said.

"Which might just mean they hit Blacklake at the same time as they did us. Can this thing go any faster?"

"No."

He swore again and sat back. I didn't say anything. I just concentrated on keeping the speeder on track and out of the way of anything that could rip its underbelly apart.

The faint glimmer of lights appeared on the horizon. Some were flickering, some weren't, suggesting the source was both electrical and fire. The sensors began to beep softly —not because we were nearing our destination but because there was movement out there in the darkness. Adlin, but not huge swaths of them.

"What do you want me to do, Commander?"

"Swing around to the right," he said, "and come into Blacklake from the other side of the river. The Adlin aren't likely to have crossed it, no matter how desperate they are."

I made a long sweeping curve to the right. While our course initially took us away from Blacklake, it was evident even from this distance that the outpost had taken a serious hammering. Smoke billowed from the gatehouse and, if the sheer size of the rubble that had been blown across not only the moat but also the ground beyond it was anything to go by, at least half it had come down. There were also fires raging within the outer bailey, the glow of them turning the skies above Blacklake a bloody red.

I hoped it wasn't a sign of what was waiting for us within.

The glimmer of the Black River came into view, although in truth it was more a lake than a river in this section, given the outpost had dammed and widened it for defensive purposes.

We skimmed across its surface, the dark water pluming high on either side as I directed the vehicle to the rear of the settlement. The walls here were at least intact and there was no indication from the radar that the Adlin—or anyone else—had reached this side.

I eased the speed and engaged the stability struts. As they unfolded from the sides of the vehicle, Trey hit the release button and opened the door. The smell of smoke and burned flesh immediately hit, and my stomach churned. Whatever else had happened here, there'd been casualties.

Trey moved back to the weapons locker and opened it up. "A sword?"

I smiled at the disbelief in his voice and shut the engines down. "Trust me, it's not a normal sword."

"I can see that—it's made of glass."

"The same as my knife, which severed an Adlin's leg with one quick cut."

He looked skeptical, but handed me the weapon, a rifle, and an ammo loop. He took the other guns, strapping them to his legs before slinging the second rifle and ammo loop across his shoulders. With a glance at me to ensure I was ready, he exited.

I leapt across to the bank then followed him along the base of the wall to the smaller rear gatehouse. The acrid stench of smoke still stung the air, but it was the hush that was more unnerving. There were no alarms, no sound of voices. And maybe it was simply a matter of the sheer thickness and height of the walls stopping any such sound from reaching us, but it was nevertheless worrying.

Unlike the gateway at Winterborne, this was protected by

a heavy metal portcullis. It was at least forty feet high and double that in width, which meant that even a sleuth of Adlin would have had trouble shifting it. There were no electronics visible, no obvious way to raise the gates or communicate with those inside, but beyond the portcullis, in the small covered area between it and the main gate, there were several cameras. Whether they were working or not was another matter.

"Do you want me to try hailing them again?"

He shook his head and squatted down in front of the portcullis. "Communications must be down. Otherwise, they'd have responded to our presence by now. Give me your knife."

I did so. After brushing away the dirt and grime from one of the stones, he jammed the knife's delicate edge into the small gap between the stones and twisted it sideways. There was a soft click, and the stone slid to one side, revealing an ancient-looking scanner panel.

"That," I said, accepting my knife back, "is a rather ingenious hiding spot."

"It was apparently the brainchild of a commander some two hundred years ago, after some of his men had been stranded by a lockdown and subsequently slaughtered by the Adlin."

"The lake hadn't been created at that point?"

"No. That came with my predecessor, after a particularly dry year left little more than a trickle of water in the river."

It undoubtedly provided them with a secondary source of drinking water, too. "Will the scanner still work if comms and power are down?"

"It should. Both gates can be operated on emergency power."

He placed his hand against the glass and then pressed one of the buttons on the side. After a moment, the screen came to life and his hand was scanned. A light flicked from red to green and the portcullis slowly began to open.

Trey closed the scanner, scuffed dirt back over the stone to cover its presence, then ducked under the portcullis and strode to the rear gate. It, like Winterborne's, was made of black stone, though the large patches of lichen and moss that decorated the surface of this one suggested it wasn't often in use. He hit a stone to the right of the doors and the portcullis dropped back into position with a clang. He pressed a second stone, and a noise not unlike a bass drum's beat began to boom out from behind the main gate somewhere.

"A doorbell?" I said, amused.

He glanced at me. Though a smile twitched at his lips, it failed to ease the tension in his eyes. "It's a door, so why shouldn't it have a bell?"

I snorted softly, but was stopped from replying when a gruff voice said, "ID number?"

I glanced around but couldn't immediately see where the demand was coming from.

"593714ST," Trey said.

"Voice and number correlation. Good to have you back, Commander."

With a heavy rumble, one of the big doors began to slide aside. There were armed soldiers on the other side, but they relaxed the minute they saw us.

"Hansen, report." Trey stepped through the gap and began striding down a long, dark corridor lined with both weapon and oil slits. While both were considered to be rather old-fashioned these days, if they'd been in place at Winterborne, perhaps the Adlin wouldn't have gotten as far as they did.

"The main gatehouse has been breached," Hansen said as he fell in step beside the commander. "There are twenty-seven known casualties so far, and three dead. The inner wall remains secure and the Adlin have been repelled."

Meaning, I hoped, that the bracelet was still here and safe.

"No civilian casualties?" Trey's voice was clipped. He was asking about his daughter, even if he didn't come out and say it.

"No, Commander. And your daughter is safe. We haven't as yet given the all clear to the raid shelters though."

The tension that had been holding Trey hostage almost immediately lifted. "And the gates? How were they breached?"

"A blast of some kind," Hansen said. "Lieutenant Ruma has just sent a recon team out."

"Under full cover, I hope."

"Yes, Commander."

"And communications?"

"Were partially destroyed when the gatehouse fell, and finished off by the Adlin."

Trey grunted. "I want them restored as a priority, Hanson."

"Aye, Commander."

We came out into the inner bailey courtyard. There were several fires burning and people everywhere, some of them ferrying wounded to the small inner bailey hospital, others either trying to put out the fires or clean up rubble. The inner courtyard might not have fallen, but it had certainly been hit—and by something more than just trebuchets. The missiles the Adlin had used during their last attack on this place certainly hadn't been capable of the damage done here. It almost looked like the stone had spontaneously blown apart—and the only people capable of causing that sort of havoc were earth witches of extreme power. Trey trusted those under his command, so did that mean someone else had slipped in here? For the most part, the outposts—other than West Range—weren't used as vacation spots, but it wasn't unknown for the kin of those serving at them to visit from time to time. Could one such visit have led to this destruction?

If the wind knew the answers to any of my questions, she certainly wasn't saying. In fact, she was being remarkably mute. But maybe she was still grieving for Hedra's soul.

No, the wind said. *She is a betrayer, and unworthy of our collective grief. But we cannot fully answer your questions. She forbade us.*

She? *Hedra, you mean?*

Yes.

If you deem her a betrayer, why do you still follow her wishes?

Because the order carries the weight of three, and while one lives, the order holds.

Meaning Saska, I gathered, given she was the only one left of the three women who'd been wearing the bracelets. *Can she countermand the order alone?*

No. Only death will break the binding.

And I certainly wasn't going to kill her. Saska might be a part of whatever the hell was going on, but she was also our only real hope of finding answers. And maybe now that Hedra was dead, she'd be more willing to talk.

Two soldiers saluted the commander as we neared inner gatehouse tower and then opened the heavy metal door. Trey bounded up the stairs; I followed, not sure what else to do. But that uncertainty had no sooner crossed my mind when he glanced back at me and gave me a nod. It was almost as if he'd heard the thought, which was decidedly odd considering he wasn't even wearing an earwig. And while I could talk to the wind, he couldn't, so it was unlikely she'd passed on the inner question.

Another two soldiers stood watch at the top of the stair-well. Trey pressed his hand against a scanner to the right of the heavy metal doors and, once they'd opened, strode inside. This room was basically a smaller-scale version of the one in the outer bailey. My gaze immediately went to the wide windows that lined the front of the room. The damage was even more extensive than it had looked from a distance. It wasn't only the left half the main gatehouse that had fallen, but a good twenty or more feet of the wall on that side. It would have taken one hell of a powerful explosion to cause that sort of damage, which surely meant that while the Adlin might have been involved in the attack—and they certainly had been given the number of bodies below in the courtyard —they weren't the brains behind this whole event.

We desperately needed to find out who actually *was*.

Ruma turned around as he entered. "Glad to have you back, Commander."

He nodded. "Any idea how the breach happened yet?"

"Unfortunately yes. We think we caught the perpetrators on video before comms went down." Her gaze flickered to mine and, just for a moment, I thought I saw a flicker of hostility. "Grant, on the main screen if you please."

"You saw them, and didn't stop them?" Trey said.

Ruma nodded. "You'll understand the lack of urgency when you see the playback, Commander."

He crossed his arms and waited. The big screen sitting above the main viewing platform flickered then came to life; what appeared was a nighttime view of the outer courtyard, with the main gatehouse front and center. Music and laughter could be heard—no doubt the equinox celebrations in full swing—but on the screen all was quiet. Aside from the watch officers making regular patrols, the courtyard was all but abandoned.

"Skip to the important part, Grant," Ruma said.

The playback rolled forward at speed. At nine fifteen and thirty-four seconds, two figures appeared. They were dressed in black and were rather small in stature, appearing as little more than shadows in the night-held courtyard.

Silver glinted on the wrists of both of them and my stomach began to churn.

They paused for several seconds, looking around carefully; one of them glanced briefly toward the camera, her face pale and thin. Shock coursed through me.

Not just because her entire face and every bit of visible skin was lavender-gray, but also because she couldn't have been any older than ten or eleven.

"No," I said in disbelief. "Two children can't be responsible for all this destruction."

"These two *aren't* ordinary children." This time there was no denying the hostility in Ruma's gaze. "They're stained, for a start—"

"Ruma," Trey said, with just a hint of reprimand. "Enough."

She glanced back at the screen, but anger still vibrated through every part of her body. Why was it when the unstained did something bad, no one thought to tar the entire community with the same brush, and yet the opposite was true when it came to us? Life wasn't fair, I was well aware of that, but it was nevertheless frustrating.

I returned my gaze to the screen and watched the two children run across the yard and disappear inside the gatehouse. For a second there was no further movement, and no sound other than the ongoing celebrations. Then a rumble began, softly at first but gradually getting louder, until it seemed as if the earth itself was screaming. And perhaps it was, because a few seconds later, it heaved upwards with such force that one part of the gate sheered away from the other, and the section of wall connected to it was blasted away. Dust, earth, and metal exploded through the air and, for several more minutes, there was nothing else to be seen. When the debris settled and the dust began to clear, the gatehouse was down, the alarms were sounding, and the Adlin were pouring through the broken section of the wall.

"And the children?" Trey's voice held little in the way of emotion.

"We presume they died in the explosion. We lost the cameras when the Adlin tore down the comms towers, but there was no sight of them before that point."

"Did any of the Adlin get inside the inner bailey?" I asked.

"No." Ruma didn't even glance at me. "The Adlin don't appear to have possessed whatever device the kids used, and the flooded moat stopped them getting too close to the inner wall. They retreated rather quickly."

The Adlin never retreated quickly; if they'd done so here, then there'd been a purpose behind it.

It was also rather obvious that kids hadn't been carrying anything. Not in their hands, and not on their tiny bodies. Whatever they'd used must have come from within—from the power of the earth or the air. I opened my mouth to say as much, but closed it again at Trey's sharp look. Once again, he seemed to know what I'd been thinking.

"How did those kids get in here?" he asked. "They're not from Blacklake."

"No." Ruma hesitated. "We found them unconscious in the wasteland a day and a half ago and brought them in. Both were severely malnourished and dehydrated, but otherwise unharmed. We had them in the infirmary but not under guard."

"Whereabouts in Tenterra did you find them?" I asked.

She gave me the coordinates and I glanced at Trey. "That's close to where I initially found Saska, Commander."

"I doubt that's a coincidence."

"No." I hesitated. "Perhaps I should go interview Treace? She might be able to tell us a bit more about the two children."

Trey glanced at his second. "Has the medical and healing staff been given the all clear?"

"Aye, Commander, but we're only using the secondary medical facilities. The main hospital was severely damaged in the explosion."

Trey nodded and returned his gaze to mine. "Return to the main hall when you finish. I'll meet you back there."

And be careful. He might not have said that, but the words whispered around me nevertheless.

I nodded, spun around, and left. My footsteps echoed in the silence as I clattered down the stairs. The guards watched me, but neither acknowledged my presence nor tried to stop me.

Most of the fires were now out, although the foul scent of the oil the Adlin had used still hung on the air. Most of the debris had also been cleared; only the smaller stones and metal particles remained to show anything untoward had happened here.

I walked across the inner courtyard and bounded up the steps to the smaller hospital. It was packed with the injured and those tending to them, and there was certainly more here than the twenty-seven Hansen had initially mentioned. The air was thick with the scent of blood and the sounds of pain, and I found myself hoping April hadn't found himself in a similar situation back at Winterborne.

I paused in the doorway and scanned the room, looking for Treace, but not immediately seeing her. I did spot Mace Dien's wild red hair, and made my way over. He was tending to a youngish man with a shattered arm, but glanced up as I approached.

"Neve March," he said, surprise evident. "I thought you'd gone back to Winterborne?"

"I had, but I was assigned duty to the commander—"

"He's back? Excellent." He returned his gaze to his patient. "What can I do for you?"

"I'm looking for Treace—have you seen her?"

"She's upstairs, in the recovery ward."

"Thanks." I headed for the exit and climbed up to the next floor. This area was less chaotic than the floor below, but the beds were all filled, and cots had been brought in to cater for the overflow of wounded being tended to. I scanned the room again and spotted Treace's familiar figure heading out the door on the far side.

I made my way through the maze and then hurried after her. "Treace," I said, as she disappeared through another doorway.

Her face reappeared. "Neve," she said, with a smile that only barely lifted the stress so evident in her. "Didn't expect to see you again so soon."

"No." I stopped. "Have you got time to answer a couple of questions?"

"Possibly not, but come along with me while I'm collecting the medicines."

"Thanks." I followed her into the apothecary. "I just wanted to ask about the two children who were found in Tenterra the other day."

"Those poor wee waifs?" She shook her head. "It's criminal what's been done to them."

I crossed my arms and leaned against the wall, watching as she began gathering various herbs, tablets, and other medicinal items into the basket she was carrying. "In what way?"

"They were little more than skin and bones, and the smell that was coming from them—it was a mix of urine and blue cheese, and totally foul." Her nose wrinkled. "The poor souls couldn't have seen water for years. Their reaction certainly seemed to indicate that—they were terrified."

A smile touched my lips. "That's not unusual for kids, is it? Many would rather be grimy than clean any day."

"This was more than the usual reluctance. We ended up having to give them a calmative." She shook her head, sadness in her eyes. "Not that it did them much good. The foul scent seemed entrenched in their skins."

"Were you able to question them?"

"We tried, but the language that came out of their mouths certainly wasn't one I'd ever heard before."

"So you weren't able to find out anything about them? Or why they might have been out in Tenterra?"

"No." She half shrugged. "Miller—one of the nurses here that has some telepathy ability—did a reading on them at the lieutenant's request, but apparently all he got was an incoherent mess."

"Is Miller around?"

The sadness in her expression increased. "He got caught when the main hospital's wall collapsed. I haven't seen him come in, so I don't think he survived."

"Oh, I'm sorry, Treace."

She sniffed and looked away. "He was a good man."

I hesitated, waiting several beats to both honor the dead and to give her time to collect herself, and then said, "I don't suppose he told you anything he saw?"

"A little." She wrinkled her nose. "But it didn't make much sense. He said he saw earth, tunnels, and darkness, and an existence that was little more than pain and suffering. He saw women strapped to beds, and the raw, bloody remnants of perfect little babies. And he saw skeletal hands that were thin, taloned, and lavender colored."

Horror stirred through me. Much of what Miller had seen in the children's minds seemed to echo what I'd so briefly caught in Saska's. Did that mean she was connected to them?

Could they, perhaps, even be *her* children?

They'd been found close to where I'd found Saska, after all, and it wasn't impossible that they'd been with her when she escaped. And yet, if that had been the case, why hadn't I spotted them? And why would she not mention them? Could any memory loss be so complete that she wouldn't feel something terrible had happened, that some vital part of her was missing?

Or was that what she'd been trying to tell me when she'd said many answers would be found if I searched the area in which she'd been discovered?

"Can you describe the two of them to me?"

Treace hesitated. "They were very badly stained—much worse than you are, I'm afraid—but one of them had the looks of an air witch, and the other could have been of the earth. They were both wearing lovely silver bracelets, which was strange given their physical and mental state. I mean, if someone cared enough to gift them something like that, why were they in such a state?"

Why indeed. But it confirmed that at least one of them *could* have been Saska's. Or maybe even Pyra's, given she, too, had given birth before she'd returned to Winterborne. "Were either of them tested for magic?"

Treace raised her eyebrows. "Why would they be? With staining that bad, lass, there's no possibility they could have held magic."

That raised my eyebrows, given Trey's daughter was both stained *and* capable of magic. I'd been under the impression everyone at Blacklake was aware of her abilities, but Trey had obviously been a lot more circumspect than that. Which wasn't really surprising since he'd given up his entire world —everything he'd ever known—to raise her himself.

"Do you know what's happened to them?"

Guilt flashed across her face and she looked away. "Aye.

They snuck out on me; I'm told they were likely killed in the attack."

So she didn't know that they were the reason the attack happened in the first place. Without their destruction of the wall, the Adlin wouldn't have gotten into the outer bailey. I wasn't about to tell her that, though. Not when she was already feeling so responsible. "You can't be blamed for what happened, Treace. No one can. It's just one of those unfortunate sequences of events."

A smile ghosted her lips. "So Mace said."

"Then believe him." I pushed away from the wall. "I'll let you get back to it."

She nodded. "At least it wasn't as bad as it could have been, given the wall fell. I never thought that was even possible. Makes life out here a little bit scarier now."

"I'm sure your witches will ensure it doesn't happen again." Although the truth of the matter was, not even the strongest witch could defend this place—or Winterborne itself—against treachery. We had to find the people—be it the Irkallan or someone else—behind this plot and stop them.

Fast.

"I hope you're right, lass. I really do."

I gave her a smile and left her to it. Once back outside, I paused and looked around. I wanted—needed—to be doing something to help, but this wasn't my home and Trey had given me orders to return to the main hall once I'd finished talking to Treace. After another moment, I reluctantly walked down the steps and headed across the yard toward the main hall. A bit of rubble skittered out from under my foot, and the sight of it had me pausing. It not only looked as if the very fabric of the stone had been stretched to breaking point, but it also had thin strands of metal entwined around it. I picked it up and turned it over in my hand. If the walls here had been built along the same lines as the ones at

Winterborne, then the inner portion would be stone over which the thick sheet of shiny black metal had been wrapped. For this stone to be a weird mix of the two, the very fabric of both had to have been altered. And while I had no doubt the strongest earth witch would be capable of such a deed, it had been two kids behind the destruction here. I could accept the possibility that between them they'd had enough power over the earth to bring down Blacklake's defenses, but surely two kids wouldn't be able to draw so much power that both stone and metal had fused? Especially given most witches, be they air or earth, didn't come into their true power until puberty?

Except, I thought with a chill, that rule didn't hold true for those of us who were stained *and* magic capable. I'd always been able to hear the wind, even if my ability to interact with her hadn't come until puberty. I might not have ever had much control over her, but how much of that was a result of not having anyone to teach me? Or the fact I'd never done the bonding ceremony with either element? Trey had said his daughter had been able to hear the earth from a very young age, and he'd been teaching her as soon as she could walk and talk in order to stop accidental usage that could have revealed her abilities to the wrong persons.

Frowning, I spun around and headed for the gatehouse rather than the main hall. Something about this stone prickled at my instincts, and I wasn't about to ignore it. The drawbridge was still lowered, and though water remained in the inner moat, the gentle current swirling toward the damaged main hospital suggested it was already being drained back to the lake. The soldiers guarding the inner gatehouse gave me a nod of acknowledgment but didn't stop me from entering the outer bailey. Maybe they remembered me from my previous time here, or perhaps they'd been sent word to let me pass unchallenged.

The destruction in the outer bailey looked even worse here at ground level than it had from within the tower. The wall and gatehouse had blown apart in chunks that were as big as some troop carriers, and the remnants of the Adlin and the few soldiers who'd been caught on the walls during the initial explosion and subsequent attack lay scattered everywhere. There was a group of men currently inspecting the gatehouse remains, but instinct had me going right, toward the workhouses, kitchens, and mess hall. I jumped off the drawbridge and walked close to the inner wall's skin, my fingers brushing the cool black metal. At first glance, it seemed the fighting hadn't gotten this far, as there wasn't even blood splatter let alone any sign the wall had been attacked. And yet the ground told a different story; there were a lot of footprints in the mud. Big heavy prints that were Adlin rather than human. They'd run along here, but for what purpose?

The wall swept around to the left, a gentle curve that soon had the gatehouse and the drawbridge out of immediate sight. The muddy footprints continued forward, and a foul smell began to taint the air. Unease prickled across my skin and I slowed. There was no sign of any damage to the wall, and no indication what the Adlin had intended when they'd come this way. The wall remained unbroken, but the gentle curve gave way to an oddly rough-looking section of wall that was a mix of both metal and stone—much the same as stone in my hand. I glanced down; in the glow of light coming over the top of the inner wall, it looked vaguely washed out—as if the explosion had not only not stretched its matter to breaking point, but also drained all color.

Not color, a voice whispered. *But power. Energy.*

That voice didn't belong to the wind: it hadn't come from the air, but rather from the ground. It vibrated across my flesh before finding its way into my thoughts. The earth—or rather, the collective consciousness of all those who now lived within it—had finally decided to speak to me.

I looked back at the odd section of wall. Just like the stone in my hand, it, too, seemed colorless.

I frowned and walked closer. The muddy ground under my boots grew heated, and with it came a sense of anger and defilement. Whatever was going on, the earth wasn't happy about it.

I stopped in front of the odd section stone and splayed the fingers of my free hand against it. There was a weird chill to the metal and stone mix, and its surface was very definitely rougher than the section it met at a very slight angle. I shifted my fingers to that portion of the wall. The metal was also cool, but the earth's anger vibrated through it, giving it life and a pulse. I returned my hand to the rougher section. No heartbeat, just a strange deadness.

I stepped back and glanced up. The roughness continued right to the very top of the wall, but I couldn't see anyone or anything up there—which wasn't surprising given most of Blacklake's watch would be concentrating all efforts on protecting the breached area from the possibility of another Adlin attack.

I followed the rough wall to the point where it met the main curtain wall. The join here was again messy—it was almost as if it had been done in a rush.

Had the inner wall been breached at some point in the distant past? Technology these days made patching any defects or imperfections easy, but maybe that hadn't always been the case, at least out here in the outposts. Or maybe they'd believed the main wall was strong enough to repel anything the Adlin might throw at it, so they simply hadn't bothered repairing small imperfections on the inner wall.

I brushed my fingers along the join between the two walls and frowned. There were more than a few gaps between the two, and while they might not be any wider than my little finger, that was enough for an Adlin to wedge a claw in and perhaps gain a means to either climb the wall or even tear it open.

I shifted and pressed an eye against one of the wider gaps. There seemed to be movement in the darkness beyond this section of the wall, and it was accompanied by a soft thrumming sound. It was coming from the earth and was almost a strangled sound of protest—as if the power and the voices that resided within her didn't want to be doing whatever task they were being set to do.

But it was the air that slid through the tiny gap between the walls—air that was ripe with the scent of unwashed flesh, urine, and blue cheese—that gave me the answer as to what was happening in that darkness. It was the scent of the children. They weren't dead. They were here, doing freedom only knew what.

I stepped back and sucked in a deep breath to try and wash the foul scent from my lungs. And though that sound wasn't very loud, all movement stopped in the darkness beyond the wall. The silence that followed was full of fear, anticipation, and awareness.

I didn't move. I barely even dared to breathe. I had no idea what was going on beyond this rough wall, or who else might be in there with the two children, but given the footprints, I certainly had suspicions—even if they made little sense. If there was one truth that had been indisputable up until now, it was the fact Adlin would never work alongside humans, be they adult or child. We were prey, a food source, *not* their allies.

After several more minutes, the noise resumed, and the beat of energy became quicker, harder, than before. I knelt and placed a hand against the earth. While I might have undergone the ceremony of Gaia with Trey, he hadn't actually mentioned how I was supposed to use that power or even how to contact the voices within the earth. And while they might now have spoken to me, I needed more than that. I needed to *see*.

I closed my eyes and reached down to that part of me that had ever so briefly become one with the energy of the earth. She stirred within me, a pulse that was reluctant at first, but one that gradually grew until it matched the cadence coming from the earth under my fingertips.

Shapes twisted in the shadows behind my eyes. Shapes that were large and hairy, armed with sharp claws and wicked teeth. Not just one or two, but what looked to be a full sleuth. In front of them, standing with one hand against the wall, was a tall, dark-haired boy. On either side of him, each with one thin, lavender-gray hand wrapped around his arm and their bodies shaking and sweating, was a pale-haired girl and a dark-haired boy.

Three children, not two.

The original two had obviously survived the ferocity of the blast that had brought down the wall, but the third must have come in with the Adlin. And now they were all behind this wall, trying to get into the inner bailey. Because of the bracelet. Because whoever lay behind this scheme was so keen to get it back that they'd risk not only exposing the fact that they were working alongside the Adlin, but also risk the lives of at least four of their major weapons—because what else could Hedra and these three children be?

The images shifted abruptly, centering instead on the almost skeletal hand on which a silver bracelet gleamed. His fingers were pressed hard against a wall that had lost its black shine, and there was a three-foot radius of lifelessness around his hand. But even as I watched, it began to creep both up and down the wall.

They weren't trying to blow this wall. They were creating

a doorway—one big enough to fit the Adlin through. And with the entire outpost concentrating on damage done to the gatehouse and defending the breached wall, they could cause untold destruction before Blacklake was able to marshal its forces and fight back.

The screaming protest of earth, stone, and metal was growing stronger, a sound that suggested they were very close to achieving a break through.

I rose, then turned and raced back to the drawbridge. "Has communications been restored? Are you able to contact the command center?"

The nearest guard frowned. "No—comms and the earwig system remain down. We're using runners—why?"

"Because the Adlin haven't left. They're still here, and about to break through the inner wall. We need to inform the commander immediately."

"I can't believe—"

"Believe it," I growled. "And just do as I'm asking—now!"

"Nightwatch March, that's impossible—"

So, he did know who I was. "So was them having the capacity to blow up the outer gatehouse and wall, and yet here we are, with both of them down."

"Yes, but—"

"Trust me, and go. *Now*," I added, when he hesitated. "Commander Stone's anger at leaving your post will be nothing compared to the wrath that will fall on you for *not* doing as I ask in this circumstance."

"There's nothing stopping you—"

"Can you talk to the earth?" I bit back. "Convince it to heal the wound in the wall rather than break it? No? Then do as I say."

He glanced at his fellow guard, then gave me a short nod and departed. I looked at the other man, but he held up his hand. "There will be hell to pay if we both left our post, especially if the Adlin are here."

Which was a fair enough point. There might be no indication of other sleuths in the area, but that didn't mean they couldn't be nearby, readying a secondary attack. Someone had to be ready to raise the drawbridge and lock everything down should that happen.

Which meant it was up to me alone to delay the Adlin—at least until Trey and his people got there. Urgency pulsed as fiercely as my heartbeat as I ran through the gatehouse and up the nearest set of steps that led to the top of the wall, but it was the earth's as much as mine. They were so very close to breaking through.

I unslung the rifle as I ran down the wall walk, making little noise thanks to the rubber matting that covered the walkway to prevent slipping during rain. As I neared the junction of the true wall and the false one, I slowed. The air stirred around me, bringing with it not only that foul stench again, but also a warning.

They knew I was there.

I stopped and leaned over the parapet. In the V-shaped space between the original outer wall and the recently raised false one over two dozen figures milled. I couldn't actually see the children, because several Adlin were now leaning over the top of them, using their bodies to protect them. But the frantic pulse rising up through the stone and metal suggested they were still trying to breach the wall.

I raised the rifle, sighted, and then fired.

Several Adlin went down, their brains spattering across the faces of the others. The others roared in fury and several attempted to climb the rough wall. But even a wall devoid of life and energy seemed resistant to the power of their claws, and they fell back before they got very far. I kept firing, picking them off one by one.

Within seconds, there were at least a dozen dead, but the frantic pulse of the earth had now shifted to the dead wall, and it was breaking down, reforming into a wave of stone and metal that quickly arched over the space to give them a rough umbrella. I cursed, heard a separate rumble in the earth, and spun around. Trey and a half dozen others were running toward me.

"The children have formed a false roof to protect the Adlin and themselves," I said. "You need to get back downstairs and brace the other side of the wall—they're almost through it."

He and his people immediately turned and headed back down the stairs. I made to follow him, but the air spun around me, urging me closer to the outer wall.

I frowned but obeyed. The wall still pulsed under my feet, but I could no longer hear the screaming of the earth. I stopped at the junction where the outer and inner walls met, and peered down. The newly created roof didn't quite meet either wall at this section and the Adlin were visible far below. A soft glint caught my eye; after a moment, I realized what it was. Silver. Not from any sort of weapon, but rather a bracelet. Only this bracelet wasn't on the children, but rather one of the Adlin. An Adlin who bore coloring unlike any I'd ever seen before. Large sections of his brown fur had been replaced by patches of lavender gray; he was stained. Just like those children. Just like me.

Despite my desperation to believe the Irkallan weren't behind all this, the proof of it was standing directly below me.

And while Saska might have been certain that her much-feared queen hadn't enslaved and impregnated the Adlin and was simply using them, there obviously *had* been some cross breeding happening.

The Adlin chose that moment to look up, and another

chill went through me. Not because his eyes were as lavender as the patches on his fur and filled with an intelligence and awareness that was as rare in the Adlin as his coloring, but because his eyes were *human.*

Either the Adlin were evolving into a more human form, or they'd not only interbred with the Irkallan during the war, but also with humans.

That was a nightmare I didn't even *want* to contemplate.

He roared, revealing teeth that were long, white, and every bit as deadly looking as that of a regular Adlin. It was a sound of defiance, and yet one that held the edge of command. As the sound echoed harshly across the silence, the remaining Adlin moved as a mass, flowing from the edge of the inner wall across to the outer one. The throbbing under my feet instantly muted, but the scream of the earth intensified.

The children, the air whispered. *They attack the outer wall.*

Which suggested the queen had given up her quest for the other bracelet and was now intent on escape. I ran across to the outer edge, peering down until I spotted Trey and two of his people. A brown-haired man stood on his left, and a woman with dark hair stood on his right. All three had their hands splayed across the wall, but Trey's hands overlapped those of the other two.

The rest of his soldiers stood in a semicircle several paces farther back from the wall, their weapons held in readiness.

They combine strength to repair, the earth whispered. *They will not hear you.*

Combining strength... *that's* what had been happening with the children. The one capable of earth magic had been using the strength of the other two to help punch a door through the wall.

And while it might be true that Trey wouldn't hear me, the soldiers below still needed to be warned what was going on. We couldn't let those kids be taken away—they were too damn dangerous, for a start, but we also needed to probe them more fully, to understand what had been done to them and perhaps even get some idea as to who was behind this whole stinking mess.

"Hey," I shouted down, "the Adlin are now trying to break out through the curtain wall."

A pale-skinned woman glanced up. I didn't recognize her, but she was wearing the colors of a sergeant. "At what point?"

"Twenty feet before the place where the two walls meet."

She immediately spoke to one of her counterparts, then as he raced toward the smaller command center, she and the remaining soldiers ran for the drawbridge. I bent and forced my fingers through the rubber matting until I touched the metal. While I had no doubt there were easier ways to contact the earth, this had worked last time. I reached down to that inner part of me again, and said, *Trey and the other earth witches need to know what is happening while they work to repair the wall. Can you please warn them?*

As the earth agreed to do so, I thrust up and ran across to the main wall, stopping just above the point where the Adlin were clustered. I reloaded the rifle and aimed for the small gap between the false roof and the wall, and then fired everything the gun had. Sparks and metal flew as the pellets caught the edges of the wall, but a lot made it through. Three Adlin went down. The rest gathered up the bodies of the fallen and held them overhead, using them as shields. I swore softly. It was an effective ploy, because even if I reloaded, I'd only be shooting the already dead.

The klaxon sound of a siren began to ring out and, as I looked up, a full squad of soldiers raced toward the broken section of wall. They were fully kitted up, but even so, there were at least seven Adlin still alive down there. It would be a close battle, even with a full squad.

The earth's screaming reached a fever pitch, the sound so loud and agonized it hurt my ears. As the wall began to vibrate and the metal under my feet grew hotter and hotter, I realized I only had minutes, if not seconds, to get off the damn wall.

I turned and ran.

The vibrations abruptly ceased and, just for a minute, I thought we were safe, that the children's strength had finally failed them.

Then a whole damn section of the wall exploded upward, taking me with it.

9

I flew high, surrounded by shards of metal and stone that sliced through my flesh as easily as they sliced through the air. My uniform was shredded in seconds and my skin became slick with blood. I rose skyward for so long it seemed as if I'd reach the stars, but gravity soon reasserted itself, sending me hurtling back to the ground. It was a long, long way down, and there'd be little more than a red stain and a few flattened remnants of flesh and bone to scrape up if I hit it at this speed.

I closed my eyes and reached for the wind. She answered immediately, her cold fingers battering away the stones and metal that continued to rain around me even as she provided a cushion of thicker air to impede the speed of my fall. I hit feet first and hard enough to rattle my teeth, then staggered forward and fell with a grunt to my knees. For several minutes, I couldn't do anything more than suck air into my burning lungs as I tried to ignore the pain reverberating through my body. Thankfully, the wind still battered away the wall remnants; they rained all around me, many of them hitting so hard the ground shook under the impact. But it wasn't the falling pieces of stone and metal that provided the biggest danger right now; it was the Adlin.

Because with the wall smashed open, they were free of Blacklake and on the run.

I couldn't see them, but I could feel them. Could follow their progress through the impact of their steps on the earth.

Some were running away.

Some were coming straight at me.

And my rifle was who knew where; I'd lost grip of it when the wall had exploded. Which meant I was about to see if the sword was as good as the knife when it came to the flesh of the Adlin.

I pushed upright. Sharp shards of stone dug into my foot; I winced and looked down. My left boot was missing. And while it was inconvenient, it wasn't as deadly as the loss of the rifle might yet prove to be.

I drew the sword from its scabbard across my back. The thick glass blade gleamed in the pre-dawn darkness, but it looked wholly inadequate against the three Adlin racing toward me.

I glanced around, looking for a more suitable place to make a stand. Although the immediate area was littered with huge chunks of stone and large sheets of metal, none of them were of much use when it came to cover. Not when I had to have the room to swing a sword. Now, if they'd formed a rough semicircle, it would have at least curtailed their attack options....

The thought had barely crossed my mind when the ground heaved and the big chunks of stone began to roll, gently at first but with increasing speed, into a half circle formation. The earth had heard me. It seemed that a direct connection, be it hands *or* feet, was the answer when it came to summoning her power—for me at least, anyway.

As the Adlin's battle cry reverberated across the night, I

spun and ran into the newly created circle. The space between the two curved ends was small enough that only one Adlin could run through at a time. It gave me time to react and kill; whether or not it would make a difference was something I'd learn in little more than a few minutes.

Because in truth, by restricting their avenues of attack, I was also restricting my escape options.

I gripped the sword tightly with both hands and waited. In the distance, through the opening in the stones, I could see the fleeing Adlin. The stained one was carrying three small bundles under his arms, and was pulling away from the other Adlin. He was protecting the children—saving them—at the possible cost of his companions.

That *wasn't* Adlin behavior. They hunted and fought as one, no matter what their numbers. I'd never heard of any Adlin providing a rearguard service to ensure one of their number got away. But that one Adlin was under the control of whoever was behind this madness, and *he* held sway over the Adlin as a whole. Unusual or not, it was obvious they would obey their leader no matter what.

The battle cry of the Adlin bit through the air. I swung my attention back to them and took a deep, steadying breath.

I could do this.

I *would* do this.

The first Adlin launched himself through the gap and slashed wildly with his claws. I sidestepped quickly and swung the blade. Its sharp tip sliced across the creature's torso, opening him up from underarm to hip. As his blood sprayed through the air, he hit the ground, rolled back to his feet, and came at me again. At the same damn time, another Adlin came through the opening. I swung the blade at the first one, forcing him to twist in midair and fall away to avoid having his head chopped off, then grabbed a fistful of air and threw it at the other. As he was punched backward, knocking the third Adlin off its feet, I ran at the first, raised the sword high above my head, and chopped it down. The Adlin twisted away, but he wasn't fast enough. The blade hit his skull, slicing through bone and brain as easily as butter, and swept down, cleaving him from head to stomach before the momentum of his desperate leap had his body falling away from the blade's touch. A roar of sheer fury had me instinctively ducking. The claws that would have taken my head off instead sailed over the top of it. I swung the sword again; the side of the blade hit the Adlin's arm and cut it clean away. Blood spurted across my face, momentarily blinding me, and the wind screamed. I threw myself sideways, hitting the ground so hard that the air was forced from my lungs. I gasped, struggling to breathe, struggling to see, and all too aware that death in the form of an Adlin's claw would be my fate if I didn't damn well *move*. I twisted around. Saw, through the blood and gore matting my eyelashes, an Adlin high in the air above me. Its companion was running through the gap and had death in his eyes. I tried to get up, to scramble away, but my strength, it seemed, had fled me just when I needed it the most.

Death might be damnably close, but it didn't have its claws in me yet, and there was no way known I'd go down without fighting to my very last breath.

I again called on the air and flung it at the running Adlin. Pain tore through my head, making my eyes water and momentarily blurring my vision. Which was probably a good thing because it meant I couldn't see the face of the Adlin above me. But I could feel its fury and sense of triumph.

I raised the sword.

The Adlin saw it and twisted in midair, trying to avoid it. At the same time, a gunshot rang out. The Adlin's head exploded even as the sword skewered him. His remains thumped down on me, forcing the air from my lungs a second time. This time, the pain was a blanket that all but smothered me. Darkness closed in and I knew no more.

I woke to the itch of wool against my skin and the brightness of sunshine flooding the room. For a minute, confusion stirred, but I'd barely opened my eyes when Trey stepped into view.

"How are you feeling?" He pulled a chair up beside the bed and sat down. His warm, rich scent teased my senses, filling every breath and stirring to life a fierce awareness.

I did my best to ignore it and lifted the blanket instead. It appeared I'd escaped both the explosion and the Adlin with little more than a smattering of bruises and a few healing cuts. "I'm good, considering I should probably be dead."

"Mace thinks you've charmed the gods, because there's no other possible explanation for you surviving two Adlin attacks *and* a wall being blasted out from underneath you." He reached over to the small table sitting against the wall and picked up the glass oft murky-looking liquid. "He also said you have to drink all of this."

I pushed up into a sitting position. The various muscle groups twinged in protest, but all in all, I'd come out of the whole thing better than I should have. I accepted the glass Trey offered, but the slight brush of his fingertips against mine had delight skipping through me. That weird hypersensitivity seemed to be back, and yet it lacked the overwhelming power of before. Was that because I'd gone through the ceremony of Gaia with Trey? Or was something else happening this time?

I frowned and sipped the drink; it was warm rather than cold, and tasted faintly of lemon, ginger, and an earthy but slightly bitter dash of ginseng. "I take it this is one of his potions?"

"It's just a few herbs to boost your immunity and strength." He scanned me briefly. While there was absolutely nothing immediately sexual in that look, desire stirred through me and found an echo in his eyes. "Blacklake might have suffered greater losses if not for you. We owe you, Neve March. *I* owe you."

I wrinkled my nose. "Hardly, given I was only doing my job. What happened to the Adlin and the children?"

"The one carrying the children escaped, but we tracked down and killed the rest."

Because the rest had been sacrificed to save their leader and the children. "And the wall?"

"Is already under repair. We've called in the earth witches from both Farsprings and West Range to help with the rebuild."

I frowned again. "Why not just call in witches from Winterborne?"

"Because the masque celebrations can't be interrupted for anything less than an attack—"

"Which is exactly what has happened—"

"Yes, but it went no further than the outer bailey in either Winterborne or here, and therefore it gives them no reason to pause or stop." A bitter edge touched his smile. "They'll never allow the day-to-day trials of the rest of us to interfere with the machinations and alliances the masque and equinox celebrations bring."

"The rest of us?" I raised an eyebrow. "You, my dear commander, are one of them."

"Just because I was born one of them doesn't mean I remain so. Not in spirit or in heart, anyway, and that's all that counts these days." He leaned forward and caught my hand in his. His fingers were warm, and filled with a strength

I found oddly arresting, even in my hyperaware state. "My daughter was wearing that bracelet, Neve. If you hadn't caught on to what the Adlin were up to—"

He stopped, but I saw the fear flash through his eyes. "Why wasn't she in the raid shelter with everyone else?"

A wry smile tugged at his lips. "She had been, but she came out with Leon, our earth witch, when I called for his help with the wall."

So the woman who'd stood on his right while he'd battled to preserve the integrity of the wall hadn't been just another earth witch, but rather his daughter. The long sleeves she'd been wearing had obviously hidden the bracelet.

"Were you drawing on their strength to reinforce the wall, or was it more a combining?"

"The latter. I doubt the former is even possible."

"Oh, it is, because that's what was happening with the three children."

He frowned. "Three?"

I nodded. "The other child must have come in with the Adlin. The small girl with the air witch coloring and the other boy were gripping the older lad; neither of them were touching the wall, so he had to have been drawing on their strength."

Trey sat back, and in doing so broke the connection of our fingers. And yet the heat of his touch remained, a beat of warmth that seemed to flow sweetly through my body.

"It still doesn't explain how two small children could not only draw and control enough power to blast open the curtain wall, but do so without going insane. They couldn't have undergone committal ceremonies, not at that age."

"I suspect whoever is behind this plot really wouldn't care whether his or her weapons were sane or not. And we stained don't appear to need the ceremony to be able to use either magic, remember." I paused and flexed my fingers, trying to keep my mind on the matter at hand rather than the man who was so close and yet so far away. "When your men were chasing the Adlin, did they notice anything unusual?"

"No." He leaned forward again, but didn't touch me. I wasn't sure whether to be grateful or frustrated. "Why?"

"Because one of them was not only stained but wearing the same sort of silver bracelet as the children and the three women in Winterborne."

"Stained?" He stared at me for several seconds, horror slowly growing on his face. "How is that even possible? As far as I know—and as far as any history books are concerned —the Adlin fed on the flesh of the dead but were never involved in the war itself. From everything I've read, the Irkallan basically left them alone."

"Him being stained is not even the worst of it." I paused, shuddering as the image of the Adlin's face rose like a ghost to taunt me. "He had human eyes."

"Impossible."

"No."

He swore and thrust a hand through his short hair. "That's not the news we needed right now. Not when there're also traitors in our ranks to contend with."

"Two of those traitors are now dead, and Saska's at least fighting the control of the queen." I hesitated. "We can't really ignore the possibility that the Irkallan are behind all this. Not now."

"No." He scrapped a hand across his jaw, the sound like sandpaper. "But if they *are*, then the two half-assed attempts to regain the bracelets makes even less sense."

"Half-assed?" I raised my eyebrows. "You can hardly call the destruction of Winterborne's gate mechanics and the walls here half-assed. They came damn close to causing untold damage."

"Yes, and that's what has me worried. They could have

pushed their advantage, and they didn't. They'd caught us unawares and did nothing with it. Whatever else history might have said about the Adlin *and* the Irkallan, it is fact that they always pushed an advantage."

"Yes, but it's not the Adlin behind this plot. Saska's queen is controlling them through their leader." I hesitated. "In truth, it's probably the offspring of the witches who are our greatest threat right now. If the three who attacked this place are any indication, they're capable of great magic."

It would also, I realized suddenly, explain Saska's comment about her captors killing her three perfect little girls. They weren't *after* perfection; they wanted the stained, and the greater the staining, the better, because it appeared to indicate a stronger capacity for unrestrained power.

So where did that leave me? Half my body was stained, and yet I didn't appear to be capable of the same sort of power those three kids had called forth.

"They undoubtedly are the greater threat," Trey said, "but given we've never been able to find the women who remain missing, tracking their offspring will be nothing short of impossible. Besides, neither Pyra nor Hedra even remembered having children."

Which was decidedly odd given Saska could. "Has Kiro sent any word about what's happening at Winterborne?"

"Nothing more than the fact that the masque continues unheeded, and that Saska seems to have become more unstable since your departure. He's got her under close guard at the moment—and he's called in reinforcements from the Nightwatch to do so."

"Really? Who?"

"I believe one of them is a friend and bunkmate of yours—"

"Ava?" I couldn't help my delighted grin. At least she'd

finally be able to see and experience life the Upper Reaches, even if only from a distance.

"Yes. He doesn't trust that the Reaches guards have not been coerced or infiltrated, so put in a request for ten Nightwatch officers to guard major points." He hesitated. "I believe he put in a specific request for two of your bunkmates because of your trust in them, but one is in hospital recovering from wounds received in the attack."

My heart jumped into my throat. "How bad are the wounds?"

"Kiro didn't say. I didn't get the impression they were life-threatening, though."

Relief spun through me. Not life-threatening could have meant anything, but at least he wasn't dead. Then the rest of Trey's statement impacted me. "If Kiro is aware of how close I am to both Ava and April, he's read me more thoroughly than I'd hoped."

"But not as thoroughly as he would have liked."

I frowned. "Surely he can't still believe I'm holding secrets that are dangerous to Winterborne? Not after everything that has happened."

"No." Trey paused. "But he does believe you're the key to unlocking what's happening."

I snorted. "A stained Nightwatch officer with uncertain, untrained abilities and who-knows-what parentage is highly unlikely to be the key to anything, Commander."

"And yet Kiro believes otherwise." He hesitated again. "And be warned, he's currently investigating your parentage."

"How is that likely to be of any help?"

Trey shrugged. "He didn't say. But he is definitely a man who'll leave no stone unturned in his quest for answers."

"Do you think he'll tell me if he does uncover my parents?"

"Would you want to know if he did?"

"I don't know." I frowned. "I mean, they cast me aside like so much rubbish. I shouldn't care—and I don't—but I guess there *is* a part of me curious as to who they might be."

"Which is only natural."

"Perhaps, but such curiosity isn't likely to end well. Not for me, anyway." Of course, it was doubtful he'd actually be able to uncover any information. It wasn't like the birth records of the stained were overly detailed—mine had nothing more than the date of my birth and the name I'd been given on being handed into state care. "But I'm glad the Nightwatch has joined us. I'll feel less alone and out of place."

Trey raised his eyebrows. "So my company has not been pleasing to you?"

"That is not what I meant, and you know it." I waved a hand. "For all your talk about the Upper Reaches no longer being a part of you, you were raised in that place and are comfortable there. I was not, and it was only the fact that I wasn't there for pleasure that stopped me running back to where I belonged."

"I know." It was so softly said that I barely heard it. "But I, for one, am glad you didn't give in to that particular desire."

His words had that odd, earthy energy surging to life between us again. It was both powerful and sexual, and far more than mere attraction. It ran over me in a wave and made me burn. But again, it wasn't just desire; it was deeper than that, stronger than that.

Something flickered in his eyes, something that set my soul racing, but it was just as quickly shut down. He thrust up from the chair and walked across to the window, staring out for several minutes without comment.

Leaving me to wonder if I'd imagined that flicker.

"Kiro wants us back tonight," he said eventually. His voice was cool and collected. "Are you feeling up to it?"

"I'm feeling up to many things." I frowned at his back and

wondered why he'd retreated. What was he trying to keep from me? "Up to and including traveling."

"Good." If he heard the half invitation in my voice, he gave no sign of it. "Mace will be here in a few minutes to give you a final check. If all is well, we will leave at one."

Which was little more than three hours from now, according to the ornate clock on the wall…. I blinked and suddenly looked more closely at my surroundings. Between the tapestry wall coverings and the richly covered furniture, it was very obvious I wasn't in the hospital.

"Have I been placed in the guest apartments?" I said, surprised.

"No. My personal quarters."

"What?" My gaze shot back to him, but he was still staring out the window. "Why?"

"Because it was easier; the secondary hospital had run out of room for beds."

"So why aren't I in the bunkhouse?"

"Until the wall is fully restored, no personnel will be staying there. All those not on duty are bunking down in the state apartments." Though I couldn't see his smile, I heard it in his voice. "It's an understatement to say they're quite enjoying the experience."

"I can imagine, but it still doesn't explain why I'm not with them."

"There are well over one hundred and fifty people off duty at any one time, and only five state apartments." He turned and sat on the edge of the sill. "Luxurious or not, the place is rather crowded."

"A perfectly legitimate and sensible answer, but I rather suspect there's something you're not telling me."

A smile ghosted his lips. "It's nothing important."

"I also suspect you lie, Commander."

"Trey, at least when we're alone. And perhaps I should

have said, it's nothing that needs to be discussed immediately."

I frowned. "Has it got anything to do with the ceremony? Kiro said it was dangerous—"

"Any ceremony involving such deep and powerful forces contains danger for its participants," he cut in. "Especially for those not specifically trained to guide such inductions."

"Meaning the ceremony has caused you a problem?"

He hesitated. "I wouldn't call it a problem. More an interesting development."

"A statement that really doesn't clarify anything."

"True, but this is neither the time nor place for such revelations." He half shrugged. "I need to get back to work. Mari will be here with a meal very soon, and I'll see you in a couple of hours. Until then, rest."

As if I could rest knowing that in saving me, something untoward had happened to him. I frowned at his departing back, but if he was aware of my glare, he didn't show it.

I climbed out of bed and padded barefoot over to the window. He appeared a few seconds later and strode across the inner bailey's yard to the smaller command center. He really was something of an enigma, and one I found rather fascinating. Not that *that* was hard—who wouldn't be fascinated by a strong, good-looking man who'd walked away from everything he'd known to care for a daughter he'd held for only a few seconds? A man who'd worked his way through the ranks like everyone else, who'd gained the trust and respect of everyone he worked with, but who nevertheless seemed to guard his feelings and his thoughts fiercely, only occasionally giving them free rein when it came to his daughter. I'd spent a lot of time in his company over the last few days, and yet I still knew so little about him. He was attracted to me, that much was obvious, but he was also fighting it, and not just for the sake of the mission. There was something deeper at play here, something that was perhaps even dangerous.

What that something was, I had no idea. And if the air and the earth knew, they remained mute.

Once he'd disappeared into the tower, I retreated back to bed. But that odd restlessness had returned. While it was nowhere near as strong, it was still bad enough that I couldn't lie down for long. The sheets were simply too scratchy against my skin. I paced the confines of the room instead, feeling like a caged animal—one whose skin was jumping, burning with pleasure and rising desire. It was so strong I was sure that if I got back into bed and closed my eyes, it would have felt as if I was actually *having* sex. And yet, at the same time, there was a distance to the sensations—as if it were happening to someone else and simply flowing across to me.

I swore softly, spun around on one heel, and headed into the bathroom. Unfortunately, the cold water did little to ease the growing rapture. I pressed my hands against the wall, needing its support as my breathing hitched, my body shook, and pleasure swept through me. And it was a very weird thing to be experiencing a climax and then fall into its peaceful aftermath without having to lift a hand.

I took a deep breath and released it slowly. The cold water continued to beat down on my skin, and it swept away the last vestiges of passion. While I had no idea what might lie behind the strange—if pleasurable—experience, I very much doubted it had anything to do with the wind or the fact I'd not undergone the ceremony to bind myself to the collective consciousness of all those within her. Binding might involve sex, but I gathered it also needed the guiding hand of a priestess or at least someone of great power, thanks to dangers involved. Besides, it wasn't as if I'd heard the voice of the wind during the strange ordeal. In fact, she'd been remarkably quiet since I'd woken.

The sound of a door opening had me pushing away from the wall. I switched off the water and grabbed a towel, wrapping it around my body as I walked out.

The woman who entered was tall and slender, with dark hair, a suntanned face with a smattering of freckles across her nose and her cheeks, and green eyes that were bright and mischievous. She was carrying a tray of food, and I couldn't help but notice one hand was as stained as my own.

This couldn't be anyone else but Eluria, Trey's seventeen-year-old daughter. And she *wasn't* wearing the bracelet.

"Wasn't Mari supposed to bring that tray in?" I asked with a slight smile.

"Indeed, but I saw an opportunity and decided to take it." She placed the tray on the small side table then studied me critically, her gaze lingering on the visible portions of my stained flesh. "I haven't met another stained person before. I was curious."

"About what?" I sat on the edge of the bed and pulled the table closer.

She shrugged. "About what your life has been like and how the staining has affected it. And about Winterborne, and what it is like to live there."

"So you know who I am?"

"The whole outpost knows who you are, especially after you saved our butts last night."

Meaning Trey hadn't said anything about me to her. But then, why would he? I smiled and patted the bed beside me. "Well, answering such questions could take a while. You'd best sit."

She grinned and did. I ate my meal, talked about my life and Winterborne, and answered her questions honestly. She then recounted her life here at Blacklake and it was obvious she adored her father and loved living here. It also became obvious she was very much his opposite in that she was open and easygoing, and yet I could see so much of him in her inner strength and determination.

We continued to talk and the hours passed too quickly. As the clock struck twelve, she gasped and thrust to her feet. "If I don't move I'm going to be late for training."

"Training?"

She nodded and grinned. "Weaponry and defense practices before lunch, history after it."

"You actually *like* history?"

"Well, no, but Dad says that the lessons of the past should never be forgotten."

"Your dad is a wise man."

"He is. Most of the time, anyway." She grinned. "Will you come back and visit me sometime? I've really enjoyed talking to someone who's stained like me."

"If I can get time off from my duties, and with your father's permission, of course I will."

"Good. And don't worry about Dad—he won't say no. He's not as fierce and as ungiving as he makes out."

"Only, I suspect, when it comes to you."

"You could be right." With a bright, cheerful laugh, she waved goodbye and all but bounced out of the room.

Leaving me to silence and some rather unsettling wisps of envy.

I pushed the tray table back to the wall and idly wondered how long it would take me to get used to the solitude of being Nightwatch again. As harrowing and as dangerous as the last few days had been, they'd also shown me another side of life. I might have felt ill at ease and out of place for the most part, but there'd still been many bright moments of enjoyment.

And it wasn't as if the experience had ended. I still had a

couple of nights to enjoy, and it really didn't matter if I'd be spending most of that time helping to track down those connected with the plot. Two days was certainly enough time to store up some pleasant memories for the years ahead.

A sharp knock at the door interrupted my reverie, but before I could say anything, the door opened and Mace appeared.

"Ah good, you're awake." His gaze scanned me critically but unlike before, when Trey had done the very same thing, there was little in the way of internal reaction. "How are you feeling?"

"Absolutely perfect, thank you."

He smiled. "You should be dead, you know that don't you?"

"Luck does seem to be favoring me right now."

"If that isn't the understatement of the year, I don't know what is."

He motioned me to remove the towel and lie down. Once I had, he placed one hand on my forehead and another on my chest, just above my heart, and closed his eyes. Warmth radiated from the epicenter of his touch in gentle waves, but again, there was nothing sexual about it. It was, in fact, weirdly impersonal.

After a few minutes of silence, he pulled his hands away. "You, young lady, are amazingly resilient."

"Meaning I pass the physical?"

"Very much so." He flicked the towel back over my torso. "Although I highly recommend you avoid another encounter with the Adlin if you can. It might be a case of third time unlucky."

I snorted. "I'm Nightwatch. It's not like I have much choice about who I do and don't fight."

"Under normal circumstances that might be true, but it

seems to me you've gone out of your way to cross their path of late."

"It wasn't by choice, trust me." I hesitated. "Did you do a similar hands-on physical with the two children when they were here?"

"Yes—why?"

"Was there anything unusual about either of them?"

He frowned. "Not really—again, why?"

I hesitated. "I saw an Adlin with human eyes, and I just wondered, given these children didn't—according to Treace —appear to speak or even understand us, whether they might somehow have been related."

"An Adlin with human eyes? Surely you're mistaken—it was dark, after all."

"Maybe." I wasn't, but I didn't want to start any untoward rumors either. Kiro was keeping the problems at Winterborne close to his chest, so I imagined he wouldn't appreciate me letting the cat out of the proverbial bag, even out here in an outpost. "So there was nothing unusual about the two kids?"

He hesitated. "Their skin reminded me a little of the exoskeletons I've seen on some insects, but I have no doubt it was probably a result of both their severe aversion to water and malnutrition."

"Could there be any other reason?"

He wrinkled his nose. "There are some known diseases— like scleroderma—that causes a thickening of the skin, but I could find no trace of such in either of the children."

Which meant we'd hit another dead end—and that was damn frustrating. "Treace also mentioned a smell—did you notice that?"

He half smiled. "Even those with the dimmest olfactory senses couldn't fail to notice it. It was so entrenched that I fear it might be a part of their physiology."

"Have you ever come across anything like that before?"

"No." He paused. "But I have to admit, your questions have piqued my curiosity. I'll check the medical library and consult with some of my fellows in Winterborne. They might provide some clarity."

"Could you let me know if you do uncover anything?"

"I will. In the meantime, you'd best get dressed. The commander will be waiting downstairs for you at one." He glanced at his watch. "You have half an hour."

"I'll be there."

He nodded and left.

Silence, I thought, as it closed in around me again, sucked.

I thrust to my feet, found my clothes—which once again consisted of a new Blacklake uniform rather than my own—and got dressed. Once I'd reclaimed my knife and my sword, I headed downstairs to wait for Trey. Watching the noise and motion of daily life here in Blacklake was far better than the solitude of my room.

Especially when that room was one of Trey's rather than a more impersonal hospital or bunkhouse.

I walked across to the waiting speeder. The door was open, and the engine was already primed and ready to go. A nearby guard gave me a nod in greeting then spun around and walked away. I sat on the step-up and waited.

Trey must have seen me, because a few minutes later, he came out of the tower and strode toward me. I rose. "Commander, do you mind if we make a slight detour on the way back to Winterborne?"

He raised his eyebrows. "No, but why?"

"Because I want to reexamine the area where I found Saska."

"There's nothing there." He tossed a small pack into the speeder and then offered me his hand. "We've already checked it out."

I placed my hand in his and allowed him to help me into the speeder. His fingers held mine just a shade longer than was necessary, but this time, only a tiny flicker of that odd energy stirred. Perhaps it had been tightly leashed—at least on his side. It wasn't like I had any great control over it—or anything, really. "Saska told me answers could be found there if we look in the right places. I don't want to chance ignoring it."

"She's part of this plot. She might just be sending you on into another trap."

"I don't think so." I slid into the driver seat. "I actually think she's doing her best to help us."

He climbed in behind me then pressed the door-close button. "I'll have to trust your instincts on this one, because Kiro's certainly not getting much out of her."

"Maybe his sort of talent just doesn't work on an unstable mind."

I punched in the coordinates and then carefully guided the speeder through the inner gatehouse and across to the remnants of the main one. Even though a little less than ten hours had passed since the attack, the outer wall was already half rebuilt. But it would be days before the outpost was fully secure again. Trey obviously put a lot of trust in his people—there could be no other reason for leaving now. Not when he was also leaving his daughter in their care—although I rather suspected Eluria was more than capable of looking after herself.

Once we were free of Blacklake, I punched the accelerate button and kept the vehicle on an even keel as she rapidly gained speed. As the dust began to plume behind us, I said, "Your daughter came to see me this morning."

"Did she now?" There was amusement in his tone. "What did she want?"

"To talk to someone else who was stained. Which

surprised me—I'd have thought that with so many people living and working at Blacklake, there'd be others who are stained."

"There are at least a dozen that I know of," he said. "But it was probably the draw of someone new that had her running to your side against orders."

I frowned and glanced around at him. "You didn't want her talking to me?"

"Oh, I'm all for her becoming acquainted with you, but not when she's skipping lessons to do so." His expression was amused. "If she wishes to follow in my footsteps and become commander of Blacklake, she has to learn to obey orders. Especially if she wants to give them herself one day."

I grinned. "I suspect following commands is always going to be difficult for her. She has her father's determination and strength of self-belief."

"That she has." He was silent for a moment, and then said, in an obvious attempt to redirect the conversation, "Did Saska give any clue as to what we might find?"

"All she said was answers," I replied. "Did you take the bracelet from Eluria?"

"Yes. The outpost will be safer if that thing isn't held at Blacklake."

"Winterborne won't be any safer—not after the success of the recent attack."

"But Winterborne has far more resources it can call on." He paused. "Did you press Saska for more information?"

"Yes, but she wouldn't—or couldn't—say anything more."

He grunted. "That really doesn't give us much to go on."

"Which seems to be something of a theme in this quest of ours."

"Unfortunately, yes."

He fell silent. I returned my attention to the controls and the miles rolled quickly by. When the sensors indicated we were nearing our destination, I slowed the speeder down and did a sweep of the area. As Trey had said, there was nothing there.

I returned to the point where I'd found Saska unconscious and stopped. Trey hit the door-open button and then climbed out, one hand on his blaster as he scanned our immediate surrounds. There was nothing and no one out there according to the sensors, and yet that odd sense of presence once again hit me as I stepped onto the sandy soil.

I stopped beside Trey and raised a hand to shield my eyes against the bright glare of the sunshine. "This really is a godforsaken land."

"Not so much godforsaken as almost totally drained of life," he replied. "It'll be centuries yet before it'll recover enough to become farmland again."

I glanced at him. "I was under the impression it would never recover?"

"That was the initial thought, but the success of the regeneration projects at the outposts has proved otherwise."

"I'm guessing the Adlin would love to see this entire area repopulated. There isn't much more than Wildebeests and the occasional patrol for them to hunt here at the moment." I took a couple of steps forward, and that weird sensation of something or someone being near began to fade. I swung around and returned to the spot where Saska had lain. The feeling reasserted itself.

"What is it?" Trey said.

"I don't know." I bent and splayed my fingers against the soil. The earth was warm against my skin, well heated by the day's sunshine. But there was very little in the way of life and energy—not even the faintest echo.

I walked forward several yards, and then repeated the process. Though faint, this time there was definitely the glimmer of power. It pulsed across my skin like a distant heartbeat, warm and welcoming.

I glanced up at Trey. "I can feel the faint pulse of the earth magic here, but there's nothing where you're standing. It's empty."

"Which isn't unusual. When the earth witches of old drew on the power of this place, they did so in waves rather than as a complete whole. There will be patches of life—places where the well of magic has already started to refuel."

"Yes, but there's something *in* that emptiness. A presence of some kind, but one that has no beat of life."

His expression gave little away, but I nevertheless sensed his doubt. "How can there be emptiness and life at the same time?"

"I have no idea. I'm only telling you what I'm sensing."

He grunted and splayed his fingers wide, reaching for the earth magic without actually touching the ground, as I generally did. His frown deepened and, after a few seconds, he swore and shook his head. "There is a barrier in place. I can't reach the earth."

"Is that barrier a result of this area being drained in the war? Or is it a new development?"

"It's new in this area, but not in others. It almost appears as if the earth's voice is being deliberately muted."

"And yet you and the other witches seemed to be having no trouble reconstructing the walls."

"Because not all of Tenterra is affected." He walked over to where I stood. "I can feel the beat of earth here, for instance."

"Are any of the dead areas near the outposts or Winterborne?"

"To be honest, we haven't tested the land near Winterborne, but perhaps we should." He frowned. "There *is* one patch that sits between Far Springs and ourselves that's a good one hundred feet wide and rather worrisome, if only because it's a more recent development."

I raised my eyebrows. "How recent?"

"It's happened in the last fifty years and runs from the banks of the Black River to the heart of Tenterra. It can almost be described as a highway of deadness."

"Have you ordered the area to be excavated to see if there's an underlying reason for it?"

"Yes, with the help of a couple of diggers from Winterborne. We went twenty feet down in various spots, but there was nothing except earth devoid of life and energy."

"Perhaps we need to go deeper. There *is* something here— I'm sure of it."

"Dead earth won't respond to my commands. Believe me, I've tried."

"Then maybe we should jointly try? I know you said it's generally impossible, but the three kids were doing it. I can't see why it won't work for us."

A smile touched his lips, but there was only wariness in his eyes. "Given you're constantly achieving the impossible, it's worth trying."

He held out his hand. Once I'd placed mine in his, we walked across to the dead patch. He flared the fingers of his free hand wide; energy shimmered through the air, and throbbed through the connection of our hands. The earth beyond the dead spot stirred, rolling away from us in gentle waves, but earth in dead zone remained stubbornly inert.

"That," Trey said, as the energy flowing between us eased, but didn't entirely disappear, "is rather annoying even if not unexpected. I'll order the diggers out from Blacklake, but in the meantime, we should—"

"Let's try one more thing first." I released my grip on his hand and then tugged off my boots and socks.

"I hardly think *now* is the time or place for such pursuits." His expression was amused.

"It would seem to me that—according to you—there's *never* a good time or place for such pursuits. At least with me." I couldn't help the slight bite in my voice. Frustration obviously hadn't entirely left me, despite the shower episode. "But never fear, I'm not intending to seduce you, Trey. It would appear my ability to call on the earth is dependent on an actual flesh to earth connection, so maybe I simply need a stronger connection here."

Something flickered through his eyes—frustration, perhaps, or maybe even annoyance. But all he said was, "That's an interesting restriction, and one Eluria doesn't have."

"But she's been trained, and I haven't. And perhaps that lack is, in this case, more of an advantage, given I'm finding my own ways to power, and I'm not restricted by what should and should not work." I held out my hand. "Shall we try again?"

We did. Unfortunately, the result was the same—nothing.

He released my hand. "Again, another not unexpected result. We should get moving if we're to make it back to Winterborne before—"

"I've one final thing to try."

He raised his eyebrows and motioned me to go ahead. I took a deep breath and reached, not for the earth but rather the air. It answered my call with a fierceness that knocked me back several steps and tore a gasp from my lips. Trey immediately grabbed me, bracing me as I directed the air at the earth. She hit it so strongly that dust and small shards of stone immediately pummeled the air, surrounding us in a halo of dead brown soil. She kept digging down, until the hole was far deeper than I was tall, and I could no longer see the bottom of it. And just as it seemed we would again find nothing, a tremor of exhalation ran through the wind and echoed through me.

The dead earth had given way to emptiness, and in the process revealed her secret.

There was a goddamn tunnel under our feet.

I released the air, but the minute I did, dizziness hit. I would have fallen had Trey not already been bracing me. I turned and rested my forehead against his chest, sucking in air and fighting the weakness that washed through me.

"Damn," I muttered after a few minutes. "That's never happened before."

"It's doubtful you've called forth *that* sort of power before now," he said. "It was a pretty damn impressive display."

I pulled away slightly and met his gaze. "Is the weakness a result of not having done the committal ceremony to the air?"

"No. All magic has its costs, even for those who *have* committed to our elements. Weakness is but one of those." He raised a hand and gently brushed the sweaty strands of hair from my eyes. "The fact is, you shouldn't have been able to call that much power, let alone exhibit such a degree of control."

I frowned. "But Kiro said it was not unknown for the stained—"

"Yes, but they have to learn the means of control first, just like every other witch. You seem to have skipped that particular point, at least when it comes to the air."

"Well, you did say I kept doing things I shouldn't be able to." I stepped back from his touch—even though part of me wanted to do the very opposite—and walked over to the shaft I'd excavated. It was a long pit of darkness.

He stopped beside me. "How deep is it?"

"It's just over fifty feet—and at the very bottom of it lies a tunnel."

His head snapped around. "What?"

I nodded. "I have this really weird feeling the tunnel is how Saska got here."

"The tunnel might be, but how did she get to the surface? Regular air witches can't interact with the earth." He knelt at the edge of the hole and peered in. "The air has a rather foul smell to it."

My heart began to race a little faster. "Urine and blue cheese?"

He glanced up again. "The senses of a Sifft are stronger than I thought if you're aware of the smell when the wind carries it away rather than toward you."

A grim smile touched my lips as I knelt beside him. "The children had the same smell."

And *that* not only meant this tunnel was somehow connected to them, but could also be connected to the plot to overthrow Winterborne.

Trey swore. "It could also mean the deadness in the earth is an indicator of them."

I glanced at him sharply. "You heard my thoughts?"

His gaze met mine with grim wariness. "Yes."

"But how? Are you telepathic?"

"No." He hesitated. "The ceremony of Gaia created a connection between us."

"Is that *all* it did?"

He hesitated again and half shrugged. "I don't know. And I can't hear them all the time."

That was a relief, given some of my more recent thoughts about him. "But you must have at least some idea of what other problems might arise."

"Indeed, but I can't see the sense in worrying about things that may not happen." He waved a hand at the trench. "Not when we have greater worries."

In other words, he still didn't want to talk about it. The

man was frustration itself. I resisted the inane urge to call him all sorts of names—although the slight smile touching his lips suggested he'd caught them anyway—and said, "I don't suppose you saw a rope in any of the storage units?"

"I had no reason to look. Wait here." He rose and ran back to the speeder.

I leaned over the shaft, wrinkling my nose against the stink that was rising. Twined within the god-awful smell of urine and blue cheese was the aroma of rotting meat. Something had died down there, and I could only hope it wasn't a child. That Saska's freedom hadn't come at the cost of another's life.

Trey returned with both a rope and flashlight. His gaze swept the width of the excavation and uneasiness settled across his expression. "I don't think I'm going to be able to get down that shaft. My shoulders are too wide."

"That's because it was created for someone my size, not yours." I held my hand out for the rope, and after a moment, he gave it to me. "Besides, it's not your task to be investigating such places, Commander. It's mine."

His expression was decidedly unhappy. "I'd rather be stuck down that hole than up here worrying about what you're dropping into."

"I'm Sifft, remember, and Nightwatch besides. I can both see and defend myself, and probably far better than either you or anyone else you might send down to investigate."

"I understand all that. It doesn't change the fact I'd rather it be me." He turned on the flashlight and pointed it down the shaft. "I can't see anything but dirt at the bottom."

Meaning the death I still smelled was out of immediate sight. I looped the rope around my waist and shoulders, and then handed him the rest of it. "Don't let me fall."

"No." He hesitated. "Be careful, Neve. Comms are still down at Blacklake and we're too far out from Winterborne for Daywatch to come to our rescue if something goes wrong."

I flashed him a smile. "Careful's my middle name, Commander."

He snorted softly, but his amusement quickly fell away as I hung my legs over the edge of the shaft. After a deep breath to gather as much fresh air as I could, I slowly lowered myself down, keeping my palms pressed against the wall on either side to help keep the strain off Trey's shoulders.

"Don't worry about my damn shoulders," he said. "Just concentrate on listening for whatever might lie just beyond sight."

"Why aren't I catching your thoughts as easily as you seem to be catching mine?"

"Oh, you're catching them. Most of the time, you're just not aware of it."

"That's rather annoying."

"Not really. Not from my perspective anyway."

"Suggesting you have thoughts you'd rather keep secret?"

"We all have those, Neve."

"Yeah, but I suspect yours might concern either this quest or me more than anything related to your life, be it at Blacklake or Winterborne."

"How about you concentrate on what you're doing rather than firing questions at me?"

I half smiled. "I'm female, Trey. We can multitask."

"Believe me, I'm *well* aware that you're female."

"I'd never have guessed it from your actions of late."

"Can we please have this discussion later?" he all but growled. "Tell me what you're damn well seeing."

"Right now, I'm seeing and feeling nothing but lifeless earth. And you really *don't* want to know what I'm smelling."

I continued to drop down into the darkness, and with each foot that passed, the stench got stronger, until my stomach was threatening to erupt up my throat. Damn it, I needed fresh air! I reached for the wind, and yet again, she immediately answered. Fingers of freshness spun around me, easing the sick queasiness in my stomach as they chased the worst of smells away.

I continued to ease my way down the shaft. The farther away from the surface I got, the deeper the darkness became. I'd never feared the ink of night, but there was something in this utter blackness that had trepidation racing across my skin.

"How much further?" Trey called down.

"Five feet. Get ready, I'm about to jump down."

"Go for it."

I released my grip on the walls and dropped to the tunnel's base. Dirt listlessly filled the air; it was almost as if the life that had been drawn from it had made it unwilling to stir.

I drew my knife and blaster, holding both weapons at the ready as I carefully looked around. There was no movement in this place, no indicator that anything or anyone had been down here recently. Seven feet to the right of where I stood, the tunnel ended. To the left, it stretched on into inky darkness. The scent, whatever it was, was coming from the left rather than the right.

I hesitated, and then went right, slipping my blaster back into its holster so I could place a hand on the solid wall of earth. Initially there was no response, and then power stirred, a beat of life that held only a little distance to it. The earth might be inert at the tunnel's edge, but life returned just over a foot away.

I spun around and walked back to the shaft. "Nothing in the immediate vicinity," I called up. "I'm going to follow the tunnel for a few minutes, and see where it leads."

"Don't go any further than the length of the rope," he said. "I can't get down there to help if trouble hits, remember."

"That restriction might not give us the answers we need, Commander."

"I'm more worried about your safety than answers right now."

It was a comment that had warmth stirring through me, even though I seriously doubted he'd meant it in the way my hormones were hoping. I walked forward cautiously, scanning the rough walls and dusty floors, looking for the death I could smell. The deeper I went into the tunnel, the stronger it got, but I reached the end of my tether well before I found its source. I hesitated, and then untied the rope. I might have orders to go no further, but Saska had said there were answers here to find, and find them I would.

I dropped the rope to the ground and proceeded on.

"Damn it, Neve," came Trey's voice. Whether it was real or in my thoughts, I wasn't entirely sure. "I can send a full team in to investigate the tunnel. It's stupid to take this risk when we have a more important mission at Winterborne."

So I was right—he wasn't so worried about my safety, but rather what losing me might mean to his and Kiro's quest.

"That's not entirely true, and you know it."

Entirely…. There was a whole lot of possible hurt in that one word. It was certainly a warning that attraction was no indicator of anything stronger.

Although as one of the stained, I should hardly be surprised at that.

I gripped my knife tighter. The glass blade gleamed with blue fire in the blackness, making the lifeless walls glow with an almost metallic sheen. Though my footsteps were soft against the dusty soil, they seemed to echo ominously in this place. If there were anything—or anyone—living in the deeper recesses of this tunnel, they would hear my approach.

The wind stirred, assuring me that I was alone, that none were near. Which was comforting, and yet at the same time, not.

I slowly continued. The air grew hotter and that terrible stench stronger. Sweat trickled down my spine and stung my eyes, and it felt like I'd been creeping through this awful place forever. But Trey would have undoubtedly badgered me into returning if too much time had passed.

In the darkness up ahead, something loomed. I paused, my heart racing in both expectation and fear. Whatever it was, it wasn't moving. And the gentle wind certainly gave no indication of danger.

I frowned and unhooked my blaster. The knife might be the better weapon for close fighting, but right now I was more than happy to simply shoot, thereby eliminating the necessity of the latter. I crept closer, and the looming shadow revealed itself to be a smooth wall of earth and stone. A created wall, not a natural one.

On the left-hand side of it, at the junction of the barrier, the tunnel's wall, and the floor, was a hand.

A small, stained hand.

A *child's* hand.

And one that was unattached to a body.

Horror filled me as my gaze darted back to the pile of rocks and earth. Did the rest of the child's body lie beneath it? And did I really want to uncover it?

The answer was a decided no, but such cowardice wouldn't provide the answers we needed. And there were answers here to be found, I was sure of it.

I sheathed both of my weapons and then stepped closer to the smooth wall and pressed my hands against the earth. Like the walls that surrounded me, there was no life in this smooth mound of compacted earth and rock. I pushed against it as hard as I could, but other than a few bits of dirt falling across my fingertips, it had little effect.

Which left me with one choice. I stepped back and called in the wind. It howled past me and literally exploded the blockage into pieces, throwing me backward with the force of it and sending stones ricocheting across the darkness.

"Neve?" Trey's voice was faint. I really *had* gone deeper into this tunnel than I'd intended. "What just happened?"

"I cleared a barrier. I'm okay."

I pushed up into a sitting position. The dust was so thick I tugged my shirt over my mouth to filter some of the muck from my lungs. It took forever to clear, even with the air doing its best to draw the cloud back down the tunnel, away from this area. I climbed upright and carefully edged forward. In what had been the heart of the rock fall, I discovered a body.

But it wasn't the body of a child.

It was thin and long, with skeletal limbs and crusty lavender skin, and a build that oddly reminded me of an ant's even though it was clearly humanoid. I followed the line of its remains and spotted its head.

It was then that true horror hit me.

I might never have seen the likes of this creature before in real life, but I'd certainly seen many a picture of them in the few history books I'd read.

What lay before me was the remains of an Irkallan.

10

As I'd feared, the Irkallan *weren't* in hibernation. And the fact that this body was here, lying so close to the severed hand of a stained child all but confirmed that they were not only active again, but also behind the plot to bring down Winterborne.

I didn't want to believe it, I really *didn't*, but there was no denying it now.

History had certainly given witness to the fact that the Irkallan could breed with humans—the staining still coming through so many of us was evidence enough of that. And the witches who'd been kidnapped had, if medical evidence and Saska's comments were to be believed, been forcefully impregnated in an effort to produce stained children. Those children were then raised by a queen they had no choice *but* to obey thanks to the existence of the silver bracelets.

There was no royalty left in Tenterra, Gallion, or Salysis. But the Irkallan lived and worked in a similar fashion to the insects they partially resembled. Not only did they exist in an apiary—which was exactly what Pyra had told me when I'd been questioning her—but there was also a caste system in place that had workers of various levels, soldiers, breeding females, and a queen who ruled them all.

The Irkallan might have been defeated, but they hadn't given up their dream of domination over all other races. They were merely undertaking a longer-term, camouflaged, and decidedly devious action this time.

Freedom, help us....

There is more to find beyond this body, the wind said.

I wasn't entirely sure I could handle finding anything else, but I nevertheless stepped over the Irkallan's remains and walked on. After a dozen or so steps, I noticed a thick trail of black on the tunnel's sandy soil. I bent and touched it. It felt hard—crusty—and though it had no scent, I had a fair idea what it was.

Blood.

Blood from a child whose hand had been severed, perhaps?

I closed my eyes against the pain and horror that rose— but once again, the former was oddly distant, an echo that seemed to be coming from someone else. And it wasn't Trey, as it definitely had a feminine edge to it.

Could both the sensations I'd experienced in the shower and the emotions hitting me now be coming from Saska? Did the connection that had flared so very briefly between us out there on the storm-held terrace somehow linger?

I'd never heard of such a thing, but then, I wasn't overly versed in the ways of psychic talents or magic, even if I did possess the ability to use the latter.

I brushed the soil from my fingers, then rose and moved onward. Twenty feet later I found the rest of the child's remains. She was naked and lying facedown on the ground, her small body so badly stained there was only a tiny patch of pale skin on her left rump. Her right hand had been severed and a large pool of dried blood surrounded its stump. Her other hand was whole, but there was no bracelet on it—just the grime marks on her wrist to indicate where one had been.

The Irkallan had been here. They'd retrieved the bracelets but left the bodies where they lay. There would be no remembrance of a life lived for this child, no ceremony to cast her soul on to its next journey. Nothing but inhospitable soil and a spirit destined to endlessly roam this unforgiving darkness.

I wanted to rant and rage against the utter inhumanity of the whole thing. Wanted to weep not just for this life, this child, but for the others who were still out there, still under the control of the Irkallan.

But such an outpouring would be little more than a waste of energy. To stop this plot—to save the children born into this madness, if it indeed it was at all possible to save them— we first had to find just how far the infiltration into Winterborne went. And, perhaps, even more urgently, just how close they'd gotten with their tunnels.

My gaze returned to the bloody stump, and I frowned. Why was her right hand lying on one side of the rock fall and her body here on the other? Given both bracelets had been retrieved, it suggested the rock fall had happened *after* both her death and that of the Irkallan. But why would they bury one and not the other? Did they do so merely to conceal the Irkallan's body, or did they, perhaps, want to ensure no one else could escape this way? Given the children they were breeding were capable of using the lifeless earth when our witches weren't, they had to know any earth-capable escapee would be able to get through the barrier. So maybe the blockage was meant to stop us from realizing the full extent of the tunnel system if we *did* manage to get through the dead earth.

Which left one more rather vital question—if this child

had been with Saska at the time of her escape, why did she then abandon her? It made no sense—not given the heartache I'd seen in Saska over the death of her babies.

I stepped away, and then stopped. I couldn't leave the child here in this darkness. At the very least, she deserved to lie in earth that had the beat of life. I couldn't guide her soul on but I could at least provide her the comfort of a resting place that wasn't sterile and empty.

I took a deep breath to gather my strength, and then once again called on the air. This time, there was no rush of power. The breeze that answered was gentle, filled with reverence and care. The child's remains were carefully wrapped and then lifted from the soil. Though her body had to have been lying here for at least a week, there was little in the way of decay or bloat. Perhaps the fact we were so far underground, with no heat or insect life present, helped delay the decomposition. Or maybe her exoskeleton-like skin was keeping the process at bay. The Irkallan hadn't stepped too far along the lines of decay, either.

The wind turned the child around, and for the first time, I saw her face.

It felt like someone had punched me in the gut. My breath left in a huge whoosh of air, and all I could do was stare.

Because the child's face was *mine*, right down to the stain on her cheek, although that patch lay on her right cheek rather than the left. The other slight difference was her eyes —hers were silver with a ring of brown around the iris rather than the golden of mine.

I fell back against the wall and pressed my hands against my knees, sucking in air as I battled the urge to be sick. Horror pulsed through me, not just because of the uncanny resemblance, but because it surely meant there was a blood connection between me, Saska, or perhaps one of those other kidnapped women. There could be no other reason for this child being my mirror image.

Freedom, help me... it was my *kin* involved in this plot, be it willingly or not.

I closed my eyes for a moment and tried to get both the shock and my thoughts under control. This latest fact didn't really change anything, even if it did add weight to my desire to see it all ended.

I pushed away from the wall and directed the air—and the child's small body—forward. As I stepped over the Irkallan's remains, I hesitated, then drew my knife and chopped off its head. Trey might be able to hear my thoughts —and therefore be well aware of everything I'd discovered down here—but others might need hard evidence before they could be convinced that the enemy we'd long thought in hibernation was instead actively plotting our downfall.

I grabbed the head by its two antennae, holding it away from my body as bits of fluid and who knew what else began to leak from it, and continued back down the tunnel. When I reached the end of the rope, I grabbed it with my free hand but didn't immediately tie it on. There was time enough for that.

"Trey, you still up there?" I said, as I finally neared the shaft.

"Where else would I be?" His voice was heavy with anger. "Damn it, Neve, I told you not to risk—"

"That risk was worth it, trust me." I paused, and frowned. "Have you been catching my thoughts?"

"Not since you released the rope. It would appear proximity is a factor."

"Then I have a whole lot of bad news for you," I said. "But first, I'm sending you up a body."

"Whose body?"

"A child's—a stained child's. She should be buried in soil

that holds the beat of life, not left in this sterile, empty darkness."

"Are you sending her up via the rope?"

"No. The air." I directed the wind to hold her vertically rather than horizontally, and then sent her up the shaft. "She's on her way."

Light flared down the length of the shaft, momentarily blinding me. I shielded my eyes against the glare and watched the child's body rise. When the air had lifted her free of the entrance, I took off my jacket, placed the Irkallan's head inside of it, and looped it around my utilities belt. Then I tied the rope back around my body and said, "Right, you can haul me up now."

He did so, quickly and efficiently. The minute I was topside, he said, "That child could almost be yours."

"I know." I undid my coat and held it out. "But this is even worse."

He quickly unwrapped the head, and his expression shifted from one of puzzlement to disbelief and horror.

"An Irkallan? It can*not* be—"

"It explains the extensive staining on the three children who attacked Blacklake. It also explains why witches are being kidnapped—they're forcibly impregnated to produce children capable of using magic, but whose actions can then be controlled via the bracelets."

He swore and began to pace, his strides long and angry. "We've been monitoring the Blacksaw Mountains since the end of the war. There's been no sign of movement in or around that place."

"Well, there wouldn't be, especially if they were going underground rather than over."

"Even *that* doesn't make sense. Young children, stained or not, wouldn't have the strength to create such tunnels—it'd more than likely kill them. Besides, it was only thirty years ago that the disappearances started happening, and they'd need far more women to produce the number of children required to make such a vast undertaking viable."

"You said the dead patches started appearing more than fifty years ago. What if witches have been disappearing far longer than we've presumed? What if this plot has been happening for centuries rather than years?"

He swore and thrust a hand through his dark hair. "We need to get back to Winterborne—urgently."

"Not before we bury that child—"

He swung around and I saw the denial on his lips. But his gaze met mine and, after a moment, he gave a short, sharp nod. He strode across to the viable earth and, in little time and with very little effort, a deep grave had been dug.

I shifted the tiny body into it and gently placed her on the bottom. "Rest well, little one. May the earth grant you the peace and happiness that was not yours in life."

"And may those that reside within the earth's magic treat your soul with kindness, and guide it on to rebirth," Trey added softly.

I watched the small body being covered with earth and tears trickled down my cheeks. It was irrational to feel so emotional about a child I'd never known, and maybe it was due in part to the link I seemed to have formed with Saska. Or maybe it was the fact she looked so like me that it wasn't hard to imagine it was my child down there in the dirt. Either way, those tears kept falling.

Trey didn't say anything. He simply tugged me into his arms and held me. "No child, whether they're kin or not, deserves to die alone like that," he said eventually. "We have to stop these bastards, Neve."

"Yes." I pulled away from him and quickly brushed the tears from my cheeks. "Winterborne needs to be warned."

"Yes." He hesitated. "Do you want me to drive?"

I smiled, and wondered if it looked as forced as it felt. "A brief if irrational emotional outburst won't stop me doing my job, Trey."

"It's hardly irrational." He picked up the Irkallan's head and swung into step beside me as I walked across to the speeder. "In fact, it's a rather nice confirmation that you *are* capable of such depth. I was beginning to wonder if the Nightwatch training had beaten it all out of you."

"If anything was capable of doing that, it wouldn't be our training, but rather the fact of being born stained." My voice once again held an edge of... maybe not bitterness, but certainly resentment. "I hope your daughter appreciates the gift you gave her, Trey, because she wouldn't be the woman she is now if she'd been raised with the restrictions that come from being stained in Winterborne."

"And yet you appear to have risen above them."

"Because I was lucky enough to have Sifft blood, and was raised to become Nightwatch." I met his gaze squarely. "Those born both unlit and stained may no longer be killed at birth, but we remain an underclass who have few opportunities and little say in what becomes of us. That needs to change, Trey. If the stained are declared unlit because we're immune to magic, why couldn't the same be true of the many who are unstained *and* unlit? Winterborne could in the future find itself under attack from within, from the very class of people they depend on for daily survival."

"All that is true," he said. "But such a change will never happen with any great speed. Remember, I was ostracized for my choice."

"Yes, but any change made for the better always starts with one small step. Perhaps, in this case, it should be the recognition—and protection—of those stained who possess magic."

"Such a ruling would have to come from the Forum—the

very people who rely on those whose station you're trying to raise."

"I'm hardly trying to raise their station," I snapped back. "All I'm suggesting is that we be given a voice—a choice—in what happens to us."

"Even that will not be so easily achieved."

I jumped into the speeder and reclaimed the driver seat. "It will *never* be achieved if it isn't even considered."

"Right now, we have greater concerns than the fate of the stained and unlit in Winterborne." Trey climbed in behind me and shut the door. "Which *isn't* to say that I don't agree with you. But I'm hardly likely to be a harbinger of reform. I gave up my right to speak at the Forum. I'm Blacklake's prime, a position that has no standing in there."

I punched in Winterborne's coordinates and then hit the accelerator. "Yet you're the one Kiro called when he needed help with this investigation. And I certainly didn't see much antagonism aimed your way during the masque."

"You're well aware of the reason Kiro called on me. And the house of Stone is one of the most powerful in the Upper Reaches—even a son who's been ostracized is given a certain amount of respect. But that respect doesn't mean they'll listen when it comes to changing centuries of tradition."

I sighed. I knew the sense of what he was saying. Knew change probably wouldn't happen in my lifetime, if ever, but that didn't make it any less frustrating—and it certainly didn't make tradition any less wrong.

But perhaps what was even more frustrating was the fact that it was only when I'd been taken out of that environment and shown a completely different way of life that I'd seen *my* life in a different light. Life as a Nightwatch was pretty damn good as far as things went for the unlit and the stained, but there were still many restrictions on what I could do and where I could go. My life *wasn't* my own. I would always be ruled by the color of my skin and by what I'd been deemed to be when I was born, even if the title of unlit no longer applied.

I might have chaffed under some of the restrictions of my life beforehand, but it had never really held much sway in my thoughts. Now though... now I had to wonder just how easy it would be to step back into the shadows of my old life. To keep going as if nothing had ever changed—as if *I* hadn't changed. But I guess the reality was, there was no other choice, and certainly nothing else I could do. No matter how strong my magic might prove to be, few would consider me partner material because of the staining and all the connotations that came with it—even if many of them were now untrue. And I certainly didn't want to become a breeder in some Upper Reaches household.

Which, when I thought about it, was little better than what the Irkallan were apparently doing.

And if Trey heard *that* particular thought, he didn't say anything. No surprise there.

As we got closer to Winterborne, I pressed the earwig and said, "Nightwatch eight-three inbound from Blacklake, approaching Winterborne with Commander Stone on board."

"Got you, eight-three. Be careful coming in—we've repaired the gates but haven't yet cleared all the debris."

"Will do, Control." I broke contact then glanced around at Trey. "Are we heading straight back to the Upper Reaches?"

"Yes. Why?"

"Because I'd like to go visit April and see for myself how he is."

He hesitated. "Will ten minutes do? Kiro wants us back at five to allow for situational updates and time is already tight."

"Ten is fine."

"Good. I'll use that time to check for dead spots immediately outside the walls."

"Surely the Winterborne earth witches would have noticed the lack of life in the soil if the Irkallan had gotten that close? Wouldn't the fact that the earth's voices had become muted or reluctant given them a warning that something was off?"

"It took those of us in the outposts years to notice, and we live in Tenterra. Most of the witches within Winterborne concentrate their efforts on either ensuring defenses remain pristine, or keeping a close watch on farm practices and the soil within Gallion so it might continue to sustain us in coming years."

"Ten minutes isn't going to give you much time to check, then. The wall is two miles long."

"I don't need to inspect its entire length to find the lifeless patches. The earth will tell me if they exist."

"One of the benefits of being trained, I guess."

"Yes."

I returned my attention to driving, but I could feel his gaze on me. Could feel the uncertainty in him—about what I had no idea. And if the growing silence was any indication, it once again appeared he wasn't about to enlighten me.

I contacted base again once we were close enough to see the wall, which meant the gate was open by the time we arrived. I eased the speeder onto the lift that would take it to the underground garage, and then shut everything down. Trey opened the door and climbed out, the rewrapped Irkallan head gripped in one hand.

"Captain November," he said, as he climbed out. "Could you please order the gate to remain open—I need to inspect the ground beyond the walls."

Mak immediately relayed the information to the gate

staff, and then said, "Anything we should be concerned about?"

"That's something I won't know until I do the inspection."

Mak grunted and glanced at me. His gaze, as ever, held a slight hint of disapproval. "Your secondment to the commander's division has been approved, March. Your personal items have been placed in storage, and your bunk reassigned until either your return or you request them sent elsewhere."

I frowned. "I hardly think that was necessary, Captain, given the secondment is only temporary."

"It's procedure, March." Mak glanced at Trey. "Lord Kiro has requested you join him as soon as possible."

"Inform him we'll be there in twenty minutes." Trey glanced at me. "Meet me at the internal gates in ten."

I nodded and, as he walked away, glanced back at the captain. "Do you know what ward Nightwatch April is in?"

"All Nightwatch casualties are being housed in Red-five. I'm sure you're capable of finding him from there."

I didn't thank him. I simply saluted and got the hell away from him. April's ward was on the fifth floor of the hospital, in the area reserved for serious but stable injuries. Nine others were in the ward with him, most of whom I knew. They all greeted me cheerfully, but my attention was mostly on April and my replies somewhat absent. His face was puffed and bruised, and there was a large gash down the left side of his face. His right arm and left leg were both immobilized, suggesting he'd broken them.

"You," he said, a wide grin splitting his bruised features, "are a sight for sore eyes."

"I'd like to say the same about you, but that would be a lie." I picked up his good hand and squeezed it gently. "How are you feeling?"

"Probably as bad as I look, but I get the last lot of treatment from the healers tomorrow, and should be mobile by the beginning of next week." He grimaced. "I'm mightily pissed that I'm missing all the damn fun in the Upper Reaches though."

"Trust me, the Upper Reaches isn't all it's cracked up to be —especially when it's nothing more than standing watch rather than getting involved in festivities."

"While that might be true, it would still be a welcome change of scenery." His gaze skimmed my length and he frowned. "Why are you wearing a Blacklake uniform?"

"I've been temporarily transferred to Commander Stone's command. Listen, were you still on watch or celebrating when the attack happened?"

"I'd just finished my shift—why?"

"Did you actually see the Adlin approach this time? I mean, they've been howling for nights, but none of us could actually see them and they seemed to disappear every time we tried to attack."

"Very true." He frowned. "The command didn't give any indication there was any sort of movement out in Tenterra until the last moment, which is damned unusual. As far as I'm aware, the sensors weren't down."

"Can you remember when—and where—they were first sighted?"

He hesitated. "We were doing quarter-shifts so that everyone had a chance to attend the harvest festivities; mine was from ten to two, so it would have been a few minutes before then that they were first spotted."

"At the walls or further out?"

He snorted. "Nightwatch may have been running a skeleton crew, but there's no way known the Adlin would have gotten that close without someone seeing them."

They could have if they were using tunnels, but I wasn't about to tell him that. "Where then?"

"Just over half a mile out from the wall."

Meaning in the time since they'd first started howling, the tunnel—if indeed there was a tunnel—had gained roughly half a mile. "Did they all appear at the same location, or was there a couple of different streams of them."

"One, according to command."

Which hopefully meant that there was only one tunnel to find and shut down. "Did command pinpoint any particular location?"

He gave me the coordinates, which were slightly to the east of the main gate, and somewhere between April's tower and mine. "So how come you managed to do so much damage to yourself?"

"Because, as I said, my shift had ended but I'd been ordered to the gatehouse to back up the crew there when the damn gate mechanics all but exploded. Don't remember much after that, but they apparently found me under a mess of stone and metal."

"Meaning you're lucky to be alive." I leaned forward and dropped a kiss on his lips. "And I'm totally glad that you are."

He wrapped a hand around my neck to stop me from pulling away and then kissed me more thoroughly. "It's just as well there're some pretty nurses to occupy my time in this place," he said eventually, "otherwise I'd be rather put out."

I smiled. "You're here to heal your broken body, not to seduce pretty nurses."

"It's only the unimportant bits that are broken. Everything else is in full working order." He paused, his expression contemplative. "And there is one very pretty redhead who has, in fact, been very obliging. I wouldn't mind spending a whole lot more time with her once I'm out of this place."

I raised my eyebrows. "That's sounding a bit more serious than a mere flirtation."

"Hardly, given we've only just met." His grin flashed. "And

never fear, I will not deprive either you or Ava of the wonderment that is my body until seriousness does happen."

I snorted and lightly slapped his good arm, even as sadness slipped through me. Things were indeed changing, and not just for me. While I'd always known the day would come when the relationship between the three of us would have to end, I wasn't entirely sure I was ready for that ending to happen so soon. Not that it was just yet, but still….

I forced the sadness away and released his hand. "I'll catch you later, April."

"You will. And be careful, Neve."

"Always."

I headed out. Trey was waiting near the secondary gatehouse. The carriage that had initially taken us into the Upper Reaches was waiting on the other side of the gate. "Did you find any dead patches?"

He fell in step beside me. "Not in the immediate vicinity, but there is a reluctance in the earth's voice, so something is near."

"According to April, the Adlin who attacked us appeared on the sensors at about half a mile out." I gave him the coordinates. "If that's the case, then the tunnel has progressed half a mile in about nine days. And that means we still have some time to stop them."

"But it is totally dependent on just how many earth-capable children they are willing to deplete unto death to get that sort of speed." Once we'd climbed into the carriage, he gave the order to move, then picked up the clothes that sat neatly folded on the seat next to him. "We both need to change. Kiro doesn't want anyone suspecting anything untoward has happened."

I accepted my dress but didn't immediately start stripping off. "Why? They'd have to be aware of the Adlin attack, even if they had no idea what else might be going on. And as an outpost commander, wouldn't they think it natural for you to seek out details of such an attack?"

"Yes, but I'd hardly take my lover to such a meeting, hence the need to pretend it was nothing more than a brief outing."

"Brief?" I snorted. "Anyone with any sort of eyes would know otherwise. We've been missing half the night and most of the day."

"Which is very easily explained away, given it was the night of the masque reveal *and* a time when alliances—new or old—are sexually celebrated."

"Meaning I missed out on the fun again?" I mused. "Damn."

"Indeed." His gaze swept me, and the heat of his desire washed tantalizingly across my skin. But he didn't move—didn't reach for me. Instead, he resolutely pulled his gaze away and began stripping off.

Stone by name, stone by nature. At least when it came to giving way to any attraction to *me*.

"So is he planning to tell the Forum about the attack on Blacklake?" I leaned down to untie my boots, and then shucked them and my socks off.

"He'll have to once we've shown him the Irkallan's head. I guess the timing of the revelation will depend on whether he's uncovered any other traitors aside from the three women."

"Hence the need for an update before we attend the masque." I pulled off my shirt then undid my bra, tossing it onto the pile of clothes.

"Yes."

He continued stripping off, and it wasn't very long before we were both naked. The heat in the air had increased to the point it felt like I was being bathed in desire, but he still refused to look at me or even acknowledge what was rising between us.

"And there is good reason for that, Neve," he said softly.

"Then tell me what it *is*." My voice held an edge of anger that was not quite contained. "Make me believe it's not my stains or my station."

His gaze jumped to mine at that and there was no hiding either his desire or surprise. "Knowing what you know about me, how can you even think that?"

"Then what the hell is it?"

He sighed and thrust a hand through his hair. "It's the connection we formed when we did the ceremony. There's the possibility of it getting stronger if we continue to be sexually involved. I thought it best not to risk forming an unwanted, permanent attachment."

Unwanted. The story of my entire life. Bitterness swirled but I somehow kept it contained and simply asked, "How serious an attachment are we talking about? More than just reading minds?"

He shrugged, frustration evident in his expression. "Possibly. It's rare for the ceremony to be performed by someone not trained, and there's really only vague warnings about permanent connections being formed."

"Meaning the risk is one of both mind *and* heart if we're sexually active over a period of time?"

"Yes, although how long that period needs to be is also rather vague."

"Is it just you that runs this risk? It can't be one-sided surely."

"It's not, but—"

"And is there a cure for this connection?" I cut in. "If it does indeed form?"

"Distance, according to the texts I've since read. But that doesn't mean we should take such a risk until we're sure it's something neither of us fear."

I leaned closer. He didn't retreat, but he didn't reach for

me, either. The earthy energy that seemed to arise whenever we were too close burned the air, and it was a force that certainly seemed to be *for* a liaison rather than against it. "Commander, isn't the possibility of one partner falling for the other and not having their affections returned something all lovers face?"

"Yes, but—"

I raised a finger to silence him, but he caught it, kissed it. "Neve, you've got it all wrong. I'm *not* afraid of a connection forming, but I don't want you trapped in a relationship you don't want and couldn't ever be comfortable with."

I stared at him for a minute, unable to believe what I was hearing. It wasn't a rejection—quite the opposite, in fact. Happiness surged and a silly grin split my lips. "I've thought myself in love before, Commander, and survived the fallout when it became obvious it was very one-sided. I'm willing to take that chance again, but only if you are."

With a sigh that was almost relief, he wrapped a hand around my waist, pulled me against him, and kissed me. There was nothing cautious about this kiss, nothing gentle; it was heated and hungry, filled with all passion that had been simmering between us since the ceremony. And it made my pulse race and my heart sing.

This time, he didn't stop or pull away. The kiss gave way to caresses, and swiftly became a heated exploration of each other's bodies, one that involved both hands and tongue. We tasted and teased, caressed and kissed, as much as the confines of time, urgency, and the small carriage would allow, until the scent of need was so sweet and heavy on the air it was almost liquid. When I could no longer stand the glorious torture, I pushed him back onto the seat and straddled him. But he gripped my hips, preventing me from fully capturing him, his gaze on mine and his expression serious.

"Never, ever, believe that I haven't wanted you," he

murmured. "Ever since that very first night in my suite at Blacklake it has been so."

With that, he released me, and I thrust down onto him. And oh, it was such a moment of utter perfection, where everything was as it should be, that neither us of dared move.

Then desire surged, and his groan was one I echoed as we began a dance as old as time and life itself. Slowly at first, and then with increasing urgency. Pleasure curled through my body, shaking me with its power, until the growing need for completion had my body wound so tight it felt like I would surely shatter. And then I *did* shatter, as did he, the force of it so strong it tore gargled screams from both our throats.

For several seconds after, we simply sat there, our bodies locked together. That odd, earthy energy continued to surge around us, a force that remained more than just sexual, and one that for the first time seemed completely united. It was almost as if two halves had now been made whole, and that energy—be it of earth or something far more basic—was now satisfied.

He dropped a kiss on my forehead and said, "I would love to take you to bed right now and more thoroughly risk that connection we spoke about, but I can't."

"No." I climbed off his lap. "I don't suppose you have towels and water in this carriage, do you?"

"Indeed do we do." His mouth twitched as he opened a compartment to the left of my seat. It revealed a small sink, tap, and above it, some towels. "This isn't the first time carriages have been used for such pursuits."

I laughed and quickly cleaned myself up. He did the same, and by the time we'd both dressed, the carriage was pulling to a halt outside Rossi House.

Our door was opened and once again, Trey exited first. I handed him the still-wrapped Irkallan's head and my sword —my knife was once again strapped to my thigh, its presence concealed by the flowing skirt—and then accepted his help down. My gaze immediately went the white stone and silver metal façade of the fantastical building. Nothing seemed to have changed, and that seemed rather weird given all that had happened since we'd left.

A liveried pageboy came down the steps as we began to climb them, meeting us halfway. "Lord Kiro waits for you in your quarters, Lord Trey."

The wind stirred around me as he spoke, whispering of dark deeds being done. With it came the urgent need to go check on Saska. I glanced at Trey. "You go. I really need to go check on Saska."

He frowned. "I don't think that'd be wise—"

"The wind would suggest otherwise."

"Which means it's a suggestion we dare not deny." He caught my hand and raised it to his lips. "Meet me back in our suite once you've finished. And be careful."

"People keep telling me that." Amusement twitched my lips. "Anyone would think I'm the careless sort or something."

He laughed and released me. I watched him stride after the page for a second, and then headed left, following the wide patio around to the rear of the huge house. I eventually entered via a side entrance then walked down the silent halls to Saska's suite. Ava and a golden-haired man I only vaguely knew were standing either side of the doorway.

"Neve," Ava said, delight creasing her features. "You didn't get dead."

"Not through lack of trying—at least if you believe what others might be saying." I glanced at the other guard. "How are you, Ranel?"

"I'll be better when our shift is over. It's almost as boring standing here as it is on the wall."

"Trust me, boring is probably better than the alternatives right now." I glanced back at Ava. "Anyone come in or out?"

"Other than Lord Kiro, no." She hesitated. "And he didn't look pleased when he left."

I smiled. "He never looks pleased."

"Yeah, but considering they had sex, I would have thought he'd at least be a little happier."

Meaning Kiro had used the full extent of his talents on Saska again. "How long ago was this?"

"Around lunchtime."

Which was about the time the pleasurable sensations had hit me in the shower. For whatever reason, a link had definitely been formed between Saska and me.

But I had to wonder what being seduced in such a way— even if Kiro had taken the time to make it pleasurable for her —would have done to her already unstable state.

"Has there been much movement since then?"

"No," Ava said. "But she must have the side doors open, because the force of wind has been strong enough to rattle this door."

Given Saska's propensity to stand outside in the wild weather, that wasn't entirely surprising. Yet unease stirred. "Do you know if there's anyone stationed on the balcony exit?"

"Yes, there is." She glanced at Ranel, who said, "I believe Gen and Luc are currently assigned there."

Two people I wasn't familiar with, which suggested they were newer recruits. "And Saska hasn't come out?"

"No."

Which didn't mean she was still there. Not given the stunt she'd pulled in Tenterra. "I need to get inside to talk to her. What's the procedure?"

"You were given all-hours access. Everyone else has to be cleared through Lord Kiro."

"Ah. Good."

Ava opened the door and I stepped through. Once it was closed again, I paused and scanned the suite. Nothing appeared to have changed since I was last here, although the force of the wind coming in through the open patio doors was strong enough that the curtains were flying like flags. The air in the room was also bitterly cold, suggesting the doors had been open for a while.

"Abee?" I had to raise my voice to be heard against the howl of the wind. "Are you here?"

There was no response, either from Saska's maidservant or from the two Nightwatch who were supposed to be stationed outside the patio doors. Maybe they simply couldn't hear me over all the noise. I walked across to the doors, caught the end of one of the violently flapping curtains, and pushed it further aside before stepping through the door. The wind skirted around me rather than hit me full force, but I nevertheless felt the anger within it. I scanned the balcony, but other than a few upended chairs, there didn't appear to be anyone out here.

Where the hell were the Nightwatch officers? They wouldn't have abandoned their posts—not without good reason, and certainly not without telling anyone. Even if they *did* have reason to leave, Ava and Ranel would have been informed.

I stepped farther out into the balcony. The wind continued to move around me but the urgency beating through it was growing stronger. I did a full circuit of the patio, my unease growing with each step. There was no one here and no indication of any sort of disturbance or fight. Both the Nightwatch and Saska had disappeared and while the latter's absence didn't really surprise me, the former filled me with growing trepidation.

I walked back into Saska's suite and looked around.

Again, there was little sign of any sort of disturbance, but I found Abee in small butler's pantry next to the bathroom, unconscious on the floor and bleeding from a long gash on the side of her head. I swore and quickly felt for a pulse. It was rapid and faint, but it was at least there. She wasn't dead.

But I feared the same would not be said of the Night-watch officers.

I thrust up and ran back to the front door. Both Ava and Ranel swung around as I flung it open. "Are either of you in direct contact with Lord Kiro?"

"He's in direct control of all the seconded Nightwatch, and our earwigs have been retuned to a communicator that accompanies him," Ava said. "Why?"

"I need you to tell him that he, Commander Trey, and a healer are to get here ASAP. Saska's maid is unconscious, and Saska and the two Nightwatch officers are missing."

Ranel swore and immediately pressed his earwig. As he began relaying information, I added, "Roughly what time did the wind get really strong?"

Ava hesitated. "It would have been about five and a half hours ago."

Which was roughly the time Trey and I had left Blacklake. I had a bad feeling it wasn't a coincidence. "And there was no indication from either Gen or Luc that there was anything untoward happening?"

"Gen was bitching about how fierce and cold the wind was, but was bluntly told to keep off the line—that we were only to contact each other if there was something wrong."

"So there's been no word from either of them since then?"

"No. And we're not due for a shift change until nine."

"How long are the shifts?"

"Twelve, as usual."

"Lord Kiro is on his way," Ranel said. "He wants you to wait for him."

"Tell him I can't. Tell him I'm going after Saska."

Ranel nodded and began to relay the information. Ava's expression became troubled. "I suspect I know how you intend to find her, but be wary. The source of your information cannot be trusted when you're using it as a means to track down a powerful air witch."

"I know."

I squeezed her arm and then spun and ran back to the patio. The wind's violence had not abated and the voices within her were mute. But the concern remained, and it was growing stronger. Whatever Saska was up to, whatever she'd done or was doing, the wind did not approve.

It was also interesting to note she was more vocal—and more willing to help me—beyond Winterborne. Obviously, the binding of three that was preventing her from either speaking to me or helping me more greatly wasn't so restricting once we'd moved into Tenterra.

My skirt flew every which way as I stepped onto the patio again but this time, the wind wasn't avoiding me. Instead, she urged me on, toward the outer edge. Darkness was gathering along the horizon and the sea far below was as violent as the wind, casting foamy fingers high enough up the sheer cliff face that I could not only see it, but also taste the salt of it. Yet there was far more to be seen than heaving seas if the wind was to be believed.

I gripped the nearby capstone with one hand and carefully leaned over the edge. On the rocks far below, held in place against the violence of the seas by the thin fingers of rocks that had skewered their bodies, were the missing Nightwatch officers.

Saska—and the wind—had murdered them.

Anger stormed through me as I raised my face to the skies and the wind. "Damn it, why didn't you stop her?"

The rule of three means we have to abide by orders given whilst one is still alive. We had no choice but to do this foul deed.

I swore and pushed away from the edge. "Can you tell me where Saska currently is?"

We have been forbidden to tell you. But we can show you, if you trust.

Trepidation stirred through me. The last time I'd been asked to trust the air, they'd told me to leap off a wall. I had a bad feeling that's exactly what they intended now. "Why can't you simply guide me through the halls of this place?"

Because that will not be fast enough. She teeters on the edge.

I took a deep breath and released it slowly. It didn't do much to calm the inner butterflies. The wind had admitted it could not go against direct orders—what if one of them had been to kill me?

If that had been so, we could have simply tossed you down the cliff or even drawn the air from your lungs until you suffocated.

Both of which was not only true, but would also be a very nasty way to go. "What do you want me to do?"

Move to the far side of the patio and stand upon the wall. We will lift you, as we lifted you both in Tenterra.

That lift had left Saska shaking with weakness, and would undoubtedly do the same to me. But it wasn't like I had a lot of choice—the urgency beating around me suggested there was very little time left.

I climbed on the wall, holding my arms out to balance as the wind's fierceness grew. Icy fingers began to wrap around me, growing ever stronger with each heartbeat, until I was once again concealed within the confines of a smoky cloud. It thrust me several yards into the air and ripped me sideways, the force of it so great it tore a gasp from my throat. Wherever Saska was, it was not anywhere here in the Rossi household. We flew over the top of it, the night a blur around me. But we didn't go far. As the gossamer cloud began to unravel, it became obvious we were heading for the stone and metal water tower that soared above much of the Upper Reaches. Though it was still used as a storage facility, it now stood marooned on the edge of a thick finger of rock that thrust out toward the sea—a lasting reminder of how much more land Winterborne had once claimed.

But what the hell did Saska intend by coming here? I doubted one lone air witch could draw a strong enough storm to destroy the structure—not when it had been built to withstand whatever the elements threw at it during the wild weather years immediately after the war.

As the wind dropped me closer, I spotted Saska. She was standing close to the edge, where the gentle curve of the roof abruptly dropped away. She didn't look up as I approached, though she surely had to be aware of my arrival.

The last fragments of the cloud disintegrated and the wind deposited me gently on the metal roof. Saska didn't turn around, didn't react. Didn't acknowledge me in any way. She just stood on that edge, her arms crossed, her wrists hidden by the heavy sleeves of her gown, and her hair streaming behind her as she stared out over the wildly churning seas far below.

Weakness washed through me, and it was an effort to keep my knees locked, to keep upright. I swallowed heavily and said, my voice slightly hoarse, "Saska? Are you okay?"

"No," she said softly. "I'm not, and never will be."

I took a few, rather wobbly steps closer. She didn't move, didn't look at me, but the sudden tightening across her shoulders warned me to be careful.

"You need to come down from here—"

"You went away, sister," she continued, as if I hadn't spoken. "You went away, and you took my strength with you. I couldn't fight the queen's will; she's too strong for me alone. She's always been too strong for me."

"Not always," I countered. "You escaped from her, remember."

"But the price I paid for that foolishness was a heavy one." Her voice was little more than a whisper, carried to me on the wind. But her pain was something I felt deep inside, and it was so sharp and real it might have been my own. "And in the end, it was all for naught."

Again, the wind warned me to be gentle, but I had to know if what I suspected was the truth or not. "And what was that price, Saska?"

She closed her eyes, but it didn't stop the tears. Didn't stop the agony that stabbed through me. "I killed her you know. I stole her breath and watched the life leak from her eyes."

Pain grew. Whether it was hers or mine, I couldn't say, because they were so entwined. "Why? Did you fear the queen would use her to stop your escape?"

"She couldn't. The child wasn't wearing the bracelets, and without them, distance communication is somewhat fragmented," Saska said. "There is only a finite number of those bracelets, and they are generally kept for when the stained go beyond the apiary or for those of us with a will of our own—which those born into that place do not have. Their only desire is to fulfill the queen's wishes."

Which explained why the children were wearing bracelets at Blacklake—the queen was communicating with them.

"Where are the bracelets kept when the children aren't wearing them?"

"They are stored in the same place as the children."

Stored. Treated as nothing more than items to be used and discarded however the queen might wish. Anger stirred, and this time it was all mine.

"Then why take the child?" I somehow managed to keep

the anger from my voice. "And why would she even go with you in the first place?"

Saska's lips twisted, though I wasn't sure if it was bitterness or regret. "She had no choice. I was her mother, and that is a bond hard to break, even in *that* place." She paused, the flow of tears getting stronger. "I needed her earth abilities to escape, but there was never any escape for her. She is better off dead. They're all better off dead."

"You can't believe that," I said softly. "Surely if they were rescued—"

"No." She shivered. "They are the queen's. They will always be hers. Those who show any sort of independence are immediately killed."

I closed my eyes against the sting of tears. I was no mother, but I didn't think you had to be to imagine the sheer and utter horror of having to watch children—be they yours or another's—being murdered time and time again. And while she might have been teetering on the edge of insanity before she'd escaped, being personally responsible for the death of one of her own had surely sent her over it.

"Why was her hand severed if she wasn't wearing a bracelet?"

"The Irkallan sent after us was aiming for me. He got the child instead."

"So the queen intended to kill you both?"

"Originally, but she is nothing if not adaptable." The smile that touched her lips held no warmth. "It felt good to kill him, even if the queen cares little about the life of one soldier. Not when there are so many more of them."

"How many more?"

"Thousands and thousands more." Her voice was bleak. "They've ramped up their breeding over the last two hundred years."

That was *not* good news, but also not unexpected, given

this plot had obviously been in development for many, many years. "How was the soldier buried, then? And how did you get out of the tunnel?"

Saska's expression was bleak. "The rock fall was the earth's response to me stealing the breath of the child."

"Then how did you get back to the surface?"

"I directed the air to dig a shaft; once I had been pulled up onto the surface, the wind covered any trace of it."

"An air witch can't interact with the earth, Saska—"

"No, under normal circumstances, we certainly can't." She finally glanced at me. Her silvery gaze was haunted with pain, horror, and the shadows of death, but there was something else there, something I did *not* expect.

Kinship.

"Have you not guessed our secret yet?" she added.

A weird mix of uncertainty and elation raced through me. It felt like I was standing on that precipice, and any sense of security I might have had about my life was about to be pulled out from underneath me. "I know that we seemed to have formed some sort of connection, but I don't understand the reason for it."

"Nor did I, not initially. But it is the reason they fear you, and the reason they want you dead."

I rubbed my arms, even though I wasn't cold. "What's that reason, Saska?"

"We're twins, Neve. You were stained and unlit, and sent into state care, and therefore kept safe from them. I was raised by a mother whose allegiance already lay with the Irkallan queen, and who betrayed me by handing me over to the apiary once I'd come fully into my powers."

I stared at her, unable to take it in but feeling the truth of it reverberating deep inside. She wasn't only my sister, but my *twin*. And Hedra... I'd killed my own mother. Horror swirled, even if I couldn't regret that action.

I closed my eyes and took a deep, shuddering breath. The truth some small part of me had always wanted was now laid bare before me, and it was one that would bring more pain before this day was over. Because the shadows of death were drawing ever closer in Saska's eyes and a sick feeling of helpless inevitability washed over me.

"It was the Adlin who attacked your train as it was coming back from the West Range outpost," I said. "Not the Irkallan."

"Those Adlin were under the control of one who is stained and in thrall to the queen. Destroy him, and you kill their allegiance to the queen."

That was obviously the stained Adlin I'd seen but failed to kill. I scrubbed a hand across my aching eyes, but she wasn't finished yet.

"Our kinship is the reason you've been able to control the air. My knowledge leaks through our connection to you, just as the stain on your skin allows us both to use the air in ways that shouldn't be possible."

Meaning she didn't know about my ability to use earth? I opened my mouth to ask, and then closed it again. Right now, despite the information she was giving me, she somehow remained in thrall of the queen. Maybe it was her madness, and maybe it wasn't, but either way, I wasn't about to give them such information if they weren't already aware of it.

"The fact we share strength and talents explains why they want me dead," I said. "Is that also why they fear me?"

She was silent for a moment, her gaze on the distant horizon and her arm muscles flexing. She was fighting the queen—or whatever the queen wanted her to do. But how were those orders being relayed? The Adlin had retrieved one of her bracelets, and Trey still had the other. Hedra's were buried deep along with her body, and Pyra's set had been thrown deep into the ocean. Had the wind been ordered to retrieve them from the sea? Was that even possible?

No, the wind said.

"No," Saska echoed, leaving me briefly wondering which question she was answering.

"Then why?"

"Because of me—because of our shared DNA—you can find her. Kill her."

The queen? "Not without a damn army at my back, Saska."

"With an army at your back, you will fail."

"Not if we blast the shit out of the mountain."

"It won't help you. They don't live in the mountain, but deep under it. Even if the entire range was flattened, you won't stop them."

"So an army won't get near her, but one person going in alone can? Saska, that's insane." And surely it was something she was being forced to say. Maybe the Irkallan queen didn't just want me dead; maybe she merely wanted to lure me into her web so she could watch me die. Or, worse yet, use me.

"Oh, I'm well aware it's insanity itself." Her gaze came to mine again. "But it's nevertheless a truth you should not ignore if you wish to end this madness."

"But how can you or anyone else be absolutely certain a mass attack wouldn't bring them down? The earth witches never took the war to the Irkallan's doorstep, Saska."

"But they did—three times, according to the queen. And each time they failed, because all life was drained out of the Blacksaw Mountains by some unknown force long ago. Earth witches cannot command such soil, and air witches, unless they are stained, cannot interact with it." She paused. "Life *does* beat deep under the mountain, in the heart of hive where the queen and the breeders reside, but the deadness above prevents Winterborne's witches from using it."

"So if I were to escort a small group inside—"

"You will die, as they will die," she cut in. "They will sense their presence long before any of you got close enough to do them damage. Even a fully armed force would have little hope—the tunnels are too tight and too numerous. Your soldiers would be dead before they were even aware the Irkallan were close."

"But wouldn't that also apply to me going in solo?"

"No, because we are two halves of a whole and both born of Hedra. *That* is what will protect you as you enter that place."

Not only born of Hedra, I realized, but also of the *Irkallan*. Bile rose up my throat and I swallowed heavily. As much as I had railed against Winterborne's treatment of the unlit and the stained, the fact was, I was only standing here today because of it.

"So if I go in alone, you're saying I have a chance of getting deep enough into the apiary to cause them damage? Maybe even destroy their queen??

"Yes. And you can retrieve the remaining bracelets and drop them into the black mirror, where no Irkallan would dare enter, and from which they will never be retrieved."

I frowned. "Is this mirror magic?"

"Once you kill her," she continued, as if I hadn't spoken, "they will be in complete disarray."

It was madness. Utter madness. And yet it made an odd sort of sense. *Freedom, help me....*

"So if I *were* to make such an attempt, would you come with me?"

The smile that touched her lips was tinged with sadness. "No. I dare not. I can fight the queen's pull and ignore her demands with some success here in Winterborne, but I would very easily betray you if I ever got near the apiary again. It's far safer that I remain here."

There was something in her voice, something in her expression, that had fear rising. I wanted to reach for her, hold her, tell her that everything would be okay, that she was safe and that I'd protect her with everything I had. But the wind was telling me none of it was possible, that she'd passed the point of being kept safe long ago, that she no longer even *wanted* to be kept safe. The tears that were tracking down Saska's cheeks were now also falling on mine.

Damn it, surely she'd suffered enough? Surely she was due some—if not happiness, then at least some peace?

Peace will only come with death, the wind said.

Meaning she would be welcome into collective consciousness when neither Hedra nor Pyra were?

No, and for similar reasons. We cannot afford to have their madness infect the collective consciousness.

But she *wasn't* like them—she was at least fighting....

It does not matter, the voices said. *She only fights because you are here. Your absence set her back, and Kiro's actions further weakened her mind. What she has done here will yet cause much grief.*

As fear rose anew, I finally asked the question I *should* have asked first. "Saska, why are you up here? What did the queen wish you to do?"

"What she wanted has nothing to do with this tank, but rather the pump rooms far below."

My heart began to beat a whole lot faster, the fear so strong I could taste it in the back of my throat. "And what did she bid you do in those pump rooms?"

"She had me inject a toxin into the water being pumped up to this tower."

Freedom, help us.... This tower supplied a good half of

the water to the Upper Reaches households. "And that toxin? What was it?"

A strange smile touched her lips. One that was almost alien. "One that is fast acting, does not need to be drunk to be effective, and for which there is no known cure."

"Saska, you need to come down from this place. We need to warn—"

"No," she said softly. "*We* do not. That task falls to you, not me."

"Which doesn't alter the fact we need to get down from this place."

For a second, she didn't answer, but her arm muscles were flexing again and the death I'd seen in her eyes now surrounded her like a pall.

"Be ready, Neve. They're coming."

And with that, she threw herself over the edge.

11

"No," I screamed, and lunged for her. But it was too late —far too late, to either stop or save her. "Air, please, you must help her! She doesn't deserve to die this way. Not for her mother's sins, and certainly not for anything she may have been forced to do since."

It is her wish and her command that we do not save her, the wind said. *It is the only way she can help you. The only way she can make amends for everything she has done.*

"Damn it, no!" I dropped to my knees and watched her fall. Tears coursed down my cheeks and splashed to the metal underneath me, glimmering as brightly as the silver on Saska's wrist.

Hedra's bracelets, I presumed. I wondered how she'd retrieved them, but almost immediately scratched the thought. The wind had witnessed Hedra's burial, and it wouldn't have been too hard for someone of Saska's standing to convince a lower house earth witch to help her when everyone else was otherwise occupied in restoring Winterborne's defenses. Although I did have to wonder if that earth witch had subsequently survived the retrieval.

No, the wind whispered.

I watched her fall for what seemed an interminably long time. Despite the distance growing between us, there was a clarity to the air that allowed me to see her expression. There was no fear there, just serenity and acceptance. As she drew close enough to the waves that their foam splashed across her body, she raised a hand and blew me a kiss. And then she was gone, swept into the fierce grip of the ocean, her body drawn down, deep down, by the currents and her desire to never resurface.

Something within me broke. I wrapped my arms around my body and screamed in denial and pain. It was a sound the air echoed fiercely. As the skies opened up and rain pelted down, all I wanted to do was sit there and cry for the twin I'd barely known.

But I couldn't. Not if I wanted any hope of honoring her final wish and stopping the Irkallan's insidious plans.

I pushed to my feet and looked around. The skies might be weeping for a sister lost, but it was also making it damn hard to find a way off the tower's roof.

Leap, the wind said. *We will deliver you safely to the ground.*

This time, there was no hesitation. I ran toward the edge that overlooked Winterborne and leapt high. The wind caught me, wrapping me tightly in her cold fingers as I plummeted toward the ground. There were two figures down there standing in front of a carriage, and though it was hard to see their features through the gray curtain of rain, I had no doubt it was Kiro and Trey.

The wind checked my speed and deposited me safely on the ground, but I'd barely had a chance to drag in a relieved breath when Trey pulled me into his arms, his hug as fierce and as welcome as anything I'd ever experienced.

"Freedom, help me," he murmured. "I think I just lost ten years of my life watching you fall like that."

"I wasn't falling." I closed my eyes, briefly allowing myself to relax in the warm comfort and strength of his embrace, then gently pulled away. "The Irkallan are coming and Saska's placed a toxin of some kind in the tank's water, one that doesn't need to be ingested to work."

Kiro swore and immediately ran for the pumping station situated underneath the tower. "How long ago?" he asked, over his shoulder.

I hesitated as the wind supplied the answer. "Three hours."

"Will the sheer volume of water being held in the tank dilute the potency of it?" Trey asked.

The wind stirred again. "Apparently not," I said.

"Which isn't an unexpected answer," Kiro said. "But a frustrating one, given three hours means entirely too many people could have already been exposed to it."

"Yes."

Kiro opened the pump house's main door and stalked inside. We followed, and discovered what could only be described as chaos. Bits and pieces of metal lay everywhere, and the huge pumps that were used to draw the water from the artesian well through to the filters and then up to the tank were silent. The place was dark and there were no signs of any life—and, at the very least, there should have been several people monitoring operations and a couple of guards, given the importance of this pumping station to the Upper Reaches.

"Spread out and try to find someone," Kiro said. "I'll contact the Forum and order an immediate shutdown of water usage in the areas covered by the tank."

"With the pumps out of action, will people still be able to access the water?"

"Yes, because it's gravity fed." He made a "go" motion with his hand and then pulled an earwig out of his pocket.

I headed left, Trey went right. In the far corner, behind several large but silent machines, I found three women and two men; two of the former and one the latter wore the basic brown uniform of Winterborne's general workers, and the other two wore guard uniforms.

"Found five people." I checked for signs of life, even though it was obvious from the odd angles of all their necks that none had survived their encounter with Saska. "All dead."

I moved out from behind the machines and saw Trey walking toward me.

"That must be everyone, because there's no one else here," he said. "Did Saska say how long we had until the Irkallan came?"

"No, just that they were on the move." I crossed my arms, trying to ward off the chill that came from not only being soaked to the skin, but the growing sensation of doom. "Our best chance of survival is to stop them digging underneath us."

"Which is undoubtedly why Saska was ordered to place the toxin in the water." Trey took off his waterproof jacket and wrapped it around my shoulders. "They were hoping to knock out a good percentage of our witches."

"Kill them, not knock them out." I pulled his jacket closed but felt no warmer for it. The chill seemed to have settled into my soul.

Trey studied me, his expression troubled. "What else did Saska tell you? Because there's a fear in you that wasn't there before you talked to her."

I raised an eyebrow. "You're not catching my thoughts?"

"Only some. Perhaps that will change as we become more intimate but for now, no."

Good. While I had every intention of telling Kiro what Saska had said regarding the only viable way to get into the hive and kill the queen, I wasn't about to be so open with Trey. Not until it was absolutely necessary. Even if we hadn't been involved, he wasn't the type of man to willingly let *any* of his people undergo what would probably be a suicide mission. For all intents and purposes, I was currently under his command and therefore his responsibility.

"Saska was my twin sister," I said. "She's the reason I can command the air as well as I do. I'm the reason she was able to order the air to interact with earth to get out of that tunnel."

"At least that explains the connection between you." He hesitated. "Are you all right?"

"I discovered I had a blood sister and then lost her all in the past hour," I said, shivering. "And I learned that I killed my mother. So no, I'm not all right."

He didn't say anything, just tugged me into his arms again and held me. That odd connection stirred, filled with a strength and warmth that flowed around and through me, bolstering my reserves.

"And the bodies in the tunnel?" he asked softly, his question whispering past my ear.

"Her daughter, and an Irkallan soldier." I reluctantly pulled away from him and scrubbed away the tear that slid down my cheek. "Saska killed her child rather than let her remain under the queen's rule."

"A monstrous act in any other circumstance but this," he said softly, "and one I fear we will have to repeat if we are to win this war."

I didn't reply to that statement. I didn't even want to think about it.

"We can't just stop them at Winterborne's walls," he continued. "Not this time. The fight has to be taken to them."

"Saska said that was tried during the war. That because

there's no life in the Blacksaw Mountains, no witch will ever be able to do much damage to them."

"Witches might not be able to, but I'm betting a fully equipped army could."

"Aside from the fact Saska said it wouldn't work, if that were true, wouldn't they have tried it last time?"

"Technology has taken some dramatic leaps since then. We now have the power to blast the entire mountain away if we want to."

"That won't help if the bulk of the apiary is deep underground."

He raised an eyebrow. "And is it?"

"From what Saska said, the queen and the breeders certainly are."

He grunted. "That may or may not be a problem. Especially given we have no idea if the tunnel coming out from underneath the mountains is at the same depth as the one we found."

"Its depth would probably depend on where the bulk of the workers and soldiers live."

"Yes." He glanced at Kiro briefly, who was still talking animatedly into his earwig, and then added, "That's not our main problem, however. And it's certainly not the one that will make us monsters."

My throat went dry and my heart began to beat a whole lot faster. I already knew what he was going to say, because Saska had also referred to it, however obliquely.

"The children," he added softly. "We have to find and destroy both the women who were stolen, and all the children they've given birth to. And we have to ensure we collect and destroy the remaining bracelets, so that they can never be used again."

I swallowed heavily, fighting the pain and the knowledge of what was coming. Of what I'd have to do. "But—"

"With or without them, those children have been indoctrinated into Irkallan society. You saw the mental damage it caused Saska—how much worse would it be for children who were born into that environment?"

"Neither Hedra nor Pyra suffered as Saska did, though—"

"Saska suffered because she fought the orders she was being given. Neither her mother nor Pyra did." Trey's voice was grim. "I very much doubt the children would even be capable of it."

There was no doubt about it—Saska had already told me that any child that showed any sort of self-awareness was killed. I was only arguing because I just didn't want to do what I knew I would have to.

I scrubbed my hands across my eyes, smearing tears. "Have you still got the bracelet you took from your daughter?"

He frowned at the sudden change of topic. "Yes—it's in my backpack. Why?"

I shrugged. "I just wanted to ensure it was safe."

Before he could question me further, Kiro approached. "I've called in all available healers and medics from both the Lower Reaches and the outer bailey to cope with whatever levels of sickness might eventuate here in the Upper Reaches over the next twenty-four hours. I've also ordered an immediate meeting of the Forum." His gaze came to mine. "You'll have to report everything you've uncovered."

"I won't reveal my capabilities," I said. "I'm not going to end up as little more than a serf or a damn breeder after all this is finished."

Amusement touched his lips. "Oh, I think there's little chance of that happening."

"I don't care how small the risk, I won't do it."

"Fair enough." He glanced at Trey. "You'll also be asked to report."

"My father will just love that."

His voice was dry, but once again, hurt shadowed the deeper recesses of his eyes. I guessed a man who'd given up everything for his child couldn't understand his own parent not offering *any* level of understanding or forgiveness.

"Your father officially retired from the Forum six months ago, and won't be present," Kiro said. "Karl's daughter is now acting second."

Trey took this news with very little change in his expression, and yet I felt the annoyance—perhaps even anger—flick through him. Obviously, the rift between father and son was now so wide his brother had feared to pass on such a vital piece of information.

But better that than being in the situation of learning who your mother was only *after* you'd killed her....

I crossed my arms and thrust the thought away. I wouldn't have changed my actions even if I *had* known Hedra was my mother, so why dwell over it? "And what's being done about the water?"

"Engineers are on their way, and a code red alert has been issued across the Upper Reaches," Kiro said. "Given it's been three hours since the toxin was added to the water supply, I've also called out the guard to do a house by house check of inhabitants to uncover the current state of play in regard to illnesses or even deaths."

In other words, they were currently doing all they could. We all just had to hope it would be enough.

"Neve, I know you're soaked to the skin," he continued, "but I'd rather you remain in your current clothes. It'll add a sense of urgency to proceedings."

I raised an eyebrow. "Meaning they'll take a bedraggled woman more seriously than they would a Nightwatch officer?"

"Yes, especially when you're introduced as Trey's second."

He glanced around as three men entered the pump room. "Ah, good. You've been apprised of the situation?"

The big man who'd entered first nodded. "We've got a second team closing down all the supply valves as we speak. We're here to fix the pumps so the tower can be emptied and flushed out."

"Excellent." Kiro's gaze met mine. "Ready?"

Not to face the Forum, I wasn't, but at least I was doing it by Trey's side. I nodded, and then took off the jacket and held it out.

"Keep it," Trey said. "You're shivering."

"Yes, but it's pointless both of us—"

"I'm hardly going to get soaked between here and the carriage," he cut in, "so just put the coat on, Neve."

I did, and then followed Kiro back out into the rain and the waiting vehicle. The Irkallan's head—still wrapped in my coat—sat on the floor. Trey had barely closed the door when the carriage took off. It didn't take us long to get to the building that housed the sitting members of the Forum, which was situated in the middle of the plateau and was a plain-looking, circular white building. It was only single story and the roof was an odd green-gray—the sort of color copper went as it aged, though I wasn't sure the roof here was made of that material. In fact, given the sleek, shiny finish, it rather looked like glass.

On this side of the building, there were three entrances, all of which were heavily guarded. The carriage stopped directly opposite the biggest of them; Kiro motioned Trey to grab the Irkallan's head and then climbed out. We followed. As we drew closer to the doorway, one of the guards saluted and said, "Lord Kiro, the arbitrator wishes to advise you that a quorum is now present and they are awaiting your presentation."

Kiro nodded and continued into the building.

"A quorum?" Trey said, as we followed him into the sweeping and surprisingly large foyer. "That suggests we might have only just met minimum quota."

"Indeed," Kiro said. "But at least we've reached it, and can therefore immediately act on whatever decisions are made here this evening."

We strode toward a set of intricately carved gold doors, our footsteps echoing on the darkly stained wooden floorboards. The doors opened as we approached, revealing a room that again was rather plain and surprisingly small. An odd light seemed to fill the room and I glanced up at the ceiling. In the place of stone, metal, or even wood, was a solid piece of green glass, and it soared gloriously over the room like the canopy of a forest. And perhaps it was the reason for the plainness elsewhere—you had no need for extravagance when such a beautiful piece of craftsmanship lay above.

The room itself was divided into two parts. The half on this side featured two rows of darkly stained wooden chairs —the back ones slightly elevated above the front—and on the other, a raised platform. A single wooden chair sat to the left of this, in which a balding man in his mid-fifties sat. Although my knowledge of how the Forum worked was only rudimentary—little more than what they taught in school, really—I knew that man was the arbitrator. It was his job to maintain order within the Forum, but he could also cast a deciding vote in the rare eventuality of such being needed. For that reason, the arbitrator never came from any of the houses, be they upper or lower, but rather from the ranks of those who—like Kiro—had personal magic, and who were well known and trusted amongst all the houses.

Almost half of the wooden chairs were occupied and, as Kiro led us up to some empty seats on the left side of the second row of seats, my gaze swept the nearby faces. I couldn't see anyone who in any way resembled Trey.

Kiro motioned us to sit then walked back down to the floor and across to the platform. Trey tucked the Irkallan's head under the seat and then nudged me lightly with his shoulder. When I glanced at him, he murmured, "Front row, middle seats, green cushions. My brother and his daughter."

My gaze fell on them. Although—at least from side on—there didn't appear to be much physical resemblance between the brothers, the young woman could have been Eluria's sister.

"Did he acknowledge you coming in?"

"No." Once again, his smile held a bitterness that spoke of hurt. "I think perhaps Father's anger has infected him."

"Maybe he simply believes the Forum is not an appropriate place for such a reunion."

"Which is undoubtedly true. It does not, however, explain his avoidance of me over the last few days."

I reached out and entwined my fingers through his. He squeezed them briefly then released me. Perhaps the Forum was also no place for a display of affection, however minor.

"What about the Rossi household?" I asked softly. "Who's taken Marcus's place here in the Forum?"

Trey discreetly pointed to seats to our left. "Who do you think?"

Jamson. I guess *that* was no surprise given he *was* heir. "Did Kiro discover who murdered Marcus?"

"It was Lida, as you suspected. She also planned to kill Saska."

Because Saska had been pregnant with a child who, if gifted, would replace Lida's son as heir. "I know Jamson had nothing to do with the murder, but it still stinks that he benefits—" I cut the rest of the comment off as Kiro began to speak. In a calm, emotionless voice, he told the assembly everything we'd uncovered, including the duplicity of the three women and exactly what they'd done. But he didn't mention the Irkallan, instead calling Trey to join him on the platform and recount his part of the story. Trey did so, but again, he made no mention of the Irkallan. That task was obviously mine.

Kiro called me to the dais. I took a deep, shaky breath that did little to calm the rush of nerves, and then picked up the wrapped head and walked down. A gentle murmur followed me to the platform, but I couldn't tell if it was due to some of the lords and ladies here recognizing me from the masque, or if it was simply because I very obviously had no right to be in such a place. I stepped onto the platform; Trey moved to one side, giving me room to stand between the two of them.

"Tell them everything distinctly and without embellishment," Kiro murmured, as he took the Irkallan's head from me. "From the moment the beacon was spotted to what Saska told you up on the water tower."

I took another deep breath and did exactly that, only omitting the fact I was Nightwatch rather than a Blacklake soldier. It took forever because there was so much to tell, and by the time I'd finished my throat was dry and my skin so cold it was beginning to leech inward, forming a thick pit of ice in my stomach.

"Do you truly expect us to believe the Irkallan have been active for centuries?" a pale-skinned man sitting to the right of Trey's brother said, "and that we've caught absolutely no sign of it until now?"

"Indeed," Kiro said. "In fact, if not for the actions of both Officer March and Commander Stone, we'd still be dangerously unaware of said activity."

"But what evidence of this do you have?" a woman at the rear said, "aside from the testimony of someone who abandoned his family *and* his position, and a stained soldier?"

"You'd do well to hold both your tongue and your

animosity, Lia," Trey said, voice clipped. "Especially given it was the actions of your sister that led to my leaving."

The woman snorted. "I believe it takes two—"

"Enough," the arbitrator said, in a voice so loud it echoed through the chamber. "We're not here to discuss old grievances, but rather a future threat. Kiro, if you have proof, present it."

He did so, unwrapping the Irkallan's head and then holding it high so all could see. Once again, a murmur filled the room, but this time it was a weird mix of unease and disbelief. But then, this was the first time anyone here would have seen an Irkallan outside the pages of a history book.

"As Officer March has already said, the Irkallan's body was found in a tunnel not far from the Blacklake outpost. The body of a child lay with it—that child was Lady Saska's, one of many born to the witches stolen from Winterborne. This insidious plan has been in operation for *centuries*, my lords, and it's now coming to fruition. The Irkallan are using their half-breeds to mine the earth and create tunnels— tunnels that not only bypass our outposts, but have, in fact, made a beeline directly to our door. The end of one such tunnel lies no more than half a mile from Winterborne's gates—and you can thank Commander Stone for uncovering its existence this afternoon. Otherwise, we mightn't have known about it until they were murdering us in our sleep."

"I hardly think *that* possible," another man from the front row said. "Their witches surely could not be as strong as any here."

"If their plan to eradicate the Upper Reaches witches via poisoning had been fully successful," Kiro noted, "they wouldn't have needed to be."

"There's also the point that they've managed to bring a tunnel to the very feet of our wall, and none here detected it," Trey said. "None of you have even noticed the uneasiness of the Tenterra earth, or the fact there are now large areas of deadness—a deadness that bleeds out from the Blacksaw Mountains itself."

"You're well aware our focus has been on the Gallion farmlands on which this place survives," another bit back. "We can't be blamed—"

"No one is blaming anyone," Kiro said. "We're merely stating unpalatable facts."

"It seems to me we have two major problems right now," a new voice said. I glanced to the left and saw it was Karl, Trey's brother. "The first being how do we stop them at our gates if their tunneling deadens the earth and prevents us interacting with it. The second is whether we even have enough firepower to dig them out from under their mountains."

"According to Lady Saska," I said. "We do not."

His gaze came to me; the green depths were so familiar and yet so foreign it sent a shiver down my spine. "And are we to believe the words of a woman who was in thrall to the Irkallan queen? A woman who is responsible for an attempted mass poisoning, and who might yet be responsible for the deaths of hundreds of people?"

"Don't forget she *did* tell me about the toxin, even against the queen's orders," I countered. "And she's also the only reason we know about the tunnels."

A small smile tugged at his lips, and again it was familiar and yet not.

"What exactly did Lady Saska tell you about any attack on the Blacksaw Mountains?" Kiro asked.

I glanced at him; in his pale eyes, I saw the awareness of secrets being kept. I drew in a deep breath and released it slowly. Now was not the time to hold back—at least not on something that would have major implications for any action taken. "She said that you can attack the mountains for all you're worth, but you won't destroy the Irkallan. The apiary lies too deep underground to be affected by weapons, and any attempt to invade on foot would be similarly doomed, not just because of the tunnels' close quarters, but because of their sheer numbers."

"But she would say that," Karl said, even as Kiro asked, "Did she offer any solution to that problem."

"She did." And he knew it. I could see the knowledge in his eyes, and the determination that lay underneath it. He might not know what she'd said, but he was well aware there was more to her warning than what I'd already admitted.

"And?" he asked, when I didn't immediately go on.

I crossed my arms, but it did little against the invading cold or the deep sense of inevitability that was beginning to flow through me. The air stirred around me, offering me comfort, offering me strength, but never once offering me hope.

"She said if we wished to destroy them, there was only one way to do so." I hesitated, well aware of tension gathering in the man standing to my left. It was a tension that flowed through me, heated and angry—not at me, but at the situation and fate. At what he obviously guessed might be coming. "She said the only way to avoid detection was to send one person—and only one—into the apiary."

"*No.*" Trey's response was immediate and explosive.

"And is that person you?" Kiro said.

"Yes," I said. "Because it turns out that Saska and I were not only sisters, but twins. The fact that my DNA is so similar to both hers and Hedra's—our mother—will me to give me the chance to slip inside when they will scent all others."

"That is *madness*—"

"Indeed, it is." I met Trey's furious gaze evenly. "But it's a madness Saska believed, and one I also do. There *is* no other option. Not if we wish to keep Winterborne and all we hold dear safe."

"Thank you, Officer March," Kiro said, before Trey could say anything else. "We'll now have to discuss options, so I'll ask you wait in the foyer."

Summarily dismissed, I left the platform and walked out of the room. Trey's gaze followed my retreat. I knew without looking it was fierce, filled with anger and frustration, even if the rest of his expression was remote. Knew it because it was a river of emotion that flowed through me, amplifying my own fears and uncertainty.

I somehow made it out the door without giving in to that flood of emotion, but once the doors closed, the trembling began. I staggered across to the small seating area to the left of the main door, then dropped my head between my knees and sucked in air.

They were going to approve the plan. I had absolutely no doubt of that. Those who lived and ruled here in the Upper Reaches were a practical lot, and if there was *any* chance that one lone, unimportant unlit soldier could do what an army could not, then they'd order it done. No doubt there would be soldiers, equipment, and witches on standby should I fail, but they would nevertheless take the chance that Saska wasn't entirely mad, that her words held some grains of truth, and thereby risk only one life rather than many.

But the thought of going to into that mountain and roaming through the tunnels alone and without any sort of assistance filled me with a fear unlike anything I'd ever known.

You will not be alone, the voices said. This time, it was both the whispering wind and the more sober, earthy tones of the earth. *We will be with you.*

Which was good to hear, but it didn't help the fear. Because if something went wrong down there, I'd die alone.

And for any Nightwatch officer, that was perhaps the worst of all fates.

Neither the wind nor the earth had a reply to that. After a few more minutes, I pushed back in the seat, rested my head against the wall, and closed my eyes. And though I didn't think I'd sleep given the turmoil and the fear, I did.

Hours passed, and night became day. Eventually the assembly room doors opened and people began to stream out. Most of them ignored me, but a couple of them—including Trey's brother—did at least glance my way and give me a nod.

Kiro and Trey were in the last group to come out of the room. Trey's gaze almost immediately came to mine, but his expression was guarded and he didn't say anything. Kiro was talking animatedly to a man dressed in gold—the color of the Hawthorn ruling house.

I pushed up from the chair as they neared. The stranger looked my way and gave me a tight smile. "I wish you luck, Officer March. Much seems to rest on your young shoulders."

With that, he strode out of the room. I glanced at Kiro. "So it's been approved?"

"In theory, yes. There are still many finer details to be worked out, however."

"Saska said the Irkallan were coming. I don't think we have the time—"

"You're *not* going out there alone and unsupported," Trey growled. "I don't care how close the Irkallan are, we'll at least ensure you have a fighting chance of getting in *and* getting out."

"Which is nice sentiment but one that could yet prove costly—"

"You are currently under *my* command, and therefore my responsibility, March." His tone was that of a commander, not a lover. "I've never sent a soldier into a situation without first ensuring all eventualities have been considered and every chance has been given for a positive outcome. I'm certainly *not* doing so now."

He might have conceded the necessity of me doing this, but he was far from happy about it. That, at least, was something we both agreed on. I returned my gaze to Kiro. "So, what happens next?"

"You go rest. I've already ordered the Nightwatch to your suite at the Rossis' to ensure no one comes in or out while you do so."

"And what about the Irkallan? And the tunnel? What plans are being made to counter both?"

"As I said, they still need refining. We currently await the arrival of the remaining outpost commanders."

"But the Irkallan—"

"Sensors are being placed under the soil as we speak. We'll know soon enough if they're coming," Kiro said. "Even if the Irkallan's witchlings *are* currently working on that tunnel, it could still take them days to reach the wall, and possibly even weeks to burrow under both it and the subterranean levels. Our counteractions will more than likely begin tomorrow."

We dare not wait until tomorrow, the wind whispered. *We do not know how long we have until the Irkallan queen realizes Saska has fallen. We have a limited window in which to act.*

Which was undoubtedly true, but I wasn't about to leave Winterborne without at least saying goodbye to those I cared about. And if I were to have any hope of achieving the task Saska had set me, then I also had to be at my peak, both physically and mentally, and that meant I needed to eat and rest.

I crossed my arms, my fists clenched against the desire to reach out for the man who stood so close. To ask him to wrap his arms around me and keep the gathering darkness at bay, if only for a few precious minutes. "There's no way I'm going to sleep right now—"

"Try," Trey said. "Because you'll need every ounce of strength to survive what comes."

And survive you must. He didn't say that out loud, but I heard it nevertheless.

"Then I'll need some sort of potion to do so," I continued, voice flat. "There's altogether too much going through my mind right now."

"I'll order a healer to attend your suite." Kiro glanced at Trey. "We must go. Neve, we'll drop you off—"

"Thanks, but I'll walk," I said. "I'm so cold now that it won't matter, and I need the fresh air after being stuck here for so long."

"Yes." Kiro paused. "I apologize for that. I should have asked for food and wine to be brought to you."

I shrugged. "I'm not going to fade away for lack of a meal."

"No, but you could have caught a chill and that—"

"Is the least of my problems right now. Go make your plans, Lord Kiro. I'll be waiting to play my part."

He nodded and walked out the door. Trey didn't immediately follow. Instead, he tucked a stray strand of hair behind my ear and said, "I'll do everything in my power to ensure you survive this. You know that, don't you?"

I nodded but didn't say anything. Everything he could do wouldn't be enough, and we both knew it. The earth and the air wouldn't be so silent if there was a sliver of hope.

He studied me for a moment longer, then dropped his hand and followed Kiro out the door. I waited until the carriage had left then walked out into the cold light of day. Though it had finally stopped raining, the air held a bitterness that cut me to the quick, adding to the ice already lying inside.

I resolutely made my way through the Upper Reaches and down the winding road that led to the outer bailey. Good-byes were in order, and though I managed to keep hold of my emotions, April nevertheless sensed there was something amiss.

"Are you okay?" he said, as I pulled away from his hug.

"Yes. It's just that this is the first time we're taking the fight to the Adlin's home ground, and I'm feeling a little antsy. You know how it is."

It seemed safer to say it was the Adlin rather than the Irkallan, given the truth behind the attacks hadn't yet been released to the wider public—and maybe never would.

"Yeah, and I'm wishing right now I was sharing those prefight jitters. Pisses me off no end I'm stuck in here while you and Ava get all the action."

"Tell you what, I'll kill a couple of them in your name." That, at least, was one promise I *could* keep.

"Excellent." He squeezed my hand and then released me. "I won't say be careful because you always are. I will say that you owe me a full recap over several beers once I get out of here."

"Done deal." I stepped back, hesitated, then bid him goodbye before he could see or sense the tears that were threatening to fall.

It had to be close to midday by the time I made it back to the Rossi household. The halls were empty and silent, and there was no music or laughter flowing from the other end of the building—which was no surprise given most would currently be asleep after partying all night.

Ava and Ranel were standing guard at the door into the suite Trey and I had been assigned.

"About time you appeared," Ava grumbled as she hit the

door-open button. "The healer's been waiting for over half an hour. Where the hell have you been?"

"I went down to check on April. I didn't think the healer would arrive so soon."

"Well, he did, and he's pretty annoyed." Her gaze swept me. "You don't look ill—everything all right?"

I forced a smile. "Yeah, it's just that I need to grab some sleep and I'm thinking I'll need some chemical help to do so."

"Ah," she said. "So what's going on? The bastards really haven't told us much. We don't even know what happened to Gen and Luc."

"They're dead, I'm afraid. Lady Saska tossed them over the cliff."

"I hope the bitch pays for that," Ranel said.

That bitch was my sister... but I kept the words inside and simply said, "She did. She's dead."

Ava frowned. She might not be able to read my mind, but she knew me better than any person alive and I had no doubt she could see the sadness within me.

"There's something else going on, isn't there?" she said. "Something big."

"There's a major assault being planned," I said. "One that involves not only both the Night and Day watches, but also all the outposts."

"Then I hope to hell we're not stuck here," Ranel growled. "I'll be royally annoyed if we miss out on that sort of action."

A smile touched my lips. "April said much the same thing."

"I can just imagine." Ava still looked concerned, but she didn't give it voice, just stepped back and opened the door. "You'd better get inside and grab some rest. We've orders to let no one else in now except Commander Stone or Lord Kiro."

"Good." I gave her a quick hug, said a silent goodbye, and then went inside.

A thin-faced man in his mid-forties rose from one of the cloudsaks. "About time, Lady Neve—"

"I'm sorry for the delay," I said. "Did Lord Kiro explain what I'm after?"

"He said a sleeping draught—correct?"

I nodded, my heart beating a little faster. "And a fairly strong one, if you have it. I want an uninterrupted eight hours rest."

"That, at least, is an easy request." He opened the satchel he was carrying and plucked a vial of clear liquid free. "This should do the trick—it'll work in a matter of minutes, and keep you asleep for at least eight hours."

"So I take the whole vial?"

"Yes." He handed it over, then closed his bag and said, "Anything else?"

"No." I hesitated. "Has there been much of a fallout from the toxin being placed in the water?"

"Numerous deaths in the ranks of the serving class, but only three so far from the ruling houses. Plenty showing unpleasant and possibly deadly symptoms, however, so I'll bid you a good day, and be off."

"Thanks for waiting."

He nodded as he left. I glanced down at the vial in my hand then placed it down on the coffee table and walked across to the discreetly placed buzzer to one side of the main door and kept my fingers crossed our maidservant was one of the ones who'd survived. It seemed luck was on my side and hers, because a few seconds after I pressed the buzzer, she appeared.

"What can I do you for, my lady?"

"I'd like a large platter of meats, breads, and cheese,

please. And some wine, too." I hesitated. "What's the water situation like here? Do we have any?"

She nodded. "The Rossi are one of three upper houses that disconnected from the old tower's supply after installing their own tanks fifteen years ago. I believe a temporary pump system has been set up so we can supply water to the rest of the houses."

"Ah, good. Thanks."

She nodded again and disappeared. I walked back over to the cloudsaks and sat down. If I wanted to obey the wind and leave tonight, then I had to do two things aside from getting as much rest as I could today. The first was to get hold of both a speeder and weapons, as having both would conserve my strength getting to the Blacksaw Mountains and give me options for destroying the apiary once I was inside.

If I got inside, that was.

The other thing I had to do was convince Trey it had to be done my way, not his.

To achieve the first, I'd have to talk to Kiro. It would be the quickest and easiest way to get what I needed, as his word was the next-best thing to law, at least around here.

The second, however, was likely to prove impossible.

I eyed the small vial uneasily. Using it might just break something that was both new and fragile, but did that really matter given survival was highly unlikely?

It was a question I really didn't want to answer, even if part of me was screaming that of *course* it did.

I closed my eyes and tried to rest as I waited for the maid to return with my meal. I must have drifted, because when I opened my eyes, there was a tray of covered meats and a bottle of red on the table, and the fading light streaming in through the windows suggested dusk wasn't very far away.

I poured myself a glass of wine and ate my fill of the breads and meats. There was still plenty left on the platter, but that was good as I needed some sustenance for my journey. Once I'd finished, I wrapped the remaining breads and cheeses in a large waterproof cloth and tucked them away for later, then slipped the sleeping draft down the side of the sofa where Trey was unlikely to see it. With that done, I stripped off, had a shower, and then headed into the sleeping chamber. The bed Pyra had shattered had been replaced as Trey had ordered, but there were still too many memories of her actions left in the pitted walls and flooring.

I tried to ignore them and crawled under blankets where, despite the turmoil and the belief that I wouldn't sleep, I did.

The room was wrapped in darkness when I awoke. For several minutes I simply lay there, listening to the howl of the wind outside but hearing no voices within her. The suite itself was silent and I had no sense that anyone was near.

I climbed out of bed and walked into the living area. As I did, the main door opened and Trey entered. He smiled when he saw me, but it held little of its usual vigor, and the redness in his eyes was matched by the weariness that cloaked him.

"You look worn out," I said as I walked toward him.

"It's been a rather long twenty-four hours."

He caught my hand and pulled me into his arms. For a moment, neither of us said anything. We simply enjoyed the comfort of each other's presence.

"So," I said eventually, "what decisions have been made?"

"I leave at dawn for Blacklake. The attack is timed for midmorning as that's the earliest we outpost commanders believe we can get supplies ready and our forces moving."

"So you're attacking en masse?"

"No. We'll cross the river from our various positions and attack the apiary's known exits on several fronts. Winterborne will send a force into the Adlin homelands to stop any sleuths from answering a call to arms by the Irkallan queen.

Hopefully by attacking them on so many fronts we'll draw their attention away from Drakkon's Head, and give you the chance to slip in, find and destroy those kids and the queen, and then lay the charges and get out."

"But what if the queen orders the kids into battle?"

"I doubt she'll risk their use unless absolutely necessary. Not if she has as many soldiers as Saska claimed."

Part of me hoped he was right. But the other half—the selfish half that didn't want to the responsibility of ending the lives of so many children, even if they *were* indoctrinated into the enemy's way of life—hoped otherwise.

I pulled away from his embrace and studied him again. "You look as though you're in desperate need of a hot meal."

He scrubbed a hand across his eyes. "I am. All I've had is coffee."

"Then go clean up and I'll order us both something. The water here is safe—apparently the Rossi have their own supply."

"Excellent."

He dropped a kiss on my lips then headed for the bathroom. Once he'd disappeared behind the partially drawn curtain, I poured two glasses of red and then retrieved the sleeping potion. With that poured into one of the glasses, I called for the maid and ordered our meal.

By the time he'd freshened up, the thick, delicious-smelling stew and freshly baked bread had arrived. I picked up the two glasses of red as he walked toward me, a towel wrapped around his hips and tiredness still riding him. It made me feel a little less guilty about what I was doing.

But only a little.

I smiled and handed him the wine that held the potion, and then lightly clicked my glass against his. "To a successful mission and a safe return."

"Amen to that." And he downed the wine in several gulps.

I poured him another, then dished out our meals and sat beside him on the double cloudsak. While it was a comfortable silence, tension nevertheless ran through me—an undercurrent that wasn't helped by the stirring air and the urgency that was becoming stronger within it.

Trey was struggling to keep his eyes open by the time he'd finished his meal. "This," he said, with a huge yawn, "is definitely not the way I'd imagined the evening going."

I chuckled softly and plucked the bowl from his hands before he could drop it. "Me neither, but we have all night and I'd rather you sleep now than tomorrow on the battlefield." I placed both bowls on the table, then rose and offered him my hands. "Come along, Commander. Time for you to hit the bed."

He allowed me to pull him up and leaned on me heavily as I helped him across the room. "I don't know what's hit me," he murmured. "I've taken part in more than my fair share of war councils over the years, and while I've been tired, it's never been this bad."

"This sort of thing happens when you get old." I forced a smile and hoped he didn't sense the gathering guilt. "Or so I'm told."

He snorted softly. "You make me sound ancient."

"When I was a teenager, anything over thirty *was* ancient."

I pulled off his towel, then pulled back the sheets and sat him down—although in truth, he all but fell down. I swung his legs onto the mattress and tugged the sheets back over him. His eyes drifted closed, and in seconds he was asleep.

I bent over and brushed a kiss across his lips.

"Goodbye, Trey," I said softly. "Please don't think ill of me in the morning. I'm only doing what has to be done."

I pushed away from him, pushed away my emotions, and strode into the other room. Once dressed, I hunted down his pack and checked the bracelet was still there, then refilled his water flask and placed it and the wrapped cheese and bread into it. I strapped my sword onto the outside of the pack, my knife to my leg, and then swung the pack onto my back. With a deep breath but no backward glance, I strode to the door and opened it.

"Neve," Ava said, surprise flitting across her face. "I thought the commander said you weren't to be disturbed?"

I grimaced. "Change of plans, unfortunately. Can you contact Lord Kiro and tell him that I'll be at the Upper Reaches gates in ten minutes?"

She nodded and did so. "He sounded somewhat surprised," she said, after a few seconds. "But he'll be there. Are you sure everything is okay?"

"Yes." I gave her a quick hug. "If you're assigned to the Adlin attack party tomorrow, please be careful."

"Ditto, sister."

"Always," I said, and left.

Kiro was already waiting by the gates before I arrived there. His gaze swept me then rose to mine. "I'm gathering you've chosen a very separate path to what either Trey or I had planned."

"Yes." I stopped in front of him. "According to the wind, there's a limited window in which I can get into the apiary unnoticed. I need to be there by sunrise if this attack is to have any chance of success."

"Meaning, I'm gathering, the potion the healer gave to you was given to Trey?"

I nodded. "He'll wake with dawn."

"The wind's advice isn't to be taken lightly, so it is perhaps for the best," he said. "But he'll be far from happy with your actions."

"I know." I hesitated. "Tell him I'm sorry."

He eyed me but didn't say what most would have—that I could tell him myself when all this was over. Kiro was a realist—as his next words proved. "What do you wish of me?"

"I need explosives, guns, and a speeder."

He immediately activated the earwig and ordered the supply of all three. Once he'd signed off, he added, "Go to armory five and collect what you need. The speeder is being prepped and will be waiting by the time you're kitted up."

"Thanks."

He gripped my shoulder lightly. "May the wind give you speed and the earth grant you passage back. And thank you, Neve March."

I nodded but didn't say anything, simply because there was nothing I could say. We both knew this was more than likely a one-way trip, and wishing it otherwise wouldn't change a damn thing.

Which didn't mean I *wouldn't* give everything I had to survive, but Kiro wasn't the only realist standing in this street.

I walked on down the hill. The wind chased my heels, her whisperings filled with the urgent need to be gone. Armory five was situated at the midway point of the inner curtain wall, just to the right of the gates and close to where Hedra had died. A soldier I didn't recognize waited at the door.

"Nightwatch March?" When I nodded, he added, "Captain July has given orders that you're to be given as much weaponry and explosives as you need."

"Excellent." I swung the pack off my shoulder and followed him inside. "I need a couple of gut busters, ammo, and some form of explosives that are basically set and forget."

He grunted. "You want a big boom or a little one?"

"Big." I hesitated. "Although a couple of smaller ones wouldn't go astray. I also want reasonably stable, as I don't want to blow myself up before I get to my target."

"Then the M185 blocks are probably best for the bigger blast. They have the power to blow up a mountain if you put enough of them together, but are quite harmless until you put the detonation timer into it."

"How long will I have to get out once I do that?"

He hesitated. "The longest timers I have on hand are twenty minutes, but I think there's—"

"Twenty minutes will do," I cut in. I couldn't afford to waste any more time. Not when the wind was beginning to hassle me again. "What about the smaller booms? I think I'll need something stronger than grenades."

Given the toughness of the Irkallan's exoskeleton and the fact grenades were primarily designed to damage via concussion and shrapnel, it was probably safe to presume they wouldn't actually cause enough damage to stop more than a couple of them. Grenades worked just fine on Adlin, but no text I'd ever read had mentioned their usefulness against the Irkallan.

"I've got a dozen or so NP10 balls," he said. "Team them with the pop cap primers and you've basically got a grenade with a more deadly boom."

"Three or four of those would be perfect."

He nodded. "And the M185 blocks?"

I frowned. "How big are they? I need to carry them a fair way."

"They not large. You can probably get six in that pack of yours easy enough."

I handed him the pack. "Fill her up then."

He chuckled softly and did so. Once he'd shown me how to insert the detonator and set the timer on the blocks, and how to use the cap primers, I threw the pack on and then clipped the two gut busters and several ammo clips onto my utilities belt. I would have loved more, but I had to be able to move with a decent amount of silence and speed. I signed for everything, thanked the soldier, and then headed out. As Kiro had promised, the speeder had been brought up from the underground level and was waiting in the middle of the outer bailey. Captain July was standing beside it.

"Haven't been told what your assignment is, March," he said, his raspy tones filled with the concern I could see in his expression, "but take care. I hate losing good soldiers."

"Thanks, Cap."

He nodded and stepped back. I climbed into the speeder, stowed the pack, then claimed the driver seat and hit the start button. As the Captain ordered the gate opened, I closed the door and strapped in.

But as I waited for the huge gates to open, fear stirred anew.

I might be Nightwatch; I might have been trained from a very early age to follow orders and fight, no matter what the odds or the cost, but right now I was also as scared as hell.

But my sister and my mother had left me with no other option; I had to do this alone. I just had to hope that Saska was right, that because we were twins and our DNA was similar, the Irkallan wouldn't be alarmed if they sensed my presence in their tunnels.

But I also had to hope I could find the strength to do what had to be done when it came to those children.

Anything else beyond that was a bonus, and that included finding the queen and bringing the mountain down on top of the apiary itself. Survival would be a miracle, and something I was realistically not even hoping for.

As the gates opened wide enough for the speeder to pass through, I pressed the accelerator and headed out into the darkness of the Tenterra dustbowl.

12

The flags of dawn were beginning to taint the sky by the time I reached the foot of the Blacksaw Mountains. They loomed above the small craft like some felled, misbegotten giant, and were as dark and as barren as they'd looked from a distance. There didn't seem to be any easy way for the speeder to get up its craggy side without receiving major damage, so I halted underneath some overhanging boulders and shut it down. The darkness closed in, thick and eerie—the latter sensation not easing as my eyes adjusted to the surrounding ink.

I opened the door, grabbed the pack, and climbed out. The air was crisp, but it was nowhere near as cold here as it had been in Winterborne. No doubt the sheer distance from the sea and the arctic winds that blew off it had something to do with that.

Somewhere high above me was Drakkon's Head, the main entrance into the Irkallan's apiary, but I couldn't see it from where I stood. In fact, there was nothing but rock and a few scrubby, ill-looking plants for as far as the eye could see.

I slung the pack over my shoulders and then said, "What

are the chances of getting a lift up there?"

The wind immediately whipped around me and, in very little time, had encased me in a bubble of gossamer air and shunted me up the dark mountainside. About halfway, the scrubby vegetation completely gave up any attempt at survival, and the landscape became little more than a wonderland of rocks of all shapes and sizes.

The speed of my ascent finally eased and, as the gossamer started evaporating, the maw-like entrance into the mountains became visible. It was easy to see why this area had been named Drakkon's Head—it very much looked like one of those mythical beasts had found its end here, with the tunnel's entrance its open mouth, complete with jagged, glinting black teeth.

The air dropped me gently onto the ground. Dust stirred around my feet, smelling and looking like ash. The fierce, rocky outcrop that was the drakkon's head towered above me, its eyes ebony pits that seemed to be aware and watching even though I logically knew they were probably nothing more than smaller caves.

I couldn't see or hear any life in the immediate area, but the stench coming out of the drakkon's mouth reminded me of the smell that had radiated from the three children who'd assaulted Blacklake, only a thousand times worse. It made my stomach heave and, for several seconds, I battled the urge to vomit. If I was to have any hope of getting deep into the apiary, I was going to need fresh air.

That we can provide, the wind said, *just as we did before. But you should not linger here. A patrol draws close.*

I swore softly, drew my knife and one of the gut busters, and walked forward. The wind chased along behind me, stirring the ash and erasing any sign of my presence.

The closer I got to the drakkon's mouth, the more my fear of it rose. I knew it was ridiculous, knew the drakkon was merely a creation of rock and erosion, but there was a heaviness and anticipation riding the wind's coattails that made it seem as if the whole mountain was about to come alive and consume me.

Which really *wasn't* so far off the mark, given what I was walking into.

I edged along one side of the drakkon's maw, every sense I had alert for any hint of movement deeper within the cave. The wind was urging me to hurry, warning that the patrol was little more than minutes away, but I couldn't afford to rush. One misstep might spell the end of everything before it had even started.

As the darkness of the quickly fading night gave way to the deeper ink of the cave, my knife began to give off a soft, blue-white glow. It was a light that picked out a similar luminance within the walls and, after a moment, I realized there were long seams of glimmer stone within the black rock. Perhaps *this* was where the Adlin had gotten the stone for their beacons.

I shoved the knife away. I couldn't risk the Irkallan patrol noticing the glinting stone, nor could I risk whatever guards there might be beyond this large antechamber seeing the knife's soft glow.

I waited for the gleam in the walls to fade and my eyes to once again adjust before moving on. There were two tunnels at the far end of the chamber, one peeling off to the left and one going straight down.

As I hesitated, studying them both, the wind said, *left.*

I obeyed. The tunnel walls immediately closed in and the air became thick with that stomach-churning stench. The wind stirred in response, brushing away the worst of it, allowing me to move on without the threat of my stomach's contents decorating my boots.

There wasn't much to see. The tunnel's walls were

surprisingly smooth but held no beat of life. Not even the memory of it lingered. If this mountain had once contained earth magic, then it had been gone for centuries, if not a millennium.

The Irkallan might not have caused it, but I couldn't help wondering who or what had—and whether it would eventually spread beyond these mountains.

No, the wind whispered.

How can you be sure? The earth has no voice in this place.

Not here, but there is life elsewhere, and she shares her secrets. Miners lived and worked in these mountains long before the Irkallan arrived. They robbed these mountains of both its minerals and its life, and then moved on to find new lands to mine and destroy.

Which perhaps explained why there was no mention of them in any history books—it had simply happened too long ago.

The deeper I moved into the tunnel, the warmer it became. Sweat trickled down my spine, and I had to keep swapping the gut buster from one hand to the other so I could swipe the moisture from my palms.

The downward incline continued, gradually getting steeper. I had no sense of time or distance in this place. There was nothing to judge such things by—no sound, no light, no life.

Then the wind slapped against me, forcing me to stop. My breath caught in my throat as I listened for whatever danger might lay ahead. After a moment, I heard it—a footstep. One that was little more than a whisper, and spoke of bare feet against rock.

My fingers tensed against the gut buster, even though I knew firing it was the last thing I needed to do in this place.

Another footstep echoed, one that was oddly different to the first—it was heavier, and accompanied by an odd, scraping sound. Tension ran through me, but I resisted the urge to move, to retreat back up the tunnel. If I could hear them, they'd undoubtedly hear me.

A soft glow began to infuse the darkness, one that reminded me of the light generated by the glimmer stone in the main cave. As it got stronger, the veins in my tunnel began to glow, providing a halo of cool brightness that thankfully didn't reach up to where I stood.

But it gave me some sense of where I now was. This tunnel ended at a T-intersection roughly fifty feet away. The intersecting tunnel was double the width of this one and, if the pathway worn into the floor's rock surface was anything to go by, saw a whole lot more traffic.

The glow of light coming from the glimmer stone seams got stronger, the footsteps closer. While the wind gave no hint as to what might be coming, she shifted direction, drawing fresh air around me and then sweeping it back up the tunnel. Taking my scent away from whatever approached rather than toward it, I realized.

Shadows appeared and began to solidify. One small, one large.

One human in form, the other the stuff of nightmares.

My gut churned with renewed vigor.

Because the figure holding the tiny light that was causing the glimmer stone to glow so brightly was a small, stained child. One with short-cropped brown hair, a face that was thin, hollow, and grubby, and a body that only held small patches of brown skin in amongst the staining. Small rivulets of moisture ran down his emaciated torso, but did little to erase the dirt caking his flesh, and he was all but dragging his feet.

The other was an Irkallan.

Though the child continued, the Irkallan paused in the middle of the T-intersection; its antennae moved back and forth as its dark, oval-shaped eyes stared right at me. After a moment, it made an odd clicking noise, its mandibles opening and shutting as if in vexation.

I didn't move. I didn't even breathe.

With another click, it moved on, and as the light began to fade, I slumped against the tunnel wall and breathed deeply in an attempt to calm my racing pulse.

Damn, that was close.

I grabbed the flask from the pack and took a long drink to ease the burning in my throat. Once it was stoppered and placed back, I cautiously moved forward. At the intersection I stopped again, looking carefully to the right to ensure there were no other Irkallan or children approaching, and then glanced left.

The soft light was slowly fading as the Irkallan and the child moved around the tunnel's gentle curve to the right.

Follow the child, the wind said. *He will lead you to the rest.*

Which was precisely what I'd intended, and what I'd hoped.

I stepped out into the larger tunnel and padded after the two of them as quietly as I could. But my footsteps were far louder than either the Irkallan's or the child's, and would eventually reveal my presence. Though this tunnel didn't appear to be guarded, it was certainly well used given the worn pathway. Just because there wasn't much in the way of traffic right now didn't mean there soon wouldn't be.

I stopped again to take off my boots and socks, tucking the latter inside the former before tying them onto my pack. The smooth stone was surprisingly cool under my feet given the heat in the air, but at least without footwear any Irkallan who were near might initially think my footfalls were nothing more than another child being escorted somewhere. At least until they actually saw me.

I continued to chase the soft glow that was the only indicator of the child and the Irkallan. Their footsteps were no longer audible, suggesting it was the wind that'd driven the sound to me in the first place.

The tunnel continued to curve around, and then began to descend deeper into the mountain. Though the wind still provided me with fresh air, I was nevertheless aware that the urine and blue-cheese stench was growing stronger, suggesting I was drawing closer to the main part of the apiary. Luck had been with me so far, but how much longer would that last?

As if in answer to that question, the pale glow ahead went out. As I stopped, my gaze searching the darkness, I became aware of the footsteps. They weren't just coming from up ahead, but also from behind.

I swore and looked around, but the tunnel's sheer walls offered nothing in the way of cover.

Run, the wind suggested.

Unhelpful, I replied, but nevertheless did just that, switching out my gun for my knife as I pelted around the corner—only to spot an Irkallan standing twenty feet away. He rose up to his full height, his mandibles clashing as he began to emit a shrill sound. I threw the knife and, as the glittering blade spun through the air, reached back for the sword.

The Irkallan sidestepped the knife, as I knew it would, but by then I was close enough to swing the sword. There was no finesse or skill behind the blow; there couldn't be, given I wasn't sword trained and had no time for anything approaching finesse anyway. All I wanted to do was stop him from alerting any of his hive mates to my presence. The glowing blade hit his left side, right at the point where his thorax joined his abdomen, and sliced the pieces of his body apart. His exoskeleton might have been no harder than butter for the ease with which the sword went through it.

As the two pieces of his body fell in different directions and his shrieking stopped, I heard the scrape of nails against stone and swung around. Another Irkallan was in the air, its razor-sharp fingernails lengthening as it arrowed toward me. I threw myself sideways and down, grunting as I hit the stone hard, but twisted around and thrust the sword upward. The Irkallan curled its body around itself, protecting its head and limbs, and presenting only its hard outer shell to the blade. It made no difference—the sword cut his spine open and the Irkallan's innards rained down upon me. I cursed softly, swiping at the gore covering my face as I thrust to my feet. The Irkallan might be cut open from neck to tailbone, but it wasn't finished yet. It was using its claws to drag itself up the wall, attempting to rise, even as its broken body continued to ooze black fluids and freedom only knew what else.

I strode toward it, blade held out in front of me like a lance. The Irkallan gave up its attempts to rise, and ran—not toward me but away, using its claws to drag itself along the smooth stone with surprising speed, and emitting a high-pitched sound as it did so.

I charged after him. The Irkallan twisted around as I neared and somehow jacked upright. I raised the sword and brought it down hard, but he twisted away from the blow. The blade's sharp tip embedded itself into the floor with enough force to send a shockwave up my arms; sparks skittered through the darkness.

The air screamed a warning; I swore and twisted away from the blow. Instead of gutting me, one of its claws skimmed my left side, slicing through my uniform and down into flesh. Pain surged even as warmth began to flood down my side. I cursed, wrenched the sword free from the stone, and heaved it upwards. Again the Irkallan tried to twist away from the blow, but the spinal injury was obviously hampering its movements now, and it was nowhere near fast enough. The sword sliced into the Irkallan's arm and pinned it to his torso, even as the blade continued cutting into his body, until it was fully sheathed in flesh. The Irkallan's screeching stopped and life leaked swiftly from its eyes. I stepped back, pulled the blade free, and let the Irkallan slump to the ground.

For several minutes I didn't move. I simply stood there as warmth continued to slide down my waist and the wind swirled around me, bringing fresh air but no further sound of life. Not that it meant anything, especially if others had heard what I presumed was the Irkallans' warning cries.

I took a deep, shuddery breath and then looked down at the broken body near my feet. *Wind, can you carry the two Irkallan into the smaller tunnel? There's less likelihood of them being found so easily there.*

As the air lifted the bodies of the Irkallan and carried them away into the darkness, I carefully stripped off my jacket and shirt, the left side of which was soaked in blood. The sword emitted just enough light to see the extent of the wound, and it wasn't pretty. The Irkallan's claws had opened me up from just under my breasts down to my hip; the upper portion of the wound was deep enough that I could see ribs, but it at least grew shallower as it skimmed down my side to my hip. I swung the pack off and fished around until I found the small medikit. I plucked one of the sealing sprays free, snapped off the cap, and then liberally applied it to the long wound. It stung like blazes, and I had to grit my teeth against the scream that tore up my throat. I waited a couple of seconds for the sealer to take hold then grabbed the sticky bandage strip and roughly wound it around my body. It might restrict some of my movements but it would also help support the sealant and stop the wound from breaking open again.

With that done, I redressed then sheathed the sword and slung the pack back over my shoulders. While I would have liked to keep hold of the sword, I'd rather not run the risk of its soft glow giving me away.

I retrieved my knife, shoved it back into its sheath, and then walked on. As the tunnel's decline grew, the heat intensified, and moisture began to slick the walls and drift in tiny rivers across the floor, forcing me to go even slower lest I slip.

A soft pulsing soon began to invade the silence. I paused to listen, but there was no threat in the sound, and nothing underneath to indicate anything approached. In fact, that noise reminded me of a heartbeat, one that was oddly comforting.

Another curve soon appeared, this time to the left. I kept close to the wall, trailing my fingers along its surface to ensure I didn't drift too far away from it. We Sifft might have excellent night sight but night usually had stars or the moon to give at least some light. There was absolutely nothing here. And while I wasn't walking totally blind thanks to the assistance of the wind, keeping contact with the wall at least gave me some warning of change.

The pulsing grew stronger and light flickered somewhere ahead. I gripped the knife's hilt in readiness and slowly edged around the tunnel's curve.

The light came from two rough archways carved into the tunnel's walls—one to the right, one to the left. Within the left, I could hear someone shuffling around, and from the right, there came a murmur of conversation, though it was no language I'd heard before. And it certainly didn't sound as if it were coming from human throats.

But then, I guessed it was logical the children born of this place would try to imitate the sounds they heard the Irkallan making rather than anything human-sounding, especially given Saska had said the children were taken away from them at birth.

I closed my eyes for a minute, gathering my strength for the task ahead, and then reached the wind. *Tell me what you see.*

It's not the children. At least, not human children.

Relief spun through me, even though it was little more than a brief reprieve. *So they're Irkallan offspring?*

No, the wind murmured. *Adlin.*

Freedom, help me…. *How many?*

Sixteen.

Even young Adlin were dangerous, especially if there was a number of them. If they caught my scent, I was done for.

You can kill them. You can order the breath drawn from their lungs and their threat would no longer exist.

Yes, I could, but I still had no idea where the children born to the stolen witches were being kept, and until I *did* discover that, I needed to conserve my strength. And surely, despite the appearance of this area being unguarded, there *would* be Irkallan nearby. They'd not risk Adlin roaming about unchecked—not if Saska was right and there was only a limited supply of the controlling bracelets.

I eased toward the doorways and stopped again. Both archways were inset with heavily barred cell doors, the metal glinting silver in the pale light coming from either room. I drew in a breath to steady my nerves and listened to the movement within the nearest cell while I watched the other. When the noise suggested they'd moved away from the arch, I scampered silently across.

Thankfully, no angry roars followed me down the tunnel. But it was becoming increasingly evident I was nearing a main living area; not only was that odd thrumming getting louder, but the strong breeze sweeping through the tunnel from somewhere up ahead spoke of life and a vast city.

There is a small, disused mine shaft on your right, the wind said. *Take it.*

I did. Unlike the circular and very smooth walls of that main tunnel, these were rectangular and roughhewn, with thick, regularly spaced wooden posts to support both the walls and the ceiling. It was obviously a remnant from the time before the Irkallan, when miners had lived and worked in this place.

A dark, slime-like moss hung in ribbons from the ceiling and oozed along the floor, making every step treacherous and forcing me to go even slower. Despite the moisture running down the walls and dripping from the moss, the heat was becoming oppressive. Every breath felt like it was burning my lungs, and my shirt and pants were so damp with sweat that they clung uncomfortably to my skin.

The old shaft made a long, gentle curve to the left and then began to drop down again. The moisture dripping from the ceiling increased, and there was now a foot-wide river bubbling down the middle of the floor—a merry sound that was somehow audible against the deepening thrum. That thrum reminded me somewhat of the hum you could hear in and around beehives, and it made me think I was at least near, if not even in, the heart of the Irkallan settlement.

But was I anywhere near the children?

The queen keeps them near her, at the very lowest level of this place, where it is deemed the safest should there be an attack, the wind said. *This shaft will take you close.*

Close wasn't what I wanted or needed. Not in this place.

No. The wind hesitated. *There is nothing between this shaft and where the children rest. Nothing but space.*

I edged around small rockslide, and then said, *Why would there be only open space? Isn't the whole mountainside little more than a maze of tunnels and shafts intersecting various chambers, be they small or large?*

There is another fall up ahead, the wind said. *One that has splintered the wall between this shaft and the main tunnel. Look through it, and you will see the true breadth of the Irkallan's city.*

It was a statement that revived the ashes of fear. I didn't want to see the true impossibility of my quest—didn't want to know for sure the flutters of hope that still beat within me had as little chance of survival as I did.

An odd mound began to loom in the darkness ahead. As I drew closer, it revealed itself to be heavily compacted slide of rock, dirt, and thick timbers, all of which was covered by the oozing moss. To the left of this, where a timber beam had once held back the earth, was a three-foot-long seam wide enough to put my fist through. I carefully climbed the rubble then grabbed the jagged edge of the seam to hold myself up and peered out.

What I saw was almost beyond belief.

It was a vast, vertical tunnel—one that had enormous proportions. It was at least a quarter of a mile wide and beautifully cylindrical. The tunnel's walls were lined with perfectly spaced archways that divided it into different levels, and each one appeared to be an entrance into a chamber of some kind, although most of them were dark so I couldn't see what lay within. But there was a stunning symmetry in the construction here, because not only did each arch appear the exact same size, but it also lined up perfectly with the one above *and* below. A wide, continuous ramp wound around the wall and linked all the levels and rooms, and it drew the eye downward. It was a long drop. Although there had to be at least fifteen levels above me, there were at least another fifty below that I could see before the darkness simply got too deep to penetrate.

But the thrumming noise I could hear seemed to be coming from somewhere close to that deeper darkness.

Saska had said the queen and the breeders lay at the heart

of the apiary, within earth that still held life and heat. But there was no life in the walls I could see, no voices to be heard. Did that mean this shaft held the workers, and that the queen, breeders, and perhaps even the witchlings they'd bred lived somewhere else?

No, said the wind. *They reside in the chambers above the current flood line.*

There's water at the base of it?

Yes. The vertical tunnel once had another fifteen levels, but over the generations, the water that leeches through this dead rock has flooded them.

How close will this tunnel get me to the queen's level?

Not close enough.

Which again was not what I wanted to hear. I shifted sideways and tried to see what was nearby but there was nothing to be seen. It was almost as if nothing had been built into the tunnel's walls along this section.

The path does pass by three feet below your position, the air said. *But because all the old mining shafts near here are unstable and constantly flooding, the Irkallan decided not to use this area.*

I blinked. *And how would the collective consciousness of the air know something like that?*

Because we asked the earth.

Air can't interact with earth.

Unless there is a conduit. You were that for Saska; when her death ended the weight of three ruling that we were not to help you, that ability to interact with earth was opened to us.

Interesting. *So the earth is aware of our approach?*

Yes. But it cannot help until you once again step onto ground that holds life and hope.

Which again, wasn't overly useful when to get to such a place I'd also be in the midst of the queen's lair.

I thumbed the sweat away from my forehead and eyes, and then squeezed past the rockfall and continued forward.

But the mine shaft was narrowing, the going getting rougher, and though I had no idea how much time had actually passed in the world above, I had a bad feeling it was running out, for both me and for those soldiers who were to provide diversionary midmorning attacks. This place had at least sixty-five levels of Irkallan and who knew how many inhabited each level. In some ways, it didn't even actually matter; the truth was, the Irkallan could put forth a force far greater than any of us had imagined, and their queen had already shown a willingness to waste her soldiers if it achieved the desired outcome.

Unless I did something about it—unless I diverted the queen's attention away from the upcoming attack—the outpost forces would be overrun and slaughtered.

I continued out down the ever-narrowing mineshaft, but it was becoming increasingly difficult. Rockfalls were more frequent and the pathway so slick with water and slime that I had to grab the roughly hewn walls to keep upright. Despite the heat in the air, my feet were so cold from constantly being in the water that I was beginning to lose feeling in my toes and it forced me to keep stopping so I could rub some life back into them.

Inevitably, I reached a rockfall that there was no getting past. But it had, at least, brought some of the inner sanctum's wall down with it. The gap wasn't quite wide enough for me slip through, but given the wet decay gripping the rock surrounding the fall area, I didn't think making it bigger would be all that hard.

I squatted on my heels and carefully peered out. I was five levels above where I needed to be, but at least I could see the water now. It was a vast lake that lapped at the edges of the circular path that swept down into its ink and then disappeared. Its black surface was mirror smooth—I blinked. *This* was the black mirror Saska had mentioned. It wasn't any sort of magic; it was a lake that was at least fifteen stories in depth and getting deeper. A lake the Irkallan feared to go near.

And that one fact made it the perfect place to hide the bracelets, because surely if the Irkallan could have drained this lake they would have rather than letting it slowly consume their home. And those bracelets, with their ability to control the thoughts and actions of others, were surely better left in some place where they were never likely to resurface than taken back to Winterborne where they'd undoubtedly be studied and perhaps learned from. Such technology had already proven to be dangerous in the wrong hands and—from what I'd witnessed over the last few days—there seemed to be more than a few such hands in amongst those of the Upper and Lower Reaches.

I studied the areas immediately above the water line, trying to find some indication of where the queen was. After a second, I spotted an arch that not only broke the symmetry of the rest, but also looked newer. If the Irkallan were constantly having to retreat from the water line, perhaps that newer arch was an indicator of where the queen and her breeders now lived.

The levels immediately above this larger arch were as still as the rest of them. Although I had no doubt there would be guards I couldn't see, it was odd that there was very little in the way of movement in this place. Of course, that might just be because the sun would have risen by now and, while the Irkallan weren't nocturnal, they did tend to be more active at night. It was a fact that might also explain why soldiers hadn't flooded the tunnel when I'd killed those two Irkallan. Maybe there'd been no one close enough to hear their cries for assistance.

I leaned forward and saw that the curving path passed by this breach in the wall. Getting out of this mine shaft wasn't going to present much of a problem, but working my way down the remaining five levels of the vertical tunnel to that larger arch would be fraught with danger. I really didn't like my chances of doing so unseen.

My gaze returned to the unmoving surface of the lake. Five stories was a hell of a jump, but it was also a survivable one into water, especially when I was Sifft rather than an ordinary human. Stronger bones came with the heritage. And if I dropped into the water quietly enough, they'd barely see or hear me enter the lake. The problem was the water itself, and the fact that I wasn't the world's greatest swimmer. Hell, I could barely even dog paddle—a fact that had amused Ava and April no end whenever we'd spent our days off in the sea over at West Range.

But it was the best choice. Taking the winding pathway might be dryer, but it also came with a bigger risk of being seen.

I glanced at the wet and fractured rock. I needed to widen the seam by another foot, at the very least, if I was to have any hope of getting my shoulders and butt through it. Thin, I was not.

Wind, can you keep an eye on things outside and warn me if there's any movement nearby?

Yes.

Thanks. I shoved my sleeves further up my arms and then got to work. It took a lot longer to break open a wide enough space to get through than I'd thought—not because the stone didn't break away easily enough, but because I had to place each piece down carefully, ensuring it didn't move or cause the main slide to shift in any way.

With that done, I swung the pack around and opened it up. I'd munched on the cheese and bread as I'd driven to the mountains, so there wasn't much left, but it was doubtful I'd need the rest of it given getting out of this place was highly unlikely.

I dropped the food onto the ground, covered it up with some soil, and then shook out the cloth to ensure there were no crumbs left. While the M185 blocks appeared plasticky and were more than likely waterproof, I doubted the same could be said of the detonation timers and pop caps. I wrapped them carefully in the cloth, then tore off an edge of my soaked shirt to keep it in place. With that done, I repacked the bag, checked there was no one on the outside walkway, and carefully eased through the hole I'd created. Once I'd dragged the pack out after me, I shoved it on and kept low as I scrambled across to the edge.

It really *was* a long way down. There was no way known I was going to hit the water without making an audible splash. *Could you ease my speed as I near the water?*

Yes, the wind said, *but wait—there is movement below.*

I waited, staring down at the black water, my pulse racing and my gut churning. It wasn't so much the fear of the situation or of being discovered, but at jumping feet first into that ink and never coming up. If I had to die in this place, I wanted to do so fighting the enemy and taking some of the bastards out with me, not by being sucked into the murky depths of an inky lake.

Right, the air said. *All clear if you're quick.*

I thrust to my feet and stood on the edge, but didn't immediately jump. I continued to eye the dark water, imagining in my mind how I needed to slip into the water, putting it out into the general consciousness of the air in the vague hope that it would be so.

Then, with as deep a breath as I could take, I stepped off the edge. The air didn't interfere, and it certainly didn't hinder the speed with which I dropped—not until the very last moment. I entered the water feet first and with very little noise, but the sheer iciness just about tore a gasp from my throat. It was only force of will that kept my mouth clamped shut. As I plunged deeper, the backpack's bulk hit the water, acting like something of a brake and just about tearing my shoulders out of their sockets. Then my head was under, the iciness and darkness all around me, and disorientation and fear set in. I closed my eyes—I couldn't see anyway, so there was no point in keeping them open—and concentrated on holding my breath, on *not* panicking as I waited for the moment when the fall stopped and the natural buoyancy of my body kicked in and told me which way was up.

It seemed to take forever.

But as my lungs began to burn with the need for air, I finally stopped heading down and instead began to float. I kicked my feet as hard as I could and surged upward, breaking the surface with a rather unwise gasp. Thankfully, it didn't immediately appear there were any Irkallan around to hear it. As I sucked in deep breaths, I turned around to see where the ramp was. It was across the other side of the shaft, but I didn't dare risk swimming—or at least, paddling—directly across to it. Instead, I gently kicked to the nearby wall and kept close to its shadowed side, trying to make as little noise as possible. By the time I reached the submerged portion of the walkway, my body was shaking with both the cold and effort, and my legs initially refused to support my weight. I staggered out of the water and then gently shook my arms and feet, trying to get my blood flowing again and some warmth back into my digits.

Be still, the air warned. *There is a patrol above you.*

I stopped moving but the water continued to drip from my body and uniform, and it was all I could do to clamp my lips down in an effort to stop my teeth from chattering.

From the level above me came the soft scrape of nails against stone. I carefully pushed back against the wall, trying to make myself as small as possible. The clicking of mandibles came from directly above me, but I dared not look. My skin might not be as pale as Saska's, but it was still light enough to be seen by a keen eye even in this ink.

A heartbeat later came a second clashing of mandibles, this time to the right of the first. Obviously, they were having a discussion of some sort, and I wished I could understand what they were damn well saying…. The thought trailed off.

I *had* heard and understood the Irkallan queen twice now, but both times had been when my skin—my *stained* skin—had been in contact with my knife.

I quickly wrapped my fingers around the hilt, but for several heartbeats, nothing happened. Then warmth began to throb through the weapon—warmth whose beat uncannily matched the throbbing that filled this place—and then both the glass blade and hilt started to glow softly. Thankfully, the sheath countered the blade's glow, but tiny beams of brightness were leaking out between my fingers, forcing me to tug my jacket sleeve over my hand in order to hide it.

"Movement," one of the Irkallan said. Its voice was oddly broken, as if it were coming through a microphone that wasn't working properly. The queen's orders had come through similarly garbled, so obviously whatever magic was allowing the knife—and even the bracelets—to translate the Irkallan language had its restrictions. "Below."

"Yes. The mirror, it moves."

"Water drips?"

"No."

"Cannot scent anyone who should not be."

"No." The Irkallan paused. "Should place guard?"

"Waste. Attack coming from above."

So I was right—the outposts were on the move. And that really did mean that I had to get moving if I wanted any hope of stopping their forces from getting overrun.

"Yes," the other Irkallan said. "Fight not ours."

"No." There was a whole lot of frustration in that one word.

After a few more minutes, the two of them moved away. I swung the pack off and fished around until I found the bracelet. Then I carefully tore off another strip of shirt end, found a suitably heavy rock, and tied it and the bracelet together.

Right, I said to the wind, *can you take this bracelet into the middle of the lake and carefully drop it in?*

Fingers of air wrapped around the bundle in my hand and swept it away. I bent, grabbed a handful of the wet ashy soil that stained the rocks here, and rubbed it over my face and hands. With the possibility of my skin giving me away so easily taken care of, I cautiously made my way up the ramp, keeping as close to the wall as possible. As it curved around to the next level, I saw the two guards on the level above me. Unlike the ones I'd come across in that wide tunnel, these two were armed, and although the weapons were shaped like the long staffs the Adlin sometimes used, these were made from metal rather than wood. They also had blunt ends rather than sharp, which suggested they were something other than a spear. They were strapped crossways across the Irkallan's backs, and I hoped like hell that's exactly where they remained. I had no desire to discover just what those staffs were capable of.

I continued creeping around until I reached the level of the larger archway. I padded across to the shaft wall and hunkered down, scanning both this level and the ones above me. Aside from the two Irkallan who'd heard my movements coming out of the lake, there were another two coming back down the circular path. Four Irkallan didn't seem anywhere near an appropriate number of guards given the size of this place, but I guessed centuries of never being infiltrated had given them reason enough not to be overly concerned about such an event.

It at least gave me a fighting chance of getting close to my targets.

I edged toward the large arch, but the scrape of nails told me an Irkallan was approaching. I swore and quickly looked around. The walkway was an open space, and there was no place to hide other than a nearby smaller arch.

Anyone in there? I asked the wind.

Many. And stirring.

So I either killed the Irkallan who approached from the queen's tunnel or I chanced my luck with those who were only just stirring.

No need for you to do either, the wind said.

I guessed that was true, although it didn't mean there would be no effort on my part. Communing with the wind might not be stealing much of my strength right now, but it would soon enough.

I hesitated, and then said, *Take the breath of those within the smaller room and make it safe.*

The air moved away from me, leaving barely enough freshness to breathe. The stink of the place hit, so thick and heavy it was felt like a blanket was smothering my senses. I gagged, and heard the approaching Irkallan briefly pause.

I held my nose closed to stop some of the stench reaching down into my throat, and slowly—carefully—backed away. The footsteps resumed, faster than before.

I ducked into the small archway and pressed my back against the wall. The footsteps reached the walkway and paused again, and the clicking of mandibles bit through the air, the sound one of agitation. I didn't move. I didn't even dare wrap my fingers around my knife lest the slight glow give me away.

After another few seconds, the Irkallan moved away. I

peered cautiously around the corner; it wasn't just one, but three. One of them was huge and an odd almost blue color, while the other two were smaller and the usual lavender. Was the larger one a general of some kind? Or maybe even the queen's consort? Did the Irkallan have such things, given they appeared to be a matriarchal society?

I pulled back and glanced around the room. When the air had said many, it hadn't been kidding. The room was only as wide as the archway itself, but it was long. The entire length of the left wall and part of the end wall of the room were lined with sleeping pods that had been cut into the stone. There were five levels of them and, like the archways themselves, each one was perfectly lined up with its neighbors. My gaze ran the length of the room as I did the calculation— seventy-five Irkallan, just in this room alone. Holy hell....

I studied the doorway at the far end of the room. *Where does that lead?*

Into another sleeping quarters.

Are there Irkallan within?

Yes.

Will going that way enable me to get to the larger tunnel?

No.

Of course not. I mean, why would things be *that* easy? I peered around the archway again; the three Irkallan had disappeared. I checked the locations of the walkway guards and then quickly slipped into the wider archway.

Almost immediately I felt the stirrings of life. Not within the darkness, but in the earth itself. While the ground under my feet remained lifeless, I could hear the distant heartbeat of it, a siren call that almost seemed to be begging me to come closer, to hurry.

But the latter would be foolish in a place like this.

Slowly, carefully, I moved deeper into the wide tunnel. The walls here were as smooth and as black as any of the others I'd seen, but as I crept farther in, I realized that instead of glimmer stone, the veins in this tunnel were slivers of brown earth. I gently brushed my fingers across one—and was just about blown backward by the power and force of the voices that immediately answered. It was very evident the earth, while it had no real beef with the Irkallan themselves, didn't like the deadness they were spreading beyond these blackened, lifeless mountains.

But that deadness wasn't really surprising given the situation. Normal earth witches were trained almost from birth to shape earth and use the power within it without damaging the soil. The only time real damage had ever occurred was during the war, when the witches had drawn so much power from the ground that they'd killed an entire district. It was doubtful the witchlings born here in the Irkallan stronghold had any such training. From the little Saska had said, the women were kept in a constant state of pregnancy, and their offspring were taken away—or killed—at birth. That meant the stained children raised by the Irkallan would have had to find their own way around their developing powers, in much the same way as I had. Subsequently, their control would, at best, be patchy, and they were more likely to drain the earth even as they commanded it.

I continued down the tunnel cautiously, my fingers itching to brush the widening seams of live earth. But I resisted—I had no idea where the children currently were; if they were awake—as the Adlin young had been—then I risked one of them sensing my presence via the earth.

This tunnel ends in fifty feet, the air said. *It opens up into the first chamber.*

Something in the way that was said had the hair along the back of my neck rising. *And what might that chamber be used for?*

It is the chamber the breeders reside in. The wind paused. *The women are also there.*

I didn't want to see that. Didn't want to witness the atrocities I'd barely glimpsed in Saska's thoughts. *Is the queen also there?*

No. She resides in the next chamber. There is a hall that links the two—the children are kept in the rooms that feed off this hall.

Leaving me with no choice but to go through the first chamber and all its breeders. *Are there guards?*

Twenty, at least, in the first chamber. Double that in the queen's.

Meaning my chance of getting through unseen was right up there with my chances of survival.

If I were lifted along the roofline, would they see me?

Yes. They will feel the air movement. It is still and heavy in the chamber.

Which didn't mean I couldn't do it—just that I probably needed something to distract the guards from actually noticing my presence.

Can you steal the breath from them?

Yes, but the departure of so much air will be felt by both those who guard the hall and the queen's chambers. You will get to neither the children nor the queen if that happens.

I silently swore but continued to creep closer. Once I was near the end of the wide tunnel, I squatted on my heels and studied the area. Though it was as dark as anywhere else in this place, my eyes were well used to it by now. The chamber was large and rectangular. There was another wide archway directly opposite this one, and between the two there were a dozen smaller doorways. The wind told me the various chambers catered to the needs of the breeders—they were cleansing areas, food preparation and medical areas, fertilization rooms, and even nurseries—and that the latter had human babies in it, their little bodies fed with the milk being pumped from the breasts of the women.

I briefly closed my eyes, ignored the horror in my heart, and silently ordered the air to steal the breath from their lungs. Whether it would set off alarms or not, I had no idea. I guess I'd find out soon enough.

As tears slipped from the corners of my eyes, I turned my attention to the breeders. The entire central portion of the chamber was filled with them. There had to be *hundreds* of them here. They were all sitting in either well-padded lounging or birthing chairs, and each of them was looked after by at least one attendant. I could only see one of the witches. She lay flat on a bed to the right of this tunnel, in amongst a group of heavily pregnant Irkallan. The first thing I noticed was the fact there were no bracelets on her wrists. The second was that—although she was gaunt enough to appear little more than a skeleton—her belly was so extended she looked ready to burst. She wasn't moving—she was barely even breathing—and there were a multitude of tubes in her arms as well as pumps attached to her breasts. I wondered if the stuff being fed into her veins was keeping her alive or merely keeping her sedated. Either way, it was no way to live.

And no way I could save her.

I dragged my gaze away from the awful sight and studied the guards again. They were evenly spread around the chamber, and every one of them had one of those strange metal staffs at their back.

There really was no way I was getting across this room without either being spotted or attacked, even if the air did project me across. I also had no doubt that the minute I did appear, the whole damn apiary would come alive and I'd be swarmed—and dead—in minutes.

Which really only left me with the one option—I needed to create a distraction.

It was time to make some noise.

13

I bit my bottom lip as I mulled over the best way of doing that without getting myself killed, and then carefully backed up the tunnel again. I swung off the pack and unwrapped the timers. The waterproofing had worked, because even though the M185 blocks showed signs of having gotten wet, the timers were all dry.

I set two of them—one for five minutes and one for ten— and then carefully placed them into the blocks, just as I'd been shown.

Right, I said to the air, *could you please put the five-minute bomb on the roof between the two Adlin nurseries, and the ten-minute one in that first wall fissure in the old mining tunnel?*

Hopefully, it would keep the multitude of Irkallan out there in the main shaft occupied with the damage and searching for a nonexistent attacking force, and give me some sort of chance to get through the breeding chamber without backup being called.

As several fingers of wind picked up the bombs and whisked them away, I pulled out two NP10 balls and carefully placed the pop cap primers into them. Apparently, once I flicked off the orange tab at the end of the primer, I had ten seconds to get the hell out of the area before the explosion happened.

But ten seconds was really all I needed if the wind assisted me.

I slung the pack over my shoulders again and then pressed back against the wall and waited. Tension wound through me as the minutes ticked by. Then, with a muffled *whoomp* that seemed to shake the whole mountain, the first bomb went off. As shrill alarms began to sound, I thrust to my feet, an NP10 ball in each hand, and said, "Wind, get me across to the other side of that breeding chamber ASAP."

Even as the wind swung into action and picked me up, the walls around me began to shudder and a grinding noise bit through the air, one that was barely audible over the shrieking of the alarms. Up ahead, two vast metal doors appeared from each side of the cavern wall and began to slide toward each other.

Hurry, I said to the air, rather unnecessarily. We were already speeding toward that ever-decreasing gap.

As I was rushed through the door and up toward the ceiling, there was a screech from below. I flicked the orange cap off the first bomb and tossed it down into the leading edge of the breeding area. Several of the nearby Irkallan immediately flung themselves upon it, even as the guards lifted their weird staffs and pointed them at me. The metal immediately began to glow and, with an odd sort of coughing pop, globs of what looked to be pale mucus were fired my way. The wind batted them away, but there were so many guards and so many weapons aimed at me that it was inevitable one got through. The mucus hit my right shoulder, and immediately began to burn into my flesh. It tore a scream from my throat, but I nevertheless flipped the cap off the remaining NP10 ball and threw it down into the midst of the breeders—and, I suddenly realized, directly into a section that held the bulk of the stolen witches. They, like the first witch I'd seen, were little more than skeletal figures that only vaguely resembled the vital beings they must have once been, and they ranged from looking old enough to be menopausal to so young they barely looked more than fifteen or sixteen. These latter women were badly stained, which made me think that perhaps the Irkallan were rebreeding with their witch offspring in an effort to strengthen the inherited magic.

It was a sight that made me angry—made me want to kill every last one of the Irkallan. Which was stupid and not what was I was here to do, but acknowledging *that* certainly didn't stop the desire to do as much as damage as I could for as long as I could.

Even as the air switched direction and we began to plunge toward the second large archway and its closing metal door, I grabbed a gut buster with my good arm and fired at the guards. One, two, three went down, and then the first NP10 ball exploded. The force of the blast was so strong it sent me tumbling through the air. I hit the far wall hard enough to knock the breath from my lungs and split the back of my head open, but the wind snatched me up again before I could fall and sped me toward the narrow gap into the tunnel leading into the queen's quarters.

In the breeding room, there was chaos. As fire took hold and screeches of fury and pain filled the air, the ceiling began to fissure. A multitude of seams raced across it, with huge chunks of black stone falling down each time two of them met, crushing anyone who might have survived the initial blast in that section. Several bloodied guards were trying to keep the metal door from slamming shut, but with little effect.

The air spun me through the second set of doors, but it was so damn close that my breasts brushed the metal as we squeezed through. The second ball exploded, and its fierce fingers of heat and destruction chased us into the darkness.

Then the doors slammed shut with a sound that rather reminded me of a death knell.

Is there a door into the queen's chamber? I asked the air.

Yes. It closed when the alarm sounded.

Meaning I had to now figure out a way to open the damn thing. I hesitated and then said, *Where are the children kept?*

In the rooms that feed off this hall.

Are they awake?

No. They, like their mothers, have tubes running into the veins. But there are only twenty-nine here. The earth says five are missing.

Does the earth also tell you where they are?

The air hesitated, and then said, *They are being escorted into the tunnel beyond the queen's quarters.*

Is that tunnel also being sealed?

No.

Then at least I stood a chance of going after them—*if* I could get into the queen's chamber, and *if* I could then survive another encounter with her guards.

Drop me down near the children, and then go steal their breaths. But do it quickly—I don't want them to suffer.

The air deposited me close to several small archways. They, like the Adlin pens, were barred, but the metal here was dull rather than silver. Thankfully, I couldn't see inside and I didn't want to, even though I was well aware I'd have to go into each cell to find the bracelets once death had made its call.

I thrust away the rising horror of being responsible for those deaths, threw off the backpack, and then stripped off my jacket and shirt. Though only a small portion of the muck had gotten through the material, it bubbled away against my skin and caused a widening circle of damage. I grabbed the flask from the pack and trickled it over my shoulder. The pain immediately eased, but I continued to wash the wound until the blistering had completely stopped. I shook the flask and discovered there was only a little bit of water remaining. Not enough to wash down another wound if I got it, but maybe there was another lake somewhere in this warren where I could refill it. I stoppered the flask, shoved it back into the pack, and then gently probed the back of my head. The lump was huge and the hair around it was sticky with moisture, but from what I could feel, the cut itself wasn't that bad. It certainly wasn't gushing blood, and given the whack I'd received, that was something of a miracle. Once I'd sprayed some sealer over it, I shoved on my shoes to stop any further damage to my feet, and swung the pack over my shoulder.

The air screamed a warning just as a blur of lavender came out of nowhere and barreled into me. We crashed to the ground in a tumble of arms and legs, and all I could see, all I could hear, was the clashing of mandibles. I shoved a hand against its throat in an effort to keep them from my face, but the creature was so damn big—so damn heavy—that it was crushing me, and every breath was becoming a struggle.

I called to the air again. As the wind ripped the Irkallan from my body, I sat up, pulled the sword free from its sheath, and swung it with every ounce of strength I had. The blade began to glow a fierce blue as its sharp tip sliced the Irkallan's head from its body, but as the wind flung the two pieces away, splattering blood and gore everywhere, I saw in the sword's glow more Irkallan approaching. I swore and jumped fully to my feet, but even as I did that odd coughing pop sounded, and globs of mucus were flying toward me. I reached out, grabbed the air, and spun it violently. As the vortex redirected the globs into the walls of the cavern rather than my flesh, I pressed it forward and charged at the Irkallan, my sword raised high.

They answered in kind, their mandibles clashing as they screamed. The vortex hit them, tearing the weapons from their grips then bending them as easily as one might paper, making them unusable. I kept pushing the vortex forward, forcing the Irkallan back, even as a slight ache began in the back of my head. Not from the wound, but from the effort of controlling the air like this.

I ignored it, and continued to force the five Irkallan backward. They screamed and fought and continued to call both for my death and for help. It did them no good; with the metal doors into both the breeding chamber and the queen's now closed, there *was* no help for them.

I pushed them back until they were pinned against the metal door that protected the queen's chamber, and then I killed them.

With that done, I dropped my knees, closed my eyes, and sucked in air in a vague effort to ease the pounding in my head. After a while, it did so, but it was very evident that I wasn't going to have the strength for too many more stunts like that.

I pushed to my feet, waited for the slight dizziness to go away, then resolutely made my way back to the children's chambers. The gates weren't locked, but I guessed there was no need for them to be if the Irkallan were keeping their witchlings under sedation.

I closed my eyes for a moment, trying to harden my heart against what I was about to see. It was one thing to order foul deeds to be done, quite another to face the result of those orders.

I slowly pushed the first gate open. There were twenty

pods in this room, ten on each side, but only nine of them were occupied. Every child was naked—which wasn't a surprise given the warmth in this place—and they were lying on thin blankets that wouldn't have provided much in the way of padding for their small bodies. Their ages appeared to run from the very young—perhaps no more than four or five —to several who would be classed as adults in Winterborne. All of them were severely stained, with at least seven whose skin had absolutely no color other than lavender. Two of those even had wisps of close-cropped lavender hair. Given the length of time the breeding program had been going, it was unsurprising that they had more children than bracelets —and as equally surprising that there weren't *more* children here than the nine in this room and the twenty in the other. But perhaps the cost of creating the tunnel that now sat on the edges of Winterborne wasn't only earth deprived of life, but also a high death rate amongst these children.

The bracelets weren't hard to find—they were sitting in a storage nook set into the wall, every one of them the exact same size. Given they fitted the wrists of the smallest child as easily as they did adults and even that Adlin, they were very obviously adjustable even if they didn't appear to be. I quickly collected them, then walked into the other room and retrieved the remainder.

Now I just had to figure out a way to get rid of them. The black lake was a chamber and two rather heavy metal doors behind me now, and while I could undoubtedly order the earth to create a wide enough tunnel around what was left of that chamber to allow the wind to carry the bracelets through, I suspected *that* would sap a whole lot more of my strength than was wise given what I still had to do.

But I still had four blocks of M185 left, and while I doubted it would be enough to bring the whole mountain down, it surely would destroy the bracelets and perhaps even create an explosion powerful enough to kill a queen. I moved out of the nurseries and walked down the hall.

The door into the queen's chambers was huge and black, although the rust running across its metal surface hinted at the decades it had been in place and at the mercy of the moisture that was so much a part of this apiary.

I stopped in the middle, where the two halves met, then emptied the pack of everything except the bracelets. After setting the timers for twenty minutes, I carefully placed the blocks back into the pack and then strapped it closed to ensure they wouldn't move. I attached the two NP10 balls onto my belt, slipped the small medikit into my pocket, and slung my sword over my shoulder.

With all that done, I sat down next to the pack and, with a deep breath to gather strength, I pressed my fingers into the rich earth.

The response was so swift and powerful it just about fried my fingertips. *What is your wish?*

I need these doors forced open enough to enable me to get through, and a hole in one of the walls large enough to hold the pack. And I need both done quickly, as I only have a limited time to place the bombs and run like hell.

Power surged and the soil thrummed underneath my fingertips. It pulsated through me, a heartbeat that my own swiftly matched. Though it wasn't actually pulling on my strength, I nevertheless felt it slipping like rain from my body. This was the cost of the earth magic and one I was more than willing to pay if it achieved my aim.

The earth in front of me began to rise; thin fingers of rock pushed into the almost nonexistent gap between the two doors and slowly but surely pried them apart, until the gap was large enough for me to slip through sideways.

In the darkness beyond, I could see figures moving. That odd coughing noise gave me warning that I'd been seen, and I spun the air through the gap and flared it out, sending the globules back toward my attackers.

A small chamber has been created to the right of this door, the earth said. *We will seal it once the pack is inside. Hurry.*

That last warning wasn't one I needed. Not when a small part of my brain was now doing a countdown of the time I had left.

I quickly primed the NP10, then brushed the vortex to one side and threw the two balls into the room, one to the left and one to the right. I pulled the air back into place across the gap then grabbed the pack and crawled to the left side of the door in order to protect myself from the blasts.

My head was back to pounding, my breath was little more than short, sharp gasps for air, and my stomach was growling so hard it was clearly audible above the shrieking sirens. Obviously, my body wanted me to replace the energy the earth had drawn from me, but the little food I'd had left was now buried in that old mine shaft.

There were two huge *whumps*, and sheets of flame and energy shot through the gap between the two doors. It was followed by screams and thick black smoke; in that chaos lay my hope of survival.

I thrust to my feet, slung the pack over my shoulder, then grabbed the two gut busters and squeezed through the gap. The queen's chamber was huge but just as stark as any of the others. She obviously had a lot of attendants, because there were body parts and gore splattered everywhere, but not all the guards were dead. Even as I dropped down onto the chamber's floor, several of them attacked, their metal staffs held out before them and spitting goop even as they charged at me. I spun the air again; pain stabbed through my brain, momentarily fading my vision in and out. I blinked away the tears, raised the gut busters, and fired. As the Irkallan went down in the rain of metal, I turned and ran along the chamber's wall, searching for the hole that had been made in the earth.

I spotted the queen first, and froze.

She was huge. Double the size of her attendants. Double the size of her guards. One of her mandibles was broken, but they nevertheless were a good foot in length, and looked strong enough to cut me in two without any problem.

She was lying on her side at the far end of the chamber, her lavender-blue body littered with wounds and a bloody hole where one eye had been. She was still alive—I could see the rise and fall of her torso—but for the moment, she wasn't stirring. It was tempting—*so* tempting—to throw the backpack at her and let the bomb-blast finish her off. But the Irkallan were obviously smart and might well be able to deactivate the M185. I couldn't risk that—couldn't risk her regaining control of the bracelets.

I continued looking for the hole the earth had created, and finally spotted it halfway up the chamber's wall, well beyond my reach—which also meant it was well beyond the reach of the Irkallan. I tossed the pack toward it, ordered the air to shove it deep in that hole, and then thrust a hand against the warm earth and asked it to seal the hole back up.

As the earth obeyed, the air screamed a warning. I swung around, gut buster blazing. Two Irkallan lost legs, the third lost his head, and the fourth came straight at me. I kept firing, shredding his chest and stomach, but it didn't seem to matter. I swore and flicked the air at him. As he stumbled and almost fell, I quickly drew the sword with my free hand and swung it down, severing his head from his neck in one clean blow.

Where's the other tunnel? I asked the air.

Directly across the room.

Directly across meant going through the Irkallan who were currently picking themselves up and looking around for trouble. But it was also the fastest way out of this damn room.

I sheathed the sword and reclaimed the other gun, shoved a fresh clip into both, and then ran directly at the Irkallan, firing as I did. As they went down in the hail of metal, that countdown in my head said time was starting to run out.

I jumped over rubble, furniture, and the dead, and ran on. More Irkallan soldiers came at me from the left and the right, some of them bleeding and broken, but all of them looking determined to get me. Weapons were raised and fired, and the mucus chased every footstep as I leapt and dodged and returned their fire.

I reached the archway and slid around the corner, only to come face-to-stomach with another batch of Irkallan. We went down in a mass of arms and legs, their mandibles clashing, tearing into various bits of my body even as I struggled to get free. The countdown in my head continued relentlessly, an ever-present reminder of how little time I had left.

I screamed in fury and fear, and began firing, even as I reached for the air and asked it for help. As the wind grabbed my arms and ripped me free from the melee, one of the Irkallan somehow twisted around and wrapped a hand around my leg, attempting to pull me back. It was lifted off the ground right along with me, but it didn't seem to care. Its grip got tighter, its claws digging deep into my calf. I screamed again and kicked at it with my free leg, smashing it in the face. It didn't make any difference and it certainly didn't make it release me.

I asked the wind to release one hand and it immediately did so, wrapping thick fingers around my waist instead as it continued to speed us away from the queen's chamber.

I switched the gut buster for my knife and plunged it past

the Irkallan's slashing mandibles and into its eye. As the Irkallan screamed and cursed me, I thrust the knife deeper into its skull, right into its brain. It died instantly, but it didn't release me. I withdrew the gore-slicked knife and slashed it across the Irkallan's limb, freeing the bulk of its body but leaving its claws embedded in my flesh. Blood was flowing altogether too freely down my leg, but those claws might also be the only things stopping that flow from being much worse.

Minutes. I only had minutes left.

Then I heard a sound that chilled my bones—a high-pitched scream of utter fury, and one that somehow had a distinctly female sound.

The queen was awake, and hunting.

Faster. I needed to go *faster*. But the wind could do only so much, and as my strength faded, so too did my control over her. If I forced more speed now, I'd have nothing left to confront the Irkallan who were with the children.

And if I *didn't*, I'd be fighting the monster who ruled this place.

I found more strength from who knew where, and the wind's speed increased. But that unholy roar of fury was drawing ever closer; the bitch was *fast*. Faster than the wind, at least right now.

I resolutely reloaded the gut busters then asked the wind to turn me around so that I was looking back rather than forward. The scrape of claws against tunnel's stone floor was clearly audible now. She was close. *So* close.

I took a deep breath that did nothing to ease the sick fear in my gut and raised the gut busters. My hands were steady, even if my heart wasn't.

The scraping grew so loud it was all I could hear, but the darkness remained resolute and still. No monsters emerged from it.

Not for several seconds.

Then the shadows parted, and she appeared. She might have a broken arm, a shattered mandible, and only one eye, but if the years of fighting the Adlin had taught me anything, it was the fact that a wounded adversary was sometimes the most dangerous.

I fired, and kept firing, as she arrowed toward me. Blood and gore flew as the bullets tore into her head, shoulders, and torso. The rain of metal should have killed her, but it didn't. Her exoskeleton was thicker than even that of her soldiers', and it was obviously going to take more than a few rounds to do any true damage.

I wasn't sure I had that many rounds left, let alone enough time. The countdown clock in my head was now flashing red.

The queen raised her good arm and slashed at my face. I jerked back instinctively, even as the air wrenched me sideways. The queen's mandibles clashed, barely missing my legs, snapping air instead. She slashed at me again, catching my hip, cutting through the ammo belt and down into skin. I hissed in pain but kept firing as I ordered the wind to brake. The queen's momentum shot her past me, her thick claws drawing sparks from the stone as she slid to a stop and then spun around. I continued to fire; chunks of armor-like flesh were now flying, but if the queen was in any way feeling pain, she certainly wasn't showing it.

The gut busters *would* kill her but nowhere near quickly enough. The countdown had reached critical point—there could only be seconds left before the bomb went off.

I shoved the guns back onto their clips and then drew the sword. In the deep darkness of the tunnel, the glass blade shone with a bright blue fire. The queen screamed in response and charged. I held my ground and waited until the very last moment—until all I could smell was her stink and her fury, and her snapping mandibles were within slicing distance. Then I ordered the wind to dodge and duck, and, with all the strength I could muster, swung the sword. It hit her thigh, sliced through flesh and bone with ease, completely severing her leg. As her limb fell in what seemed like slow motion to the ground, the queen screamed, and somehow swung around on the other leg, slashing wildly with her claws. I swung the sword and met her blow with the blade, slicing the fingers from her left limb, her wrist off the right. Then I brought it around again and stabbed at her eye. She jerked back, unbalanced, and fell.

In that moment, the countdown in my head stopped and that imaginary red flashing light seized. What followed was a weird moment of silence. It was almost as if the earth and the air were holding their collective breaths.

Then there was an ominous *whoomp*, one that was far deeper than other two, and the earth all around me started to shake. A heavy rumbling noise ran through the tunnel behind us, getting louder and louder, gaining speed as a heavy orange glow began to light the darkness. Huge chunks of earth and stone started raining around me and the air gained urgency even as the heat and dust and freedom only knew what else battered my body.

Go, I told the air. *Now.*

She obeyed. But the rumbling had become so loud it was beginning to hurt my ears and it wasn't just the ceiling tearing itself apart now, but also the walls. The queen disappeared under a pile of rubble and dust.

The air tore me sideways, into another, smaller tunnel. But the heat and the energy of the explosion continued to chase us, and this tunnel also began to collapse inward.

I didn't want to die. Not before I'd completed my mission, anyway, and stopped the remaining children—for their sake just as much as much as anything else.

Where are the children? I asked.

They are ahead, the air said. *But if we stop, that explosion will kill you as surely as it will kill them.*

I can't leave those bracelets on them.

You will die with them if you stop.

Then I'll die. But not before I got those bracelets and somehow ensured they could never be used again.

So be it. Shall we once again steal their breath?

Yes. I hesitated. *How many Irkallan are with them?*

Only two.

Can you steal their breath as well?

Yes, but with each order, and each death, you are further weakened.

And I still needed the strength to order the bracelets hidden. Surely I could cope with two Irkallan. It was certainly better than facing two Adlin.

The air continued to sweep me through the shaking, breaking tunnel. Breathing was becoming more difficult thanks to the dust choking the air, and I couldn't see anything now. Nothing more than the dusty orange glow that was the firestorm of energy and destruction pursuing us.

The children are down, the wind said. *Be ready—the Irkallan are around the next corner.*

I swapped my sword for the gut busters as we entered the sweeping corner. But the air was so thick with heat and dust now that I had no hope of seeing the Irkallan. And if I couldn't see them, they surely couldn't see me. I asked the wind to sweep me up to the crumbling roof as we neared the end of the turn. Dirt and rock thumped into every inch of my body, the force of each blow so strong it felt like a thousand fists were pummeling me.

It didn't matter. Nothing did except killing the Irkallan and getting those bracelets. As the tunnel straightened and I got a vague glimpse of lavender flesh up ahead, I began to fire, filling the entire tunnel with a hail of metal.

As both guns clicked over to empty, the wind swept down from the ceiling and deposited me onto the ground. There wasn't much left of the Irkallan after my barrage—just a mess of lavender pulp interspersed between the bits of bones and mandibles. The children lay under these bloody and broken carcasses, their grimy faces covered with gore and yet oddly serene—it was as if they'd felt death's coming and had welcomed it.

I ran to the first child, knelt, and quickly pried the bracelet off his wrist. It would have been far easier to simply order the earth to bury both the children *and* the bracelets, but that would take for more strength than I had.

The air was so thick and hot that my body burned and every breath was now a struggle. The rumble that was the earth collapsing on the tunnel system was dangerously close again now, and the chunks of stone raining down from the ceiling were becoming body crushing. I didn't have the time for finesse. I had to get the remaining bracelets off these children and then get somewhere safe enough to bury them deep into the soil before that raging storm of heat and destruction hit me.

I sent a silent prayer of forgiveness to the souls of the children then thrust to my feet and ran to the remaining four, quickly slicing the bracelets from their wrists.

As the ceiling directly above me fissured, I grabbed the last two bracelets and then screamed for the air to get me out of there. I was lifted up and flung forward in an instant, but the ceiling and the walls were chasing me now, snapping at my heels like a drakkon hungry for flesh.

The wind flung me around another corner and, just for a second, we were free of it all. I asked to be put down again, and the air obeyed so rapidly I did a stumbling run forward before falling to my knees. My whole body shook with fatigue and pain, and there wasn't an inch of skin left that wasn't bloodied or bruised. But I wasn't finished yet.

I dropped my collection of bracelets and severed hands onto the ground in front of me and then buried my fingertips into the soil. There was no response from the earth and, after a moment, I realized why. The ground in this tunnel was dead. I swore and punched it in frustration, then called to the air and bid it to start digging. As dust began to spin around me, choking my vision and filling my lungs, the walls began to tremble and shake. Damn it, just how much farther would the explosive power of the M185 blocks travel? Surely it would have to ease off soon?

As the wind dug deeper into the dead soil, I began to hear the voice of the earth. I thrust a hand down into the hole and felt the slivers of power curl around my fingers. It pulled at me, draining the last remnants of my strength even as it answered my call.

Bury the bracelets so deep they can never be found, I said.

Our pleasure, the voices of the earth answered. *And now, run. Or you die.*

As fingers of clean earth rose up from the hole and collected the bracelets, I pushed to my feet and staggered away. But my head was spinning, my legs felt like water, and there was absolutely nothing left in the tank now.

The wind tugged at me, begging me to go faster, grabbing my arms and propelling me along as hard as it could. But my weakness was being reflected in its strength now, and we were both fading fast.

Somehow I pushed on, but I was running on nothing more than sheer determination. Then the walls started moving around me, the ceiling became fluid, and the floor started bucking and kicking. I stumbled and fell, landing hard on hands and knees. The air screamed at me to get up, to move, and I tried, freedom only knew, I tried.

But I couldn't. My body was a dead weight that refused to move.

I closed my eyes and prayed for the end to be quick.

Then the earth fell on top of me, and I knew no more.

14

It was the voices that woke me. At first I thought it was simply the air, begging me to get up, to move, to not die, but some of those voices had a timbre that reminded me of the earth. Perhaps the tunnel's collapse had cleared the dead soil and uncovered the living earth in this area.

But even if I'd had the strength to move, I couldn't have. There were several weights lying across my body, pinning me, and my legs were numb. As for dying... breathing was becoming a struggle and there was a part of me that was more than ready to give up the fight, to let go and find peace and an end to the pain.

No! the voices said. *You will not die in this place. Fight, damn you.*

I tried to open my eyes, but couldn't. I shifted slightly, realized I had movement in my right arm, and raised a hand to gently probe my face. It was covered with sticky moisture, dirt, and freedom only knew what else, and it was *that* muck that had glued my eyes shut. I carefully rubbed it away, and then opened my eyes.

Three feet in front of me was a massive rock that was

jammed hard against what remained of the nearby tunnel wall. It had stopped on an angle, in the midst of falling flat and, instead of crushing me, had protected me from the worst of the tunnel's collapse. The air swirling around me was heated and thick with dust, suggesting I hadn't actually been out for long. I twisted to the right, trying to see what, exactly, was pinning me, but the left half of my body wasn't moving properly. I turned to see why, and saw the mess that was my left arm. Not only could I see bone, but blood—blood that already stained the earth and whose flow showed no signs of abating.

I was going to bleed to death before anyone could get here to help me.

We are close, the voices said.

Only it was one voice now, not many, and its tone was as rich as the earth itself and oh so familiar.

Trey.

But why was he here, in this place? Why wasn't he mopping up the Irkallan with the rest of the outpost forces?

Hang on, he continued. *We are little more than ten minutes away from you now.*

"Everything hurts," I said, though whether I gave that reply voice or it was merely said in my mind, I couldn't say. Not that it really mattered—he'd hear me either way.

I know, he said. *And we'll fix that. Just hang on.*

"I'm hanging," I said, even as I wondered if that would be enough.

I shifted my good arm and slowly reached down into my pocket. Despite everything that had happened, the medikit was still tucked safely inside. I dragged it up toward my face, pried it open, and then freed the second canister of sealer. It wouldn't do a whole lot for the mangled state of my arm, but maybe it would stop the worst of the bleeding. It might not, in the end, make much of a difference given I had no idea if there were worse wounds elsewhere, but I had to at least try. Whether it would give me ten more minutes or not was anyone's guess.

I tore the cap off with my teeth then slowly but carefully eased my good hand over to my left and sprayed the sealer. It hurt so bad it tore a scream from my throat, and even though the sound came out as little more than a garbled cry, I thought I heard its echo in the near distance.

I kept spraying back and forth until the canister was empty, and then dropped onto the ground. Pain was a white-hot lance that continually stabbed into my brain, and it quickly consumed what little strength I had left. As unconsciousness began to claim me again, the earth around me shook.

Whether the earth remained unstable because of my bombs, or whether it was Trey and his people coming to get me, I couldn't say.

All I knew was I didn't have the strength to remain awake. I closed my eyes and let the blackness claim me.

The second time I awoke, it was to bright sunshine above me, and the softness of bedding underneath me. I remained completely still for several minutes, simply enjoying being able to breathe in and out without the flicker of pain. Then, remembering the numbness in my legs and mashed remnants of my left arm, I cautiously wiggled my toes and then my fingers. When they both responded, I felt like cheering. There was a decided tightness in my calf where the Irkallan's claws had dug in, and a similar tightness along my arm that spoke of new skin and scarring, but I didn't care.

I was alive, and I could move. Nothing else really mattered right now.

I opened my eyes. It was immediately obvious that I wasn't in Winterborne—that I was, in fact, back in Trey's quarters at Blacklake.

But the first face I saw was Ava's, and while I was more than happy to see her, I couldn't help the sliver of disappointment that ran through me.

"What the hell are you doing here?" I asked.

She rolled her eyes. "Is that all the thanks I get for sitting by your bedside for weeks on end, waiting for your lazy self to decide you actually needed to wake up?"

"You know that's not what I meant." Then I blinked as her words impacted. "Did you say *weeks?*"

"Yes." She leaned forward and caught my hand in hers. Though a smile still played about her lips, her eyes were all seriousness. "You had us all really scared for a while, there."

"Don't tell me April's here as well?"

Her smile grew. "Well, no, because he's too busy bumping uglies with that pretty little nurse of his. But he's been in regular contact for updates. I meant the docs, the healers, and of course, your commander."

I scowled at her. "He's not my *anything.*"

"Yeah, right." She squeezed my fingers lightly and then leaned back in the chair. "So how are you actually feeling? Because let me tell you, the list of your injuries was pretty impressive."

"I don't think I really want to know that information."

"You should, because by all rights, you should be dead. The healers are saying it's only thanks to your Sifft heritage that you're here at all, but April and me, we think it was something else."

I knew exactly what she meant, and it wasn't either the earth or air magic. I lightly slapped her knee. "Enough, woman. We barely even know each other."

"Yeah, but it was the connection—the spark—between the

two of you that not only saved you, but also pulled you through. I saw it, and so did the healers."

I didn't reply to that, asking instead, "How did you manage to get so much time off from the Nightwatch?" I knew for a fact she wouldn't have that much leave left, as both of us had a tendency to use it as soon as a new allocation came in.

"The captain wouldn't give me leave, so I did what any cot sister would do, and transferred my ass over to Blacklake. The commander was more than happy to have me, especially given the current state of the wall and the continuing attacks by the Adlin." She paused. "Those bastards are seriously pissed off."

I frowned. "How bad are the attacks?"

She shrugged. "They're almost daily. Nothing we can't cope with though."

I smiled. "It sounds like you're enjoying life here."

"I am, surprisingly." A wicked gleam appeared in her eyes. "And let's just say the manpower in this outpost is mighty impressive."

I chuckled softly and dragged myself up the bed. Ava immediately rose and adjusted the pillows to support my back. My left arm was decidedly weaker than my right, and there were thick, ugly scars crisscrossing its entire length. I was also missing the tip of my ring finger, but all in all, the healers had done an amazing job.

I thanked her, then glanced toward the bedroom door, my heart suddenly racing with anticipation. Trey was approaching.

The door opened and he stepped in. The grin that stretched his lips was warm and delighted, but there was little in the way of surprise. He would have known I was awake, just as I'd known he was approaching.

"Commander," Ava said, immediately rising and offering him a salute. "Our girl has finally awoken."

"So I see," he said, his gaze not leaving mine as he strode toward the bed. "You're relieved, Officer March. I'll take over from here."

"Yes, Commander." Ava gave me a wink then quickly walked out of the room.

I didn't even hear the door close. I was too busy getting lost in the gaze of the man who'd saved my life.

"Thank you," I said eventually.

He raised an eyebrow as he sat down on the bed and twined his fingers through mine. "For what? Doing what any good commander would do?"

I half smiled. "I'm thinking you went a little beyond the call of duty to save me."

"Perhaps just a little."

My smile grew. "How did you know I was there? And *why* were you even there? I thought the outposts were attacking the known exits?"

"We did, but after the initial explosions in the mountains, the Irkallan went into retreat and the Adlin attacked instead."

My breath caught. There was still one bracelet out there, one I'd forgotten about, on the wrist of that lavender Adlin.

"Not anymore it's not," Trey said. "We finally killed that bastard three nights ago."

"And the bracelet?"

"The silver was melted and made into cutlery. The inner band of technology which we presume was what allowed both control and communication was smashed and spread far and wind by the four winds."

Relief stirred through me. "That means every one of them has been dealt with."

"Yes, and if they had been able to replicate them or find more, they would have done so by now."

"Indeed." I paused. "So why were you close enough to rescue me? As far as I'm aware, Drakkon's Head is the only major entrance along that portion of the Blacksaw Mountains, and that's not where you were supposed to be."

He raised that eyebrow again. "Obviously you have no idea just how far into that mountain you traveled."

"No." I hesitated. "Did the bombs I set off do much damage? I asked for big booms, but the armory custodian didn't really say how big that was going to be. It felt bad, but that could have been because I was so damn close to it."

"Trust me, it was every inch as destructive as it must have felt. But let me show you." He rose, slipped his hands underneath me, and then picked me up, sheet and all, cradling me close to his chest as he crossed to the window. Sunshine bathed the inner bailey and there were people everywhere, not just soldiers, but metalsmiths, stonemasons, and witches, both earth and air. Obviously, it wasn't only Ava who had come to Blacklake to help them rebuild.

But that wasn't what I was here to see. My gaze rose to the long dark stain that was the Blacksaw Mountains. The main entrance into the Irkallan apiary was still very much present; indeed, from this angle, the drakkon appeared to be roaring in fury, as smoke was still billowing from its maw. But the arching back of the drakkon was now broken; the mountain had caved in for a good mile or so before the jagged peaks reappeared to dominate the skyline again.

I'd done that.

And, amazingly, had survived.

"It was rather touch-and-go for a while there," Trey said.

"So Ava said." I reached up and ran my fingers down his cheek to his lips. "And you still haven't given me an explanation as to why you were close enough to sense my presence underground."

"Ah, yes." He kissed my fingertips lightly then turned

around and sat down on the sill, resting me on his lap but still cradling me gently. Under normal circumstances I might have protested that I wasn't an invalid, but right now, being treated so tenderly felt rather nice.

"When the second lot of bombs went off and the mountain above the apiary began to collapse," he continued, "the Irkallan soldiers went into retreat. I presume their intentions were to save as much as the hive as they could. We gave chase, of course, and it was in that process that I sensed you. But it was damned hard work getting through the dead earth."

"Then how did you?"

A wry smile twisted his lips. "I didn't. The air did. It contacted me via this link we seemed to have formed, and asked me if I was interested in saving you. Rather naturally, I said yes."

"I would have come back and haunted you if you'd said no."

He laughed softly. "We didn't dig directly down—it was very apparent even from up top that the combination of the dead soil and the explosion had made the entire tunnel system unstable, so I created a new tunnel in the live earth and came in at you sideways. Once I hit the dead soil, the air took over and tunneled the rest of the distance." An odd sort of bleakness briefly touched his face. "We almost didn't make it. The tunnel you were in totally collapsed not five seconds after we'd dragged you out of it."

I rested my head against his chest, listening to the steady beating of his heart. "Thank you."

As words went, they were totally inadequate, but it was all I had.

"You're welcome." There was a smile in his voice. "Of course, now that you *are* recovered enough, there are a few decisions that need to be made."

I looked up at him and raised an eyebrow. "Like what?"

"Like your permanent transfer to Blacklake. I must warn you, I will vigorously oppose anything else."

I tried to restrain my smile, but it nevertheless twitched the corners of my mouth. "A permanent transfer would totally depend on what's being offered. *I* will vigorously oppose anything less than a full combat position equal to what I had in Winterborne."

"I'd expect nothing else," he said. "The next decision, of course, is the matter of accommodation."

My smile grew. "Aren't all soldiers quartered in the barracks?"

"Indeed, but it would hardly be seemly for you to be quartered there."

"And why would that be, Commander?"

"Because we can hardly explore what lies between us under so many watchful eyes. The gossip alone would be horrendous."

I laughed. "And that worries you?"

"Hell no." He hesitated, and then added more seriously, "But I'm well aware you've already suffered more than your share of hurt and gossip thanks to a relationship with a senior officer that went sour, and I don't wish to be the cause of such again if things don't work out between us."

"And that is, of course, a risk."

"Indeed, but not so great a one, I'm thinking."

"I'm tending to agree."

"Good," he said. "It's settled then."

I blinked. "What's settled?"

"You and me. Living here in my quarters, away from the prying eyes and the gossips."

I laughed. "As if *that's* going to stop anyone. I'm classified as unlit *and* I'm stained, Trey. That's going to raise more than a few eyebrows, and not just here in Blacklake."

"And you think I care?"

"Well, no, but—"

He pressed a finger to my lips, cutting off my protest. "I don't care whether or not you have magic. I don't care what color your skin is or isn't. I only care about the person inside that skin, and you, my lovely Neve, have proven yourself to be a strong, caring, and totally amazing woman, and I very much want to spend both my near and distant future with you."

Tears stung my eyes and I blinked them away rapidly. "I'd very much like that myself, Commander."

"Perfect," he said, and kissed me.

And it was, indeed, perfect.

ABOUT THE AUTHOR

Keri Arthur, author of the New York Times bestselling Riley Jenson Guardian series, has now written more than thirty-nine novels. She's received several nominations in the Best Contemporary Paranormal category of the Romantic Times Reviewers Choice Awards and has won RT's Career Achievement Award for urban fantasy. She lives with her daughter and very old Sheltie in Melbourne, Australia.

for more information:
www.keriarthur.com
kez@keriarthur.com